NOTHING TO DECLARE

NOTHING TO DECLARE

Fauna Perkins and Rita K. Read

With Regards
Rita K Read

iUniverse, Inc.
New York   Bloomington

NOTHING TO DECLARE

This is a work of fiction. All of the characters, names, incidents, organizations, and dialogue in this novel are either the products of the author's imagination or are used fictitiously.

iUniverse books may be ordered through booksellers or by contacting:

iUniverse
2021 Pine Lake Road, Suite 100
Lincoln, NE 68512
www.iuniverse.com
1-800-Authors (1-800-288-4677)

ISBN: 978-0-595-47510-0 (pbk)
ISBN: 978-0-595-91781-5 (ebk)

Printed in the United States of America

Dedications

For my brother, Raimo,
Without whom this book would not have been written
RKR

For my children
AND
Their children

FP

PART ONE

▼

1950 – 1968

I was small, and lost my father,
Very small, and lost my mother...
I was left with icy shoes –
They forgot my slushy stockings-
Left to walk on frozen tracks,
Over rolling causeway logs,
Stumble into every swamp,
Sucked down in every mud hole.

But as yet now I'm not ready,
Not at this age to become
A stepping log across a swamp,
Or a plank for muddy places –
Will not sink into a swamp
As long as I have these two hands
And can stretch out these five fingers
Or can lift up my ten claws.

The Kalevala, Runo 34, Lines 77-94

She came skipping through the farmyard
Head held high and eyes a shine,
With red roses in her cheeks, and -
Oh! so beautiful a face.

The Kalevala , Runo 10, Lines 244-247

CHAPTER ONE

▼

Helsinki,Finland
August 1950

Seven-year-old Mila snuggled under her covers, reluctant to let go of her last grasp on sleep. She reached under her pillow for the bright red airplane Anders, her older brother, had carved for her, the one she refused to share with her other brother, Martti. Then she remembered this was the day they were going to America and her blue eyes popped open.

Across the room of their apartment, her mother, Kaija, was busy packing a small suitcase, so small that at first glance it appeared to be a woman's handbag. It was constructed of compressed cardboard with thicker cardboard reinforcements to protect the corners and thin metal hinges and clasps. Even the cheap metal handle had been painted dark brown to match. There was no lock. Into the small space, Kaija placed Mila's meager belongings. On top of the clothing, she placed three small copper teakettles.

"What are those for, mama?"

"They're gifts to give in America," she answered. "Don't get started with all your questions; we have a lot to do," Kaija said.

She helped Mila into the new blue dress Mumma Tehelia had smocked and embroidered with flowers on the collar and bloomers to match. Mila twirled around as soon as the dress was slipped over her head.

"It's not the time to dance," mother scolded.

In spite of the warm August day, Mila insisted on wearing the blue velvet beret from Mumma. "It goes with my new dress," she said, clamping it firmly on her braids.

"I don't have time to argue with you," Kaija said, flicking her dark blond hair back with her hand, a gesture Mila loved to imitate.

"I don't need my coat," Mila said.

"It might be cold on the ferry," Kaija told her, closing the door behind her.

They walked past Mumma's apartment where she sat in her rocking chair at the window to knit because of the light, and Mila stopped to wave.

Kaija pulled her by the arm. "Don't dawdle, the streetcar's coming and we have a long walk to the harbor."

At the ferry terminal office, Kaija stopped and picked up tickets and cash for their expenses. She counted the money, and smiled for the first time that day.

"Why did the man give you money?" Mila asked, but received no answer.

"Come along, we'll go to the Esplanade," she said, surprising Mila. The Esplanade along Helsinki's waterfront was dotted with small outdoor cafes. The area was linden green with summer foliage; afternoon clouds blotted the sun and lent a smell of rain to the hot asphalt. Mila noticed men looking at Kaija as she passed their tables and thought it must be because she looked as though she were dancing. Mila was a small replica, imperial in her bearing and attitude.

When the waiter came, Kaija said, "I'll have coffee and pastry. What kind of ice cream would you like?" she asked Mila.

Mila's eyes sparkled. "Strawberry," she said, thrilled by the rare treat.

"What is America?" Mila asked, attempting to get her attention.

"There are lots of toys and everyone has enough to eat." Kaija poured cream in her coffee, dropped in three sugar cubes and stirred it, then gazed back at the men at the next table who nodded and smiled at her. Small birds hopped around the tables hoping for scraps. She closed her eyes and turned her face to the wind.

After the all night trip by ferryboat, they boarded a train in Stockholm for the trip across Sweden to Goteborg. At first Mila was fascinated by each new sight, but after endless miles of southern Sweden she grew restless.

"How much longer?" Mila asked.

"It's a long way yet," Kaija answered. She lifted the hair from the back of her neck and blotted it with her hankie, then pulled at the neckline of her damp dress and blew down the front. She stretched, took out a deck of cards, put Mila's suitcase across her legs for a game of solitaire. "Don't get into mischief," she said, glancing at the queen of Diamonds in her hand.

Mila held her airplane tightly. The rhythm of the train lulled her into sleep and she fell against her mother's shoulder.

"Wake up," Kaija said, shaking her shoulder. "We have to get off now."

Again they took a trolley and finally reached a busy market square bordering the harbor at Goteburg.

"Wait here," her mother told her. Kaija went through the door of a large building on the wharf. Mila pressed her nose against the window and watched and then turned to look at the harbor, her senses engaged by the swooping sea gulls, the hot cobblestones, the odor of frying doughnuts, but in spite of the distractions, her gaze returned to her mother who looked upset. Mila sensed that it concerned her. As soon as she opened the door Kaija took Mila's hand, hesitated, and crossed the cobblestones to a huge white ship.

A man in a dark blue uniform came over to them. Abruptly Kaija bent and hugged Mila, something she seldom did and Mila caught the whiff of her mother's scent, full of forest and sunshine.

"Remember to be a good girl and always curtsy when you speak to your elders. And don't forget to say please and thank you."

The man took Mila's hand and Kaija gave her the cardboard suitcase. They seemed to belong together, the child and the suitcase; it seemed custom made for the small hand that held it. The man led her to the wooden stairway and she twisted around to make sure her mother was following but there were so many people and so much noise she was swept away in the crowd.

CHAPTER TWO

▼

The ship turned from the dock, the crowd disappeared, and the rail seemed an endless fence. The man who led her aboard tapped her shoulder, she turned to look up at him; in the bright sunshine he became a black figure looming over her and she backed away. She noted the portholes, strange round windows like mirrors framed in gold that she'd seen from the dock. He led her to a heavy door, then a stairway and down two flights until they reached a long narrow hallway with rows of doors. She followed in a dreamlike trance while slithers of fear started behind her knees and worked up her spine. What was this stranger going to do to her? His smile reminded her of mama's friend, the one she didn't like who gave her pennies and told her to go outside and play.

"Come along now," he said in Swedish, but she didn't understand. When he tried to take her suitcase, Mila held it tightly. The cabin had bunk beds, but no round window and the gray walls absorbed the dim light.

"They told your mother you weren't supposed to travel alone." But again she did not understand. "I'll send the maid along to help you."

Mila stood in the middle of the room. When she complained at home, Mumma Tehelia asked where her *sisu* was. *Sisu* was Finnish for guts, intestinal fortitude, pride and perseverance. She didn't feel brave, but she would try to act it.

Anders wouldn't let anything bad happen to her. She knew he had to go to the hospital because of the blood he coughed up. She'd been angry and hurt when he left because he hadn't let her hug him goodbye, but she loved him with reverent devotion. Mumma explained that he'd been protecting her from his sickness. If only he were here now. She ran her airplane up and down her leg. It was real, familiar, and for a moment made her feel safe, then she stood immobile, rocked by the increasing motion of the ship.

After an eternity of waiting, she rested on the lower bunk and pulled up her legs. Mama would come soon; sometimes it took her a long time, but she always came.

With one hand she clutched the airplane and with the other pulled the bedspread over herself. She was exhausted from her fright, but instead of the ship's motion lulling her to escape in sleep, she felt queasy. Her mouth started to water and the nausea rose in her throat. She tried to swallow it back down, but it erupted in a projectile of curdled milk and undigested cheese, leaving a sweet after-taste. The convulsion made her body shake and she held her hands to her mouth, but before she could stop the next attack, a long stream of mucous washed up and vomit dirtied her new dress and the bedspread. The slick muck clung to her and she wanted to rip it away and rid herself of the slimy mess. There was no air in the cabin and the smell made her sick again.

She thought of home. Mila couldn't imagine a more wonderful place than Linkala Lane. The area was more like a rural hamlet than a suburb of Helsinki. Woods and creeks, tilled vegetable gardens, rambling wild roses, carpets of soft grasses and sun-warmed pine needles surrounded them. The buildings were similar in their plainness, free of ornamentation except for curtains tied back from sparkling windows and an occasional splattering of color from window boxes.

Then she remembered all of the times she'd been naughty - the day she persuaded Martti to help pull all the new young carrots from their aunt's garden. It was far too early and the entire crop was ruined. Being older, Martti was punished. They often fought and he called her names and referred to her as The Little Princess. She liked the words, but not the tone. If only she were home, Martti could call her anything; she'd even give him her airplane.

"Mama," she called out in anguish to the gray walls, "Please. Don't send me away."

Mila's heart jumped at the quick knock on the door and she sat up, relief flooding her. A stocky middle-aged woman wearing the blue outfit of the ship's cleaning crew crossed the room and stepped around the puddle of vomit. Mila waited, afraid to move for fear the nausea would start again. She hovered beneath the covers, only a pair of frightened blue eyes visible.

"My name is Helga," the woman said in Finnish, setting down a tray. "Do you need the toilet?" she asked. "Let's wash your face and hands." Mila shrank from her.

"Come, I won't hurt you," Helga told her.

"When is my mother coming to take me home?" Mila asked. "Please, I live on Linkala Lane."

"Your mother's not coming," Helga told her.

"You're wrong," she insisted. "Anders would never let this happen."

Helga searched the few drawers for clean clothes. "Where is your other suitcase?"

"That's my suitcase," Mila replied. "I have a new blue coat." For a moment her hopes rallied. "Mama forgot it. Maybe that's where she is." She tried to keep up her courage, but now feared mama wasn't coming.

Helga slipped off her soiled dress and helped her into the pants and shirt, her only other clothes. "I'm going to spend time with you on the boat," Helga said. She pulled the smelly bedspread off the bed, sat down and held Mila against her comfortable body. "You'll feel better when you eat something." She took the metal lid off the soup and helped Mila eat. "Take the biscuits," she advised. "They'll help settle your stomach."

Mila started to cry and Helga's eyes clouded. She brought a washcloth and wiped Mila's face. "Try to get some sleep," she said. "I'll be back."

Mila shrank under the covers and gulped her tears in huge bites of longing and waited for another day.

The next morning Helga arrived with a worn sweater much too large. She slipped Mila's arms into it and rolled the sleeves until they became thick donuts around the wrists. "This will help keep you warm when we take our walks in the air," she explained. As they walked around the deck, Mila peered at every passing woman, but failing to see a familiar face, tugged Helga toward the stairs asking if they could search for her mother downstairs. After a few more days she stopped asking when her mother was coming and saved her tears to shed alone at bedtime.

Early on the eighth day, she heard feet rushing down the halls outside and the whistle blowing as it had in Sweden. The motion of the ship slowed and she felt unfamiliar clanking noises, felt bumps, heard motors grinding. The smell of diesel oil drifted under the door. Mila understood nothing of the jumble of noises outside the door until Helga came in and hurried to brush out her hair and help her into her dress. "We've reached America," she said.

CHAPTER THREE

▼

America, 1950

Hundreds of Finns immigrated in the 1800s to work in the shipping industry in northern Ohio. Marta and Felix Liukkonen settled in Fairport Harbor, a small village on the shores of Lake Erie, and separated from Painesville by the Grand River. Their daughter, Frances, grew up there as the eldest of eight children and assumed early responsibility for her younger siblings.

Frances was nearly six feet tall. She'd never looked girlish and although attractive, somehow missed being pretty; she was the kind of woman one would describe as imposing. She had an uncompromising mouth, a straight nose and dark hazel eyes that darted like a ferret's, missing nothing.

She became a teacher but when she couldn't yank the ears or pull the hair of her unruly students, she felt unable to exercise the discipline necessary to teach and so returned to Ohio State University. In order to support herself, she lived with the family of a professor of medicine and acted as nanny for his two children. The wife was an invalid and disapproved of Frances's methods with the children and her attitude toward her husband. He, however, was impressed with Frances's brains and told her she ought to go to medical school, but Frances said she wasn't interested in being around sick people. Instead she became one of two women in law school. The professor remained the great love of Frances's life despite finding soon after becoming a lawyer that her real erogenous zone was power.

She was in her mid-thirties when one of her brothers introduced her to an Army buddy visiting from New York. Donald Robertson was tall, well built and focused on his appearance; he wore vests and always a hat: felt in winter,

Panama in summer. In the Army he entertained his buddies by juggling, a skill he'd learned working in small carnivals during summers. He believed in predestination and in the stock market. His older sister who doted on him after their mother died in childbirth had raised him. When he met Frances he was working in low-level management for Standard Oil of New York and although his salary was minimal, he amassed a great many stock certificates. He loved big cars and felt the day he owned a Lincoln Continental would be the day he arrived.

Despite the fact that Frances considered sex was for animals, she took her vacation to visit Donald in New York and proved her premise. Finding herself pregnant, she entered marriage with some gratitude, an incipient attitude of hope and the thought that, for political reasons, it was better to be married than single.

Her brush with feminine dependency ended with the birth of her baby by C-section. They named him Christopher Robin; he lived for only two weeks. Frances never forgave Donald for listening to the doctor rather than to her. She'd begged him to get her and the baby to the Cleveland Clinic for treatment of Rh incompatibility; instead Donald believed the doctor who told him the baby could be treated in Painesville. Their second child, Zeke, was born at the Cleveland Clinic two years later.

Donald now worked for the Lake County Title and Guarantee Company of Painesville. The owner was a client of Frances's. He started as a Title Officer and progressed to the dead end job of Escrow Officer. Although he missed his sister's even-tempered kindness, it seemed natural to shift his reliance onto Frances.

When World War II ended, Frances was the only Finnish-speaking lawyer in Fairport Harbor. The town became a client pool for a lucrative enterprise with her cousin, Erkki Niemi, an attorney in Helsinki. Their business was child procurement.

The Rintas were second generation Finns who still had ties to the old country and wanted to adopt a Finnish child. They felt too old for a baby and specified a girl of three or four. When Frances heard about Kaija and Mila she felt it would be an ideal arrangement, but while Kaija hesitated the Rintas decided Mila would be too old and reneged on the adoption. By then Mila was on her way to America and Frances was compelled to take temporary custody. Her sister, Helen, would care for Zeke while Frances and Donald made the trip to New York to bring Mila home.

"Do all the children you handle make the trip by themselves?" Helen asked. "I would think it overwhelming."

"It's the steamship company's job to take care of her. They wouldn't have allowed her aboard if they considered it a problem. It's only a seven day trip," Frances said.

"I don't know about all this, Ulle," Donald said, cajoling her with his pet name.

"I don't want to jeopardize the business," Frances answered. "It gives us a nice income. Adopting a war orphan might help my election when I run for judge."

"I suppose if he likes her she might be a good companion for Zeke," Donald said.

"Yes, and help around the house," Frances said. "Anyway, we won't have to make up our minds right away. If it doesn't work out, we can send her back."

New York was in the grip of a late summer heat wave and the oily harbor waters added to the assault. Although it was early morning, the air was sultry. The smell of diesel fuel permeated the still air causing Mila to feel nauseous again.

A ship's officer held Mila's hand as they started down the gangplank. Dwarfed by the crowds, she tried to catch sight of her mother. Throngs of people pushed this way and that while she stood in an open-air room with lines of long benches loaded with luggage. With one hand she pulled up the socks that dangled around her ankles, then reached up to make sure her beret was firmly on her head. The metal handle of the suitcase felt warm in her hand. A woman with a clipboard handed the ship's officer some papers, smiled down at Mila's serious expression, patted her on the head, and took her hand.

"Mr. and Mrs. Robertson?" she asked the couple standing there. "Why was the child traveling by herself?" she asked. "She should have been accompanied by an adult."

Frances soothed. "Yes, poor child. I don't know what happened, but you can be sure I'll get to the bottom of it." Frances frowned at the clerk, then turning to Mila she said, "*Tervetullut* America, Marja Leena."

Mila craned her neck when she heard the Finnish welcome. Mumma taught her to speak correct, polite, old-fashioned Finnish and to always remember her manners. Frantic to communicate with anyone, she used the polite form of 'now' that was not a demand.

"*Olkaa hyvaa, Rouva*," she said, curtsying. "Please, madam, I want my mother now."

"I am your new mother," Frances said.

"No. I have a mother, but I don't know where she is." Tears of frustration and disappointment cascaded down her cheeks. She had nothing to guide her but odors and this woman had a sharp smell, like metal. Her fleshy hands looked soft as she reached for Mila, but her fingers felt hard and uneasy on Mila's skin; Mila pulled away.

"I am your mother," Frances repeated, "and this is your father."

"I don't have a father. I have Anders."

Donald stooped to pick Mila up, and she detected the mildest scent of something pleasant. His voice was gentle when he pointed to himself and then to his wife: "Daddy," he said, "and mama." Then he handed her the biggest doll she'd ever seen wearing a ruffled dress with a matching bonnet and panties. His arms felt comforting.

They moved up the line to a man stamping passports with rhythmic regularity. "Is this her only luggage?" he asked looking at the suitcase.

"Yes," Frances answered.

He flipped it opened, shook his head, opened the immigration papers and stamped: NOTHING TO DECLARE.

CHAPTER FOUR

▼

Painesville, Ohio

Stone steps led to the screened porch of a white two-story house with gray trim. As they started up the walk, a woman holding a boy by the hand came toward them smiling. "I'm your Aunt Helen," she said in Finnish, took Mila in her arms and gave her a big hug. "This is your new brother, Zeke." She smelled of roses.

Mila curtsied and looked over at Zeke who eyed her shyly and handed her a stuffed animal. "Aboo," he said, pointing at the teddy bear.

"Zeke helped me bake some cookies and I made lemonade. I thought it would taste good after the long drive." Turning to Frances and Donald she smiled and said, "I thought it would be cooler on the porch."

Zeke was a large child for his four years, a bit fleshy and big boned like his parents. He had blue eyes, blond hair and an engaging grin. He held out the plate of cookies for Mila then sat quietly with her on a striped porch swing that creaked when the metal chain rocked them back and forth.

He motioned for Mila to follow him inside. The rooms were crammed with furniture appropriated from estates Frances represented. "My play-room," he said, leading her into the dining room. In addition to the other furniture, there was a hobbyhorse and a toy chest. She followed him upstairs. "My room," he said, and showed her toy automobiles, baskets with stuffed toys, and a bookcase bulging with games and children's stories. Last he led her across the hall to a room with dotted Swiss curtains and a rag rug like Mumma Tehelia made. It was larger than the room she'd shared with her mother and her brothers. There was a small wooden bed and a dresser. Mila only guessed at what Zeke was telling her until Frances and Helen came upstairs.

"This is *your* room," Frances said. "Look, here's a cradle for your new doll."

Mila walked to the window and looked out. The sturdy chestnut cast shadows in the mid-afternoon heat and the weeping willow blew gracefully in the breeze. She felt lost in this vast strangeness and wondered if she was ever going home.

There was a light knock on her door the next morning and then it opened a little. Mila lay in bed holding her blue beret, feeling its soft comfort next to her cheek. She slid further under her covers, and then opened one eye to see Zeke standing in the doorway, motioning for her to follow.

"Mama says come to breakfast," he said. "We're going to grandma's."

The kitchen was the brightest room in the house, a cheerful yellow with white trim. Sun flooded through two large windows, one looking out on the house next door, the other facing the backyard trees burgeoning with plums and cherries. In the center of the room was a round table covered with a yellow oilcloth. Donald looked up from his paper, smiled, and patted the chair next to him. Frances poured cereal to the rim of Mila's bowl, filled it with milk, and filled a glass with orange juice.

Tentatively Mila sipped the orange liquid, wondering what it was. Looking at all the food in front of her she murmured, "Too much."

"Breakfast is the most important meal of the day," Frances said, pushing a bowl toward her. "Here's the sugar."

"Thank you," Mila said in halting English.

"That's a good start. You'll have to learn English quickly. School starts in two weeks."

"Anders said I'll go to school with Martti," Mila said. "I won't have time to go to school here."

"What is she jabbering about?" Donald asked.

"Eat your food," Frances said.

"Please. I'm full."

Donald folded his paper. "Is something wrong?" he asked. "What's the matter?"

Mila looked down at the bowl, took another bite of the unfamiliar o-shaped cereal, then pushed it back and forth in the bowl with her spoon. She tried not to gag, but it tasted cold and woody.

A look of impatience crossed Frances's face. "As poor as they were, you'd think she'd know not to waste good food," she said to Donald and snatched the bowl and carried it to the sink. "We'll let it go this time, but after this you must learn to eat what's placed in front of you," she said to Mila in Finnish.

"Let's go play," Zeke said.

"Play inside, so you don't get dirty." Donald said. "Maybe you could show Marja Leena your toys, little buddy."

In the dining room, a dark wooden table was pushed against the wall with six chairs crammed around it. A pale blue and gray hutch with open shelves held Pennsylvania Dutch plates with hex symbols. Against the opposing wall an upright piano with a round stool stood next to a wooden cabinet that held a radio and record player. Zeke opened the lid of a large chest, took out a box of crayons and began scribbling on a pad of colored paper. Mila watched as if he'd performed a magic trick. Zeke passed the box to her and she took a purple crayon, a sheet of green paper and began drawing. Zeke watched, then said, "boat," and laughed with delight. She looked at him and said "boat." Next she drew a house with trees, and flowers, and stick figures of Mumma Tehelia, Anders, mama and Martti.

Zeke took another box from the trunk and spilled it onto the floor. Mila's eyes lit up with pleasure when she saw a set of blocks like Anders made to teach her the alphabet. These were different, she noticed, two sides were blank but Anders filled all six sides with big and little letters and numbers. Mila carefully matched the color on the borders of Zeke's blocks and began filling in the blank sides with the crayons. Zeke was busy playing with his stuffed animals. The red crayon broke and she went into the kitchen to get a knife to sharpen the point as she'd seen Anders do. She was startled when she heard Frances's alarm, "What in the world are you doing with a knife?" Then seeing the block Mila had been decorating snatched it away. "Why are you ruining the blocks?"

"I was fixing them," Mila answered, taken aback by Frances's tone.

"What's the trouble?" Donald asked.

"She's coloring all over the blocks."

"Please," Mila said. "I want to go home. I miss my brothers."

"You'll get used to it soon enough, I imagine," Frances said. "Put the toys away. We're leaving."

Mila and Zeke waited in the living room for Donald to get the car. The pictures on the wall carved from thick wood made her catch her breath. The first was of three older women in an old fashioned sauna: one woman throwing water from a wooden pail onto the hot rocks, one beating herself with a bundle of young birch leaves, the third washing herself with water from a wooden pail. Mila stood lost in a haze of memory, of going to the sauna with Mumma Tehelia, a Friday night ritual. She could almost smell the sharp aroma of the birch leaves, the dry hot smell of her hair, and hear the hissing noise of the cold water being thrown on the rocks, and how good it felt when Mumma put a cold cloth on her forehead.

Donald drove through central Painesville. A one way street circled the park that had a white gazebo in the middle. Benches had been placed beside flowerbeds and old trees; people visited with each other or sat alone reading newspapers. Around the periphery were small businesses: a drug store, a bakery, a barber shop, Carlisle's Department Store and Sears & Roebuck; the courthouse and post office were next to an apartment complex and on the far side were City Hall and the Presbyterian Church.

After a few blocks, Zeke brightened when Donald stopped in front of a white house. The front yard looked cared for. The red flowers reminded Mila of home.

An open front porch held chairs, and a wide swing with bright colored pillows. "Mother," Frances called, opening the door. Geraniums and African violets covered the window ledges; plants had been crammed into every nook and cranny of the room. "This is where you'll come after school," Frances said, urging Mila into the room.

Grandma Marta was tall and big boned, like Frances, her posture, straight and proud. She wore her gray hair in a bun like Mumma Tehelia.

"This must be Mila," she said in Finnish. Mila curtsied. She smiled so sweetly Mila felt tears start.

Uncle John and Aunt Clara sat in straight-backed chairs and Mila curtsied to them as she was introduced, but her eyes lit up when she saw Aunt Helen who gave her a hug and kissed her on the cheek. "This is your Uncle Howard, my husband, and these are some of your cousins, Annie and Russy."

"You needn't curtsy to them," Frances said.

"In Finland young girls are taught to curtsy," her mother said. "The custom is natural to her."

"How are things going with her?" Howard asked, inclining his head toward Mila. "She's a pretty little thing, and seems bright."

"Children adjust quickly in these situations. I doubt that anything was explained to her, but what can children her age understand? Erkki told me it is a blessing for her. Kaija Ahlgren, her mother, vacillated for over a year and then was in a rush to send her this summer."

Mila looked up on hearing her mother's name.

"Mama," she said.

"We were talking about these adoptions before you arrived," Helen said. "I just can't understand you and Erkki. It's like going into a market and choosing a product," she continued in English. "I think it's wrong taking children away from their families. If they must be adopted it should be handled through an orphanage."

"There are too many problems with institutionalized children," Frances said. "Erkki checks out all the children my clients adopt to make sure they're healthy and normal. We don't bother with children who have problems."

Helen looked over at Mila uncomfortably. "Are you sure she can't understand what we're saying?"

"Of course not," Frances said, "but she'll learn quickly. You know how Donald feels about foreigners. I've made arrangements for her to be in Linda Katilla's second grade; Linda's mother is a client and it will be easier because Linda speaks a little Finnish."

"How is Felix doing?" Donald asked Marta, deflecting the conversation.

Marta sighed. "Not so good. It's hard for him to breathe and the doctor says he won't last long." She picked up some crocheting in the basket beside her chair to hide the tears that sprung to her eyes. Marta had nursed him for nearly four years; only in the last year had he been diagnosed with lung cancer.

Frances's brother John leaned forward in his chair and asked, "Has any headway been made in the hearings on behalf of dad?"

Finns who worked for the Harbor Alkali Plant in nearby Fairport Harbor, shoveled chromate salts from railway containers into mounds on the factory grounds. The yellowish green poison ate into their lungs. Many, like Felix Liukkonen, gave their lives before reaching sixty-five. Frances and a handful of other attorneys led the fight for Workmen's Compensation for those with respiratory problems.

"It's not final yet, but we expect the Board to render their decision within the next two weeks on whether to include injuries from exposure to chromate salts as one of the covered compensation benefits, and…"

"I thought they were supposed to reach a decision last week. What's holding them up?"

"Politics, as usual," Frances replied. She was in her milieu now. "It's been difficult to get enough votes on the Board for our side," her eyes sparkled and her voice was full of challenge, "but I did meet with the governor last week." She turned to see the effect on everyone, then turned back to John, "I thought I told you that. He's agreed to intercede on our behalf and he has influence with the Board." She sat back in her chair with an air of satisfaction. "It's always the same story," her voice grew more strident, again she moved forward in her chair. "Only a few of us are involved in the *real* struggle; the so-called 'workers' advocates' pulled out when things got difficult. Weak sisters who call themselves men and don't have the courage of their convictions." She jabbed her finger in the general direction of the world.

Her mother rose from her chair and turned to the children. "I've made *Nisu*. Come to the kitchen and I'll pour you some milk to go with it." "*Nisu*,"

Mila repeated, she loved the braided egg bread seasoned with cardamom and topped with an egg wash sprinkled with sugar.

Shyly Mila asked if she could help and Marta put her hand to Mila's cheek, her etched face turning to a smile. "Call me grandma," she said. "You can carry the silver."

Mila helped her put the bread and butter on the table, then went back and sat next to Zeke and smiled at her new cousins.

"Well, I know all the workers and their families certainly appreciate everything you've done," John said.

Barely acknowledging him, Frances bent to pick up the briefcase beside her chair. "They should," she said rummaging through papers and pulling out a folder that she handed to her brother. "Here's your payment schedule, by the way. I've figured out your mortgage for the next sixty-five months, and this shows the payments you've made so far." She tapped the paper full of columns.

As Helen returned to her chair, Frances said, "I'll have your schedule ready next week." Helen looked uncomfortable, as John raised his voice.

"So we don't really know if father will get any benefits?"

"He'll probably be dead before we get the results, but Mother should be able to draw monthly widow's benefits. It will make it easier for her to remain here, in the house. It won't cover all her needs." Frances looked around the room. "We'll have to get the whole family together and decide how much each of us will contribute for mother's care since she doesn't drive and refuses to master English."

In the car going home Frances snapped her purse shut. "What a bunch of losers," she said. "Father and mother just kept grinding out children. None of them have a dime to speak of and they're still expecting me to take care of them, carry their mortgages, go to court to win the battles."

"You're so good at it, Ulle," Donald patted her leg and smiled at her.

"Pathetic," she said. "I promise you I'll never die poor."

That much I already know,
That I'm in a foreign country
Utterly unknown to me,
I was better off at home
More respected in my homeland.

Ibid., Runo 7, lines 197-201

CHAPTER FIVE

▼

Two days later, Frances said, "Chip Brooker from the Times will be in my office this afternoon for an interview."

Frances went upstairs with the children and changed Zeke out of his overalls. She helped Mila into a yellow dress that highlighted her blond hair and tied yellow ribbons at the ends of her pigtails. Mila felt quite beautiful, and started to spin. She hoped she could take the dress back home so mama could see it.

Donald waited for them in the Buick. His skin had a pink scrubbed look, his clothes fastidious. The Panama hat gave him a carefree air tilted ever so slightly to one side, covering his baldhead. Frances looked dowdy sitting beside him.

Mila still felt queasy riding in the car. She concentrated on a newsboy delivering papers on a bicycle.

"Park here," Frances said. Donald trailed in his wife's wake, smiling pleasantly and holding each child by a hand. Frances seemed like a different person when she entered the front door of her office building.

Rows of books lined one wall, an enormous desk held stacks of long manila folders thick with papers unevenly sticking out the sides. In the center of the desk five or six books, one on top of the other, lay opened. To the right of the books was a telephone and behind the desk was a long table heaped with more files and books.

"This is where I work," Frances told her.

Mila was fascinated by the file cabinets, wondering what they were and what they held, but before she could ask, there was a knock and Chip Brooker came in followed by two other men, carrying equipment.

"Good afternoon, Councilwoman," he said. "I see you have everyone gathered for the photos." He shook hands with Donald and said hello to Zeke. Looking at Mila, he said, "This must be our newest acquisition," he laughed pleasantly.

"She doesn't understand you, but this is our little Marja Leena," Frances said.

Mila curtsied.

"You're a real little cutey," he told her.

His helpers began setting up bright lights and screens. "Let's have you all stand here," he said, directing them in front of the desk. "Mr. Robertson, you sit in the chair holding Zeke on your lap, with the little girl standing at your arm." He turned toward Frances, "Or would you rather hold her?"

"She can stand next to me," Frances said. "Now you'll make sure and write that we've adopted a war orphan and are taking her into our home to ease the trauma she has suffered in Europe?"

"Indeed we will," he assured her, "as well as your formidable career: City Councilman, City Manager, Acting Judge, and member of the Democratic Central Committee. Have I left anything out? The notes you sent were useful. I won't have to do much rewriting," he said. "So, both parents are dead? - from the war?"

"The father is dead. The mother is alive but living a life of poverty."

"I know you've arranged other adoptions. Wasn't that enough - to help others?"

Frances's expression took on a look of benevolence. "It was incumbent on us, I felt, to help on a more personal level. That's why Donald and I decided to adopt Marja Leena and give our little Zeke a sister."

"That's inspiring. If only the world had more good people like you." Chip shook his head in admiration. "I understand you'll be the keynote speaker at this year's Labor Day parade and picnic at the Fairgrounds," he said. "We don't want to forget that."

"It's my honor to have been chosen this year and this is truly a time to celebrate the rights of workers. We've just received word that the employees, in some cases the widows and children, will be eligible to receive compensation for the lung injuries they've suffered as the result of chemical exposure at the Harbor Alkali Plant."

Brooker scribbled on a pad, "Anything else?"

"That about covers it," she said.

Donald turned to Zeke who was restless. "As soon as mother's through we'll go to the ice cream parlor."

Zeke jumped up and down. I want chocolate," he said. "A double decker, Daddy."

Donald rumpled his hair while Frances and Chip continued chatting about some proposed legislation at the state capitol.

Mila stood mesmerized in front of the broad expanse of windows overlooking the sidewalk leading to the building. An elderly black man was walking up the sidewalk clutching a large basket.

"Mr. Brooker, would you please excuse us for a minute?" Donald's voice was strained and he took Frances by the elbow and led her to the front antechamber of her office. In a whisper he said, "I don't ask much of you, but if you can't get rid of these... these so-called 'clients,'" he pointed at the man who was now climbing the few steps to the landing, "then I will. It's degrading; it cheapens your stature as a lawyer. God! bringing baskets of food, jugs of cider - like - peasants. I won't have it."

They were interrupted by a knock at the door, and Frances opened it. "Good afternoon, Mr. Thomas. I'm busy at the moment."

"Not meaning to bother you, Mrs. Robertson. Just didn't get a bill for your help to my boy, and my Missus thought you would enjoy fresh sweet corn and a loaf of her homemade bread. Good day to you, Ma'am."

"You don't even charge them," Donald exploded. "I don't want Negroes coming to this office!"

"They can't afford anything else; this *is* the way they pay me. We'll talk about it later," she said and walked back to where Chip stood talking to the children.

"Daddy," Zeke interrupted, "let's go get ice cream now."

The days tumbled together until the summer days grew shorter and crispness began to enter the evenings. Each day Mila went to bed longing for home and family. Zeke became the bookends for her day, waking her in the morning and hugging her good night at bedtime and playing together in-between. They each found the affection they lacked from the adults in each other.

Sunday nights became Mila's favorite time of the week because they listened to music before dinner. She and Zeke sat together wrapped in a blanket and often Zeke fell asleep with his head in her lap. Frances believed play and learning should be combined.

Frances introduced her to the magic by saying "This is a phonograph record," pulling a large black circle with a tiny hole in the middle from a cardboard jacket. "You mustn't get any marks or scratches on it and don't drop it because it will break." She placed it on the machine beside the piano. In Finnish she explained to Mila that "The name of this symphony is 'Sleeping Beauty,'" and she told her the story before she started the music. Mila had never heard anything so beautiful. If only she could be like the Sleeping

Beauty, she thought, to disappear into sleep until someone came and carried her home.

While they listened to the music Mila forgot for a moment that tomorrow was the first day of school and although she loved her new clothes, she felt scared. She knew so few words of English, only the words Zeke used and a few words for food. No matter how she struggled, the sentences tumbled in her ears like a puzzle making no sense.

She was quiet at dinner, picking at her food until Frances asked "Why the long face?"

"I don't want to go to school," Mila said.

"Once you're used to it you'll be fine."

Mila moved closer to Donald feeling safer, and wishing she could talk to him, and tell him she was frightened. He often held her in his lap in the big chair while he read or listened to the news on the radio. No matter how she tried she was unable to think of Frances as mother, and continued to call her madam or nothing.

"You children go get undressed for your bath," Frances said. "It's late and I'm tired."

Frances lifted the children into the tub, rubbing soap on the cloth and washing them. "Hold still," she told them, "Let me wash your ears."

She laid out Mila's red corduroy jumper and the white blouse with puffy sleeves and red trim and the new white socks with lace tops and shiny black buckle shoes. Of all her new clothes, those were Mila's favorites.

Donald came in and kissed her on the forehead. "Good night," he said as he did every night, running his fingers up her arm like a bug, "Sleep tight, and don't let the bed bugs bite."

Mila didn't understand the game, but liked the attention. He turned out the light and she lay in the dark. She hid her memories in a pretend box that held everything she loved, there were the stories Anders made up for her, mother danced to the radio, Mumma took her to the sauna, and Martti played with her in the snow. She tried not to think of everything at once, but saved the best ones until she really needed them, but tonight she felt angry. She hated mama and wanted to tell her how horrible she was for sending her away. America felt so lonely, and she feared mama didn't know where to find her.

After Zeke popped in on Monday morning she dawdled coming downstairs. The first thing she heard was Frances's voice.

"I've got a three thirty hearing in court today and then tonight's the council meeting, I thought I'd grab a quick bite at Carlisle's and go straight to the seven o'clock meeting. Would you pick up the children from mothers? There's left over roast beef for dinner."

Donald looked up from the morning paper. "But the Bridge tournament is beginning tonight. I told you that weeks ago. I won't be home until late."

Frances slammed the glass bottle on the kitchen table, sloshing milk over the top. "That's too late for the children to stay at mother's on a school night. I might have known it. It's all on my shoulders again."

Mila's stomach knotted. Each moment meant school was getting closer.

"Come here," Frances said. "You're going to be late." She buttoned the back of her blouse, then asked for the brush to braid her hair into skin tight braids, if mama had pulled so hard she would have put up a terrible fuss.

"Hurry up," Frances scolded. "I have to get you to school, Zeke to mother's, and still get to my office on time. Eat! And don't waste your food."

Mila pushed back her chair and carried her glass and bowl to the sink, still half filled with food.

"You sit right down and finish." Frances said.

"I can't eat any more."

Frances grabbed the bowl, emptied the milk and poured the cereal into the triangular shaped colander in the corner of the sink.

"If we weren't in a hurry I'd make you finish," she said.

Mila's stomach rebelled and she started gagging. In an instant Frances grabbed her by the arm and rushed her into the bathroom, while Zeke sat still at the table with wide frightened eyes, saying nothing.

Mila stood over the toilet bowl as breakfast streamed out of her nose and mouth. Grabbing her by the back of the neck Frances plunged Mila's head up and down, up and down into her vomit until her arm grew tired and her rage subsided. In a daze Mila arrived at school. Her clothes had been changed, but her shoes were wet and her hair was still damp and dripped cold beads of water down her neck. She could smell traces of vomit. At recess Miss Katilla asked her to stay.

"Did you have an accident with the drinking fountain?" she asked. "Your pretty ribbons are all wet."

Mila shook her head trying not to cry. She had forced the terrifying incomprehensible scene deep into her mind, refusing to picture it.

"You look so sad. Is there something you want to tell me?"

Mila looked down at the floor and spoke in a voice so quiet Linda Katilla leaned closer to hear. "My brother Anders must still be too sick to come and get me, but can you tell me when my mother is coming to take me home?"

Chapter Six

▼

Helsinki, Finland
Late September 1950

The head nurse of the tuberculosis ward at Helsinki's Central Hospital motioned for the young man to join her at the nursing station. Anders was a favorite of the nursing staff; he walked toward her, tall and graceful, his dark hair slicked back, his gray eyes deep and expressive, he looked older than his sixteen years. Reaching into a drawer she handed him a single sheet of paper and a few streetcar tokens. "Remember, Anders, this is only a forty-eight hour pass. Take these too," she said, handing him some coins.

Anders smiled faintly, but his tone was firm, "Thank you nurse Bensonnen, but that's not necessary. Two dollars is a lot of money."

"Just take it." She closed his long slender fingers over the coins. "Now don't forget – Wednesday at nine - or you'll get us both in trouble." Then she turned and walked away briskly down the polished linoleum corridor.

Forty-eight hours. As if he could forget. It had been late June when he entered. The warmth of summer had been at its peak. He and Mila and Martti had gone swimming and sunned themselves on slabs of glacier polished granite. Now it was late September and the weather was brisk.

He must settle for such occasional furloughs and eventual release. If he stayed away from the hospital, the Helsinki police would show up. So many young people succumbed to the disease, the authorities enforced hospitalization of those already afflicted. He understood the reasoning, but he felt like a common criminal. His bacteria count had been lower than ever before and he was slowly gaining weight. If his luck held out he could be released for good in two months. He couldn't afford to get sick again.

It felt good to stretch his legs during the half-mile walk to the massive bus and railway station in the middle of Helsinki where he would pick up the streetcar to Saimaantie Street. He pulled up the collar of the warm jacket and trousers Aunt Sofi had left for him at the hospital. He wondered why she hadn't waited to see him. Unlike his mother, she wasn't afraid of visiting the ward. She must have come while he was at his weekly check-up. The jacket still smelled of Uncle Victor's *tupa*, the workingman's cigarette. The trousers gathered where he belted them, the seat was worn, the legs short, like the sleeves of the jacket. He longed for the day he'd dress in new pants and a decent jacket that fit properly, the way he liked. The TB ward was like a small village where the patients learned skills from one another. He remembered seeing his father sew and mend and now he had learned in the same way; he planned to alter the clothes when he got home.

His new leather shoes made walking easy. They were the nicest shoes he'd ever owned. Old Jarkko, whose skin resembled the leather he worked with, taught cobbling in exchange for haircuts. Anders had learned to barber from a woman patient, a hairdresser, and the skill earned him enough money for personal necessities, like a toothbrush from the hospital canteen. He'd learned photography from Pekka Sandstrom, a frail Swede in his early twenties, who was glad for a friend. Most of the Finnish patients didn't speak Swedish and didn't want to. Anders wanted to keep up with the Swedish he'd learned as a child.

The cost of one of Pekka's cameras could have paid his family's rent for months. Anders photographed patients and staff, catching them in daily routines, glimpsing signs of life in flirtations, capturing anxiety or relief on the patients' faces as they sat in the weighing-in chair, a weekly ordeal.

His friendship with Pekka had blossomed despite the differences in their backgrounds. They shared a love for the ocean though for different reasons: Anders fished for dinner; Pekka sailed for fun. They loved books and Pekka's eclectic library augmented the ward's spotty collection. Pekka taught him Bridge, Anders taught him chess on the small portable set left to him by his father.

Depression was common on the wards, often as deadly as the disease. The doctors had resorted to electroshock in an effort to improve Pekka's deteriorating mental state. He rarely left his bed, but lay in a daze asking Anders to stop the voices coming from under his pillow. Anders told him to turn off the radio and the voices would go away. There was no radio, but the suggestion seemed to work. Anders didn't understand Pekka's constant moroseness since he appeared to have everything: books, clothes, cameras, and a family who visited and brought him fresh fruit.

Anders hadn't seen his family since he'd entered the hospital. Kaija, terrified of infection, never came to visit. He no longer missed her, but he was anxious to find out about Mila and Martti. Mila should have started school and she'd be bubbling with stories. He smiled. God the child never stopped talking. He laughed remembering her attempt to understand what a 'chatterbox' was after he called her one. *What does a chatterbox do? What does the box look like? Is it pretty? Is the box inside me? Does Martti have one too?* All the while dancing about.

The din of voices bounced off the high ceilings in the railway station, a radio played tango music. It was warm inside and the steamy windows sent beads of moisture down the walls. Young boys with shoeshine kits solicited business. He caught sight of reddish blond curls and a stocky build moving gracefully across the room and disappearing behind the glass and steel doors of the station. Martti's walk was unmistakable. Anders hurried to catch up. Martti had stopped on the steps leading to the open entrance hall and Anders watched him reach into a greasy bag and pull out his favorite treat, a deep-fried, sugar covered pastry.

"Hey, Martti, the shoeshine business must be going well," he said coming from behind and placing his hand on his younger brother's shoulder.

Martti sputtered, choking when he heard the familiar voice.

"Afraid of the truancy officers?" Anders teased.

"No," Martti laughed. "I'm too fast for them."

Last year his teacher reported that though mathematics came as naturally as breathing for him, Martti had difficulty with reading.

"Mother didn't say you were coming home," Martti said running his hand through his unruly hair.

"She doesn't know. I'm only home for a few days. You've grown taller in three months."

Martti smiled, "I'll be eleven in a few weeks."

Anders pulled the coins from his pocket and handed a few to his brother. "Call it an early birthday present," he said.

Martti broke into a smile. "Thanks," he said, counting the money.

Anders looked serious. "Why are you here this time of day? School isn't out this early." Anders cursed his illness. He should be there to keep an eye on Martti. His mother was useless in dealing with his brother. The burst of optimism he'd experienced earlier faded. Damn his tuberculosis, damn his father for dying and leaving him to cope with everything. He had to get strong and soon. Averting his eyes, Martti pointed across the wide expanse of the station. "I left my kit over there. I'll be right back."

As Anders waited he saw a blond woman come out of the restroom and grab Martti by the hand. He saw Martti gesture and the woman turn in his direction. Together they walked over to him. Her dress left little to the imagination. She had red lips stark against her white skin, and big bright eyes. She wore black ankle strap pumps and her legs were bare; the hem of her dress uneven. She let go of Martti's hand and smiled provocatively at Anders, looking him up and down.

"A friend?" she asked Martti, staring into Anders's gaunt face. "A bit young, but... not too young." Leaning down to whisper in Martti's ear, loud enough for Anders to hear, she said, "Did you tell him the rate?" She reached into the purse hanging from her wrist. "Here," she said, handing Martti some coins, "go get another donut for yourself."

"Forget it. Go get your shoeshine kit and wait for me at the front door," Anders said, his voice was hard edged. He looked at the woman and in the same voice said, "I don't care what business you're in, but my brother isn't part of it. Understand? He's not your errand boy. You and your friends keep your hands off."

"You've got it all wrong," she answered. "No one's bothering the boy."

"*Satana*" he swore. "You're in trouble...the boy's only ten."

She moistened her lower lip with her tongue. "Forget the money this time. There's a room back here," she said, gesturing behind her.

Anders nodded. "I know. The broom closet." Anders felt disgust at the tawdriness of it all, and anger at seeing Martti scramble for a few coins as he had done at the same age. Martti seemed so young.

The streetcar stopped to pick up passengers and Anders turned to his brother. "Keep away from her or you'll have more than the law giving you trouble."

Defensive, Martti said, "You did it."

"Yes, and now I know better. We'll find another way. I'll be out of the hospital soon and I'll help. The most important thing for you is school."

Anders looked out the window as they passed the familiar buildings. "Aren't you supposed to pick Mila up from school? Why were you at the station this time of day?"

Martti twisted in his seat. "My friend Ivan lives down that street," he said.

"I asked you a question," Anders repeated. "Why were you at the station so early? Is Mila at Mumma's?"

Martti jumped up and pushed the button to get off. "This is our stop," he said.

It was drizzling when they got off the trolley. As they walked the three blocks home Anders asked, "Where is your jacket? It's getting colder."

"I'm not cold," Martti answered.

"You haven't changed. Even as a baby you kicked off your blankets," Anders said. "You'll get wet even if you don't get cold."

"I'm not a baby. Stop treating me like one." Martti reached into his ruck-sack and pulled out his jacket. "Okay," he said, slipping his arms into the sleeves. "I'm going to hang out with Ivan for awhile."

"See Ivan tomorrow." Anders reached for Martti's shoulder, egging him down the street. "I just got home and I want to see you, play some chess with you tonight."

Anders thought about all he and Martti had been through. The first time he'd been in Sweden was early 1943, he was nine and Martti was four and refused to talk or leave Anders' side. Lars was in the sanatorium and Kaija was pregnant. During the war the Finnish government evacuated children from Helsinki whose parents couldn't get them to the countryside. Anders didn't know or care about that, he was excited since he never expected to have a chance to fly and considered the trip a grand adventure.

Two small planes left together from the Malm Airport on the outskirts of Helsinki, one carrying a small contingent of Finnish military and political figures traveling for war discussions, and the other carrying forty-five Finnish children. The planes were white with big red crosses painted on both sides of the plane. A half-hour into the flight, machine guns fired and the children watched speechless seeing the plane next to them fall into the sea.

When they landed they were taken to a schoolhouse where they remained until Swedish families came to pick out the child they would foster. Martti was a beautiful child and was selected time after time, but refused to let go of Anders, who was tall and ungainly with straight home cut hair and a som-ber expression. Finally the Hedlunds agreed to take them both. After a few months, another family came and took Martti. Harold Hedlund had grown fond of the eager and bright boy, calling him 'son,' and since they wanted an older child who would be of more help Anders remained with them and one child of their own, six-year-old Trudi.

Anders loved his life. He went to school, had friends and even a used bike and his own room. He was required to do a few chores, like shovel-ing snow and chopping wood, but nothing he considered hard. During the long winter evenings, Hedlund and Anders played chess and together they designed and built model boats, especially the narrow long boats that navigated the Swedish canals. Mr. Hedlund was lockmaster of the Swedish water-ways and in the summers sometimes took Anders with him on his rounds. The Hedlunds were church going folks who forbade alcohol, smoking or swearing, but they did not stint on affection for the enthusiastic eager-to-please young boy. Calling Hedlund 'Papa Harold' came natural since he still thought of his own father as Lars. Lars had been more like an older brother, only eighteen years older than his son. Most of all Anders remembered Lars' orders, impatience and temper. Not until the perspective of years did he understand his father. Now he empathized, realizing what illness and fear of dying at an early age had done to him.

He'd grown tired during the short walk. He stopped at Olaf's store and bought a wedge of cheese and a loaf of dark rye with the rest of his money. When they got home Martti raced ahead, taking two steps at a time.

"Anders is home," his voice echoed down the stairway.

Anders expected Mila to rush out and throw her arms around him. Instead Kaija sat at the table, a game of solitaire spread in front of her. Her hand was poised to lift a cup sitting next to a half empty bottle of vodka. She folded the cards together as he entered. "I didn't know you were coming home," she said.

"How would you?" he asked. He sat down. "Is Mila at Mumma's?" he asked.

Kaija got up from the table and went to the cabinet next to the pot-bellied stove. She unwrapped the package from the grocers, sliced the bread and cheese and put them on a plate. She pulled a metal canister from the shelf and busied herself at the stone sink. Filling the kettle with water she asked, "How about some tea. You're wet. I've got real black tea." Not looking at Anders she turned, "Martti, go bring up some wood." She shivered, rubbing her arms. "We have sugar cubes, too."

"Black tea and sugar cubes? You must have a new boyfriend." He caught Martti at the door, "First go to Mumma's and get Mila."

Kaija's back was to him. "Is that a new dress?" he asked. "That shade of blue is nice on you."

Kaija turned and walked back to the table, dropping to the chair. "I have something to tell you."

"I know, I know. I saw him," Anders interrupted. "Do you know he's running errands for the prostitutes?"

"He's stubborn. I can't control him."

"You don't try." Anders said.

"You sound just like your father. It's easy to criticize while you're in the hospital leaving me to do everything."

"Neither of us chose to be there," Anders said.

"Lars's vanity kept him from having the operation on his lungs. He could have lived. He just didn't want his body disfigured. He was crazy, drinking cow's blood, eating boiled ants, and sitting in the sun. Those old home remedies never helped anyone. Damn him."

"Is it easier to blame him than to take responsibility?" Anders asked.

Kaija poured vodka into her cup.

"Where's Mila?" Anders asked. "Martti needs to get her from Mumma's."

"She's not there. She's gone," Kaija said in a rush.

"Gone?" He pushed back his chair, roughly turned his mother around to face him. "She doesn't have TB? Is she sick?"

"No, not gone like that. She's gone - to America."

"I thought you were over that crazy idea." He collapsed in the chair and put his head in his hands.

"Money has been tight. It's hard to get food. Martti can eat at the station, but..."

"What's wrong with you?" His voice rose in a blur of despair. "She could have stayed with Mumma."

"Mother's been sick, her heart isn't strong."

"Sofi, then. Sofi would have kept her. No wonder Aunt Sofi didn't want to see me when she came to the hospital."

He grabbed her and shook her. "She's only a little girl. She eats like a bird." He picked up the vodka and hurled it across the room, shattering glass, the liquor dripping down the bare wall. "You have money for vodka. For tea. For a new dress." A black looked passed over his eyes as he raised his fist. "You got *money* for sending her to America. You sold her. You..." His fist crashed against the table scattering the cards to the floor.

"I did it for her. I wanted something better for her. What can *I* give her?" Her anger rose for an instant as she looked around the room and sneered. "What kind of life could she have here? Now she has a chance. Do you want her to end up like me, emptying other people's trash? She'll have a good life now with a rich family. She'll have everything."

"Lars knew you all right. He told me you'd send us away. The last thing he told me was to take care of Martti and Mila, to keep the family together." He shook his head, "I can't even do that."

"She'll be back, Anders. Once she finishes school she'll be back."

"How can you be so stupid? If you signed papers that means they have her for good. What have you done? I can't stay here." Ashen-faced he went out the door and slammed it. He leaned against the wall drained of all energy and sank to the stairs unable to go up or down. He lost track of time and place, unaware of Martti coming to help him into bed. In a troubled sleep he pictured Mila's face, her laugh. He couldn't remember ever feeling so hopeless.

As the days passed, the weather grew colder and seeped through the walls. His cheeks reddened like a rouged woman's. He turned all night while his body burned with fever and his blankets grew heavy with sweat. He heard harsh breathing, saw blood on the pillow. In his delirium he wondered if it was his father's blood or his own.

After a week the policemen came, and the men dressed in white uniforms. Anders floated down the stairway with them.

He heard Nurse Bensonnen's voice. "Take a last look at your son, Mrs. Ahlgren. He won't make it through the night. Why didn't you contact us sooner? He was doing so much better."

CHAPTER SEVEN

▼

The days got shorter and the first snow began to fall. Mila felt like the trees, unprotected against the cold of winter. Fear of Frances and the look of disapproval on Daddy's face when she spoke in Finnish made her try harder to learn English. Zeke helped her by speaking in simple sentences and showing her the names of things through pointing and pantomime. Her grasp of English impressed Miss Katilla, "I've never seen anyone learn so fast," she told Mila in front of the class, and rewarded her with a small part in the Christmas pageant.

What happiness she felt in the house came from Zeke. He expressed no jealousy at sharing with his new sister. When he struggled to pronounce Marja Leena, she told him, "In Finland they call me Mila."

"Me?" he asked, pointing to himself.

"Yes. Me-la."

"Me-la," his face lighted with pleasure.

He was a quiet child, content to watch, keeping his thoughts to himself. Frances seldom kissed or held him, but sometimes gave him a pat on the head. He rarely provoked her. Mila gave him the attention his mother was too busy for; they became peaceful companions.

"Aunt Helen will pick you up from school today," Frances said at breakfast where she issued orders for the day. Mila noted her moods like a barometer of storm warnings.

Being with Aunt Helen soothed Mila. "Will she pick Zeke up too?"

Frances took four bowls from the cupboard. "No. You and Zeke are having your pictures taken tomorrow and I want you to look your best. Helen is going to give you a permanent."

"What does *look your best* mean?"

"Don't you ever run out of questions?" Frances said. Anders encouraged her vivacious personality and probing mind, but those attributes irritated Frances. After a moment Mila risked another question. "What is a permanent?"

"It makes your hair curly."

Aunt Helen was in the hallway outside her classroom when the dismissal bell rang. She held out her arms for Mila to nestle close while she visited with Miss Katilla. She was tall like Frances, with a flare for fashion that gave the simple slacks and blouse she wore elegance.

Mila loved going to her house; she praised her for the simplest task. There was neither the somberness nor the slightly musty smell of Frances's house. Here it smelled of roasting meats and baking bread. Pinks, golds and greens made it seem like springtime. White dotted Swiss curtains were immaculately starched, pulled back with colored ties inviting light through the spotless windows. The round kitchen table held a mixed bouquet of flowers. Books and artwork were everywhere. And music.

"How about a glass of milk and some cake before we start?" Aunt Helen asked. Before Mila answered, the snack was on the table. Aunt Helen sat across from her with a cup of coffee.

"Miss Katilla says you're doing well learning English. Frances must be pleased."

"Pleased?" Mila asked.

"Yes, of course. Shall we get started? Your hair is so fine I don't want to burn it," she said, undoing Mila's braids.

Helen massaged the shampoo into Mila's scalp and gently worked up the lather, toweled her nearly dry and propped a hand mirror on the table so Mila could watch.

"You have such beautiful blond hair," Helen said. "How short shall we make it? About here?" she asked, pointing the scissors to just above Mila's shoulder.

"I won't have braids anymore?" Mila asked.

"No more braids."

Helen handed her a packet of thin rectangular papers. "You hand these to me when I ask," Helen said. When she finished, she applied the lotion; Mila flinched.

"What's happened here?" Helen asked. "You have bruises and sores on your scalp. Did you hurt your head on the playground?"

"When am I going home? I don't want to be here anymore." Mila blurted.

"You mustn't talk like that," Helen said.

"But I miss my mother and Mumma, and Anders and Martti."

"Talking about Finland just causes you trouble." She held Mila in her arms. "You must learn not to make Frances cross. She holds all the power."

Mila didn't understand the words so much as she felt the hopelessness in Aunt Helen's voice.

Looking out at the falling snow Mila asked in a quiet voice, "What if they can't find me anymore?"

At school the next day, Miss Katilla had her stand in front of the class to show off her new hairstyle. "How pretty you look!" she said. The Christmas season seemed to excite everyone with a new friendliness. Ribbon streamers hung from the streetlights in the center of town and windows were decorated with trees. The gazebo in the center of town was decorated with Christmas lights and a Crèche of the nativity sat in front of City Hall.

Each day, starting December first, she hurried to grandma Marta's where they opened a small door on their advent calendars, then grandma gave them each a piece of candy or a toy and read fairy tales. Mila never tired of the story of Hansel and Gretel and the wicked stepmother.

After Zeke went upstairs for his nap Mila helped grandma make Christmas cookies.

"Grandma, am I a bad girl?" she asked.

"What makes you ask a question like that?"

"I do things and get punished."

"What kind of bad things?"

"I get sick to my stomach," she hesitated to go on. "She says not to wander around the house at night, but if I don't go to the bathroom I have an accident and then she spanks me."

"She was strict with her brothers and sisters too. You just have to try harder not to make her angry."

Mila sat with the beater in her hand. "I do try," she said, "I try very hard. She doesn't like me. I think Daddy likes me, but..."

Mila felt the same as she had with Aunt Helen. She couldn't make them understand.

"Would you like to put the cookies in the oven all by yourself?"

Mila got down from the stool while grandma held the oven door open like in Hansel and Gretel.

Frances came into the house carrying groceries, her briefcase, and a bulging purse. She dropped into her rocker and put her briefcase on the floor next to her. "There are presents in the trunk and another bag of groceries on the back seat. Did John and Clara drop off the children? Where are they?"

"They're cutting out paper chains. I haven't heard a peep from them. I gave them hot chocolate and cookies." At the door he paused and in a softer voice said, "I thought John looked a bit worried."

"I can't imagine why John's company is holding the Christmas party so late this year. I hope he doesn't get bad news after the first of the year when they hand out pink slips. I'll have to refigure his mortgage if he loses his job."

"Too bad when folks can't take care of business the way you do," he said slipping into his jacket.

Frances smiled at the compliment.

Donald returned from the car, his arms laden with bags. "Brrr, it's cold out there and starting to snow harder. A real Christmas."

Frances reached into her briefcase, and waved some papers, a smile brightening her face. "Two big checks arrived today. One for the Lattimer estate and another from the Olsons for the adoption."

"No wonder you're so happy," he leaned over to squeeze her knee. "We'll have to see what Santa brings you tonight," he said, pushing her dress higher on her thigh.

Her mouth turned up in a provocative smile, "Hard work pays off." She straightened, "But this is what I wanted to show you. Marja Leena's mother sent a letter and a Christmas card to her."

"Is she asking for money again?"

"No. That's what I thought. Translating, Frances read: *Mila my daughter, this is a letter and Christmas card from your Finnish mother, wanting to know how you are in America. Remember to be the good girl you can be and don't be lonesome. You have two families now, one in America and one in Finland. Love from your mother.*'"

"She's just making it worse," Donald said.

Annie and Mila came into the room. Although there was only four months difference in age, Annie looked older than Mila. She was tall like her mother, with the same brown curly hair and Clara's gentle demeanor. Annie was Mila's best friend and without laughing or ridiculing mistakes helped Mila learn English. Like her mother, she could correct in such a considerate way Mila remembered the new word with pleasure and rolled it around in her mind and on her tongue.

"Hello, dear," Frances said to her niece. "Have you finished the paper chains already?"

"Yes, *Tante*. Russy and Zeke can't paste at all. We did all the chains and most of the popcorn. Mila and I gave them Lincoln logs and cowboys and Indians to play with. Doesn't Mila's hair look pretty?"

Mila held a long green and red paper chain. "Look what Annie and I done," she said.

"Did," Frances corrected. "'Look what Annie and I did.'"

"Did," Mila repeated. "We done...we *did* it all."

"Yes, that looks nice." Frances took the chain. "Why don't you girls help me wrap this around the tree and then we'll see about dinner. We're having a special treat tonight. Sloppy Joes."

"My favorite, *Tante*," Annie screeched. "Are we having buns too?"

"Of course." Frances stepped away from the tree. "Doesn't that look nice? After dinner we'll get the stockings and hang them next to the tree. Mila, show Annie the knitted stockings grandma made for all of you."

"Knitted stockings?" Mila looked puzzled.

Annie pointed to her knee socks, "Knitted stockings."

Mila's face brightened and she took Annie's hand. "I go look."

"*I will go look*," Frances said automatically, releasing a sigh.

"They get on well," Donald said, settling back into his chair and picking up the newspaper. "I'll be glad when she sounds less like a foreigner."

"Linda Katilla says children her age are natural mimics and learn languages rapidly. She said the girl is learning faster than she expected, understands more than she speaks, and will be reading at grade level before long."

"Since the adoption is final; there's no reason for her to know about the letter."

"I'm glad you agree." Frances reached for the letter she'd poked into her briefcase. "As of now all communication is severed. I'll write a short letter to the mother and make it clear she'd better not cause any trouble."

Donald looked up from his paper. "What kind of trouble could she cause?"

"Probably nothing. I'm not sure how much her lawyer in Helsinki told her about the change of plans; she did think the Rintas were adopting her. I'm not going to rush to have her become a naturalized citizen. That way if anything comes up it'll be easier to send her back."

Mila went to bed happier than usual after spending so many hours with Annie, but when she got into bed she thought about Christmas in Finland. She wished she could see the ice candles and she was sure Anders must be back by now. He would find her, she knew he would. She held Aboo close.

What are you crying for, poor sister,
My sad sister – and so young?"

Kalevala, Runo 4, Lines 53-54

CHAPTER EIGHT

▼

Helsinki, Finland
Helsinki Central Hospital
Christmas, 1950

As Anders faded in and out of consciousness, all he could think of was Mila, failure, and a desire to drift away, away from problems, away from thinking. He felt like someone had reached deep inside and pulled out an intrinsic part of his body - the part that made him want to live. Pekka hovered around him like a mother hen. Anders heard him through a fog of disinterest.

"Here Anders, mother brought this egg custard, eat some, just a few bites."

"This pillow is softer, if you raise your head, I'll slip it under for you."

"Anders, Mrs. Niemi has been leaving messages in the men's ward every day for the last two weeks, she says you're the only one who can cut her hair."

"Kirsten has been hanging around again madly in love with you, and doesn't believe I'm giving you her messages."

Through it all Anders lay comatose. After all the gentle efforts to cheer Anders failed, Pekka lost his temper and screamed, "For God's sake Anders, you've got to snap out of this. You're not dead; you're alive, so act like it. You can't give up now."

Listening to his voice, Anders remembered his own distress over Pekka's health. His health seemed under control then and now the tables had turned

- that was life. His decision to return to the living occurred within seconds and his voice came unbidden. "Feeling better now are you, Pekka?"

Pekka jumped back, startled by the familiar sound. He clasped Anders's bony hand and his voice cracked with emotion, "Thank God. What a Christmas blessing! We've been so worried."

The traditional Christmas candles glowed dimly through the windows of Einer's Bar on Porrintie Street. Martti paced about outside trying to keep warm. He could hear the music and laughter that seeped through the wooden walls. He found a stump of wood and climbed up on it to peer through the double paned winter windows but the steam and cigarette smoke circling the hazy air made it hard to see. The familiar gesture of his mother brushing the hair out of her face caught Martti's attention. She was leaning back in her chair, laughing at the man with his arm around her shoulder. Martti jumped off the stump and pounded on the door. The man who opened the door asked good-naturedly, "What have we here? Someone seeking the Christ child's parents?"

From the bar, Mikhail, a portly man whose arm had been shot off in the winter war of 1939 said "Hi, Martti. Come to get your mother? You're early tonight."

Martti clenched and unclenched his fists. "Tell her to come out."

The warmth that briefly enveloped him was gone when the door closed and he buried his hands under his arms to stay warm. If Mila had been along she would be oblivious, dancing to the tango music. He didn't miss her. Even if she was company on nights like this he felt grateful not to have her along with her incessant running and talking. He dreaded these nights and hated his mother's drinking, the men she brought home, her moods, one minute happy the next swearing at everyone or crying about her life. He threatened to kill himself if she didn't stop drinking, but she only smiled sadly at him and didn't change. Only Anders had any influence on her and he was gone, maybe dying, like their father.

A few minutes passed until Kaija came out knotting her wool scarf under her chin. "You shouldn't have come tonight. It's freezing out here," she said pulling on her mittens. She had to shout now, as Martti ran ahead of her. "Where's your hat?"

"You promised you wouldn't go to the bar tonight," he called over his shoulder. He kicked a stray pinecone. "You said we'd go to Mumma's."

"We'll go tomorrow night instead. It's too late tonight." She caught up to him and tried to put her hand on his shoulder, but he shrugged her away.

"You promised," Martti said.

"She's not feeling well, her heart is giving her trouble. Tomorrow she'll have something good to eat and she'll be anxious to see the pictures."

"What pictures?" Martti asked.

"Pictures of Mila from America. She is wearing a beautiful dress."

"Why did it have to be Mila? Why didn't you send me?"

They reached the rutted backyard of their building and he jerked the doors open and flew ahead while Kaija wearily climbed the stairs. She kept her coat and scarf on as she re-lit the fire while Martti stomped around the room.

"Shh. It's late, people are sleeping," she scolded. As she put kindling into the pot-bellied stove she asked, "What do you mean, why didn't I send you? Why would I do that?"

"Mila gets everything. She doesn't even know America is a country. She's stupid."

"I'm too tired to talk about it. The people in America wanted a girl. Go to bed."

She walked to the bureau to look at the picture of Mila, but instead picked up a smaller picture of Lars and herself, one on each side of a tall thick spruce, leaning their heads toward each other. Her face was luminous; Lars's thin body graceful, his expression softening the angularity of his face.

She thought back to the day it was taken, eight years ago. They'd made their own world that warm September when Lars waited for her outside the Sanatorium. Their passion obliterated her fear of TB. They made love in the forest, lying down under the low over-hanging bows on the fragrant bed of pine and spruce needles. Mila had been conceived that day.

Afterwards, a fellow patient watched them return to the hospital and said, "Let me take your photo on such a fine day with the birdsong in the air."

She hungered for Lars. "Damn you for dying," she said, and threw herself on the bed.

The day felt uneven, uncertain. Dustings of snow fell, alternating with brief glimpses of a weak December sun. Wrapped in woolen blankets, Anders lay on a wooden lounge chair on the fifth floor solarium, his mind spinning.

It was the week between Christmas and New Years of 1943; he had just turned nine. Eight years ago, to the very week, the last time he saw his father, heard his voice, and saw the concern in his eyes. Lars was ordered to report to Meltola Sanatorium, the long-term care facility for those with chronic tuberculosis, located seventy miles southeast of Helsinki. He was too weak to make the two-mile trip from their home to the railway station by himself. His mother, pregnant with Mila, planned to accompany Lars; but the night before she didn't feel well enough and stayed home with Martti. They didn't consider a cab since even if petrol wasn't rationed, there was no money, so Anders got the sled chair out of the shed, hoisted his father's duffel bag on the seat, and rather than argue with his ailing father, wore his woolen hat and earmuffs.

The trip seemed to take forever, Anders' arms weak from cold and fatigue. "Hurry home before it gets too dark," Lars said. "You don't have to be afraid. Nothing in the forest will harm you, only people do that."

The holiday season hung like a dirge, the very air tainted by his father's wracking cough, the snow colored by the blood that fell drop by drop. Blood and sleigh tracks marked their trail through the woods and Anders thought that if it didn't snow any more he could follow the stains home.

When they reached the station, snow was falling. Lars reached into his coat and handed a couple of his treasured sugar cubes to Anders. "You'll be responsible for the care of the family now. I don't know when I'll be home, but no matter what; you must do what you have to do to keep the family together. Tehelia will help you; she's getting old, but she's strong." He hesitated, "Your mother has her weaknesses...You understand, son?"

The sound of a throat being cleared broke his reverie. The sight of Kaija at the entrance of the solarium was a shock. They hadn't talked since his home leave. She came into the room and then sat perched on the end of one of the lounge chairs.

He knew she hated the hospital and suspected someone had called her. "What brings you out in the cold?" he asked.

"Is that all you can say to me? Can't you try and understand why I did what I did?" she asked, as if they were continuing their conversation from three months earlier. She reached into her purse for a cigarette, changed her mind and clicked it shut.

"No. I can't understand. There's no excuse. You just wanted the money for yourself. You know father wanted the family kept together. I promised him."

"Lars left me a widow with three children to raise before I was thirty. He could have chosen surgery; his pride killed him because he didn't want to be disfigured."

"The surgery was risky," Anders said.

"At least he had a fifty-fifty chance," she said.

"It was a difficult decision," Anders said, looking over her shoulder, not meeting her eyes. He wanted to hurt her as she'd hurt him. "I don't think you ever loved father. He was still alive in the hospital and you were already seeing other men."

"How the hell do you think I managed to put food on the table except for the men?" she challenged. "The end of the war didn't end our poverty, and the government says things are still going to be hard for a long time."

"What do you think life was like for me with Lars away in the sanatorium when Mila was born? He saw her only once, when she was six months old."

"Is that how you justify it? I asked you not to send her away to America. You know how important she is to me."

He could influence her behavior when he was home. Like his father, he was the only person able to give her stability. She was still young and pretty and part of him was sympathetic to her. It was her weakness he hated, the vicious cycle of her escape through vodka and men and the aftermath when she got depressed and felt hopeless. He wished she hadn't bothered coming, she just dredged up his feelings of frustration.

She buttoned her coat and took her gloves from her purse, snapping it shut. "Think what you want. What difference does it make?"

He didn't look up again until he heard his Aunt Sofi's voice.

"Good Yule," she said.

"Good Yule," Anders answered. "I didn't expect you."

"And Kaija? Has she been to see you?"

"She was here. You just missed her." A look of distaste crossed his face. "No one would guess you're sisters."

His aunt handed him a soft package wrapped in red string. Anders untied the bow and the paper fell open. "A wool scarf." He draped it around his neck, "nice and warm," he said.

Sofi took the paper and folded it. "Try to understand your mother. There's a lot you don't know. Jail changed her. She wouldn't live in the house Lars built because she was afraid to walk through the forest. She became afraid of everything, and terrified of ever going back to jail," Sofi said.

"If she was so afraid of jail why didn't she take better care of Marjetta? What kind of mother leaves a five-year-old child with a man she met at a bar? Where was she when Marjetta fell from the window to her death?"

Anders had been only four, but he would never forget watching his sister's blood drip from one step to another, her small body a limp heap against the stone. He remembered how scared and lonely he'd felt when he was sent to an orphanage during the six months Kaija spent in jail for child neglect. When Mila was born it was like having another chance to have a sister to love.

Anders's voice was full of contempt. "She's turned to Stalin - a father who will protect her. There's a picture of him over her bed."

"Anders, I think Kaija was trying to give Mila a chance for a better life."

When Sofi left he felt the emptiness return. He'd be glad when Pekka got back. His physical progress was slow and assimilating all the memories made him feel helpless, grief threatened to overwhelm him. He would do what he always did: pull out the drawers of his mind where he placed things until a later time - a drawer for illness, a drawer for Martti, a drawer for Mila, a drawer for future plans.

Nurse Bensonnen interrupted his reverie.

"Good, there's still some daylight," she said glancing out the window. She plumped his pillow and smoothed the blanket over his legs. "There's someone else here to see you."

Anders turned his head to see the small erect figure of his grandmother bundled against the cold. "Mumma! It's too cold for you to be outside."

"Cold, cold! Sure it's cold. I've lived too many years in this country to be bothered by it." She pulled off the heavy mittens. He noticed her gnarled hands and distorted knuckles and the deliberation with which she settled herself into the lounge chair, slowly straightening her legs, covering them with the blanket Anders handed her.

"So," she said, "what's this I hear about you laying around not eating or doing anything? You don't look near death, like I'd heard." She unbuttoned her coat and loosened the scarf around her neck.

"Who have you been talking to?"

"My neighbor, Mrs. Laitinen. There are no secrets here; you should know that. Her daughter Sirka works in this ward."

"Sirka? The one with the curly red hair."

Tehelia relaxed. "Well, you sound like yourself, asking about the pretty girls." Reaching into her cloth bag she pulled out a dark gray wool cardigan with a green shawl collar and stripes of the same green at the cuffs and hem. "For your seventeenth birthday. Don't look so surprised. There's nothing wrong with my memory. I remember it's only two days off." She smoothed the sweater on her lap. "I just finished it last night. Stand up and put it on. Let's see if Sirka got your size right."

The sweater enveloped his thin body. "You need to eat more," she said. Once more she reached into her bag and pulled out a porcelain bowl covered by a saucer and handed Anders a spoon.

His face lit up with pleasure. "Rice pudding with raisins and cinnamon. And *nisu*," he said, as she handed him the bread she'd folded in a piece of cloth.

They sat in companionable silence looking out the large low window until only a red streak remained between the dark winter sky and the outline of the city.

"Only three o'clock and it's like midnight," Anders said.

She rested her hand on his arm. "I must go," she said, putting the dishes back into her bag. She glanced at Anders and pulled out another small parcel wrapped in newspaper. "I have a surprise." Carefully she unwrapped the contents and handed Anders Mila's photo in a wooden frame.

Anders stared at it like he was looking at a stranger. His eyes met those of his grandmother. "What has happened to her? There is no sparkle. All of the light is gone."

Tehelia let out a deep sigh and looked down at her lap, shaking her head. "Kaija thought only of the luxuries of America. The child looks homesick and lonely."

Anders continued to stare at the picture. "It's her face. Even the big doll she's holding doesn't make her happy: my little chatterbox, always laughing and dancing and full of mischief. Look at her hair, all fancied up with curls."

Tehelia wrapped the photo. "I must return it to Kaija," she said and slowly got up and began buttoning her coat.

"I'll get her back from America," Anders said. "It's just a matter of time."

Give her lessons with the switch,
With a birchen branch correct her.
Teach her in a room four-cornered
Where the chinks are caulked with mosses;
Do not do it in the open,...

Kalevala, Runo 24, Lines 239-243

CHAPTER NINE

▼

Painesville, Ohio
1951

Frances's rancor toward Mila escalated. It erupted for reasons Mila was unable to fathom and she started to bite her nails, then the flesh around them until they bled. She envied Zeke his days with grandma Marta and dreaded coming home. She'd made no friends at school, partly because she was shy and partly because she had no free time given her responsibility for Zeke and household chores.

At dinner, Mila could feel the anger seething, keenly aware of the metallic odor Frances gave off at such times.

Donald had gone to his weekly evening of bridge at the Elk's Club.

"You can listen to music, but be careful with the records," she said, "Pick them up by their edges, and keep your fingers off the surface. I have to do some work, so play quietly." Her voice was a growl.

Mila treasured the records, placed them on the spindle and then placed the needle on the narrow edge before it reached the grooves. Frances watched her and then went to the living room. Music was one of Mila's comforts. The notes and rhythm reached her at some deep level.

"Change the record," Frances yelled when the side ended. "Don't let it keep going around like that making looping sounds."

Mila jumped to reach for the arm and dropped it with a thump and knocked the needle across the face of the record. The sound caused Frances to jump from her chair and stomp into the room.

"I told you to be careful," she said and grabbed her by the arm. "Can't you do anything right?"

"It was an accident," Mila said.

"Don't let it happen again. There will be no more accidents. Now put the records away and get ready for bed."

The rain pounded against her bedroom window. She heard low rumbling and then lightening flashed. Her door opened and she cowered, tucking her face into her pillow, sure that Frances had come about the record. Zeke rushed across the room to her bed.

"Mila, I'm afraid of the storm," he whispered.

She held up her covers while he climbed into bed and nestled next to her.

"Don't be afraid," she said and remembered the frequent thunderstorms in Finland. "It's only Old Man Thunder," Mila said, repeating Mumma's words to her. "Old Man Thunder works in the clouds. He's rolling his wheelbarrow filled with stones across the dark clouds and the cobblestone sky; that's what makes the noise. And when he throws out the stones, they hit each other; that's what causes the flashes of lightning."

A clap of thunder shook the house and Zeke snuggled against her as she had snuggled against her Mumma Tehelia. Flashes of lightening lighted the room, but Zeke went to sleep and a terrible feeling of loneliness filled Mila. She tried not to believe the things Frances had screamed at her: that her family didn't want her; that she'd never go home; that she was garbage. Only Zeke's warmth comforted her.

She retreated inside the memory box in her mind: square, midnight dark, with a tight fitting lid. Inside were her secrets and memories: Mumma's house, the curtains pinned to the wall so the sun could come into the room; the smell of the thick round loaves of bread with the hole in the middle on a long wooden pole hanging by leather straps from the ceiling; Anders and Martti pushing her through the snow in the chair sled as they searched the woods for fallen tree branches for the stove.

Their routine was the same until weekends. Frances spent Saturdays in her law office while Donald took Mila and Zeke with him to an old barn they were converting into a house twenty miles east of Painesville. They'd kept the old name, B bar B, from its days as a working ranch, only shortening it to B-B on a painted sign. The property was in a tree studded area with a creek and a bridge and extended a half-mile to the shores of Lake Erie.

Donald often stopped to buy hamburgers or ice cream. It was one of the few times Mila laughed and felt light-hearted and useful acting as "gofer." Anders loved working with wood and had taught her the names of tools, and now she could translate the names into English. She remembered Anders planing wood, the curlicues she twisted around her fingers like hair curls and his patient sanding to smooth the wood, and the tender way he smiled at her as she watched.

This weekend a heavy rainstorm kept them in town and she and Zeke built a fort under the table.

"Make it darker inside," Zeke said from under the table.

"I'll get another blanket while you put the toys in," she said running upstairs to her room to get the blanket from the foot of her bed.

"Help me put it over the chairs," she said when she returned. Mila felt safe in the dark. She was again allowed to put the records on the spindle, but she usually asked Zeke to do it. She wanted to listen to Sleeping Beauty, or Cinderella but Zeke insisted on Peter and the Wolf. Frances had told them about how the instruments helped tell the story. Mila didn't like the story.

"Okay, but you change the records," she said.

"We have too many toys in here," Zeke said, shoving some out.

The first record came to an end and Zeke made no move to change it. Mila scrambled from under the table to keep the needle from scratching the surface. In her excitement, the record on which the duck quacks inside the wolf's stomach was swept to the floor by the corner of the blanket. Her heart stopped as she watched it fall, but it didn't break. She bent to pick it up, but in her haste, she stumbled on a stuffed animal and stepped directly in the middle cracking it into big pieces. Her hands were icy with fear and she stood paralyzed.

Zeke poked his head out, his eyes big and round seeing what happened. "I won't tell," he said.

Where could she hide the pieces where Frances didn't look? Mila had no place that was private; then she remembered her suitcase under the bed and raced upstairs. The suitcase now held clothes for her bigger doll and paper streamers from the SS GRIPSHOLM; she placed the record under them, and then shoved the suitcase all the way under the bed. She ran back downstairs and put the remaining records back inside the album trying not to look at the picture of the grinning wolf.

Mila began to relax - going whole days without thinking about the broken record, but when she remembered she felt lightheaded with anxiety.

Attuned now to every nuance of Frances's moods and movements, Mila heard the back door slam shut and a shiver of dread passed through her. She listened to the heavy footsteps, fearing that today her secret would be discovered.

Frances came into the music room. "Clean up for dinner," she said.

"Shall I set the table?" Mila asked.

Frances used the stare that meant she was stupid for asking and Mila got out the silverware, willing herself to shove thoughts of the broken record from her mind since she was convinced Frances could see into it. Mealtimes were ruled by Frances's moods and tonight dinner was tense; it was Donald's bridge night. They were careful not to provoke her.

"Did you have a difficult day?" Donald asked.

"What would you know about that?" she answered. "You don't think about what I have to do every day, dealing with clients, doing their dirty work, then coming home to clean and cook and put food into your mouths."

"You refuse to get help," Donald said evenly.

She shot him a black look. Donald's lips tightened, but he remained quiet. After he finished eating he stood, avoiding her gaze. As he habitually did each night, he said, "Thank you for such a good dinner."

Mila watched him get his hat and jacket from the stand, and leave without a word.

"He thinks all he has to do is go to the office all day and his job is done. He doesn't even give me enough money to feed you." Mila tried to keep her hands steady as she cleared the table. She dried the dishes and longed to go upstairs and get into bed but was afraid to leave.

"What are you standing there for? Get Zeke ready for bed."

Relieved, Mila ran out of the room. She heard furniture being shoved around downstairs and the vacuum cleaner blasting through the house. Cleaning house at night was an indication that her anger was in the top range. "Please let Daddy come home soon," Mila prayed.

Frances continued to bang cabinets and drawers, then Mila heard footsteps fly up the stairs, down the hall, and light flooded her room. Frances stood over her bed holding a wooden broom.

"What did you do with the record? Her voice was full of menace. "Answer me this minute and don't start lying. You'll sit there all night until you talk."

Mila sat as still as possible on the edge of the bed, more terrified than ever while Frances yanked open her dresser drawers and went through the closet like a mad woman.

"I suppose you threw it away? You broke it, didn't you?"

"I want to go home," Mila said.

"Your own mother sold you. Yes. For a few dollars and we got stuck with you." Frances was screaming now, out of control, and started toward Mila with the broom.

Reverting to Finnish, Mila cried *"Aiti, Aiti, apuaminelle,"* "Mother, mother, help me."

"Speaking Finnish won't help."

When the blows began Mila fell to the floor. The pain was too great for her to absorb what was happening.

"Frances! Stop! You're going to kill her," Donald shouted and grabbed the broom from her.

"She's not normal," Frances insisted as Donald took her by the shoulders and led her out of the room.

Mila moved her bleeding legs; the skin had been gouged out. The back of her head felt swollen, she crawled to her bed and huddled with her blanket.

After a few moments Donald came back into her room and sat on the edge of her bed, stroking her hair with his big hand. "Now, Mila, tell me what happened to the record from Peter and the Wolf," he said. His voice was soothing, reasonable, and kind. "Tell me the truth."

"Zeke and I were playing and it fell to the floor. It was an accident," Mila said and started to cry.

"Now you know you have to tell the truth when you do something wrong. Then nothing will happen to you."

Mila stiffened at his words. He doesn't understand at all. It doesn't matter whether I explain or whether I don't, she thought, the same thing happens.

"Now, Mila," Donald continued, "tell us where you hid the record and this will all be over."

Frances came back into the room and stood with her arms across her chest.

Her voice was a whisper. "I put it in my suitcase, under the bed."

Frances strode across the room, reached under the bed as Mila moved closer to the wall. Frances yanked the lid open and the pieces of record fell out. She threw the suitcase across the room and it bounced off the wall and fell to the floor. Donald took Frances's arm to lead her from the room.

In the dark Mila lifted the corner of her box and pulled out her other life: chasing Martti through the woods, sitting next to Anders as he read Martti's school books to her, and last, of mama standing below at the harbor, her hand shading her eyes, waving, getting smaller and smaller.

CHAPTER TEN

▼

Bath, New York
1951

The weekend passed in a blur. On Monday Mila woke in a blot of pain. She looked at her legs, wondering if knee socks would hide the bruises so no one at school would notice them. Frances's angry words pounded in her head: "your mother sold you." She wished she could grow smaller like Alice in Wonderland, smaller and smaller until she disappeared.

Donald poked his head in. "Better hurry," he said. "You don't want to be late for school." She tried to button her blouse. "Here, let me help," he offered.

Downstairs it was as if nothing had happened. Frances stood at the counter with her back turned.

Donald cleared his throat. "I've decided a change of scenery would be good for all of us. Ulle has been working too hard and needs to get away and have a vacation. When school is out next week, we're going to visit my sister, Betty."

Mila looked down at her cereal, afraid to ask any questions.

"You'll stay with Aunt Betty while we visit Washington, D.C." Donald told her.

"I like Aunt Betty." Zeke's face lit up, but his smile faded when his mother turned around.

Bath, New York, was a town of about 12,000 people, with tree lined residential areas. The front lawn at Aunt Betty's looked manicured, and flowers blossomed in neat beds. A swing and rattan chairs looked out from the porch. Aunt Betty smiled through the screen door before she opened it wide and encompassed Donald in a prolonged hug, rocking him back and forth. She embraced Frances briskly, and then bent to give Zeke a big hug. "And this little mite must be Mila," she said. Mila curtsied. "Well bless your heart," Betty said. "What lovely manners. We're going to be great friends."

She smelled of lavender cologne and wore a freshly ironed cotton dress and an apron embroidered with flowers. "Come on," she urged and put her arm around Mila's shoulder and guided her into the house. "Sit down and have something to eat before you unload the car," she told Donald. "I just baked a cake and made a pot of coffee; maybe we can convince the children to share their lemonade on such a warm day."

Betty was tall and slender with hair more gray than brown, styled in a flattering short cut. Her voice was deep and reminded Mila of mama.

"Tom was sorry he couldn't be here," Betty explained. "You know how it is in sales work. He's lucky if he gets home on weekends with all his traveling."

Being with Betty was like a soothing unguent. When she cleared the table, Aunt Betty said, "What a good little helper." Donald seemed more childlike and even Frances seemed to relax under Betty's fussing attention. Donald and Frances sat side by side on the big sofa in the living room holding hands and smiling at each other when she and Zeke came in from playing. Frances didn't scream once.

Mila reminded Zeke to wipe his feet before coming into the house from the yard. He pulled on her arm.

"Come on, let's play ball," he begged as she stood at the back door to the kitchen. She overheard Aunt Betty and Frances talking.

"She must learn quickly. Her English is excellent for being in America only a year."

"I guess so," Frances admitted. "But it's a struggle teaching her."

"What do you know about her background?" Betty asked.

"I only know what I hear from my cousin, Erkki. The girl doesn't come from much. Her father died early and left a wife and three children. The mother is the lowest of the low and a drinker; there are two older brothers, one has TB."

"She has beautiful manners," Betty said.

"She's lucky to have so much enrichment - music, art, educated companions. She doesn't appreciate it," Frances said.

"Still," Betty said, "you can't teach natural charm and grace at her age."

"I haven't noticed much of that," Frances said. "Donald was upset having a foreigner in the house but he's more tolerant now that she can speak English."

"Donald was always a loving child," Betty said. "I'm sure it's more than that."

Frances brushed the remark aside. "We thought it would be beneficial if Mila learned the basics of house cleaning this summer," Frances said. "It will be a great help to me if she stays here with you. I'll be away in Washington, DC on business this summer and it would be easier having only Zeke."

"We'd be delighted," Betty said. "How lucky she found a good home."

Quietly Mila backed away.

It was agreed that Betty and Tom would drive to Ohio at the end of summer and return Mila before school resumed. Mila watched Donald drive away, Zeke at the back window looking sad.

Betty had been the town librarian for years, but resigned because of health problems. She ran the household on a fixed schedule. Monday she washed clothes, Tuesday she ironed - everything, including socks and Tom's shorts, t-shirts as well as the dishtowels. Wednesday she cleaned upstairs, Thursday downstairs. Friday was shopping day. The housework was done in the morning leaving time for an afternoon of bridge, an afternoon for baking, and lots of time to read. She was involved in social activities, volunteer work in the library and running the church socials. Disbelief spread across Mila's face when Aunt Betty asked her after lunch, "What would you like to do this afternoon? Where would you like to go?"

"Anywhere?" she asked after a moment. "*Anything* I want?"

Betty laughed. "Well, almost. You think about it, and if I think it's okay, we'll do it."

"Two things. Could I ask for two things to do?" she asked, unable to make up her mind and stunned by a question no one had asked her before. "Ice cream. Could I ask for an ice cream cone? Straawberry? It's my favorite."

"Of course. What else were you thinking about?"

"The library, where you took Zeke and me for story hour. Could we go there and look at the books and listen to story hour? Do you think the story lady will read the Box Car children again?"

"I don't know. What else would you like besides the Box Car children?"

"The Bobbsey Twins."

"That's what you *want* to do?"

"Oh! Yes."

Betty's face lit up. "We'll get a library card for you. Do you have one?"

Mila shook her head. "What is that?" she asked.

"You must have your own library card. You can borrow the books and keep them for two weeks

For the rest of the summer Mila spent long afternoons with her aunt on the porch swing or upstairs on the window seat in her room under the eaves where she sat hour after hour reading.

A small radio in the kitchen was tuned to music and Mila danced as she had done in Finland. Betty noted her balance, her graceful arm gestures, and enrolled her in a summer dance class.

She followed her aunt around like a shadow, getting the silver from the drawer where it was carefully arranged, arranging the place mats, removing the flowers from the dining room table and putting them on the sideboard. The housecleaning skills Frances wanted her to learn went down like the ice cream at Aunt Betty's church socials. It did not feel like work; Mila was eager to help. Betty never failed to complement her. "You do such a good job."

Mila blossomed with the nourishment of the soft voice and gentleness. Aunt Betty made her small aprons like the ones she wore, and taught her how to starch and iron them.

When they went out in the afternoon, Aunt Betty changed into a dressier outfit, put on coordinated jewelry, changed into pumps, and even on the hottest days, wore nylons.

"Frances makes fun of me," she confided. "She spends her time on better, more important things and thinks I can't be doing much with my time, always changing clothes to go out." She gave a faint little laugh. "I was brought up to believe ladies didn't sweat and one should never leave the house without looking one's best. I just can't change."

Mila felt anger rising, wanting to protect Aunt Betty. She hadn't thought of Frances, but now she remembered the soiled clothes and dank smell of perspiration.

They were in the kitchen frosting a cake for the weekly bridge game. A serious look crossed Mila's face. "Aunt Betty, do you have any children?"

"No, dear. I was lucky to have your daddy to raise, but Tom and I weren't blessed with little ones."

"Can I live at your house?" Mila asked. "I like it here."

Betty, moved by the question, took a moment to compose herself. "I wish that were possible," she said.

"Maybe Zeke could come here and live. I can help take care of him. I already do that. I play with him and pick up his toys and clear the table and wash the dishes and even help mop the floors late at night." Looking at her aunt's face she added shyly, but with conviction, "I'd be good. I wouldn't make any trouble."

Betty did not trust her voice. She put her arms around Mila and held her close. "My dear child," she said. "It's not that at all. I'd give anything to keep you. You're a beam of sunshine. And your endless chatter!"

Taking it as criticism, Mila said, "I can be quiet. Anders was always laughing at me and saying I talked all the time, but I've learned to be quiet."

"Anders?" Betty asked.

Mila got a far away look. "I'm not supposed to talk about him."

Betty lifted Mila to her lap. "It's all right...was he...is he your brother?"

Mila brightened a little, relieved that she wouldn't be scolded. "Yes, he's my older brother. I miss him," and she started to cry as Betty held her tightly.

When Tom came home from his route they had a long talk before Betty took out her stationery.

Dear Donald, she began. She felt she was walking through a minefield, but wondered why Frances had adopted Mila. From the short time she'd seen them together Betty was convinced Frances didn't like the child. Even with Zeke, her own son, Frances seemed the most unmotherly person Betty had ever met. She rewrote the letter several times before dropping it in the mail, asking them to consider it and they'd discuss it more fully when they drove Mila back to Ohio.

For once Frances was shocked into silence when Donald gave her Betty's letter to read.

"They've always longed for children," Donald said. "She'd have a wonderful home."

"Betty's fifty years old," Frances said. "You'd think she'd know better than to want that defiant troublemaker."

"We could ask cousin Erkki to get us a younger child," Donald suggested. "Maybe another boy."

"Zeke misses her and she's someone for him to play with. She's a good baby sitter. She's just getting to the age where she's some use and we'll need her when we move to B-B."

Zeke danced up and down when the car arrived, throwing his arms around Mila he said, "I missed you. Guess what? We have a new puppy. Mama says he's a mongrel like you. He's into everything, so we named him Mr. Peepers."

Mila stood between Betty and Tom, a hand in each of theirs, all three of them silent.

CHAPTER ELEVEN

▼

Painesville, Ohio

Like a snuffed out candle, the dancing happy child of Bath, New York, quickly dimmed. Frances had evaluated Betty and Tom's request and summarily dismissed their petition to adopt Mila.

Before Betty and Tom drove away, Frances said, "I'm going to run for Judge. I'm sure Mila will be a help with all you taught her this summer."

Hope was sucked from Mila; like an implosion she collapsed. She developed a nervous tic in her left eye and stomach aches so severe she often couldn't walk. The only vestige left of summer was her love of books.

It was a cold and blustery October morning. Most of the leaves had fallen and those left were blowing away with the wind. Mila thought of Winnie the Pooh and the blustery day, wishing she could read or play with Zeke. She put off going downstairs as long as she could.

She hated what they were doing, distributing the literature on people's windshields each Sunday. Instinct told her it was wrong, taking unfair advantage while people were worshiping, but Frances worked out a timetable of churches she planned to canvass.

"Why are you dressed like that?" Frances looked up from browning the roast. "Go change; put on warm pants and a heavy jacket; it's cold out and hurry up." She swiveled around to Donald who sat reading the Sunday paper. "Since you've refused to get involved, at least keep an eye on the pot roast while we're gone. If we haven't come back by noon, add the vegetables. They're soaking in cold water on the sink, and put in some more beef bullion if it's low on liquid, and keep the heat low, and make sure Zeke is wearing something clean since he didn't get a bath last night."

"I hope at least you aren't going to the colored section of town." Donald looked up from the paper. "They don't even vote. Why do you bother with them?"

"Because the ones who *do* vote will vote for me and every vote counts." Charlie Slocum was her republican opponent and shared Donald's disdain of minorities of any kind and general intolerance of those he felt below him.

Fifteen minutes after services began, Frances drove to the Presbyterian Church on Main Street and remained in the car. "It looks like lots of cars in the lot and I want to get to the Catholic Church just after eleven o'clock mass begins. If anyone asks you what you're doing, tell them you're campaigning for your mother who's running for judge and you hope they'll vote for her." She handed the leaflets to Mila. "Be sure to put each brochure firmly under the windshield wiper on the driver's side. And put them photo side up so the first thing they see is the picture of you and Zeke. Understand?"

Mila nodded. She ran from car to car, hoping she'd finish before services let out so she wouldn't see anyone from school. Friends seemed like such a nice thing to have, she thought, not that she had any. Elaine and Judy invited her to their houses to play after school, but Frances told her "There's no time for playing. You have to take care of Zeke." Judy had a younger brother, and said it was all right to bring Zeke, but Frances still refused. Friends were not welcome to visit either, but since Frances's anger was so unpredictable it was better not to risk the embarrassment.

Her heart sank as a car drove into the lot and a man and woman hurriedly got out. She prayed they would go in the front entrance, away from her, but instead they approached the side entrance near where she was standing. She wanted to hide, but saw Frances watching and swallowed as she handed them a pamphlet.

"What's this?" the man asked, and smiled.

Mila stammered, "My mother is going to be judge."

"What?" He scanned the brochure, "Not from my vote," he said angrily. "Campaigning on Sunday? A day of worship?"

As his voice rose, his wife tugged at his sleeve. "Jim, you're scaring the child. Let's go."

The man threw the brochure on the ground making sure to step on it and crush it with his foot. Mila stared down at the picture of Zeke and her holding their signs.

She ran to the back of the church, checking to make sure no one was watching and dropped some of the remaining brochures on the ground, she stamped them into the ground as the man had done, and kicked them under a car; she distributed the rest of the stack with icy hands.

"What did the man say?" Frances asked when she got back into the car.

Afraid to tell her the truth, Mila stammered, "He was ... angry." She didn't look at Frances who started the car and drove off. "I think he was angry because I was doing it on Sunday," she added. "Maybe we could do it on a different day."

"Nonsense. I don't have time and this way I can get the information to a lot of people. If your father would help," she said, "but he's too high and mighty." She paused in her thoughts and then brightened. "But some other parking lots might be a good idea. You come to my office after school, after you drop Zeke off at mother's. You can walk to the A&P and put pamphlets on the cars while people shop."

The air was crisp, but the day sunny. Fall leaves swirled around the crowd gathered in the park. The bandstand had been draped in red, white and blue. Politicians and Candidates mingled with the town dignitaries.

Frances was animated and vibrant with the attention and excitement. She smiled appealingly as she milled through the crowd, putting her hand on an arm, letting it linger there, giving jaunty waves to people she knew, stopping to chat with clients, then wending her way to the podium where she bent down to speak to those who came up to her.

Charlie Slocum was already seated next to his wife, Ruth. Sitting beside the seat reserved for Frances was Lester Skolnick, the county democratic committee chairman. Donald looked uncomfortable and disgruntled. He despised calling attention to himself; the entire exercise went against his grain. Mila's face was sullen and downcast; blank at times. She knew Mr. Slocum's children who were not on the bandstand as she and Zeke were, but in the crowd with their friends. Leaning against the metal chairs Mila and Zeke sat on were signs three feet tall: OUR MOTHER, read Mila's, FOR JUDGE, read Zeke's. As Mila fidgeted, her sign started to slip to the ground. Frances frowned at her as she straightened it, then reached across Donald and put an arm on Mila's shoulder and smiled at her.

Zeke, at six, fidgeted with a toy car in his jacket pocket. He reached toward Mila and she pulled a mint from her sweater pocket and handed it to him, in return he gave her an engaging grin. The cloud cleared from Mila's face as she looked at his chubby face and new crew cut.

The crowd settled and grew quiet. Hazel Wilson, the President of the Women for Democrats, rose to the podium.

"Each candidate will speak for ten minutes with time afterwards for questions. I urge you all to exercise your civic duty and the privilege of voting on Election Day."

"The next person really doesn't need an introduction," Hazel Wilson said, "Almost everyone here has met her in one of her numerous civic capacities. Some of you know her from her early days as the conscientious and able city solicitor, others of you are familiar with her untiring work on behalf of the citizens of this city as a city council member," her voice droned on with a sing-song monotony, "past president of the council...her judicious, impartial, and fair hearings as fill-in Municipal court judge...unfaltering advocate in and out of court." She turned toward Frances, with a look something like a supplicant at Lourdes, "in all of her numerous civic responsibilities she has insisted on unwavering honesty and integrity, not only for herself, but for all those around her. And those of you not familiar with her professional endeavors know her as Donald's wife and the loving, caring mother of Zeke and Mila." Frances smiled at Donald. At a nod from Frances Mila reached for Zeke to hold up his sign while she positioned hers to obscure her face from the crowd.

Under her breath Mila chanted to herself, "She's not my mother. She's not fair, she tells lies. I hate her." Her fingers were white from gripping the sign and she wanted to fling it away. Mila prayed that Frances failed to win the election.

After she lost, Frances was like a live electric wire writhing, shocking anyone who came near. Mila was sure it was her fault but the thought that Frances had lost was still delicious. Frances spent long hours at her office burying herself in work. As her career flourished, life at home was more turbulent than ever. Mila was used to having Frances rage at her, but never so much at Daddy or Zeke. "You make me laugh," Frances yelled, "all your complaints about my clients' skin doesn't stop you from keeping your chubby little Italian secretary."

"Carmi's only doing her job. You don't have to be gone so much, Ulle. You do it because you want to. The only time I see you go to trouble fixing yourself up is when you leave for business in Columbus."

"You and Betty with your obsession with bathing and changing clothes. I'm too busy to go shopping like other women."

Frances bought three or four dresses a year and wore them interchangeably. They were always belted prints with pleats in front, a collar and a bodice that buttoned to the waist; in winter they had long sleeves and in summer, short. On Sunday she spot cleaned them and if the weather permitted, hung them outside to air, unwilling to spend the money to have them dry cleaned.

At the end of the year she bought new dresses that looked like the ones she'd discarded.

"Maybe if you supported my efforts to win the election for Judge I wouldn't need to find my support other places."

"The only time you act intimate is in public, either with political friends or with your colored clients - not with your own family," Donald countered in his low reasonable sounding voice. "How do you think that looks to people?"

"You're so worried about presenting a nice face to the world. You don't complain about the money I earn."

Mila fell asleep as the argument roared to a crescendo and she was jerked awake by the slamming of their bedroom door. She heard the word *divorce* unsure of what it meant. Frances started sleeping downstairs on the chaise lounge. Then Frances surprised Mila by announcing it was time for her to pick a godmother and godfather. Unclear about what constituted godparents, Mila daydreamed that Helen and Howard would be her parents and a ray of hope opened. If she were denied Aunt Betty, Aunt Helen would do nicely.

Three weeks later Aunt Helen arrived with a special dress for Mila. It was made in a warm brown taffeta with woven strands of green ribbon and matching green ribbons for her hair.

Frances looked on with disdain. "You'll spoil her," she said. "She already puts on enough airs. She came home from Bath wanting dancing lessons."

"That's a lovely idea," Helen said. "She has natural grace and balance. Howard thinks she'd make a good horseman." She laughed, looking at Mila, "maybe even a jockey if you don't start growing taller."

Changing the subject, Helen said, "Donald and the children have done a wonderful job with the conversion of B-B. It's such a beautiful location and a lovely place to live."

"It's lucky they can do something to help out." Frances said.

Helen's jaw tightened and she turned to Mila. "Let's just slip the dress on to make sure it fits."

Mila looked shyly at herself in the mirror.

"You look beautiful," Aunt Helen told her. "I'll take the dress home with me and shorten it."

Mila loved her dress and felt a stab of disappointment, not knowing it was Helen's way of making sure Frances didn't pack the dress away, or give it to someone else as she'd often done with other gifts.

"Well, we may as well kill two birds with one stone and combine Mila's christening with our move to B-B" Frances said.

In church Mila prayed, but God never heard her. She absorbed the disillusionment of learning that having godparents didn't mean adoption. They drove home from church in a light rain. Donald built a fire and when Mila smelled the wood smoke her heart gave a jump, the smell so familiar yet so distant.

Uncle John and Aunt Clara arrived with Annie and Russy and Grandma Marta and shortly after, Aunt Helen and Uncle Howard. The dining table was set with a white linen cloth and Mila folded the napkins and set out the silver and china while the adults visited in the living room. Grandma Marta held out her arms when Mila joined them and from there Mila smiled at her cousin, Annie.

"Well, this is your special day," Aunt Helen said. "Isn't it nice to be celebrating in a new home?"

"You've done a wonderful job, Donald," John said.

Frances came into the room in her apron, her cheeks flushed from standing over the stove. "Dinner," she announced, looking put upon.

"Congratulations on your promotion, John. That's quite a turn around. Your worries about being fired were unfounded," Donald said as he carved the pot roast and passed the plates.

"Yes. Thank goodness," John answered.

"Helen says Howard wants to give Mila riding lessons, that she's a natural at riding," Clara said.

"She doesn't need to learn how to ride horseback anymore than she needs to learn how to do a *plie.*" A silence fell over the table, but Frances laughed derisively. "Where have the horses gotten Howard and Helen except further in debt? And who bails them out?" She left the question hanging. The answer was obvious.

"Too bad about the election," John said. "It was a close race; losing by a few hundred votes has to be disheartening."

"It was all for the best," Donald said.

Frances looked up from the bowl of peas she was holding, "What makes you say that?" Her voice was cold. "Do you think it was predestination?"

"I just meant that you have more time now that the election is over," Donald answered.

"Next time I won't lose," Frances said.

"You'll run again?" Clara's question came out in an incredulous gasp.

"Of course. Perseverance is what's needed to succeed." The table fell silent.

"Well, today is Mila's day," Helen said. "Annie, you help me clear the table and we'll have desert. Mother made *Nisu.*"

Tonight it was full moon and before crawling into bed Mila stared up at the starry sky. From the upstairs window she could see Lake Erie to the north. She heard Daddy put Zeke to bed. Then he came in to play their nightly spider game. The spider traveled up her arms, and down her legs, and over her tummy.

"Did you have a nice time on your special day?" he asked.

"I didn't feel like it was my special day."

"You mustn't talk like that. You should be grateful for all the nice things you're given."

On special occasions, like today, her loneliness and longing to truly belong threatened to overwhelm her. Mila had found a new place, a place better than her imaginary box where the faces and memories were fading. Now she escaped into a dark place of safety, a tunnel. In her tunnel she didn't have to think or feel anything. Sometimes she wasn't even aware she'd been away.

CHAPTER TWELVE

▼

Helsinki, Finland/Stockholm, Sweden
Summer, 1953

After midnight, when the sun turned to twilight, Anders went for walks. There was something primal about early morning during mid-summer. Mystical. He felt it must be like the beginning of the world, as if time had stopped while nature gathered its thoughts. It was a time when silence was so profound one could hear one's own heartbeat - even the birds forgot to make a noise.

At nineteen Anders had matured into a tall handsome man whom women turned to admire. Out of the sanatorium for over two years, the life he'd dreamed in the hospital failed in the reality of post-war Finland. The country remained poor; it was difficult to get sugar, coffee or cigarettes - the staples of Finnish life. Gas was still rationed, although few except the wealthy had automobiles.

The weight of family responsibility and duty remained. Mila had put her trust in him. His determination to find her became an obsession, but nothing could be done without money. Mumma Tehelia's health was dubious and it hurt to watch her deteriorate. He was concerned about Martti, thirteen, on his own, stubborn, defiant. Kaija had lost all control over him.

Living with Kaija was tedious. She was involved with Aleksis, who was anxious to marry, but Kaija wanted no part of marriage. Although he couldn't have been more than six at the time, Anders remembered a fistfight between Aleksis and Lars that started because Lars suspected Kaija of being unfaithful while he was hospitalized. His father made him stay in the house, but he watched from the window. All Anders could really remember was the knock-out; evenly matched by height, Aleksis had the advantage of being physically stronger, but Lars had a quick left hook and jealousy on his side. Aleksis's boxing career was flawed only by his fondness for vodka.

Her inhibitions loosened by the liquor, Kaija now felt comfortable discussing Aleksis with Anders, telling him about her satisfaction in weekends drinking and dancing. She told Anders intimate details - how she frequently performed an impromptu private strip tease for him. Anders felt his stomach lurch with both disgust and sadness for her.

Aleksis was a master carpenter and head foreman of a construction firm. He got Kaija jobs as a cook at the construction sites. Aleksis treated Martti like a son and with paternal pride got him a summer job as errand boy fetching supplies for the workmen. He was strong and sturdy for his age, ran up ramps and climbed like a monkey. Martti also had good spatial abilities and was quick with numbers.

"You can work up to a better job," Aleksis told him.

Out of necessity, Anders accepted a job at one of Helsinki's few parking garages where he washed cars, pumped gas, and chaffed at the mindless work. Things were more bearable when he mastered the skill of driving and parked the American and European cars. He impressed the manager by his quickness and dependability in every job and after a few months he was in charge of daily accounting.

"Never has anyone balanced the receipts at the end of the day so consistently and efficiently. You'll go far," the manager predicated.

Despite the added responsibility, the pay remained low and when Anders heard he could make more money in Sweden, he felt no qualms about quitting.

With Aleksis assuming the role of husband and father, Anders's decision to leave Helsinki was easier. It would be a relief to get away from Kaija. Aleksis gave Anders money for a third class ticket.

The SS Wellamo was one of three steamships that plied the waters between Helsinki and Stockholm. Although relatively small, carrying a maximum of one hundred passengers, they were beautiful little vessels with one main deck made from wood, Finland's main natural resource.

By nine the sun was high in the sky and the air was warm when the ship docked in Stockholm. The freshly caught fish was already on ice in the open market stalls and housewives were busy picking and selecting their evening meal. Anders stood stretching in the sunshine for a moment and then approached the first well dressed man he saw.

"Excuse me, sir, but could you give me the name of the best and biggest restaurant in Stockholm?"

The man looked at him and answered without hesitation. "That would be Sundstrum," he said and gave him directions on how to get there.

Relieved that he had not forgotten his Swedish he set out, savoring the hustle of the city, not missing the gloom of Helsinki. The wide boulevards seemed alive and the people he passed looked well fed and walked with purpose. Several times he stopped at the sidewalk stalls to make sure he was headed toward Alexander Street. Discreet gold letters on a pale blue background identified Sundstrum located in the exclusive shopping section in the center of the city. A desultory young man swept the sidewalk and Anders walked around him to enter the restaurant.

At the manager's station a harried looking man stood smoking a cigarette, a phone balanced on his shoulder while he wrote in a lined blue ledger.

"No more excuses," he said, "I need them by noon."

Anders waited for him to place the phone in the rocker, then with his hand outstretched and a charming smile, he said, "Anders Ahlgren here and ready to work at anything you can offer."

The manager looked up with a puzzled expression. "Who sent you?" he asked.

"I sent myself."

Somewhat amused, he asked, "I'm very busy. What exactly can you do?"

"Anything you can give me," Anders answered. "Anything at all."

Having just fired a useless dishwasher, the Manager appraised Anders. "Through those swinging doors is the kitchen. Let's see what you can do about the stacks of dishes from last night. You can ask the cook to give you breakfast before you start."

Anders couldn't believe his luck. With a full stomach he cleaned the dishes and then the pots and pans. After a few hours he went back to the manager. "What can I do now?" he asked.

"Can't anyone think for themselves?" the Manager asked. "The pots and pans," he muttered starting off for the kitchen. Before the doors stopped swinging he looked around the spotless kitchen. The pots and pans were ready for use on the ranges; the dishes were stacked on the long counter. The cooks looked up and smiled.

"I'm Peter Ostermann," he said. "You're hired. Keep the dishes washed and the kitchen clean." He left shaking his head, saying "I was beginning to think nobody knew the meaning of work anymore."

The manager locked up that night without noticing Anders still working in the kitchen getting things in order. When Anders came into the quietness of the closed restaurant he found everything bolted. Without a place to stay, he fell asleep on the banquette that ran alongside the wall facing the windows, covering himself with one of the linen tablecloths. He was folding it in the morning when Ostermann entered.

Brusquely, Ostermann growled, "You start early. How did you get in here?"

"You locked me in last night. It's okay. I arrived from Helsinki yesterday without a place to stay," he explained.

"And no money," Ostermann said.

Anders straightened his shoulders. "I didn't touch anything," he assured him. "I can have everything washed by midnight, sweep up and air out the restaurant so everything is ready for you if you allow me to sleep here."

Ostermann considered the argument. He liked this young man who seemed so eager to work. They struck a deal; he agreed to let him sleep in the restaurant, gave him an advance on his earnings and told him he could have all the food he could eat. Anders' salary was double the amount he'd earned in Finland.

Within weeks he was helping translate the menus from Swedish to Finnish to accommodate the increasing number of businessmen now traveling to Stockholm. He advanced quickly to busboy. He was even allowed to sleep upstairs in the manager's office where he could use the adjacent bathroom.

One afternoon a few months later the manager called him into his office where a heavyset man sat smoking and sipping vodka from a small icy glass. Anders recognized him as a regular patron named Oskar Lundquist.

"Herr Lundquist is the owner of the company that provides food stuffs to passenger ships that dock here," Ostermann told him. "He is looking for a hard working, honest, strong young man who speaks Swedish and Finnish. He also wants someone who can drive."

"I can drive," Anders said.

"I want someone to make deliveries from the warehouses to the steamships," Lundquist said. "Too many mistakes are being made."

Anders looked at Ostermann. "It's a good opportunity," Ostermann said. "You shouldn't pass it up, although I hate to see you go."

"You'll work seven days a week," Lundquist told him. "Every day one of three steamships arrives from Helsinki, sometimes two. Your job will be to take the orders from the cooks, write them down in both Finnish and Swedish, then go to the supply depot and deliver the goods to the boats. Do you think you can do that?"

Anders nodded.

"This is important," Lundquist said, "so listen carefully. When you arrive at the dock, you have to go to the Customs Toll Office and show the inspector the written order, a form you need to fill out showing what you're bringing. Sometimes they inspect everything, so you can't leave anything in the truck." He watched Anders, and then went on emphasizing his words. "Everything you take on board must be written down and weighed. If you've got ten liters of milk in the steel containers, that's what you write down. If four kilos of bananas or eight kilos of potatoes, that's what you write down. You must not be caught with a mistake because the Customs Office weighs the crates and checks your figures."

Ostermann sat listening, and said, "Anders is accurate with his work and he learns quickly. I wouldn't have recommended him unless I believed he could do the job."

Lundquist took a drink of vodka. "Yes. That is fine, but I've had nothing but problems with my last few workers. They were always forgetting to put something on the Customs form."

"I understand," Anders said.

Ostermann refilled his glass, and Lundquist nodded his thanks and said to Anders, "Pay is once a week and Peter tells me you have no place to stay. You can sleep in the back room off my office for now. Well. Does that suit you?"

"Yes, sir, it does. When do I start?"

"Tomorrow," Lundquist said.

Peter Ostermann shook Anders's hand. "I hate to lose the best worker I've ever had, but we'll keep in touch," he said looking over at Lundquist and winking.

When Anders saw the Customs Inspector for the first time he thought perhaps he was looking at the President of Sweden. He was dressed in his summer uniform, navy blue trousers with a gold stripe down each leg, a matching jacket with gold braid at the shoulders, a Napoleonic hat, and a sword that hung nearly to his feet. Anders instinctively clicked his feet together and saluted the large, rawboned man. The Swede smiled. After their initial meeting the inspector was even more favorably impressed because Anders's order forms were always correct to the gram, everything was neatly listed. After a few weeks, the inspector grew lax and rarely bothered to weigh or inspect the things Anders delivered to the steamships.

Lundquist complimented him on his good work. "Everyone seems happy with you - the Customs Inspector, the cooks." He shook his hand.

"When will I be paid, sir?" Anders asked.

Somewhat puzzled, Lundquist said, "Your paycheck has been deposited in the bank."

"Where is the bank?" Anders asked; he'd always been paid in cash.

"Across the street where it's always been," Lundquist said.

"I've never been in a bank before," Anders told him.

Lundquist broke out laughing. "Ahlgren, you're a good one for a joke."

"You mean my check is *in* the bank?" Anders said.

"Yes, of course. Just give them your name." He walked off still laughing.

Anders went directly across the street and up to the cashier. "My name is Anders Ahlgren," he said. "Is it true my paycheck is here in your bank?"

The teller smiled at the youth. "Yes. It's here," she said after checking his name.

"How much is in your bank for me?" Anders asked.

"Six hundred *Kroner*," she replied.

Anders was incredulous. "It's not possible. Let me see it."

"Are you serious?" the cashier said.

"Yes. I don't believe it."

The cashier showed him his name and the six hundred *kroner* deposit, but unsatisfied, he insisted. "No, let me see the money, not the writing."

"All of it?" she said.

"Yes."

She opened her cash drawer and counted out six hundred *kroner*, shuffled it into one stack and handed it to him.

"This is mine?" he asked.

"Yes."

"All of it?"

She nodded.

"Can I keep some of it here?" he wanted to know.

"Of course. That's what a bank is for." She was unsure whether to be impatient or amused.

"All right. Give me," he paused calculating, "one hundred kroner."

She counted out the money.

"And I can come back for the rest whenever I want?"

"Yes," she said. "Whenever you want." She smiled. "I'll look forward to seeing you again."

Anders received his paycheck every second week, and before his third check Lundquist dropped by the dock. "You're doing a fine job," he praised. "I'm well satisfied with you."

Anders could tell he wanted to say something else, and after a few moments of watching him work Lundquist said, "Are you smart enough to figure out how to get Vodka from Finland?"

"I believe I could figure a way," Anders told him after a long pause. "But it's dangerous. Let me think about it." The next day Anders asked, "How much would I be paid?"

Lundquist sputtered. "You're already getting paid handsomely."

"Yes," Anders agreed, "and I appreciate it. But work is work, business is business, and smuggling is risky."

After some haggling, they settled on one thousand *kroner*. "In cash," Anders stipulated.

Anders already knew that the Finnish cooks were anxious to get coffee and cigarettes, still strictly rationed in Finland, and he would need their cooperation. The Customs Department put paper tape on each crate of bananas the cooks ordered, but it was easy to unseal it and put coffee and cigarettes in the bottom. The skill came in adding and subtracting the weight until there was an exact match after which Anders replaced the paper seal so skillfully it appeared it had never been disturbed.

The alcohol was harder, but after careful thought, Anders decided the stainless steel milk containers held the solution. There were containers of both ten and twenty liters with tight fitting lids that were filled with milk when they went through Customs. Anders carried them aboard ship returning with the empty containers from the previous journey, and then took them to the depot for refilling. Soon they were not empty, however. The cooks wrapped bottles of vodka from Finland in burlap to prevent them from rattling and protect them from breakage. Under the watchful eye of the Customs Inspector, Anders carelessly tossed them in the truck.

"Every paper in order, no mistakes," the Custom Inspector told him. "If all the delivery men could be like you my life would be easy."

Anders said a silent thank you for the Swedish penchant for proper order on paper.

He felt buoyant when he mailed clothes to Martti, money to Kaija and for the first time in his life could buy good clothes for himself. He bought a leather jacket, a soft shirt, and good leather shoes. He soon found women admired the way the clothes draped over his tall lean frame and across his broad shoulders. The first one he asked out was the bank teller, but she was small change to the ones that followed.

CHAPTER THIRTEEN

▼

Painesville, Ohio

They were alone when Aunt Helen gave Mila a present for her eleventh birthday.

"I think you're the right age for a diary," Aunt Helen told her. "Most girls like to have a diary in which they can write down all their private thoughts. You can put down how you feel or anything special that happens to you." The idea appealed to Mila, but there was no corner of her life that was private.

She propped her pillow behind her back, undid the little gold clasp with the small key, ruffled the blank pages with the dates at the top, sat poised with the pencil, and began:

July 25, 1954 - We had a busy day preparing for the arrival of Erkki Niemi, the woman's cousin from Finland. She baked two sheet cakes and decorated one with the United States flag and one with the Finnish flag. He and the woman have some kind of business together, Aunt Helen said.

Mila closed the diary, pushed the two prongs back into the holes and locked the book, then hid it in her suitcase and shoved it against the wall under her bed, turned out her light and snuggled under the covers.

July 26, 1954 - Erkki Niemi is obese, and he perspires and smells bad like her. Ida, his wife and Helvi, his daughter sit with their hands folded in their laps, and don't talk. Last night the woman left the cakes on the back porch - where Mr. Peepers sleeps in hot weather - and he took a big bite out of the middle of the cake with the Finnish flag. When Zeke and I were eating breakfast, we heard her yell and when we found out what had happened I thought she'd blame me and throw the cake in the garbage, but instead she carried it to the kitchen table, banged open cupboard doors, grabbed the powdered sugar and food coloring, dumped a cube of margarine into the bowl and mixed another batch of frosting. Then, she jammed blue frosting into the places Mr. Peepers ate, like daddy spackles holes in the wall. Her dumb old cousin never suspected and told her how clever the decorations were and how good the cake tasted and had two pieces from each cake. I didn't have any and Aunt Helen didn't eat hers either.

Since she and Zeke no longer spent their afternoons with Grandma Marta she seldom heard Finnish and struggled to understand everything Erkki Niemi said. She did overhear the conversation in the kitchen.

"Later we must talk about the letter I've received, but I expect you to handle it without complications," Frances said.

"I think it's the brother that's causing the trouble," Erkki said.

"I'll draft a letter to the U.S. Consul in my official capacity, advising them that if she wants to come to America to visit her daughter I won't go through with the naturalization."

"She'll want money," Erkki said.

"We'll pay her something. They're all the same," Frances said, "always wanting something from me."

The sauna was the one indulgence Frances allowed herself when they moved to B-B. Mila flicked on the electricity to heat the stones, filled the pails with cold water to throw on for steam once they were hot, and went out to cut off a small bundle of tender birch saplings with a pliable one for a band around the bunch. As she opened the door to the sauna the smell of heated birch wood walls gripped her in a pang of longing that caught her breath as the old sense of loss and loneliness engulfed her. She remembered the happy times with Mumma and strained to picture her face - but like wood smoke it was gone.

July 27, 1954 - I expect the chair to split when cousin Erkki sits down. She finally told him to speak English since Daddy couldn't understand what he was saying. When Daddy wasn't there they spoke in Finnish and kept looking over at me. Even though I'm not exactly sure what they're talking about, I like the sound. It's comforting, not as harsh as English.

It was different living at B-B. The family spent more time doing things together at home during the summer; they often spent afternoons at Lake

Erie. Frances was a strong swimmer and outfitted Mila with one of her old bathing suits. The crotch hung low and the suit had to be tied around the waist and when it filled with water the bosom inflated like balloons. Mila's body tensed when Frances placed her hands on her stomach to support her and showed her how to put her face under water and turn her head to breathe, but with her natural buoyancy and determination to swim on her own she quickly mimicked Frances's crawl. Donald made a step with his hands for Mila and Zeke to do cannonball jumps. When they weren't swimming, they played shuffleboard or checkers. Most evenings Donald grilled hot dogs or hamburgers and they ate outside at a picnic table.

Frances seemed different, happy and relaxed, and Mila allowed herself to hope things had changed. They ate early so they could watch Lawrence Welk. To make Saturday night more festive, Donald brought home a small porcelain dachshund that had tiny mugs hanging on its back from hooks. He filled Frances's and his with Mogan David wine and gave Zeke and Mila a few sips in their own mugs. Frances danced with Zeke but since Donald was so tall, Mila stood on his shoes and he twirled her around the room. He was a good dancer, but after the third waltz Mila felt Frances's disapproval and rather than spoil the evening, she danced with Zeke and showed him the box step from dancing class. One night she danced with Mr. Peepers, who pranced around on his back feet. The sight made Frances erupt in laughter. Saturday nights Mila went to bed humming polka music, and for a brief moment she saw her mother whirling around in a small apartment. As quickly as the image appeared, Mila banished it; she wouldn't allow herself to remember anymore.

At Aunt Clara's suggestion, Frances had relented and Mila attended ballroom dancing classes with Annie on Friday evenings in the gym at Riverside High, where Annie would go to school in another year. Frances told Mila she could attend the dance classes only as long as she did her schoolwork. "If your grades fall below C after you start high school, the classes are over," she warned.

August 12, 1954. I danced with Sammy Lammi most of the time. Most of the girls won't dance with him because he's skinny and has a big nose and they make fun of his name. During the break two girls were giggling behind his back. Sammy heard them. I was surprised when he growled: 'that's Samuel J. Lambowski, III, to you.' He can't dance, but he's funny. He talks all the time and says he hates the dance classes but his mother makes him go. I've got to get good grades because I love dancing. Leroy also asked me to dance, but I won't dance with him again. He has fat wet hands.

A few weeks before school started Frances said, "It's time for you both to go to Sunday school. Mila will go to Pastor Bickle's communion classes."

The children looked at each other with puzzled expressions. "What's 'munion'?" Zeke asked.

"Communion," Donald said. "You'll hear Bible stories and learn how to become a good Christian like mother and me."

"You'll learn about the *Ten Commandments*," Frances said. "They are rules like the law. They teach you not to tell lies or steal and to do what your mother and father tell you."

"Do you know what *The Golden Rule* is?" Donald asked.

Two serious faces turned from side to side.

"It teaches that you should do unto others as you would like others to do unto you."

August 18, 1954 - I've started praying. If God can do everything, maybe He can help me.

Donald never attended plays or the symphony; if he had an evening out he went to the Elks Club, so it surprised Mila when Frances said after dinner one night, "You've been acting more responsibly. You can go to Rabbit Run with me tonight to see *A Doll's House*."

"Is it about dolls?" Mila asked.

Frances gave one of her rare laughs. "No. The play is about a strong woman who is expected to behave like a nitwit. Most critics consider the playwright, Henrik Ibsen, the father of modern drama. He wrote about social issues, like marriage."

Rabbit Run was a little theater in a converted barn a couple of miles from B-B. Young New York actors anxious to gain experience in summer stock made up the cast.

Frances had on her public personality, smiling and gracious as they approached the theater where a number of people she knew milled around.

"You remember my daughter, Mila. This is her first play." Mila shook hands. "Mila, would you like some hot chocolate?" She handed her several bills. "The concession stand is over there. Get me a cup of coffee."

The theater was cavernous and drafty. There was no heat, but when the lights dimmed Mila was transported to the world on the stage. When Frances said it would be about social issues she'd been afraid it would be like listening to political speeches. Instead she became totally absorbed. When the lights went on she was surprised to see Frances sitting beside her, so lost had she been to everything around her.

"How did you like it?" Frances asked.

"It was wonderful," Mila said. "Better than a movie." They drove in silence until Mila asked, "Was Nora free after she walked through the door?"

"No woman is ever free," Frances answered. "Some are more self-sufficient than others. Some women enjoy being treated like dolls." Then she added, "Nora wanted to be treated like a human being. Women have to decide what they want."

Before Mila went to sleep still filled with the glow of her night out, she took out her diary.

August 26, 1954 - God is listening to me. The woman took me to a play tonight and hasn't screamed or hit me for a long time. She even bought me hot chocolate.

CHAPTER FOURTEEN

▼

Painesville, Ohio
1956

In the morning the family piled into the car for the drive to Painesville where Donald parked behind Frances's law office and crossed the square to work. While Frances started her day, Mila walked Zeke to her old grammar school. Mila attended Harvey High School a half-mile from Frances's law office.

Every afternoon when school let out she picked him up and they went back to the apartment above Frances's office until it was time to drive to B-B. It was her responsibility to take care of Zeke and make sure he was entertained so he didn't come downstairs and pester Frances. This was a special Friday because Annie was going to spend the weekend. Aunt Clara was dropping her at the apartment and they would leave from there for the dance. She watched for Aunt Clara's car and when she heard it she ran downstairs. Annie squealed when she saw Mila and threw her arms around her.

"Run on upstairs," Frances smiled. "Let me get my work done."

"Mom sent some stuff for you," Annie said handing Mila a large bag containing summer dresses with matching sweaters. Mila noticed that the dresses had been hemmed for her. Twelve years old, still thin, unaware of her inherent grace, she did her best to dress becomingly in hand-me-downs from Annie. Colors were important and instinctively she knew which were best for her. She had to cinch Annie's pleated wool skirts with a belt and cover them with sweaters. On her feet were black and white saddle shoes, *de rigueur* among the girls, Annie said. They were too large and she feared she would walk out of them.

"Let's get ready for the dance," Annie suggested, putting on some Tangelo lip gloss.

"Your skin is so clear," Mila said. "Mine's all breaking out. It looks awful."

Annie pulled out her touch up tube, "Keep it," she said. "I have another one at home."

"Really? Thanks."

"Can I use it too?" Zeke asked, causing the girls to giggle.

"Why are you laughing at me?" he asked.

"It's for girls," Mila explained.

"Why don't you let me fix your hair?" Annie said. "I think it would look pretty down." Annie's hair was done in a perfect pageboy while Mila's was pulled straight back from her face and hung in a ponytail.

Zeke watched them for a few moments and returned to the table to draw.

"I wish it looked like yours," Mila said.

"Yours is beautiful," Annie said. "I wish mine was blond and curled a little."

Her hair was the one thing about herself she actually considered pretty and she felt pleased. "It's unruly," she said. "Aunt Helen gave me a wooden handled brush and matching mirror," Mila said. "I brush it 100 strokes every night."

"No wonder it's so shiny," Annie said. Annie styled it so that a wave fell over Mila's forehead almost covering the faint spots of acne.

"It looks nice," Mila said, looking in the mirror. "You make it look so easy."

"Do you want me to do your nails too?" Annie asked, taking out a bottle of clear nail polish.

Mila blushed and tried to hide her hands.

Annie took them in hers. "What have you done to your nails? They look like they hurt."

"Daddy bought some stuff for me."

"It didn't seem to help," Annie said.

"It's bitter, so I stopped using it." She blushed and promised herself to try harder.

"Where are your overnight things?" Mila asked.

"Oh! I forgot to tell you. I've joined the girls' baton-twirling group and the first meeting is tomorrow, so I won't be able to spend the weekend." Involved in her own enthusiasm, Annie failed to notice Mila fighting back tears. "Can you keep a secret? Nobody knows, but I have a boyfriend and I'm sure he'll kiss me soon," Annie confided. "Kissing is the same as sex."

Mila didn't correct her, but felt sure Annie was mistaken. She felt subdued at dinner, knowing her quietness made her less fun. As soon as they got to the dance, Annie was swept away by her friends. In the bathroom the girls giggled together and talked about make-up and boys. She envied their easy camaraderie and stylish clothes. Mila's only experience with boys was Sammy and Zeke. She glued herself to the wall where she wouldn't be noticeable.

Mrs. Albright, the Home Economics teacher, was patient and soft spoken like Aunt Helen. Each student was required to make an apron. Mila seemed unable to make a straight seam and ripped out the stitching until the fabric was threadbare. She hated sewing and the sight of her hands as she fed the material through the sewing machine.

Her schoolwork in general began to sag; dropping from As and Bs in her first semester to Bs and Cs. The school nurse felt the problem was Mila's inability to see the blackboard, that she needed glasses. "We're not wasting money on expensive glasses when you're not doing your work. I went through your English notebook last night. You haven't done any work the entire semester. The pages are blank!"

"I did the work in class," Mila said.

"We'll see about that," Frances said.

Etta Lee, Mila's English teacher, was a sweet-faced woman with snow-white hair. The class was just getting underway the next day when Frances burst through the door. Mila could almost smell her rage from her seat near the front of the class. She recognized the look on her face and prayed for a fire drill or a nuclear attack, anything to stop time.

"Why good morning Mrs. Robertson," Miss Lee said, surprised at the interruption.

Pointing to Mila, Frances proclaimed to the astonished students, "I want this girl to apologize to her classmates for taking up a seat. She doesn't deserve to be in this country where she's been given a free education and every opportunity. And what does she do with that opportunity? Nothing! Not even homework." Frances waved the grammar book in the air.

Miss Lee's voice was quivering. "Now, Mrs. Robertson..."

Frances was undeterred. "She doesn't deserve to be among students like these boys and girls who work hard in school. She doesn't deserve to be in the United States. She's an alien in this wonderful land of ours."

The class had never been so quiet.

"Stand up, you," Frances said stabbing her index finger in Mila's direction. Mila flinched, shrinking in her seat, praying the woman wouldn't strike her in front of her classmates. Frances demanded, "Apologize to your teacher and classmates."

"I don't think that's necessary," Miss Lee said. "Marja Leena does good work. There's no reason for her to apologize. I…"

Frances interrupted. "She certainly will apologize, and if she doesn't she won't be attending school any longer." She grabbed Mila's arm and forced her to stand and face the class.

Mila's head was lowered, her voice choked with tears as she whispered, "I'm sorry."

"Sorry for what?" Frances demanded. "Tell everyone what you're sorry for."

Mila scanned her mind groping to find what Frances wanted her to say. Sorry for being alive? Sorry for being here? Sorry… sorry… sorry. Let me die, she prayed, if there is a God, let me die now. Her classmates twisted in their seats. Now they knew she was different from them, an alien, not a citizen as they were. The words gagged in her throat. "I'm sorry I wasted the seat." She stood rooted. Nothing else would come out. She dared not look up, but she heard the abrupt opening and closing of the door.

"Take out your books, students, and turn to the reading assignment." Miss Lee placed a gentle hand on Mila's shoulder and led her to the teacher's lounge. "You can rest here until your next class," she said. "I'll come back then."

Mila sank into the couch and buried her head in her arms. She wanted to cease to exist.

"Is there anything I can do?"

The voice sounded like a husky whisper. Mila lifted her head and saw a tall, willowy woman, her curly black hair pulled back with a colorful scarf. "I'm Mrs. Lammi," she said. "I'm the drama teacher."

"Sammy's mother?"

"Yes," she said, "and you're Mila Robertson. You're brave enough to dance with him, he says." Her smile was lopsided, similar to Sammy's.

Mrs. Lammi was considered eccentric by many of the students. They made fun of her flamboyancy and outspokenness, but the students in her drama class adored her. Before anything else was said, Miss Lee came back.

"Are you feeling better, dear?"

"What happened?" Mrs. Lammi asked.

"Mrs. Robertson visited class. There was a bit of a scene." Miss Lee said.

"I'm not surprised. I served with her on the school board. She's something else."

"Yes, well…" Miss Lee fumbled, and shot a warning look at Mrs. Lammi. "I have to get to my next class," she said. "You can stay here until you feel better," she told Mila.

Mrs. Lammi followed Miss Lee out and came back. She put her arm around Mila and pulled her next to her until Mila's head rested on her shoulder. "If you'd like to talk about what happened – it won't go past me."

Mila stared at the floor. "Why didn't I die?" Then she lifted her head and looked directly at Mrs. Lammi. "How can I go back to my classes? Now everyone knows how much she hates me." Haltingly she related what had happened.

"What she did was hateful and unforgivable. But you can survive her. That's something we learned from the war; people do survive all kinds of horror." She touched Mila on the shoulder as she rose from the couch. "You stay here as long as you need. I have to get to my class, but I'll tell your teacher you'll be a little late," she said.

At home the incident passed like the others. Once over it was as if it never happened. Word got around, Mila knew, because her other teachers treated her with greater care. She wanted to be liked for herself, not to be an object of pity. None of her classmates commented; instead of consolation they were unable to look at her directly, and passed with a hurried, "Hi." Except for Sammy, who looked directly into her eyes and said, "Hi, Mila. I'll see you Friday night."

In the middle of the night she heard Frances call for help from the downstairs bathroom. She remained in bed expecting Donald to go downstairs; the second time she heard it she went to the hall and stood barefoot listening until she heard the plea again. When she went downstairs she found Frances leaning against the bathroom wall. There was blood on the floor and all over the tile. "Get Donald," Frances said.

May 31, 1956 - Maybe there is a God and my prayers are finally being answered. The woman has a bleeding ulcer. I hope she never comes back home.

CHAPTER FIFTEEN

▼

Since Frances refused surgery, she was being treated with medication and the ulcer continued to plague her. She issued her orders from the living room that was now arranged for her comfort. The Maalox was one more disagreeable smell. Frances called for a capful several times a day and Mila stopped whatever she was doing to carry it to her.

Just before school resumed in the fall, Frances returned to work. Although it wasn't as pleasant as having her in the hospital, it was better than feeling her gaze searching for an excuse to vent her disapproval.

On the way home from school the following Monday, Mila said, "I wish I didn't have to go to communion classes anymore."

"Yeah," Zeke agreed. "They sound really boring."

"Sometimes I wonder about God," she said. "Do you really think he watches and hears everything everyone does?"

"Like farting?" Zeke snickered.

"Well if he does, you're in trouble," she said.

"Daddy farts," Zeke said.

Mila gave him a playful shove. "You're hopeless," she said. You can't be serious about anything," then put her arm around his shoulder and pulled him to her.

October 12, 1956 - If God is always around, why do so many bad things happen? I wonder if God can really see my thoughts? I wish I had someone to talk to, like Mrs. Lammi. Sammy is lucky to have a mother like her. I'm afraid of my tunnel. I go into it almost every night because my mind doesn't have to think when I'm in it. Sometimes at school I go there or even when I'm in the car. Only sometimes I have trouble coming out. I have to move my big toe or my first finger before I can leave. What if I forget to move and I couldn't get out? I solemnly promise to myself that I will only use it when I can't think of anything else.

She wondered if God knew what she was planning, that instead of what happened to Raskilnokov's landlady in *Crime and Punishment*, Frances would die from her ulcer. Mila worked it all out. She would use a mortar and pestle to grind up glass to add to the instant coffee she made for Frances every morning. When she started to bleed, people would think since she refused to have an operation it was from her ulcer.

October 21, 1956 - Annie told me she's had her first period last month. Aunt Clara took her out for a mother-daughter lunch at Helregals Inn and she had a steak sandwich on toast. When it's my time I'll bet the woman won't take me out for lunch.

Mila's body was changing. Often she felt like crying. She read *Welcome to Young Womanhood*, the pamphlet about menstruation, with curiosity, but didn't understand 'fallopian tubes' or exactly what kind of eggs they were talking about or why they called it a 'period.' She looked at the illustration of a happy girl going to the store with her mother to buy a belt and sanitary pads and wished Annie was closer so she could talk to her about things she didn't understand and couldn't ask Frances.

November 4, 1956 - All week I've had pain in my stomach, but it's not like my usual stomach aches. I think I'm having my first period. There were spots of blood in my underpants yesterday and a few today. I told the woman and she asked if I'd read the pamphlet she left on the stairway. I HATE HER MORE THAN EVER - She gave me rags cut from daddy's old undershirt and told me to pin them to my underpants with Zeke's old diaper pins and said she didn't want to see my filth around. I'm supposed to wash the rags out every day. I'm going ahead with my plan.

Mila walked with small, mincing steps trying to keep her legs pressed together. She was sure the bulky pads protruded through the folds of her pleated skirts. Her legs were raw and chafed and every step was agony; she was sure everyone could smell the blood.

She dreaded Gym class. Hot shame flooded her face when she had to change clothes - it was bad enough to still wear undershirts when most of the girls were wearing bras. The gym baskets were unlocked and Mila began stealing pads and sanitary belts. The problem was that one or two pads were not enough so she began stealing money. Nearly being caught in the act, she grabbed a purse and wrapped it in her coat. Knowing Frances looked through her dresser drawers, she left the purse in her locker at school, but someone spotted the purse and she was caught.

CHAPTER SIXTEEN

▼

She knew the school had notified Frances but when Mila stood before her she denied everything.

"They have incontrovertible evidence. On top of everything,you're a liar. What's wrong with you? Do you have a brain tumor? Get out of my sight," Frances said. It's not enough to steal money, but sanitary pads. "You're sick."

Mila stood mute and looked at her defiantly.

December 10, 1956 - It will be so nice when she's gone. We'll all be happy and like a normal family. I'll take care of Zeke, clean house, and cook the meals just like I do now, and then dinner will be like it is in other families where no one fights.

Donald was outside straightening the garage and she approached him hesitantly. "Can I talk to you about, you know, what happened at school?" Frances was one thing, but she dreaded disappointing Donald and decided she'd explain to him on Saturday after Frances went to her office

"I think that's a good idea," he said.

"I...I really didn't want to take the money."

"That's what's so hard to understand," he said. "Why didn't you just go to Ulle and tell her you needed those things. Or ask me. That's all you had to do. She'd have been glad to go to the store with you." He shook his head.

"I ... told her I needed ... needed those things and I kept waiting to go to the drugstore, but she didn't take me and..."

"She just didn't understand; you have to make yourself clear."

"She understood. I asked her to take me to the drug store like Annie and the other girls. She said no, she didn't want to buy them for me. She's hardly ever nice. You know I can't talk to her. She hates me."

"Now, now. You mustn't go on like that. You have to learn the things that irritate her and try not to do them; Ulle's fine if you learn how to treat her."

"It doesn't matter what I do."

"She's an important woman ... and busy. She gets annoyed by little things that don't bother other people. I guess you could say in the big book of life you have to accept things how they are; you can't change very much in life - most things never change. They're written out that way." Leaning over he gave her a quick hug, got up, and then smiled down at her. "Aren't you glad we had this little chat? Don't we feel better now?"

Under her breath, Mila muttered, "Maybe you feel better. I don't."

"What was that?" Donald asked.

"I don't," Mila said.

"Before that, what did you say?"

"Maybe you feel better, I don't." The words flashed angrily from her mouth before she could stop them.

"Don't you get sarcastic with me, young lady. After all the times I've stuck up for you. Don't *ever* take that tone with me again. Do you understand?"

Mila had never heard him sound so angry with her, but rather than scaring her, it made her angrier.

"Answer me when I ask you something," he said. "Do you understand?"

A reluctant "yes," came out.

"All right then," Donald said, his tone stern, "I think you'd better go to your room and think about how you just talked to me."

December 13 - I'm not going to tell him anything nevermorenevermorenevermore. I wish I could be like the black raven and fly away. God won't help me. I've prayed for two years every night. You are the only one I can talk to. Daddy doesn't want to understand me. It's just you and me, dear diary.

It was Donald's habit to empty his pockets when he got home from work putting comb, wallet, and spare change on the dresser in plain sight. In all innocence, Zeke told Mila, "Daddy counts his money, even the pennies, when he puts it on his dresser and mother hides her purse in the closet."

"How do you know that?" Mila asked.

"He was giving me a lesson and said that children should never lie or steal."

December 16, 1956 - Christmas vacation will be here soon and I won't have to go to school. The girls no longer bring their purses to gym class and when they are forced to have me on their team during volleyball or softball I can see their discomfort by the looks that pass between them. The only place I fit in is with the other squares, but they get good grades and I don't anymore.

It was easy to steal the mortar and pestle. Mila hurried Zeke to school and got to first period science class before the other students arrived. The science equipment was kept in a glass cabinet in the storage room off the science room. The shelves were lined with Petri dishes, conical flasks, beakers, apothecary jars, test tubes and a row of mortars and pestles. She walked quickly between the long wooden rows with Bunsen burners and ring stands to the teacher's desk. She knew Miss Peacock kept the key to the cabinet in a small box in back of her top drawer. Mila moved quickly, shoved the mortar and pestle in her lunch bag and put the key back in the box well before hearing students in the hallway.

What bothered her most was where to hide it at home. She put the small mortar on her windowsill and filled it with shells from the beach. If Frances asked, she would tell her she found it. She wrapped the pestle in an old gym sock and put it in a pair of worn out gym shoes. When Frances was at her office on Saturday morning, she smashed a small chipped glass and carefully ground pieces of glass into a fine powder, wrapped them in small packets of tinfoil and hid them in the pocket of a worn out overcoat that hung in the wardrobe in the garage.

Each morning she smiled to herself. *Not this morning*, she would think. *I have time. If things get worse, I know what to do.* The mere fact that she had a plan and could do something to protect herself seemed to be enough for now.

She decided long ago Raskilnokov sniveled too much, but she began worrying about whether she was capable of carrying out her plan. Jail sounded all right because she wouldn't live with Frances anymore, but she began to wonder about herself. When Frances told her to kill the spiders in the corners of the bathroom, she couldn't do it. Instead she gathered them in a glass, put a piece of toilet paper over the end, and carried them outside. She cried over books in which animals were destroyed and couldn't imagine anyone hurting Mr. Peepers.

On Wednesday evening before Christmas vacation Mila was reading and Zeke was on the floor playing cars when she heard Frances pound on the ceiling, her method of summoning Mila down to her office. She sat scowling, a letter clutched in her hand; she rummaged through the files scattered over the desk, occasionally jerking her head in Mila's direction to glare, but saying nothing. Mila refused to give her the satisfaction of asking what she'd done wrong. Instead she became acutely aware of her surroundings, the furniture, and the changing patterns of the sky, the sound of Zeke playing upstairs. Frances got up and walked toward her and Mila's stomach tightened in a knot of anxiety. She stepped back smelling the familiar acrid odor of rage.

"Do you know what this is?" Frances screamed. She held a crumpled letter and waved it in Mila's face. "It's a letter from your mother."

Mila stood puzzled. What she was saying didn't make sense. Years ago Frances had told her that her mother was dead.

"My mother?" she reached for the letter but Frances pulled it away.

"You wouldn't understand. It's from an attorney. I don't know where your worthless mother got the money for attorneys, but none of them know who they're up against when they start threatening me. Now that you're getting old enough to be of some help, she wants you back. My guess is she's getting too old to work and needs you to support her."

Mila felt a swelling of hope.

"You'd be dead if it wasn't for me," Frances ranted. "I've supported you for years and do any in your worthless family appreciate what I've done? No. They're not going to intimidate me with their threats, I can assure you of that. If it's to be a legal contest I'll win. It's a good thing I've never let you become a citizen. We're going to get your passport photo taken and the faster the better. I've had all I can stand of you."

The photography studio was upstairs in the bank building. Frances was out of breath when she opened the glass door with the gold letters saying: OSCAR PETERSEN, PHOTOGRAPHER, and below that: Passport Photos.

"Good afternoon, Mrs. Robertson. Are you going on vacation?"

"She's returning to Finland," Frances answered, pointing to Mila.

"Wouldn't you like to comb your hair?" he asked Mila.

"It doesn't matter," Frances said.

He looked uncomfortable and after he took a few poses, disappeared into the darkroom and returned with the pictures. "I'm afraid they didn't turn out too well," he apologized. "I think I'd better take them again."

Frances looked at the grim photos. "It's fine," she said.

December 20, 1956 – I may not have to use the ground glass. I don't understand what is going on, but I had a passport picture taken. I don't dare think I might be going back for fear something will go wrong. I've been reading about Finland in the library and I picture it as a white country. I picture myself in a snowstorm. I want to stand at the rail of the ship and feel the wind and snow from home blowing in my face.

Do not call out for your daughter,
Do not cry or make a clamor;
She cannot come back to you…

Ibid, Runo 34, Lines 238-240

CHAPTER SEVENTEEN

▼

Helsinki, Finland
Winter 1956-1957

Memory and nostalgia washed over Anders as he entered the steamy warmth of the Helsinki train terminal. So many of his twenty-three years had been divided between hospitals and travel terminals. Seldom was anyone waiting to greet him. This one was a farewell of another kind, he was in Helsinki to attend Tehelia's funeral.

He decided to go to the pensioner's home first before going home to Kaija and Martti. The home had the familiar feel of poverty and futility. Sadness settled over him as the orderly took him to the room in which she'd hung herself. Her old rocking chair stood in place beside the table near the window looking out to the field of birch and pine trees. There was nothing else in the room except the bed.

"Are you a relative?" the orderly named Ilsa asked him.

"She is my grandmother," he answered.

"I don't remember seeing you visit."

"I've been in Sweden," Anders said.

Ilsa told him what he already knew from Tehelia's letters. Her voice was flat, void of emotion.

"Her arthritis was bad," Ilsa said. "She couldn't knit anymore, but she still read the newspaper every day." Ilsa's shrug dismissed such practice as lunacy. "She had a stroke, you know, and couldn't walk without a cane. I don't know how she managed to climb up and hang herself. I think in the end she must have changed her mind because she left claw marks on her throat." As an after thought she added, "Maybe it was just the pain of it."

Anders tried to imagine what it must be like working in such a place. How many neglected souls had she discovered dead by their own hand? He ran his hand over the rocking chair, where Mumma had held a family of children on her lap as she read stories. What strength, guts, intestinal fortitude, pride, perseverance, he thought. She instilled *sisu* in us all. Mumma endured while needed and when it was time, left. We should all be so brave, he thought.

It had been two years since he'd last been home. The only change was the painting. It was the first thing he noticed when he opened the door - *Iltarusko*, winter evening light. A winter landscape with an ice filled stream, bare birch trees cast in the eerie light of afternoon just before the sun sets leaving a soft cast of mauve, pink and rose on the snow. An ornate carved wooden frame completed the picture. Old man Juusonen, as Mumma called her husband, received it as trade for one of his jobs. Tehelia had never considered selling it despite her years of hardship. The colors had lost some of their vibrancy due to wood smoke, but like Mumma, its beauty remained.

Martti came in from school and seemed unfazed at seeing Anders. He greeted him like they'd said goodbye after breakfast. Martti's quick and graceful movements always struck Anders. He was shorter than Anders by a good four inches, but strong. Anders felt pleasure seeing him dressed so well on the money he'd sent home.

"Quite a man," Anders said, greeting him with a bear hug. Martti's soulful eyes glinted with a hint of laughter.

"We weren't sure you'd come," Martti said. "Whether you could get away."

"They know I'm trustworthy," Anders said. He noticed a look wash over his brother's face and wondered at the cause. Perhaps it was a fear of losing the money Anders regularly sent, but Martti was easily offended and capable of hearing "trustworthy" as an insult.

"I'm getting bored with the work," Anders explained. "The money's good, but I'm interested in electronics. It's exciting. I've been working part time at a store in Stockholm that sells home appliances. I'm good at selling and I like it."

"They have stores like that in Helsinki," Martti said, "but not many can afford to buy, they watch TV in the store windows." Martti rocked back and forth as if ready to bolt.

"Just wait. I'm convinced, TV will be the new sensation."

Anders could see that Martti wasn't interested. "How are you doing in school?" he asked.

"My math grades are high and my instructor wants me to stay in school for the additional two years. I'll be sixteen in another month and I won't have to go anymore."

Anders was ready to argue with him but Kaija arrived. Work agreed with her, but while she remained slender her face was aging and slightly puffy. She unwound the scarf and took off her hat, then hung her coat near the fire to dry.

Never demonstrative, she patted him on the arm, "So you're back," she said and busied herself boiling water for tea.

"I visited the home. It's hard to believe Mumma's gone."

"She had a number of small strokes and didn't want to live that way. She said if she had more energy she'd go into the forest and die of exposure. I'm going to miss mother. It seemed like she'd always be here." Kaija poured hot water in the pot to heat it. "She left a will of sorts. She gave Sofi her ring and since I'm the oldest daughter she left *Iltarusko* to me."

"And nothing for me," Martti said in a flat voice. Anders could see Martti hadn't changed, still full of anger and self-pity.

"She had little enough to leave anyone. You know the painting is to pass on to Mila since it belongs to the women in the family. You'd better bring some more wood," Kaija told Martti.

"We were just speaking of school," Anders said.

"He's more interested in girls," Kaija smiled at Martti as if sharing a special bond. "The girls are crazy about him."

Martti looked at his hands.

"He's shy," Kaija said. "But don't let that deceive you. They chase after him. He can have his choice."

After he left to get the wood Kaija told him, "He's uneasy around girls. He always brings them here for coffee, or stops by to get approval from Aleksis or me."

Martti is different from me, Anders thought. I wouldn't ask Kaija's approval for anything. "You're still working?" he asked.

"Yes. Cooking for the workmen is better than cleaning offices and I make extra money cutting their hair. Aleksis is a foreman now." She poured the hot water into the teapot and brought three cups to the table.

"Have you heard anything from Ohio?" Anders asked.

"I've written letters to Mila, but she never responds. I feel things aren't going well for her," Kaija said. I thought it was the best chance she had. Mrs. Robertson sends photos but even with the pretty clothes Mila looks so sad."

"And the lawyer?" Anders asked. "You've hired a lawyer with the money I sent?"

"Yes," Kaija assured him. She held her cup in both hands and took a sip. Looking over the rim of her cup she said. "You remember my friend who sent her daughter to America?"

Anders nodded, his face grim. He stirred sugar into his tea.

"She's had a nervous breakdown. She married well and money is no object for her. They hired a lawyer, but she cannot get her daughter back."

Anders's jaw tightened. He was determined not to lose his temper.

Martti dropped the wood with a loud thump. "Why do you worry about Mila? The little princess has everything she could want in America," he said.

Anders exchanged a look with Kaija. "We don't know anything about her," Anders said. "Have some tea while we have a game of chess."

They both loved chess. Anders taught Martti just as Lars had taught him, but there the similarity ended. Chess provided them a way of communicating and a brotherly fellowship, despite their different temperaments. Good players with equal skill, Anders played for the love of the game while Martti played to win. Anders opened each game with the same move, but played intuitively, holding the entire game in his head and visually projecting the moves ahead. Martti played methodically according to the standardized moves, his mathematical ability serving him well. They played long after Kaija went to bed.

"Check mate," Anders finally said.

Martti's tolerance was at an end. He swept his arm across the table spilling the game onto the floor and screamed the worst of Finnish insults. "Devil dog take you. I'll never play with you again." He refused to speak for several days.

On the weekend Aleksis arrived to take Kaija to his cabin by the lake where they ice fished by day and drank by night. Aleksis shook hands and in an effort to be friendly, offered Anders a drink.

Anders could see the conflict in Martti. He was close to Aleksis, but Anders saw how disapproving and angry he looked when he heard the bottles clink in the bag Aleksis carried.

Anders declined. "Thanks, no."

Aleksis shrugged. "I am a typical Finnish man," he bragged. "I drink Friday and Saturday nights until I pass out, but I go to my work every Monday. You? You look like a man and act like a man but you don't drink." He seemed truly puzzled.

"Father didn't drink; not all men do." Anders replied.

After they left Martti set up the chess game without speaking. The chair screeched as Martti pulled it out and sat down, then looked at Anders. "Now we play," he said.

"Okay." Anders smiled.

After an hour they stopped for a break and Martti said, "At least she doesn't go to the bar alone now. Aleksis is good to her - to me too. He's good at what he does - his work, and he's teaching me."

Anders nodded.

"You haven't been here the last few years; you don't know what it's like. I live with her every day and when she's drunk I'm the one who listens to her cursing the unfairness of her life; I'm the one who listens to the same stories time after time; I'm the one who picks up the broken bottles she throws against the walls and cleans up because I'm worried she'll fall and cut herself; I'm the one who cleans up her vomit," he caught his breath. "And I'm the one who watches her cry over Mila. She drinks more than ever since Mila left."

"It's hard on you," Anders said. "You can't change her; no one can."

"I try to get her to stop. I beg her not to drink. I want to leave school in May to get a job and a place of my own. If I were old enough I'd join the army."

A cloud of disapproval crossed Anders' face. "You've got to stay in school. You're a genius with numbers; you could be an engineer, get work in the electronics field. Don't be a fool."

"I don't care for reading," Martti protested.

"Don't be a fool," he repeated.

Martti turned the pawn around and around on the table. "Who wants to sit around reading? It takes too long. I'd rather be active, outside, doing something."

They resumed the game ending the discussion. Martti won and while he set up a new game Anders said, "So the girls follow you around?"

"That's what she says," Martii said. "Girls are complicated."

"Do you have a girlfriend?" Anders asked.

Martti shrugged, pushing the chessboard toward Anders. "White or black?" he asked.

The following week, Anders and Kaija climbed the three flights of stairs to the law office of Arne Arnerio. His name was in gold on the opaque glass panel of the door that opened onto a small reception area. Before they had seated themselves, the inner door opened and a small man came out. He smiled at Kaija and motioned them into the inner office.

"Thank you for coming, Mrs. Ahlgren," he said, holding her hand in both of his, "and this must be the son you've mentioned."

"Good day, sir. I'm Anders Ahlgren."

"Please, sit down." Arnerio indicated the round backed chairs as he returned to his seat behind his desk.

Anders leaned forward. "We're anxious to hear about the letter you've received from America."

"Yes. Well, I'll get right to it. I'm afraid it's not good news. I have a letter from Mrs. Robertson stating a number of things." He ruffled through the papers on his desk. "First, Mrs. Robertson included a copy of the letter she sent you in 1950 shortly after your daughter's arrival in America." He picked up the letter and started to read it out loud like a school lesson. "It will be solely at our discretion to decide, should the issue arise, whether the child shall be returned to Finland."

Before he could read further, Kaija interrupted. "I always thought Mila would return after she finished school."

"Let me continue," Arnerio said. "I know this is difficult for you." Again he picked up the letter. "Second, and most important, the adoption is legal and binding." He looked from Kaija to Anders. "I now have a copy of the adoption papers filed in Painesville, Ohio." Anticipating protest he opened a file on his desk to fortify what remained to be said. "I've consulted with the United States Consulate's office here in Helsinki. If the Robertsons want the child, you don't have any legal recourse."

Anders stood up and paced the small office his face a mask of fury. "Then why isn't Mila a U.S. citizen? If they want her, you'd think that would be the first thing they'd do. She's been there over six years, and you say she's still a Finnish citizen."

Kaija looked from Anders to the lawyer.

In a soothing voice, Arnerio agreed. "That puzzles me too. I've never heard of adoptive parents waiting so long to have a child naturalized. It was the strongest factor for getting your daughter back," he coughed into his hand, then continued. "It did appear they weren't interested in keeping her."

"What about her new passport?" Anders asked. "Where is that?"

"Mrs. Robertson has received it and states she will hold onto it." Arnerio shook his head looking puzzled. "When they sent those passport photos so a new Finnish passport could replace the expired one, I was sure they were willing to return her." He looked uncomfortable, but continued. "Otherwise why go to the bother...except for the last item." His voice fell as he looked down at the letter, again put his hand over his mouth for a nervous cough before reading. "After repeated questioning by us, Marja Leena says she doesn't want to return to Finland. She doesn't remember anyone in her family, not even their names."

Anders jumped from his chair. "I don't believe that for one minute. I want to hear that from Mila's own mouth. All you have to do is look at those photos to see..."

Kaija agreed. "My daughter's face looks dead." Tears of guilt and sadness filled her eyes. "Those photos keep me awake at night ... she looks ... she looks like people who have been in jail."

"There must be something more you can do." Anders's voice was a plea.

"I'm truly sorry," Arnerio said. "There is nothing we can do legally. They have her passport, and unless they change their minds," again he coughed. "Well, we can only wait."

Arnerio stood. The meeting was over. Kaija gathered her things and they left the office. On the stairs Anders said in a low voice, as much to himself as to Kaija, "I've decided to stay in Helsinki."

It wasn't until they were on the street that he told her, "I got a job at Lampi's Radio Store downtown. I've learned some English - that's how I got the job. The pay is good. The staff from the United States Embassy shop there. I'll learn more English and go to America myself to find Mila."

CHAPTER EIGHTEEN

▼

Painesville, Ohio
1957

The New Year brought hope. Each day Mila waited to hear when she'd be leaving; since taking her passport photograph the subject hadn't been mentioned, but she assumed it took time to make arrangements. Each night before going to sleep she contemplated her return home, wondering who would meet her, if they remembered what she looked like.

Nineteen fifty-six had been a nightmare of mistakes and failures; now she could leave all that behind and start again surrounded by a family that loved her. Mila strained to remember the faces and names so dear to her; they'd faded after seven years and returned only as feelings of longing.

Frances had been in a period of quiescence, but Mila knew she brooded for months over the slightest infraction. Her silent treatment had become a favored method of adding the element of uncertainty to her torment. Mila matched her with her own silence and it became a contest of wills. As the thaw started and the first harbingers of spring broke through, Mila's anxiety mounted, her dreams reflected her apprehension.

Mila woke with a pounding heart, still dazed from her dream. It was the second time she'd had it. Zeke was little again and they were on the beach, but she was standing on the grassy bank watching him play in the sand. Suddenly all the water rushed away from the beach. She could see what looked like miles of sand and rocks where the water had been moments before. In the distance she watched a wave higher than anything she'd ever seen, and it was moving toward them. She called Zeke over and over and tried running to him but her legs wouldn't move because they were sinking deep in the sand. Zeke was oblivious of her and the approaching danger. It was her job to take care of him; she felt overwhelmed with her love for him. She strained to pull her feet loose and managed to reach him and grab his hand just as the wave froze in midair and all she could see was a towering wall of greenish water ready to collapse on them. There was no one she could call; she was helpless. Though she tried to push the dream from her thoughts it kept intruding.

Mila promised Zeke they would go to the lake on the first warm day. She finished her Saturday chores and made peanut butter and jelly sandwiches and fixed a container of lemonade. Donald was painting the trim on an outside window and Mr. Peeper ran after the stick Zeke threw. She carried a glass to Donald who stopped to wipe his forehead with a handkerchief and sat down on the porch steps.

"Can we go to the lake now?" Zeke begged. "Mila promised she'd ask you."

"I can't stop painting," he said. "It's still too cold to go in the water anyhow."

Zeke kicked a clump of crab grass. "Please, Daddy."

"I'll tell you what, Mila will be fourteen soon and I know I can depend on her. I'll let you go, but you must promise not to go near the water."

Zeke's face broke into a big smile. "Okay," they promised.

Mila hurried to get their towels and lunch things together. They waved goodbye to Donald and walked away hand-in-hand.

They found a grassy bank near a tree overlooking the water. Mila took out their sandwiches and poured them each a paper cup of lemonade. Recalling her dream she cast uneasy looks at the lake to make sure it remained calm.

"Do you think Daddy will let us go swimming by ourselves this summer?" Zeke asked.

Mila handed Zeke his sandwich before answering. "There's something I've been meaning to talk to you about," Mila said. "I probably won't be here this summer."

"Where are you going?" Zeke asked, taking a big bite. "You're not going to Aunt Betty's again without me, are you?"

"Don't talk with your mouth full," Mila said. "No. I'm going back to Finland."

Zeke looked puzzled. "What's in Finland?"

"My family."

"What are you talking about?"

"My family - where I was born."

"We were born here," Zeke protested.

"*You* were born here," Mila said. "I wasn't. You know I'm adopted. My real family is in Finland."

Zeke's face took on a look of stubborn incredulity. "I'm real." He threw the rest of his sandwich on the ground, "I'm your brother," he insisted and ran toward home.

Mila chased after him, out of breath. He was in his room.

"Can I come in?" she asked, but he didn't answer. She went in and sat on the edge of his bed where he was hugging his pillow to his face.

"Why do you want to leave me?" he mumbled into the pillow

"I don't want to leave you, but nobody here really wants me."

"I do," he said. "Can I go with you?"

"It's different for you," Mila said. "They don't get mad at you."

"What if I tell mom that I don't want you to go. Please don't go."

"Some day you'll understand," Mila said. "I'll write to you and when you grow up you can come and visit."

"It won't be the same," Zeke said. "I don't believe you. I'm going to ask daddy."

Mila followed Zeke downstairs and outside where Donald was now whitewashing the fence.

"Are you back already?"

"Go ahead," Zeke said and challenged Mila. "You ask him."

"Ask me what?" Donald said.

"Mila says she's going to leave and go back to Finland," Zeke said. "Is that true?"

"Where did you get an idea like that?" Donald asked Mila. "Your home is here now. I thought you were over such nonsense."

"But..."

"But nothing."

Mila's disappointment made her weak. "But the passport?"

"That was nothing but a false alarm," he said.

> *March 12, 1957*
> *The raven wings into the night*
> *until it is one with the dark.*
> *With air currents its only guide*
> *the raven flies far and free.*
> *Dear Diary if only I could be like a bird.*

Lake Erie College in Painesville used Harvey High School as a testing ground for its psychology students to administer IQ tests. Mila was among five students chosen from her class. Pressure to perform on tests made her mind blank even when she knew the material, but when she was told there would be no grades she was able to concentrate. Mr. Applegate, her school counselor, said, "Your parents will be told the results after they're evaluated." A fellow student, George Szukinic, spent most of his time looking at the floor out of shyness. When he and Mila were asked to return for a second exam, Mila assumed she'd done poorly.

The third Friday after the test, before she herded Zeke upstairs, Frances called her into her office. Her hopes soared thinking it was to tell her when she'd be leaving after all, but it was clear that wasn't the subject. By her tone Mila anticipated anger, assuming her low grade would mean another haranguing. Frances glared at her and waved a letter in her direction.

"Do you know what a Stanford Binet IQ test is?" she began. Mila shook her head, no.

"It's a test you can't cheat on. It measures your intelligence. Do you know what that means?"

"No," Mila answered.

"It means with the brains you have, you could do anything - if you only had some drive and guts like I have. What do you do instead? Nothing."

Mila thought of the packets of ground glass.

"It won't matter," Frances predicted.

It wasn't until Mr. Applegate called her into his office to explain about IQ tests that she learned her scores.

"You've placed very high," he told her. "Your first score was one hundred forty-three and it was even higher the second time. You could be an outstanding student if you tried." He tapped a freshly sharpened pencil on the edge of his desk. "What are you most interested in at school?" he asked.

No one had bothered to ask her anything before and what difference did it make? Her anger flared and the corners of her mouth turned down in sullen determination not to cooperate.

"What about reading or poetry? Do you write stories or poems? Maybe just for yourself?"

"Sometimes," she admitted.

"I see you're not involved in any after school enrichment activities," he said turning the pages of her folder.

"I don't have time," Mila mumbled. "I go straight home and take care of my brother."

"What about lunch time? Have you thought about the Chess Club?" Sammy Lammi was the president of the Chess Club.

"The Chess Club is all boys," she said, although her interest was apparent.

"I'm sure they'll let a girl in," Mr. Applegate assured her. "And I'm going to have you talk to Mr. McGrath about your interest in writing. You know he publishes our school paper and I'm sure he would encourage you to submit some of your work."

Mila's grades began to improve under Mr. Applegate's increased interest, but her disappointment in not returning to Finland festered. Sammy was setting up the chessboard when Mila dropped down opposite, scratching the legs of the chair against the floor. "You look down. What's up?" Sammy asked with a silly grin.

"I feel trapped," she said. "I feel stuck here - forever."

"Can I help?" he asked.

Mila's eyes clouded. Before she could answer, he said, "Would it help if I gave up dancing?"

Mila laughed.

"I think life is a little like a chess game," he said. "When the game starts you lose pawns, sacrifice knights and bishops, but if you pay attention and learn - before you know it you're saying 'checkmate' and you've won the game."

july 10, 1957 – i peeled potatoes all morning for my fourteenth birthday party. we had a picnic again. no more capitals for me! aunt betty sent me a book of poems by e e cummings. my favorite is about the little lame balloon man who whistles far and wee.

daddy gave me a charm shaped like a book because he said i have my nose buried in one all the time. aunt helen gave me a pair of blue pedal pushers and a striped top and a bathing suit annie had picked out and everything fits. next week we leave for vermont and then to maine. I can't wait to see annie.

Frances wore a light cotton dress and appeared cheerful as they put the bags in the car. Donald leaned in the opened window, "I'll have the house painted when you get back," he said. "You children do as mother tells you." He waved them out the driveway.

Ollie Browning, a good friend from Frances's University days, was a recent widow with four children. They lived near Lake Champlain in a big sprawling house surrounded by cornfields and vegetable and flower gardens. The screen door opened as the car pulled into the driveway as if the anticipation had been mounting. Frances jumped from the car and the women rocked back and forth wrapped in each other's arms. Surprised at the uncharacteristic display of affection, Mila watched them disappear into the house.

Susan, the oldest daughter, assumed responsibility for entertaining the children and every day was filled with exciting things to do. She took them swimming, on long hikes, and when it rained she popped corn while they worked jigsaw puzzles. One afternoon she took them to pick fresh corn for dinner.

Frances was relaxed, usually sitting on the front porch with Ollie talking or reading. One muggy afternoon Mila went to the kitchen for a glass of water and heard them through the opened window.

"I'm going to Washington in October. "I wanted to run for judge again, but Donald's difficult."

"Is that why he didn't want to come?"

"No, we have other issues. You know he's always uncomfortable when we're together, especially if Billie's with us," Frances said. "He never got over those pictures of the three of us, although he never talked about it."

Ollie's eye twinkled with mischief and she gave a short laugh. "Too bad he had to see them."

Mila stood still, empty glass in hand, waiting for the women to continue, but Zeke's arrival, announced by the banging of the screen door, cut short the conversation but not Mila's curiosity about the photos and this person named Billie.

The days sped by and at the end of two weeks they left Vermont to drive to Maine and pickup Annie who was vacationing at her grandmother's house. Frances held Ollie's hand until the last moment, pulling apart until only their fingertips touched.

Mila shared a bedroom with Annie and when they went to bed they read teen magazines, and tried to scare each other by holding the flashlight under their chin and giggling over nothing.

"Can you keep a secret?" Annie asked.

"I always keep your secrets," Mila said.

"Remember I told you I had a boyfriend? Do you want me to show you how he hugs and kisses me?" Annie asked.

With some trepidation, Mila agreed, lured by the chance of discovering a dangerous secret. She still didn't have a realistic idea of how babies were made, but hugs and kisses had something to do with it, she knew.

Annie put her arms around Mila and told her to turn her head, "like this," she said, "so our noses don't get in the way."

Their lips were just touching when the lights snapped on with an angry flick and for a brief second the late night quiet became even quieter. They each drew back as if they'd been prodded with an electric current, then Frances's voice hissed through the humid air.

"I knew you were up to something, but this! This is beyond *anything* you've done."

Startled and trapped the girls sat in bed stock still, their eyes adjusting to the light and the words pouring over them.

"Are you all right, Annie? What did this animal do to you?"

Annie was wide eyed with fright. "Nothing, *Tante*. Nothing." Eagerly she tried to explain, "I was the one who was showing Mila how my boyfriend..."

Before she could explain further Frances cut her off. "There's no need for you to concern yourself, dear. Don't try to defend her." Grabbing Mila by the arm she yanked her out of bed and shoved her from the room.

"How can I explain this to Annie's father? He'll be livid."

"I wasn't... I wasn't doing anything wrong. Annie..." Mila said trying to pull away.

"Lesbian. I knew it. Lesbian slut. Seducing my own family. First flirting with Donald and now Annie. No one is safe around you. If you ever touch Zeke I'll kill you."

"Is everything all right?" Annie's grandmother knocked at the bathroom door. "What's wrong?"

"Go back to bed. I'll handle it," Frances said.

Breathing hard, she stopped and pushed Mila into the bedroom with Zeke, pointing to the floor, "You stay there. I'll decide what to do with you later on."

Mila lay on the bare floor trembling. She heard Zeke get out of bed. "Here's my blanket," he said spreading his blanket over her, and then padded back to bed.

She fell into a troubled sleep and a troubled dream in which she had the feeling she had killed a child and cut it up in pieces, terrified someone would find out. She found herself in a basement where she'd hidden pieces of the child, burying them near the furnace. She was frightened and alone. Then the dream changed and it was her being threatened by someone with a hammer. Mila felt death was her only hope.

So she moved still lower down
Toward the Underworld's abysses,
Raking, raking thoroughly,
Lengthwise, crosswise and aslant.

Ibid, Runo 15, Lines 259-262

CHAPTER NINETEEN

▼

B-B, Ohio

There was a forced normalcy to their routine after their return home. No one spoke to Mila. When she sat down at the table, Frances said, "If you must eat, wait until we're gone." She returned to her room, heard Donald leave for work, then Frances taking Zeke with her.

She looked around her room, impersonal except for a stack of books on the linen chest, the lone hint at the personality of the person who slept there. Unlike most teenagers' rooms there were no photos, no bottles of lotions, no records, no radio. The things that mattered to her were tucked away in her cardboard suitcase. To ease her loneliness she pulled out the small suitcase examining her treasured possessions: the clay bust of Cyrano de Bergerac she sculpted in art class, some stones and shells she thought beautiful and small pieces of driftwood. A poem she'd written, called Sandpipers in which she spoke of their fragility as they danced to the tide, tripped by the shadows, quivering with the breeze and dancing on a thread of sand. Reading it over she took it as a sign, an omen that her decision to kill herself was the proper course. Her window looked toward the lake, a shining brilliance. She took out her diary, the pencil resting on her lip as she thought, and then she began to write.

august 13, 1957 - this is my last entry. i don't want to die, but i can't think of what else to do.

She stuffed the poem in the pocket of her shorts, put the suitcase back in the corner of the closet, and left the house.

The air was soft. She was acutely aware of everything, the cooing of the mourning doves, the breezes rustling the tall elms and maples. It seemed only a moment until she reached the beach where she stepped out of her shorts, pulled the shirt over her head and threw herself in the morning water. Shivering from the chill she started swimming straight north toward Canada, until her arms refused another stroke. She thought it should take only a few minutes to drown and hoped it wouldn't be too painful. She couldn't judge her distance from shore or the depth of the water, but with her last reserves she dove as deeply into the water as she could. She couldn't see the bottom, but continued deeper, she squeezed her eyes closed and tried to ignore her burning lungs until everything turned black. She stopped struggling. Natural buoyancy made her rise to the surface. She let the water rock her like a leaf blown from a tree, floating on the surface too weak and tired to rally the energy to dive again. She floated and drifted until she was washed ashore.

Time stopped existing but when enough strength returned, she hobbled back to the house. The rest of the day passed and as dinnertime approached her anxiety grew. Her plan had failed. She was trapped. What would they be like when they arrived? Should she make dinner? She put potatoes on to boil, cooked meatballs, made a salad. When they got home no one spoke to her, even Zeke wouldn't look at her. She ate alone, cleaned up the kitchen and shrank into her room soundless, desolate, abandoned.

The next morning was the same. She resolved to go back to the lake and do the job properly; perhaps a heavy rock in each hand would do the job. Through the kitchen window she saw a small bird flitting in and out of the rose covered white trellis where it had made its nest. The mother bird would protect the baby, she thought, protect and feed it and teach it how to fly. Even small birds loved and protected their young.

She sat down at the kitchen counter and put her head on her arms. The linoleum felt warm and comforting. After a moment she felt thirsty and reached for a glass and caught sight of the aspirin bottle. Yes, she would do it. She wondered how many it would take. It was a bottle of fifty and almost full, surely it would be enough.

The first few went down easily, but the taste was bitter. She poured a glass of milk. They went down easier, a sip of milk and a couple of aspirin. She poured the contents of the aspirin bottle on the counter beside the milk carton to get at them faster, but the bile and grainy texture rose in her throat; she gagged, forcing herself to swallow. She finished the milk, and took out the plastic container of orange juice. When that was gone she spooned apple-sauce down after each batch of pills. For the first time she was convinced she would die and it was too late to do anything. The room went around and her ears buzzed, her stomach churned. Every part of her body ached.

She carried the empty bottle to the garbage and stumbled upstairs. It seemed natural to curl up beside the door to her room and lie on the smooth floor wanting something, someone. "Anders," she whispered. Her mind groped to connect the name with a face before she fell asleep.

"My God Donald come here. She's lying in vomit."

Hard hands were shaking her, but for once she didn't care, then Donald's voice. "Don't be so rough. She looks sick."

Frances covered her nose. "It smells awful in here. Open the window."

"What have you done?" his voice was edged with irritation. "Did you take something?"

"Thirsty," Mila said in a whisper.

Donald helped her to bed and brought her a glass of water. Time passed and then she heard his voice again.

"Try and eat this," he said. "It's your favorite: Campbell's chicken noodle soup."

The smell made her sick and again she vomited.

Frances stood in the doorway.

"Shouldn't we call the doctor?" he asked.

"I did call him."

"Does he want us to bring her into the office?"

"No. He says she probably has the flu and the best thing to do is let her sleep and give her a couple aspirin."

The walk to the bathroom was a struggle. She couldn't get rid of the taste of aspirin. Why couldn't she have died? She went back to bed and hugged the pillow tightly to her chest. Escape was all she wanted. The tunnel beckoned her to slip in and stay.

Despite her illness they all continued to shun her. Donald brought her tray without exchanging more than bare essentials: "Here's your tray," or "I'll take your tray away now."

august 19, 1957 - i don't know what else can happen to me. maybe the woman is right and i have a brain tumor and i'm crazy. i am so lonely. now zeke goes to grandma's house every day. i hate the idea of going back to school. i'm supposed to write three book reports this summer to stay in honors english but i just can't make myself do it.

As she improved she snuck into Frances's room and read from the Harvard Classics and Nietzsche. She replaced the books in time to go downstairs and have dinner ready, like a ghost who invisibly boiled potatoes and set the table and cleaned up afterward, still not allowed to eat at the table with them.

august 29, 1957 – at last i will have company. she is going to let zeke stay home with me until school starts. it will be wonderful to have someone to talk to. when we were alone for a minute zeke looked sad and asked me why i was bad. i wonder what she told him.

Conversation between Mila and Frances was limited to Frances's orders, but she was again allowed to eat with the family and to watch television with Zeke. Aspirin never appeared in the kitchen cupboard again.

It was the annual fall ritual of taking out the summer screens and putting in the winter storms. Mila sat on the windowsill of the second floor bedroom lost in a daydream. She had removed the screen and was trying to wash the uppermost portion of the immovable outside window, but her arm wasn't long enough. Frances came in to check on her.

"Can't you see all those streaks you've missed?" Her voice startled Mila and her grip loosened on the window's edge. Frances approached for a closer inspection. "I've already finished the windows in the other room," she said.

Mila lowered her body so she could explain. "It's hard to clean because I can't reach the top and I'm afraid to lean out any further."

"Don't talk back," Frances snapped.

"I just need help. I'm afraid..."

"I'll give you something..."

She didn't complete the sentence, but moved swiftly toward Mila holding the broom, her face contorted with rage. Her eyes were black bullets as she raised the broom to push Mila out the window. Mila pictured herself falling, her feet made scissor motions to find purchase on the floor. In one smooth motion she pulled her body into the room and propelled herself toward Frances, all her frustration exploding.

With a strength born of fear and pent up rage Mila wrestled the broom away from Frances. *Sisu* that isolated Finnish word came back to her. "Don't. Don't you get any closer to me. *Never* touch me again." She advanced toward Frances who took a surprised step backwards.

"Donald. Donald Robertson," Frances screamed. "Get up here right now. This girl is trying to kill me."

Mila heard his footsteps rushing up the stairs and watched him stand frozen taking in the silent tableau. Frances stood rooted pointing to Mila who stood with the broom raised across her body.

"She's lying," Mila said. "She tried to push me out the window with the broom. I was defending myself and I don't care whether you believe the truth or not. I don't care what you think."

CHAPTER TWENTY

▼

Painesville, Ohio
1958-1959

Initially the pain was slight - a mere annoyance, but when Mila couldn't run in gym class, she went to the school nurse. "Perhaps it has something to do with your menstrual cycle," the nurse suggested. "Does the pain seem worse then?"

"I'm not sure," Mila answered.

"If it continues, you should talk to your doctor," she said.

Mila knew it would do no good to tell Donald and hesitated to approach Frances until the pain became severe.

"My stomach hurts," she said. "The school nurse said I should see the doctor."

Frances let out a sigh. "Stop being such a whiner."

On a rainy bleak Saturday morning in November she was helping Frances in the law office. "That stack of papers needs to be filed," Frances said.

Mila stood alphabetizing by client's name before carrying them to the file. She felt warm and nauseous trying to stand up straight. The pleats in her skirt bulged in the front, although she was losing weight.

Unexpectedly Frances caught her by the shoulders and held her at arm's length. "Why is your stomach so big?" she demanded. "Go see Dr. Smith immediately," she said jabbing the air with her rigid index finger and with a sweeping motion pointed to the medical building across the street.

The cold hard rain felt refreshing and she dashed across the street relieved that she would finally have an answer. As family physician, Dr. Smith was always kind to Mila and she felt comfortable with him.

"Your mother just called," he said. His voice was soothing and calm. "Some problem with your stomach?" He led her to the examining room and told her to put on a gown.

"Just lie back," he told her. "I'll have to examine you." With gentle hands he felt her abdomen. She tried to relax, grateful to feel a gentle touch, but winced as he continued exploring.

"You're a brave girl," he said. "Get dressed while I call your mother."

As soon as the door closed, Mila got off the table and moved closer to the connecting door.

When Dr. Smith spoke it was not the kindly voice he'd used with Mila, but stern and angry. "No, she's not pregnant. Didn't you listen to her? She's been in pain for months."

Mila backed away from the door. The steam heater hissed and the smell of her wet wool skirt gagged her.

When Dr. Smith knocked and returned to the examining room he put his arm around her shoulder, giving her a hug. "Your mother wants you to go to the hospital and wait for her. She says she'll come as soon as she finishes with her client."

Mila pushed open the glass door at the hospital, went through the second set of doors, and followed the arrows to Admitting. Everyone looked busy, but finally a nurse noticed her. "Can I help you, honey?"

"I'm Mila Robertson. Frances Robertson's..."

"Oh! yes. Dr. Smith called. I'll take you to your room."

Mila followed her to a room with two beds; the nurse pulled a curtain around one of them. "Take off your clothes and put this on," she said. "It ties in back."

Mila left her underwear on and sat on the high bed. A gray haired woman came in and handed her a pencil and a menu. "Time to mark your dinner choices," she said. Mila ticked off two vegetables and ice cream for dessert, delighted; it was like a restaurant. In a few minutes a tall man in his thirties came in. He wore a green coat and had a stethoscope around his neck.

"I'm Doctor Pollock. I won't hurt you but I have to examine you." He edged Mila's panties down and percussed her stomach. "How long has this been hurting?" he asked.

She tried to remember. "I was working for the City Recreation Department last summer. I remember running with the little kids and it hurt."

"Last summer? That's a long time. We'll know more after we take some x-rays. You may have a tumor, but we'll take good care of you, so don't worry."

Mila was finishing dinner when Frances and Helen arrived. Aunt Helen walked to the bed, kissed Mila, and handed her a box tied with a large pink bow. Mila gasped when she folded back the layers of tissue. "Oh! a satin robe and matching slippers. I've always wanted a quilted robe."

Dr. Pollock came in carrying the x-rays. "I'm glad you're here," he said to Frances. "We've scheduled Mila's surgery for Monday morning."

"Is it a tumor?" Mila asked.

He nodded, yes.

"Is it malignant or benign?" Tumors was one of the things Mila had read about after Frances's constant accusations about her having a brain tumor.

The question took him by surprise. "We won't know until after the operation."

Mila woke feeling groggy and didn't want to open her eyes. She heard the door swing open and felt daddy kiss her. He whispered to Frances sitting in the chair beside the bed. "She looks so thin and frail."

Frances stretched and rubbed the back of her neck. "The doctor said the tumor was big; he had trouble excising it and apparently nicked her bladder in the process. She's catheterized and they'll watch her to see if she develops urinary problems."

"I'll stay with her," Donald said. "Go home and get some rest."

"Now that you're feeling better, I'd like to tell you some things about your surgery," Dr. Pollock told her. "It was benign, a growth the size of a grapefruit on your ovary - what we call a dermoid cyst filled with tissue, hair and nails."

"Now maybe you'll stop biting your nails," Frances interjected and turned to the doctor, "We've been after her for years."

"This has nothing to do with nail biting," Dr. Pollock said. "Mila's tumor grew from a single cell - very similar to a cell that becomes an egg. It's the most common tumor of young women." He hesitated. "There's another thing - it won't concern you now, but your mother and I think you should know."

Mila tensed as she did whenever Frances was involved, waiting for something awful.

"We had to remove an ovary." He looked closely at Mila to see if she realized what he was telling her. "You know that the ovaries are where your eggs are stored and that each month -"

"Yes," Mila assured him. "We learned about that in health class."

No wonder Frances wanted him to tell her while she was there; she'd told Mila for years she had bad blood; that must be why the tumor had grown.

"Good," he said. "It's quite likely that you may have trouble getting pregnant when you're married, but you won't be thinking about that for a long time." He stood at the end of her bed and wrote something on her chart. "You'll be in the hospital four or five more days," he continued, "but as I told your mother earlier, when you go home you must take it easy. No lifting, no gym class. And you're going to have to eat more; you need to regain your strength. You're much too thin."

Learning she was to stay in the hospital was welcome news. Her inability to conceive failed to concern her since she reasoned it was better not to have children; she wouldn't want to pass anything bad on to them. The nurses fussed over her, she got to eat what she wanted, and was free to read for hours. Frances seemed concerned enough to stop by with books.

Her stitches still pulled and she closed her eyes and dozed. When she opened them again it was to see Sammy imitating Miss LaRue, their French teacher, who had a habit of pulling up her bra straps. He stood miming her and in a high voice he said, "*Bonjour, les etudiants.*"

Mila laughed and pulled a pillow to her stomach. "Oh! stop. It hurts," she said. "*Ferme la bouche*, Sammy."

Only Sammy could make her laugh like that. It was his sense of humor that Mila loved best of all; only with him could she be silly and carefree. She loved his goofy looks, the gawkiness that betrayed the intelligence in his eyes. He was growing into his height, but as usual he needed a haircut and his curls looked completely out of control spilling down his forehead.

"You're in the big time," he told her handing her a copy of THE CLARION, their school newspaper. "They printed your poem - page four," he said.

UNDERTOW

The violent dream recedes
Before night waters
Still and strangely bright
Until in one fine curve
The last wave crests
And stands a moment brightly crowned
Enough. The sea is strangely bright.

"I guess your parents will be pleased," he said.

Mila thought about the double life she and Frances lived, the private and the public, and didn't answer.

He changed the subject. "I'm getting out of Hicksville. I hope to be accepted at Stanford."

"In California? That's wonderful," she said. "My cousin, Annie, is going away too. I'll be the only one left around here."

"Why don't you go away to school?" he asked. "There are lots of good schools in California."

"Nice idea. California is another world."

It was well after visiting hours when Frances stopped by after her Council meeting.

"I brought your school assignments," she said. "I've talked to your teachers and they tell me you're more than keeping up with your work. It's a shame you didn't apply yourself earlier."

"Thanks for bringing the books," Mila mumbled.

Pulling the chair closer to the bed Frances spoke in a lowered voice. "It's possible the tumor has been affecting you for some time. It might explain some things. If you continue to do well through your senior year we'll have to think about where you'll go to college - perhaps Ohio State. Clara says Annie is talking some nonsense about Penn State because of a boy. She should go to Ohio State like her father did."

Unexpectedly Frances said, "I've sent in your green card for you. We're going to have to get you naturalized before you're eighteen."

Each year Mila renewed her green card and remained a Finnish citizen. Being naturalized before she turned eighteen was at Frances's discretion.

Frances noticed the paper next to Mila's bed opened to the poem, "Undertow by Marja Leena Robertson," she read, scanning the poem. "Don't let this go to your head and allow the rest of your work to suffer while you write poetry," she said.

After Frances left, Mila felt infused with hope and thrilled at the thought of going away to school like Annie and Sammy. She'd like to go to Kent State, but Ohio State was rumored to be harder scholastically. She knew she could study hard until graduation and resolved to make first honor roll, with Sammy's help in math. And she would finally be a citizen.

She didn't want Frances to change her mind and resolved to do everything perfectly. If she were accepted, Frances would have to be proud of her. She picked up the poem and read her lines: The violent dream recedes...

Writing in an agony;
Turning, twisting, this way, that way
Without finding any easement.

Ibid, Runo 9, Lines 520-522

CHAPTER TWENTY-ONE
▼

Meltola Sanatorium
Finland - 1960

Finland was primarily a glaciated flat, a low-lying country full of bogs and marshlands, the lakes so plentiful that bridges connected parts of middle Finland. Meltola Sanatorium was sixty miles west of Helsinki, built in the pine and spruce forest on a high and broad scimitar, a gravelly glacial moraine that provided drainage and kept dampness from the ground. The pale sun made ribboned stripes on the driveway leading through the trees. The yellow brick building glowed against the snow like an elongated artificial sun in the forest. The only adornment was a square turret from which the Finnish flag flew. The white painted window sashes looked like rows of crosses.

To the left of the hospital entrance was the path that led to the gigantic granite outcropping that comprised Cake Hill where only a few straggly pine trees managed to gain a toehold in the crevices of cold stone that were remnants from the ice age. They stood like crooked candles on a child's birthday cake. Every few months a patient managed the slow walk along the soft pine needles that lined the path. After the labored climb up the quartz speckled granite he reached the sturdiest of the pine trees, shoved a stump in place, strung a rope around his neck and hung himself.

There had been talk over the years of cutting down the trees, but those patients who were determined to kill themselves would have been harder to find in the thicker part of the forest. Desperate patients ended their lives through a variety of methods. Construction workers favored dynamite;

women stockpiled sleeping pills or chose to drown in the small lakes dotting the area, the young jumped from the upper floors.

Suicide was frequent, not so much because of the illness itself, but because of the isolation. The patients felt hopeless. Most families chose not to visit for fear of contracting the deadly disease and medicine was unavailable. In the two years since Anders succumbed again to illness, Kaija visited him once.

Anders looked up from his book with a mixed expression of surprise and pleasure. It was Martti's first visit since being conscripted to serve two years in the army.

"Hey, little brother. Can the Army get along without you?"

Without smiling Martti answered. "Just for the weekend."

"How did you find me?"

"It wasn't easy. The post mistress told me," Martti said.

"Tarja?" Anders asked.

"She didn't give me her name. She was rather haughty, but she knew where to find you."

"They call her the ice queen," Anders said. "Every man in the place wants to bed her."

"Is that all you people think about here - sex?" Martti asked.

"It's all we have to think of," Anders answered. "Sex and death." Anders motioned at the chair. "Have a seat. How is the Army?"

"I hate it," Martti said. "I can't wait for the two years to be over so I can get on with my life."

"Have you seen Kaija?" Anders asked.

"She is drinking more and more. Often she misses work now. I'm afraid she'll lose her job," Martti said.

"What about Aleksis?"

"They drink together, especially on weekends, but he never misses work. You know how he brags about that. She cares for Aleksis but refuses to marry him."

"Has she heard anything of Mila?"

Irritation clouded Martti's face. "Better Mila stay in America with the other capitalists."

"You're brainwashed with that red propaganda."

"You will *never* understand," Martti answered, "without communism the working man has nothing."

"We had nothing with it. Is Papa Stalin still hanging over Kaija's bed?"

Martti's face turned red with anger and he knocked over the chair as he stood up. "I have to get back to camp," he said.

"Don't be so rigid. You just got here. You close your mind and allow no room for other ideas," Anders said.

"You always goad me. You know how I feel." He turned and left the room without saying goodbye.

The visit left Anders agitated. There was so little he'd been able to do for Martti other than send money from Sweden. He turned toward the wall and closed his eyes. He wished there was someone in the family he could talk to. It wasn't Martti; he was too tied to Kaija and too full of hostility, torturing every conversation into combat. Dr. Rintala interrupted his thoughts. He stood leaning over the foot of the bed, his hands on the iron railing looking at Anders with a satisfied smile.

"The government funds have finally come through," he said. "Now there's no reason to wait."

It took a moment for Anders to answer. "I had a better chance a couple months ago. I was ready then; now I'm weaker and the surgery will be more extensive for the wait."

"Don't be so stubborn. You're getting weaker by the day and this can't be put off any longer. Doctor Eskola says you're just like your father. He tried to talk Lars into having this procedure but he always refused. Both of you are too vain about your bodies."

"Leave my father out of it," Anders snapped. "What do you know about his reasons? Or mine. What if it doesn't work?" Anders pulled at his sheet, as if to straighten it. "I'll have to think about it."

"The last x-ray shows invasion of the entire left lung. Collapsing it is your last chance."

"So there's nothing left but surgery," he said and then gave a short bitter laugh. "Unless I die *during* the operation. I'll give you my decision tomorrow."

With equal decisiveness Dr. Rintala said, "I'm scheduling the thoraplasty for the morning."

"I saw Dr. Rintala leave your room," Tarja said from the doorway. "I guess it's safe to come in." She came to his side and leaned down to kiss him on the forehead, her long hair covering both their faces.

Tarja Stenberg was not a great beauty, but she exuded a sexual tension that caused men to turn their heads with longing. Her long shapely legs moved with graceful strides and her thick wavy hair framed green expressive eyes. She was five foot eight and had a presence and proud aloofness. She was impressed by Anders's eclectic knowledge and insatiable love of books.

Besides working in the hospital's post office, she managed the patient's library and attended classes at the university.

Anders loved her mouth. It reflected her emotions better than anything else. Her lips were soft and full and he longed to kiss her, but denied himself the pleasure for fear she would become infected.

"I've missed you," he said.

"I came back yesterday afternoon, but every time I stopped by, you were gone. The nurse said you've been getting lots of tests."

"Every test they can think of. My heart is healthy, my blood is good, my weight is dropping, my left lung is shot, and surgery is set for tomorrow."

She pulled a chair next to the bed. "So you've agreed?"

"I said it was scheduled. My doubts circle like vultures."

"What an image! Why hesitate? The surgery will help you."

"It's not that certain," he said. "I have a fifty percent chance of surviving surgery and if I don't have it, less than fifty percent chance of living to the end of the year. I'm damned if I do and for sure I'm damned if I don't."

"You've got to go through with it - the odds are better." She stood and enfolded him in her arms. "You've got to try."

Anders sank back onto the pillow. "I may as well get it over with one way or another. It's all I think about anyway. I even dream about it."

"And not about me?" she teased.

"You know the answer to that," he said.

They wheeled him to surgery early the next morning. It was cold and he wanted to ask for a blanket, but he was too doped up to form the words.

Dr. Rintala made an incision near the neck and threaded a catheter into Anders's heart to monitor it during the operation. It was risky and he sighed with relief that it went well. Next he made a twelve-inch incision at a diagonal through the major muscles in the back starting just below the shoulder blade. No anesthesiologist was available and the surgeon repeatedly administered local anesthesia, but still Anders flinched. Next he sawed three ribs at both ends and lifted them out in order to cut through the sac covering the lung. It was three hours before Rintala could suture him up. He stretched his arms to relieve the tension and motioned for the nurse to wheel Anders back to his room.

In his drugged state his thoughts turned to his mother and Mumma and in his delirium he focused on a scene from his childhood.

It was wartime and bombs were falling. They were issued pieces of wood to hold between their teeth so their eardrums wouldn't burst from the sound waves. He and his friends had become experts in the Doppler effect: from the sound they could detect where and when the bombs would fall and how long it would take. War was an adventure they didn't understand - death only a word. Kaija never wanted to go to the underground shelters carved into the granite; she preferred staying in the apartment and blocking out the reality of war. Fear seemed to overtake her and she became paralyzed until Anders insisted and then she followed, docile.

Mumma Tehelia was hurrying before the doors of the shelter closed when Anders heard the bombs falling and saw an elderly neighbor hurry toward the shelter. A flying piece of shrapnel severed his head and it rolled down the street. His body crumpled to the ground as Mumma caught Anders's arm and dragged him into the shelter with her. "He's gone," she told him, "nothing can be done for him now."

Anders's breathing was labored and his movements agitated. He lay on his right side, legs and feet alternately curling toward his chest, then kicking out straight. The rails were pulled up on both sides of the bed and his hands clutched the bars. Intravenous lines were attached to both arms by tight strips of white tape to hold the needles and tubes in place. The long rubber tube of the catheter snaked from the hole in his lung to drain the fluid to the bottle under the bed. His chest and back were covered with thick bandages. Tarja pulled the blankets to cover him as he tried to shove them aside. His morphine induced dreams made him moan.

"Hot," he complained. "I need morphine." His voice pierced the quiet of the room. "The pain. Morphine. Now."

Tarja bent and took his hand. "It's not time yet. You just had some."

"No. Now. I need it now. Help me."

"I can't do anything. It's the doctor's orders. I am helpless."

Dr. Rintala left orders for the morphine to be tapered off. Anders had been heavily sedated since the surgery and had become addicted to the large and frequent doses of the drug. His behavior was erratic and crazed.

"*Satana Rintala.* To hell with him. Tell him. Find someone. Only one shot." His voice rose to a shout as he tried to hoist himself from the bed.

"Please," Tarja was frantic. "You'll pull the tubes out. Oh! God, Anders. They'll restrain you again if you try to get out of bed."

Anders shouted, "Get the bees out of this room," in a mixture of Finnish and Swedish. "The noise hurts my head."

Tarja looked puzzled, the windows were closed, and there were no insects. "Try to sleep," she said. "I've chased them away."

In a pleading voice he begged. "Don't let them put the winding sheets on me. I can't move. They wrap me like a corpse already."

He fell back on his bed, his eyes wild. "I'm freezing," he said pulling the blanket around his shoulders and fell into a restless sleep.

Tarja walked to the window and leaned on the sill. Dawn was barely visible beyond the towering spruce that surrounded the east side of the sanatorium. She hugged her arms across her chest as her eyes were drawn to the hill beyond the trees. In his delirium Anders kept repeating the words *Cake Hill* and called out for someone named Tehelia.

On a sunny, clear morning three weeks later, Tarja walked into Anders's room, stopped, and smiled. Anders's bed had been pushed against the wall and he was inching his left arm up the wall - a strengthening exercise to regain mobility.

"I might be disfigured, but I will not walk all hunched up tilting to one side like a broken windmill."

"Doesn't it hurt?" she asked.

"Not as much as a migraine," he said. He inched his fingers back down and used his other hand to cushion his left arm against his side. "I think that's enough for now."

"You look wonderful," she said and gave him a long embrace. "It's nice to have the privacy of a private room."

"Yes. And it's wonderful to feel the softness of your body again."

"We need to talk about something," she said.

"Anything. Why the serious face so suddenly. You're ready to leave the hospital, aren't you?"

"Yes...no. I mean that's not what I want to talk about," she said sounding uncharacteristically unsure.

His concern was immediate. "What is it? I haven't given you TB? Nothing bad about your health is it?"

"No. I didn't want to worry you before the operation. I'm pregnant. I'm not sure what I should do about it."

"Pregnant," he repeated, stunned. "You're sure? How? When?"

"The usual way," she replied, laughing now. "Almost four months...you know when...the night you shoved the chair under the doorknob." She waited for him to say something, and then went on. "At first I thought I should get an abortion, but I'm not sure, maybe it's too late. I haven't thought about having children, but now I sort of like the idea of having a baby...our baby."

"If you're at all ambivalent then you shouldn't have an abortion. I'm uncomfortable with that idea anyway. We can work it out. People have babies all the time."

"I love you." The words hung softly in the air. Their love had never been acknowledged with words. Gently she placed her hands on his cheeks. "We don't have to get married, but if I go through with this I want to know if you'll be involved."

"Involved? I've been involved since we met."

"And you don't think I'm the Ice Queen of the Bering Sea." She smiled enticingly and moved toward the bed. "I've heard everyone talk, but what do you think made all the ice melt?" She pulled back the sheet that covered him. "That South Pole, right there..."

"Mr. Ahlgren! Miss Stenberg!"

Tarja's movements were mechanical. She jumped back. "Dr. Rintala. I was just helping straighten the bed...but I have other things to do." She walked briskly from the room.

"Indeed," he said. He turned back to Anders. "I'm glad to see you're doing better. You'll be able to get it up today."

The men looked at each other and laughed.

CHAPTER TWENTY-TWO

▼

Cleveland and Painesville, Ohio
1961

Mila sat up straight in the examiner's office for her final interview before the swearing in ceremony. She smoothed her skirt; her hands nestled loosely inside each other in her lap. She felt her heart thumping. "Do you promise to shovel coal in the defense of your country?" the examiner asked. Mila was silent for a long time. "Do you understand the question?"

For once she spoke what came into her head. "Yes, but I don't see how that would help," she answered. "If there's a war I don't think shoveling coal will help because we'd be using another source, like atomic energy."

"The girl knows better than that," Frances said, then turned a scowling face to Mila. "Don't act so smart. Don't forget when you arrived you had nothing. Those words are stamped right on your immigration entry form: Nothing to Declare. Everything you have you owe to this country."

"Actually," the official said, "it was a good answer. Perhaps we need to delete that question and ask if you would help the United States during war time."

"Yes. Of course," Mila replied.

After completing the interview Frances stood and shook hands with the Examiner. Mila followed suit. "Thank you," she said.

Frances took her to Eisley's for an ice cream sundae; otherwise her naturalization was to be completed without fanfare.

Sammy called to congratulate her on being a citizen. "I've got something to tell you," he said. "Can you go for a walk?"

"I'll ask," she said. When she came back to the phone she told him she could go "for a little while."

Zeke came racing from the backyard when Sammy drove up. "Mila and Sammy sitting in a tree, k-i-s-s-i-n-g. First comes love, then comes marriage, then comes Mila with a baby carriage," he screamed. If it had been anyone but Sammy, Mila would have died of humiliation. Donald came around from the back of the house and she introduced him.

"Don't be too long," he said.

They sauntered toward the lake.

"Things are really going to change pretty soon," Sammy said. "I guess we're practically grown-up."

"I guess," Mila said.

Since the surgery Frances demonstrated a subtle change in her attitude. Mila was wary but hopeful. She sent off her applications to Ohio and Kent State. She now had purpose and continued to excel at school, maintaining First Honor Role. She continued with the chess club and became active in the Young Democrats. Her interest in politics gave them a common interest and Mila felt a grudging admiration at Frances's formidable knowledge. Frances encouraged her since Donald, as a Republican, had little tolerance for the liberal left, believing that minorities should keep their place and that the majority of Democrats were socialists

"Have you heard anything about college?" Sammy asked.

"No, not yet. I hope I'll hear soon. How about you?"

Sammy hesitated, then said, "I wanted to share the good news: I just heard; I have a scholarship to Stanford."

Mila stopped on the path. "Wow! That's terrific. Congratulations." Without thinking she threw her arms around his neck and gave him a hug.

"Boy!" he said, "all kinds of special things are happening today."

"I'll miss you," Mila said. "You're just about my only friend."

They walked in quiet contemplation until Sammy stopped. "Well, I might as well get this over with," he began. "I figured since you already know how I dance you might be willing to go to the prom with me."

"Sure," Mila agreed, trying to match his nonchalant tone. "I didn't expect *anyone* to ask me."

"That's encouraging," Sammy said. "I didn't expect anyone to go with me."

They both laughed.

Donald was reading the paper when she came back. Frances sat in her rocker reading file folders.

"What was all that about?" she asked.

"He came by to tell me he has a scholarship to Stanford, and to ask me to the senior prom."

Mila was surprised when Frances said, "He's a nice boy, and smart."

"He might be a nice boy," Donald said looking up from his paper. "But isn't his family Jewish?"

"What difference does that make?" Frances asked. Her mouth turned down in a frown.

A few days before the prom the seniors spent the afternoon passing their physical education requirements. They were timed on walking the length of the yard, treading water in the pool, and having their heart rate monitored after fifty jumping jacks. The boys were also required to climb a rope and do push-ups. Mila heard about Sammy's accident as she was changing out of her gym outfit.

"Leave it to clumsy old Sammy Lammi to fall off the rope and break his leg," they laughed.

"Yeah. Not only does he look like a goofball, he's clumsy."

"He may look stupid, but he'll probably walk away with all the awards at graduation even in a cast."

When Mila got home, Frances was there. "Mrs. Lammi called me at the office," she told Mila. "It's too bad, but you probably know he's fractured his tibia. Mrs. Lammi apologized, but obviously he can't take you to the prom."

"Is he all right otherwise?" Mila asked.

"Yes."

"I'd like to visit him in the hospital."

"He'll be home tomorrow," Frances said.

The next day Sammy called about the time he should have been picking her up for the dance.

"Your corsage is wilting," he said.

"Are you in pain?" Mila asked.

"Only when I try pirouettes," he said. "I'm sorry about the prom. Are you disappointed?"

"With your lame excuse? A little, I guess, but then you don't have a leg to stand on."

"I'll give you a rain check," he said, "and learn to limbo."

Since she'd heard the girls in the gym she'd tried to prepare herself for the disappointment, but it hadn't helped. She sensed that Frances actually felt a bit sorry for her since she hovered near enough to hear Mila's conversation.

Frances routinely did the washing on Friday night so it could dry outside over the weekend. Mila picked up the basket of wet clothes from the laundry room and carried it outside where she could be alone. She glanced up at the stars and stared at the clusters of the Milky Way, struck by the vastness. Her life was like that, she thought, filled with areas of blackness, but dotted sometimes with sparkling light that gave her hope. If only the acceptance from Kent or Ohio State would arrive.

When she went back into the house Zeke looked up from his comic book. "Mom made hot chocolate," he said, reaching for one of the cookies.

Mail was delivered to Frances's office and not to B-B. Frances brought it home and left it on a small table in the downstairs hall. There was seldom anything for Mila, but her eyes were drawn to a large brown envelope with the flap opened and the words: Kent State. It had been a fantasy before, but now the reality of going away to college was within her grasp. She felt euphoric, but resented the fact that she didn't have a right to open her own mail.

"I see you've found the letter," Frances said. "Your hard work paid off."

"What happens now? Do I need to write back or anything?" Mila asked.

"We'll talk about it some other time," Frances said. "Let's see what happens with Ohio State."

The brusqueness with which she dismissed the subject made Mila feel uneasy. Had she detected something more than dismissal in her reply? Daddy was even more tepid.

A few days later Frances called her into her bedroom. She was sitting at her dressing table in a robe brushing her long thick hair and Donald sat on the edge of the bed. Mila seldom went into their room and felt alien standing there, too intimate to be comfortable.

"We've been talking about college," Frances began. "You know how busy I am. Daddy can't be expected to work, then do everything at home, and watch Zeke as well."

Mila felt her limbs go numb. She watched Frances's mouth open and close barely listening to the words.

"We've discussed it and we've decided you're still too immature to go away to college. We've decided you should attend Lake Erie College for Women here in town for the next year. You can start taking summer classes and then, if your grades warrant it, we'll consider it again," Donald said.

"But you promised. You said if I did everything well I could go away to college. You promised me."

Frances cut her off. "No. What we said was we'd *think* about it. And we have."

Mila turned and walked from the room. Her head felt full of static. When she put it on her pillow it felt fragile as if it would blow apart if she moved too fast. Why do I ever believe things will get better and change, she wondered?

What she and Sammy lacked in social acceptance they made up for at graduation. Time after time Sammy was called to the stage to receive an award. Mila listened to the drone of words. The white prom shoes felt tight. None of it made any difference to her. Anger consumed her.

"One of our First Honor Role students has demonstrated outstanding skills in a wide range of subjects. As well as belonging to the Chess and Art Clubs her poetry has been published in the Annual Anthology of High School Poetry chosen from the Regional Anthologies to be among the best poems chosen for publication in Songs of Youth. Harvey High School is privileged to hear a poem written by Marja Leena Robertson."

Mila rose from her seat and climbed the five steps leading to the stage. The podium eclipsed her, the microphone buzzed as her words bounced and echoed through the quiet auditorium, mocking her.

"Portals," she began, "thresholds to fame - doorways to the future, open them as you will..."

CHAPTER TWENTY-THREE

▼

The gathering at B-B seemed like a stage prop: table decorations by Aunt Helen and Aunt Betty, predictable bland menu by Frances - the cast of characters forced into their parts. Mila felt detached, acting a part in a play. Aunt Betty was the only one who expressed pride in her, so sure her life would be exciting and successful. Mila wanted to collapse in her arms feeling a rush of gratitude for her unflagging love. She swallowed, clenching her teeth to avoid tears.

She thought of the classmates she would no longer see. Their celebrations would be different from hers. She wondered what Sammy was doing to celebrate. Mrs. Lammi had given Mila a small book of poetry by Emily Dickinson. The day seemed out of joint, anti-climatic. "I'm sorry you won't be going away to college," Aunt Helen said when they were alone in the kitchen. "You must be disappointed."

Mila shrugged. "I'm registered at Lake Erie College," she said. "I sign up for classes in a couple weeks."

Aunt Helen's words were clipped and out-of-character. "You're old enough to understand now." She glanced toward the door. "There's something wrong with Frances." She continued rapidly. "She was cruel to all of us. She's been mean since I can remember. She was always jealous of me and tried to get me into trouble when I was small; I was too weak to defy her. She could out talk all of us - talk, talk, talk. But Frances has never been able to control you, not really. You stood up to her; that's what's made it so bad for you." Helen grasped her hand and looked into her eyes, "Get out of here before it's too late." Her mouth was pressed into a tight line and for an instant Mila saw a reflection of Frances's mouth.

"You knew all along?" Mila couldn't look at her. "Why didn't you say something before? Why didn't you help me?"

"Where would you have gone?" She put her hands on Mila's shoulders, "You were only a child. You're grown now. Leave before she kills your spirit - before you're in debt to her." She hurriedly picked up the cake.

Mila remained alone in the kitchen shaking with rage. She took a few deep breaths to compose herself.

"Open your presents," Zeke begged. "That's the best part of parties. Open mine." Zeke gave her a Mickey Mouse alarm clock. "Because you hate to get up," he said.

She opened the present from Frances and Donald last wondering what they would give her. It felt like a book but when she untied the ribbon the last thing she expected to find was a white Bible, her name printed in gold. She wondered if Frances had underlined pertinent passages in red.

Inside it said: Love, Mother and Father and below that: Matthew 25:40.

After everyone left, Mila cleaned up the kitchen. She was putting things away when Frances and Donald came in. They stood silently and Mila wondered whether they would berate her for something, but Frances broke the silence by saying, "We haven't had a vacation alone for years and we've decided to make a trip to Europe; we think you're old enough to be left alone now."

Mila stood in mute disbelief and astonishment.

Frances went on. "Donald thinks it's foolish to make such a long trip and not visit Dover where he was stationed during the war so we'll be gone a month. We're depending on you to act responsibly and to take care of Zeke."

"We're trusting you with a great deal of responsibility," Donald repeated. "I hope you won't disappoint us. We'll leave you spending money, but use it wisely."

"I've arranged a job in the County Recorder's office at the court house," Frances said. "Since it's only afternoons you'll have plenty of time to do your homework - and don't get behind with my filing."

"How will we get back and forth to town?" Mila asked.

Frances had refused Mila's request to sign-up for drivers' education in her senior year and it was impossible to make the trip back and forth to B-B without transportation. Frances hesitated and looked at Donald. "We've decided you'll be allowed to live in the apartment above the law office while we're gone," she said. "You can keep the wages you earn working at the court-house."

What a present, both of them gone for a month Mila thought, trying not to look as happy as she felt. Before she turned out her light that night, she looked up the passage from Matthew:

For I was hungered, and ye gave me meat: I was thirsty and ye gave me drink: I was a stranger and ye took me in:

Naked and ye clothed me: I was sick and ye visited me: I was in prison and ye came unto me.

Inasmuch as ye have done it unto one of the least of these my brethren, ye have done it unto me.

How long Frances had searched for that passage, Mila wondered, for one more way to indicate she should be grateful for charity, but Frances wasn't God, even if she wore that mask. *Judge not that ye be not judged*, Mila thought.

She and Zeke settled into a relaxed and unstructured existence for the most part.

"It's fun when it's only us," Zeke said.

"Don't forget they'll be back so we have to be responsible." Mila loved Zeke and had been hurt by his easy rejecting during the trouble over Annie. She told herself he was just a little boy at the time. "You're getting older," Mila said. "I have to be able to trust you."

Zeke grew serious. "I know, sis. I promise you can trust me. I'm not a little kid anymore."

"Promise?"

He crossed his heart, and then crossed his eyes as he smiled. "Promise," he said. "But don't forget I'm bigger than you are and you can't push me around anymore." Almost fourteen, Zeke was husky and wore his blond hair slicked back in a 'ducktail'. He excelled at math, baseball, and archery but wasn't interested in 'dry books', his term for the rest of school work.

For the first time, Mila felt a sense of autonomy. She and Zeke worked out their routine. During the day he attended a sports day camp and went directly home afterward or met her at school.

Even though she wasn't going away to university, enrollment day for summer session at college was exciting. She sat on the lawn going over her catalog, watching the students mill across the campus. Her first choices for classes were unavailable, but she managed to get into English Literature as well as one of the few remaining spaces in Drama. She treated herself to a coke in the student union feeling the excitement of being amidst the noisy voices, but too shy to join any of the groups.

Lake Erie had a good academic reputation and the evening classes had a different feel since many students were older and serious about their education. The students in the drama class seemed to have a special kind of camaraderie; they were vivacious and full of fun. The evenings flew by dotted with cups of coffee, droll humor and laughter.

She was drawn at once to a woman named Pam who was in charge of the Drama Department's scenery. Pam had an effortless ease in making others feel comfortable. She seemed to feel Mila's shyness.

"You should try out for a part," Pam said.

"Oh, no," Mila said. "I love being part of the production, but I could never act in anything."

Pam shrugged, "Me either. You can be my helper: They also serve who only sew and paint," she laughed.

Pam worked at Huntington Elementary School during the day as a special education teacher teaching a mishmash of physically and emotionally disturbed children. Even slow learners fell under the rubric of Special Education. Pam's gregarious nature and love of people flowed over the production. Mila was impressed that her cheerfulness and spontaneity belied the seriousness of her professional life. She learned Pam was dedicated to her profession and respected for her effectiveness with her students.

"I've got to get out of here on time," Pam said during rehearsals. "My baby sitter needs to leave early tonight."

"You have children?" Mila asked.

"Yep, two: David is twelve and Julie is seven." There was a pause. "I'm divorced," Pam added, "so there's no one to catch the slack at home."

"I'd be glad to baby-sit for you sometime," Mila told her.

"Really? That would be a blessing, but you should meet them first. Why don't you and your brother come over for dinner Friday," Pam said.

The simple invitation sent a shiver up Mila's back. "We'd love to," Mila said. "Can I bring something? Dessert?"

"Great," Pam said.

Wearing dark green linen Bermuda shorts, a gauzy print sleeveless shirt, and pink sandals, Pam greeted Mila and Zeke with hugs.

"I like your pink sandals," Mila said. "I feel so bland."

"You always look well pulled together," Pam said.

Pam's lived-in house, cluttered with art, records and magazines, over-flowed with half-finished projects; books were scattered everywhere. As they entered the kitchen, a tall barefoot man in loose shorts and a black tee shirt looked up from chopping herbs, onions and grated zucchini into ground meat.

"This is Colin," Pam said. "You're in luck - he's cooking tonight." Looking at Zeke she asked, "how about some lemonade?" Without waiting for an answer she made each of them a glass.

A trumpet solo pealed from the radio. "Great music," Mila said. "What is it?"

"Miles Davis's rendition of "I've Always Got the Blues," Colin answered.

Pam led Mila and Zeke to the backyard. "Come meet my kids," Pam called to the children playing croquet. "They're supposed to be setting the table." The children came across the yard with the same smile Pam wore. "These scalawags are David and Julie," Pam said. "If you're going to eat," she told them, "you've got to help."

"I know you from day camp," David told Zeke as they smiled in recognition.

Colin appeared with a plate of hamburgers and checked the grill. Pam took the silverware Mila had picked up and handed it to Julie, admonishing her with a smile. The children spread a checkerboard tablecloth on the picnic table and distributed the napkins and paper plates. When they finished they invited Zeke to join their game.

"Come talk to me while I make the salad," Pam said. Mila helped cut up vegetables and then wandered around the living room. It was decorated in the same cool greens and blues Pam favored for her clothing.

"Your house is wonderful," Mila told her. "I love this painting."

"I did it from a photo a few months after Julie was born. It's my favorite too." Pam laughed, "it's my stab at Madonna and child impressionism and good enough for an honorable mention at the Cleveland Museum's May Show last year. That's where I met Colin. He got a second prize for a huge abstract."

"I'd love to be able to paint," Mila said.

"I can give you a few pointers if you want to try."

"I'd like that," Mila said.

"Do you have any hobbies?" Pam asked.

"I like to read," she said, "and I write poetry."

The screen door banged shut and two men came in; one held a bottle of wine and the other a guitar. They each gave Pam a hug and kiss. "Okay, here's the wine, where's the food? We smelled the grill from next door and heard Colin's voice so we knew there'd be plenty."

"Meet Paul and Greg," Pam said, "my next door neighbors. Paul and I work together. The poor man is a roving music teacher, a sad testimonial on how the public school system treats artists. Greg owns the Chanticleer Book Shoppe."

"I love that place," Mila said.

"A literate one," Greg said in a soft southern drawl. "I like her." He was tall and slender, prematurely gray at the temples, and had a neat Van Dyke beard and moustache.

"Pam said you met at LEC," Paul said. "What's your major?"

"I'm thinking of teaching, elementary level," Mila said. "I'd like to work with children with learning disabilities."

"It takes a special kind of person," Paul said. "Pam's an expert."

Dinner was long, leisurely and full of eclectic conversation that made Mila tingle. After dinner Paul played song after song and they sang. Zeke and David hollered out songs they learned at the YMCA day camp. Mila's dessert was the final sweetness of the evening.

"I hope everyone likes lemon pie," Mila said. "I usually have trouble browning the meringue."

"You mean you made it yourself?" Pam said.

"Not everyone is like you," Colin kidded her.

"Mila's only flaw," Greg announced, "is the poor child doesn't know how to drive and I have offered to teach her."

"In my car, of course," Paul laughed.

"Of course," Greg said. "Now let's have another sliver of that lovely pie."

"Does Greg mean that?" Mila asked while she helped Pam clean up the dishes, "about teaching me to drive?"

"Absolutely," Pam assured her. "He wouldn't offer otherwise."

Mila didn't know there could be evenings like they'd spent with Pam in which everyone was cheerful, and felt free to say what they thought. And the laughter. For the first time in eleven years, Mila felt independent and she loved it.

Aunt Helen dropped by to check on them, but except for dinner on Sunday, she and Zeke were mostly on their own. The apartment was stocked with potato chips, soft drinks, and ice cream. They played cards or watched television in the evenings unless she was at school. Zeke often waited for her after class. "Come on," he urged, "let's go out for hamburgers." Or they went to Eisley's for chocolate shakes.

"I wish we could be like this all the time," Zeke said.

"We can't though. We'd run out of money."

"We could get jobs," he said.

"You have to graduate and go to college," Mila said.

"I don't want to go to college," Zeke protested. "I want to go to sea."

"That won't happen if they have anything to say about it," Mila said.

"When I graduate they won't be able to tell me what to do."

"I hope not," Mila said.

Mila's driving lessons were a mixture of frustration and hysteria. She learned to loosen her grip on the steering wheel, and finally to coordinate clutch and shifting. When she was most tense, Greg would crack a joke and they would breakup in laughter.

She often stopped by his bookstore, sampling new books or visiting. "I have a present for you," he said one day, handing her a small anthology of poetry. "I think you'll enjoy *High Flight*, by a poet named Gillespie." He'd copied the opening line from the poem onto the flyleaf: *Oh! I have slipped the surly bonds of earth and danced on laughter tipped wings.*

Never had anyone seemed so sensitive to her feelings. That was exactly the way she felt. The lines became a talisman she carried in her pocket on a small index card.

Mila and Pam fell into an easy way of picking up in the middle of sentences, as if raising the arm of a recording and putting it back in the same place. Pam casually included Mila and Zeke in impromptu dinners and Mila immediately established herself as a favorite with Pam's children who became as familiar and endearing as the mismatched kitchen chairs. Like Zeke, she too wished it could go on forever, that Donald and Frances would never come back from Europe. The days were too perfect to be real, but the days turned into weeks and summer was drawing to an end.

CHAPTER TWENTY-FOUR

▼

At Sunday dinner Helen reminded them that Frances and Donald would be back the following week. Mila didn't need reminding. The thought of returning to the drudgery of B-B was anathema, but it motivated Mila to get busy catching up on the filing. After Zeke was in bed that night, she went downstairs to the law office, closed the shades to the street, and turned on the light. She'd done Frances's filing for years, but had never opened the drawer marked *personal* until now. She scanned the labels and was surprised to find one with her name. As she reached for it, she inadvertently pulled out two files. The one behind fell opened and several large photographs spilled to the floor. As Mila stooped to pick them up she stopped in surprise. They were pictures of Frances and two women; all three were nude. She recognized Ollie, but not the other one. Could it be Billie? The person Frances had mentioned? Two by two they posed provocatively behind trees or looked into each other's eyes while hugging. She was stunned. The pictures felt alive in her hand and she rushed to put them back.

She continued to rummage through her own file, barely recognizing the passport photo of herself. There were a number of letters in Finnish, a few looked like business letters from someone named Arne Arnerio, and she decided on impulse to take them. The others were handwritten and signed Kaija Ahlgren. She grabbed them; they could be from her mother. She also decided to take her naturalization papers and her Finnish passport; they were hers and Frances wouldn't give anything to her willingly.

For the first time, Mila felt comfortable offering Pam small confidences about Frances.

"I don't understand those pictures," Mila said.

"She's a closet lesbian. Lots of people have those tendencies. It would explain a lot about her." Pam said.

"But, at least two of them are married."

"That's not so unusual," Pam said. "Sometimes marriage is a cover. I'm not saying she is," Pam continued. "I can't imagine her ever letting go of control enough to get much satisfaction from anyone."

"You don't know how I dread having her come home."

"A friend of mine was one of her clients for awhile. Lee thought she was a bitch on wheels and found another attorney; and another friend on the City Council was always talking about her temper."

"If he only knew," Mila said with a tight smile

"Why do you stay there?" Pam asked.

"I guess I've been afraid of what she'd do. I don't know where I'd go."

"What can she do? You're old enough to make your own decisions."

"Not according to her," Mila said.

Pam was stuffing celery with peanut butter. "You could move in with us. The kids love you and I have an extra bedroom."

"Are you serious?"

"I wouldn't ask otherwise."

"I wouldn't want to cause you any trouble - you know, repercussions. And I don't have much money," Mila said. "My job doesn't pay enough to live on."

"Repercussions?" Pam shrugged and blew out a puff of air. "Can you manage fifty a month?" she asked. "And help me with the kids? Baby sitters are expensive."

The next evening at the apartment, before Mila cleared off their plates she told Zeke about Pam's invitation.

"You mean leave home now?" he said. "What about me?"

"If they'd let me go away to school the way they promised, I'd be gone now," Mila said. "We'll see each other whenever you want. I promise. You could even spend weekends."

"They'll never let me do that," Zeke said. "Can't you wait awhile? They've never taken a vacation without us before," Zeke argued. "Maybe they'll come back and everything will be better. Maybe it will be different now that you've graduated."

Mila got two bowls and put a quart of ice cream on the table. "That's a lot of *maybes*. She doesn't like me, Zeke."

"Sure she does," Zeke said. "She's your mother."

"She's not my mother. She never will be."

"Then aren't I your brother?" he asked.

"Of course you are. That's different."

"Then don't leave. Wait for me. When I graduate I'll go to sea. I'll join the Merchant Marines, or the Navy and we won't have to worry about money."

She smiled and hugged him. "I love you, Zeke. You'll always be my brother."

After the initial inspection of the files and the apartment Frances seemed satisfied. The first stories of their travels faded to memory and they settled into their old routine.

As enrollment for the fall semester drew closer Mila summoned her courage for the confrontation she expected when she told them she wanted to move. The taste of friendship and freedom was heady. Now she knew there was another way to live where life could be fun, instead of orders and complaints, laughter could ring and smiles could rule your face, not grimaces and disapproval.

On Sunday after Donald and Frances were settled, Mila took several deep breaths, stood up straight and went into the living room. Her throat was dry and her pulse was racing. "I need to talk to you about something," she said.

Curtly Frances asked, "Yes? What is it?"

"I need to talk to both of you," she raised her voice so Donald would put down the paper.

She put her hands into her pockets to control, or at least hide, their shaking and fingered the poem, *High Flight*. "I've made plans to move," she said.

They seemed struck dumb, then Frances asked, "Who is the boy?"

"It's not a boy. It's a friend from school. She has a spare bedroom and since I don't drive I can walk to classes."

"Who is this woman?" Donald asked, his paper forgotten. "What have you gotten yourself into?"

"Nothing. I need to be on my own and it seems like a good chance to try."

"You haven't answered me," Donald said. Mila was taken back by his gruffness. "Just who is she?"

"Her name is Pam Davies. She lives a few blocks from school, so it will be more convenient."

"I know the woman." Frances found her voice and gave a knowing nod. "She's a common divorcee, running around with some long-haired artist. I know the type."

"Why are you doing this to us?" Donald asked, his face angry and puzzled. "This woman won't be a good influence on you and everyone in town will know you're living with a loose woman. How could you even dream of embarrassing us like this?"

"I was hoping you'd understand," Mila answered.

"I don't understand at all," he said, "making a decision like this by yourself. You should have consulted us. Just when we were beginning to trust you again." He grabbed his paper and shook it before burying his face in it.

"Who else have you talked to about this?" Frances asked.

"No one," Mila said.

"Well, young lady," Frances said, "this time you've made your own bed. We've been talking about sending you to Ohio State next fall, but now that's out of the question. Go to your room."

Mila started up the stairs. The worst was over.

"Come back down here," she heard Donald call before she got to her room.

"We're trying to understand. We know you were disappointed about college, but we've agreed that you've acted responsibly up to now. We'll pay your tuition at Ohio State starting next semester. Now what could be fairer than that?"

The compromise was surprising. It would solve so many of her problems. Mila's mind raced until she remembered all the broken promises and disappointments. She wouldn't compromise herself for their money. "I have to try," she said simply. "It's important to me."

"We're giving you one chance to reconsider your decision," Frances said. "If you leave this house you'll never get a penny from us, so when you fail don't come begging for help." Her index finger grew more rigid with each word until it resembled an iron poker stabbing at Mila.

Mila stood without answering and Frances seemed to sense her resolve. "You'll have to live with your decision, but I want you out of here by tomorrow night."

Facing them without shrinking or cringing was the bravest thing she'd ever done, and she'd succeeded. She'd done it! She was free and she felt a new sensation: utter joy. She felt herself expanding and wanted to laugh out loud, to dance, to jump, to twirl, to smile.

Greg insisted that she borrow the car to move.

"But I don't have my license yet," she said.

"It's only a few miles," he assured her. "You'll be fine, just don't go too fast."

"Maybe I should come along," Pam said.

"I don't think that would be a good idea," Mila said. "I can do it. The worst is over. My things are ready, all I have to do is get them."

Zeke stayed in his room all morning. Mila rapped softly and opened his door but when he saw who it was he turned his face to the wall.

"Zeke?" she said.

"Go away," he answered.

"Don't be angry with me." She went into the room and sat on the edge of his bed and put her arm on his shoulder, but he jerked it away.

"I promise we'll see each other. We can meet for lunch or a soda after school. You can come to Pam's whenever you want."

"It's because I didn't talk to you after Mom got so upset that summer, isn't it?

"No, Zeke, of course not."

"Then why are you going?"

"I've told you before. You know what it's like here for me."

Reluctantly he said, "Yeah, I guess so, but..."

"Nobody can change our memories. We've grown up together. Just think how many things we can remember about each other that nobody else knows about and remember what fun we had while they were gone?"

"Yeah. And remember," Zeke said, "I'm still going to sea. You'll see. Then things will be just like I promised."

"I'll miss you so much," Mila said, fighting back tears. "But you're the only one I'll miss."

She knew Frances had gone through everything, but she made sure she'd packed Aboo, the comforting stuffed animal Zeke had given her. Zeke carried her bag to the car.

Frances and Donald stayed in the backyard until she put everything in the car. Neither asked whose car she was driving, or when she learned to drive.

"Well, I guess that's it for now," she said. She tried to smile, but her emotions caught up with her. "Please don't look so sad. It will be okay."

"Zeke?" Frances called through the screen door, but he ignored her and remained at the curb as Mila pulled away. She watched him in the rear view mirror standing alone at the curb.

She felt light headed and her stomach churned. She rolled down the window and leaned her head out to feel the wind blow her hair. The farther she got from B-B the more her sense of freedom accelerated.

The trip went fine until she turned into the driveway coming back to Pam's. Inexperienced in sharp turns, the car was going too fast and before she could slow down she'd missed the driveway and knocked down Greg and Paul's fence. The car was unharmed but she turned off the motor and rushed to their door. There was no answer. Pam helped her unpack the car and they were sitting in the kitchen over a cup of tea, Mila worried and apprehensive.

When she heard the doorbell and Paul's voice she expected him to sweep into the kitchen, red faced and screaming.

"I see Mila was out driving," he laughed. His tone was jocular, but Mila burst into tears.

"I'll never drive again," she vowed. "Your beautiful yard!"

Paul put his arms around her. "It can all be fixed," he said.

It took a minute to absorb what he was saying and then in a small voice she sobbed, "I'm so happy."

PART TWO

▼

1961 - 1980

All the leafy groves were merry
And the clearings always joyous
While the flowers waked to frolic
And the seedlings set to dancing

The Kalevala, Runo 44, Lines 88-94

CHAPTER TWENTY-FIVE

▼

Pam's House
Late Summer, 1961

Mila felt like she'd been living in black and white and the world had exploded into color, liberated into the stream of life. Getting up each morning filled her with anticipation of what new experience was waiting.

"This is for you," Pam said, placing a small package on the kitchen counter at breakfast Sunday morning. It felt heavy and when Mila tore away the paper she held a flat rock on which Pam had painted a sunflower and in the center the word JOY.

"Oh! That's just the way I feel."

"I know," Pam laughed. "I got the message when you walked around saying joy-joy-joy all the time!"

"I'll always keep it," Mila said, throwing her arms around Pam.

Colin treated her like a younger sister and Mila liked his easy way with David and Julie. "You're as adorable as a kitten," Colin said. "It's like you've always lived here."

Like so many times in the past, as she was getting ready for bed she stood studying her face in the bathroom mirror: the arch of her eyebrows, her long thin nose, the dimple in one cheek; she searched her face as if to memorize each feature. If she ever encountered a face like hers would she recognize her own family, she wondered, her long ago family? For the first time in eleven years Mila knew a feeling of belonging and yet, in the midst of her happiness she was seized by a pang of nostalgia for something she couldn't name.

Saturday marked her thirtieth birthday and she wouldn't be able to graduate from Harvey High School unless she passed her exams. She rushed down the hall, fearing Frances's fury if she failed. She nearly tripped on the stairs running in a frenzy to find the classroom, but her shoes didn't fit and her feet came out of them causing her to turn her ankle, and she couldn't pull the broken zipper up on her skirt.

Mila woke up in a twist of sheets, her nightgown damp. Stunned with dread, she waited for her heart to stop racing, the panic of never breaking free still tangible.

In late August shortly before the fall semester began Zeke came to the courthouse. "They're sending me away to military school," he said. "A military prep school."

"Aren't you excited?" Mila asked.

"I don't want to go to military school. I want to go to sea," he said.

"What made them decide to do that?" She noted Zeke's distress. "Let's go get a coke," Mila suggested.

They slid into a booth and ordered.

"Mom says you were a bad influence on me this summer." Zeke stirred the coke with his straw. "It's different with you gone. I wouldn't have to go if you hadn't left."

"You know perfectly well that's not true." She reached across the table to cover his hand with hers, softening her voice. "If they'd kept their promise to me, I'd be away at college this fall. Besides, it might not be so bad once you've given it a chance. And if you're serious about going to sea, the training you get at the academy might be good preparation for the Navy." Mila glanced at the brochure Zeke had given her. "Seems like they've got a great sports program. You'll like that. I'll be anxious to hear how things are going with you, so be sure to write."

He gave a doubtful shrug. "Okay. I'll send you my address. I won't be able to see you before I leave." He made a loud noise with the straw as he finished his drink.

Mila watched him walk away and to her surprise found she was irritated with him for being so obstinate. She wanted to shake him, tell him, "You don't know how lucky you are to get away." She also realized getting away was her desire, not Zeke's, and that he was afraid of military school. She vowed to write every week so he would know she hadn't forgotten him.

Mila soon realized Pam's total disinterest in cooking and took over. She thought of Colin's comment the first time she gathered the ingredients to make lasagna. "Pam's idea of dinner is canned hash with green pepper rings."

After dinner Mila dropped a plate on the tile sink as she did the dishes and it broke into pieces. She caught her breath waiting for Pam to explode. "I'm so sorry," she apologized. "I'll replace it. Your beautiful China." She picked up the pieces.

Pam sat with David and Julie correcting papers as they did their homework. She looked up. "It's no big deal. Don't get so upset."

"But I've ruined the set."

"So I'll go to Goodwill. They have open stock," she laughed. "The kids break dishes all the time; that's why nothing matches." Pam got up and took the pieces Mila held and dumped them in the garbage, then gave her a hug. "What's going on? You seem quiet tonight."

"Zeke came by to see me today. He's being sent away to Military school and he blames me."

"He's had good training in blame from his mother," Pam said.

"I got a sailboat kit to send him. He's crazy about sailing. I don't want him to think I've forgotten him."

"That was nice of you. You're a good sister."

"They were talking about Frances at the courthouse today. President Kennedy might appoint her Ambassador to Finland because of all she's done for the Democrats."

"Wow!" Pam said.

"Yeah. Poor Finland," Mila said.

"Did you know Paul almost lost his job last semester?" Pam asked. "The school board wanted to force him to quit because of the rumors that he was homosexual. You'll never guess who saved him: Frances Robertson, of all people. She challenged the school board and argued that he was an excellent teacher and his record was flawless and his personal life was just that, personal."

"She likes causes," Mila said.

"Whatever her reasons, her arguments saved Paul's job and now she is being recognized by the new Democratic administration," Pam said.

"It intrigues me that one person can make such a difference to so many people in so many ways." Mila remembered their mutual interest in Democratic politics and fleetingly wished she could discuss politics and points of law with her. She caught herself, surprised to admit that she longed for her respect, if not her love, but over the years when the slightest ember of connection glowed, Frances snatched it away leaving ashes of bitterness and rejection. It was seeing Zeke that dredged up the past and she mused out loud, "Funny, after eleven years to be more or less cut off from everyone."

"It seems like there should be *something* you could do to find out about your family in Finland," Pam said.

It's like trying to remember a tune," she told her. "I can almost remember sometimes.

"Why don't you write? They must have records."

"There are a few letters from some years back on what appears to be a lawyer's letterhead, but...I don't want to be disappointed. What if he doesn't have any information or isn't practicing law anymore?" Mila put the clean dishes away. "Maybe some day," she said in a wistful voice.

CHAPTER TWENTY-SIX
▼

On Tuesday and Thursday neither Mila nor Pam had night classes. Pam sat grading a stack of test papers and marked a large red B then moved it to the stack she'd already corrected. She stretched her arms overhead and rubbed the back of her neck.

"Are you seeing Colin this weekend?" Mila asked.

"I don't know yet. He hasn't called. If he's on a painting spree he'll be holed up and won't answer the phone or eat until it's over. Maybe I can get some sewing done."

Pam accepted his idiosyncrasies with equanimity. She seemed untroubled by where their affair would lead. She accepted the fact that Colin lived in Cleveland and worked as a graphic illustrator to earn enough money to paint and play the saxophone with a small jazz quartet. He was in his late twenties, a few years younger than Pam, and hadn't been married. He was not truly handsome, but ruggedly good-looking. His hair was longish, wavy and as black as the turtlenecks he wore; his dark eyes burred through you with their intensity. People were attracted to him like iron filings to magnets and he doted on Pam and jazz.

Mila wasn't sure she understood jazz, but slowly her ear was becoming attuned to what she considered the disharmony; she now prided herself for recognizing Dave Brubeck, Miles Davis, Thelonius Monk and John Coltrane. She listened by the hour to Bach. There was logic and symmetry to the orderly progressions of his harpsichord and piano concertos that pleased her. Her popular taste ran more to Nina Simone, especially her Plain Gold Band recording and she liked the new beat coming out on the Motown label. Her own collection was balanced by the classics, especially Mozart whom their neighbor, Paul, had brought into her life; she played music to match her mood. When Lou Rawls sang *Love is a Hurting Thing* she felt his anguish and wondered what it would be like to love someone who could make her feel like that. She saved for a small portable hi fi player and couldn't imagine anything more luxurious than lying in bed Sunday morning listening to recordings. She couldn't imagine a day without music.

Colin called Saturday and asked Pam to drive to Cleveland because the band had a gig. Mila had accelerated her class load in order to graduate early and had little time for relaxation.

"You need a break," Pam told her. David and Julie are with their dad. Come to Cleveland with me."

Mila protested. "I feel like I should study."

"One afternoon won't make that much difference. The drive to Cleveland gets boring all alone – fields and fields and then more fields. Good old Ohio."

Colin promptly hurried down when Pam honked. "My regular drummer is sick. We have to get Truman Okubo. He lives off Chester."

Pam gave a shudder. "That's a tough area."

"This guy's okay. He's from Nigeria, I think; a good back-up drummer."

Mila watched as the neighborhoods changed. Euclid Avenue was a main street running east from downtown. Formerly elegant homes had become run down; poverty and harshness were made uglier by the absence of trees. Even though the spring air still held a chill, a few women sauntered down the sidewalk in short skimpy skirts with halter tops glancing over their shoulders at the passing cars.

Mila noticed two nuns walking briskly. "Seems like a funny place for them," she said.

"There's a convent at the end of the block and they can't afford to move away. The righteous sisters are trying to convert the other sisters." Colin laughed. "Turn here," he said at Eighty-First Street, "Truman's boarding house is down this block."

A bald middle-aged black man in a wheelchair answered the door. He wore a pink kimono and fluffy pink slippers and he and Colin high fived each other. Mila tried not to stare, and looked at Pam who betrayed nothing by her bland expression.

"This is Uncle Clifford," Colin said. "He runs the place. I'll go get Truman."

Pam led Mila to the communal kitchen, an enormous room with an old-fashioned gas range on which a bubbling pot filled the air with the smell of spices. A young man surrounded by books and graph paper sat at the kitchen table in the middle of the room where a radio played exotic rhythms. He looked up without speaking, nodded in an abstract manner and bent back over his work. He had a compact body and the darkest skin Mila had ever seen; it seemed to shine from within like a beautiful ebony statue. He wore a colorful loose fitting shirt.

Pam filled a glass with water, walked to the range and lifted the lid. "Smells delicious. You're Kwasi, aren't you?" she asked holding out her hand.

"Kwasi Achampong. You have a good memory."

"This is my friend, Mila Robertson, who lives with me." Mila shook hands, surprised by his English accent. He had a warm firm handshake and standing next to him Mila caught the scent of spice.

Waving his hand over the table, he said, "As you can see, exams are coming up and there never seems enough time to study."

"You sound like Mila," Pam said.

"Where do you go to school?" Mila asked.

"Cleveland State; I'm taking electrical engineering."

"Well, that must be exciting. I mean – I don't know anything about engineering, so I don't know if it's exciting or not," she said.

"Only if you hold the wrong wires," he replied, laughing suddenly. His laughter transformed him.

"I'm in school...well, I'm working too...not that school isn't work. I work during the day and go to school at night. It seems endless." She rambled and couldn't seem to stop.

"I know what you mean. Here, sit down," he indicated the chair across from him and held it out for her. As she sank into it she noticed that Pam was gone. "I go to school one semester, the next I work," he said.

"Where?" Mila asked, feeling calmer.

"Lakeside Electric Illuminating Company. Not that they're illuminating," he quipped. "What about you? Where are you working and going to school?"

"In Painesville, about thirty-five miles east of here," she explained seeing his puzzled look. "I've got another semester and summer school and then I'll be teaching here in Cleveland, I hope."

Pam's voice made her jump. "Are you ready to go? Colin's helping Truman carry out the drums." Pam turned to Kwasi, "He's got a gig at Kimball's. Want to come?"

"Not this time," he said. "I keep putting this stuff off and I'd better stick with it since I promised myself to do it this weekend."

"It was nice meeting you," Mila said holding out her hand. "I hope we'll see each other again."

"I'll be here," he said. He let go of her hand and it was with reluctance she felt their connection end. She raised her hand to her face; it smelled of spice.

Truman and Colin were making room for the instruments in Pam's station wagon, and Mila whispered to Pam, "Where's he from? Do you know?"

Truman answered. "Ghana, north of Accra. He's the son of a tribal chief."

"How do you know?" Pam asked. "Did he tell you that?"

"No, man. He doesn't have to. Those two small slashes on each cheekbone – they don't come from fighting. No, man. He's a chief's son. Proud, quiet and proud. All the time in the books. Well, not all the time. The man can dance. The women, they go for that kind…silent…but a mover." Truman was short and stubby and wiggled his behind as he placed the drums in the trunk of the station wagon. "If only I looked like him. Man, oh man."

"Where does he go to dance?" Mila asked.

"The International Students' Center," Truman said. "Saturday nights. It's jammed with students and some non-students. High life, reggae, good dance music. If you look and sound African, they don't ask, man."

Mila wished she could hear the music and see the dances that went with it. Music went straight to her feet; she couldn't sit still, she had to move.

Both Colin and Pam kidded her "You must have been born with a special dancing gene."

It was several weeks before Colin had a practice session in Cleveland. "I'm picking up Truman. Want to come with us?" he asked Mila.

It hadn't occurred to her that Kwasi might not be there and she felt a profound sense of disappointment until she heard his voice. He came into the kitchen wearing white shorts and a navy blue shirt and she resisted a desire to reach out and stroke the softness of the material. His smile was equally friendly to both Pam and Mila.

"How did your tests go?" Mila asked in an attempt to remind him of their last conversation.

"Rather well," he said.

"What does rather well mean?" she asked. "All A's?"

He didn't answer, but his smile validated her guess.

"What does ISST stand for?" she asked, pointing to his shirt.

"International Student Soccer Team," he said.

"Last time I was here you said you'd like to hear Colin play; they're having a practice session this afternoon."

"I would like to hear him, but I have a game."

"Some other time," she said, trying to keep the disappointment out of her voice.

"Why don't you come with me?" he asked.

Mila looked at Pam with a smile. "Have a good time, we'll pick you up when we bring Truman back."

"Sally is around the corner," Kwasi said.

"Your girlfriend?" she asked, and again she heard his rich full laughter.

"Sort of," he said.

He walked on the balls of his feet, every movement graceful like he was dancing. Struck by his bearing, Mila straightened her own posture. He was shorter than Colin and she found it a relief not to strain to look up.

They arrived at a disreputable Mustang faded a dull shade of red with a dented right rear fender. "This is Sally," he said. "Her full name is Mustang Sally, after the song. It belongs to a friend, but I'm hoping to buy her."

"At a bargain price I hope."

Sitting beside him she was again aware of the tantalizing scent of his skin and felt a visceral response.

Later at the soccer game, she had no idea of who was winning, but intently watched him maneuver the ball with his feet, appreciating the intricacy of his movements.

"I couldn't make sense of what was happening," she admitted afterwards. "It seemed like everyone was running every which way."

"In a way they are. The players can play the ball in any direction; they can use any part of the body, but essentially it's kicked, or headed. Only the goalkeeper is allowed to handle the ball and that's only in the penalty area of the goal he's defending."

"Headed?" she asked.

"Yes, didn't you notice?"

"I guess I figured it was a mistake, but using one's head always helps," Mila remarked.

"Indeed," he smiled. "In my opinion it's a better game than what you call football."

"I don't know anything about soccer."

"It's been in the Olympic Games since 1908."

"About the closest I get to a sport is dancing. I love to dance."

"Me too. Dancing is part of our life in Ghana," he said.

"Did you learn to play soccer in England?" she asked, wondering if that was where he'd acquired his accent.

"I've never lived in England; Britain ruled Ghana until 1957. I boarded at an English prep school in Accra from the time I was eight until I was seventeen."

"Truman said you are the son of a tribal chief."

Kwasi seemed surprised. "Well, yes. My father is the tribal chief in the Ashanti Tribe," he said.

"What does it mean…to be a chief? I don't suppose it's like putting on a suit and going to the office."

He laughed. "No, not hardly. My father owns cocoa plantations. We live in a compound and each wife has a separate house. And, before you ask, we are not cannibals and we do not eat missionaries."

Mila smiled. "That's a relief."

"But he does have a solid gold throne. Actually it's more like a stool, but beautifully carved."

"It must not be very comfortable."

"It's more of a tribal symbol. It's passed on to the oldest son of the first wife. My mother is the third youngest of his four wives."

"Four wives?"

"Yes. She's low on the scale, since wives have status by virtue of their seniority. My brother, Michael, the oldest son by his first wife, is in medical school in Boston; my sister, Grace, is a doctor in Canada. She married a Canadian and doesn't plan to return home, but that's unusual."

"Do you go back often?"

"No. The government is having problems. It's forbidden to send money out of the country. Father used to pay my tuition automatically and my allowance arrived monthly. No more. Money sometimes doesn't arrive at all. Ghana is in the throes of building the Aksombo Dam on the Volta River to generate hydroelectricity; water is the problem. Father is depending on all of us to complete our educations and return home."

"I don't know much about your part of the world."

"You must have heard about the Ivory Coast, where all your slaves came from." He laughed wryly. "There are lots of black cleaning people from Ghana working for the electric company, but no engineers."

She tried to figure out what it was about him that intrigued her most. She enjoyed hearing his soft tones when he talked. His voice lulled her, so soothing after years of the raucous voice of Frances and she enjoyed his full-bodied laugh, head thrown back, leaning back in his chair, feet lifting from the floor. From the first time she saw him sitting at the scarred wooden table at Uncle Clifford's she was struck by his look of absolute concentration. She'd seen that look on Sammy's face when he played chess, and even Frances when she was absorbed in law. It was the same way she lost herself reading poetry, and Pam when she painted. Mila was attracted to people who became absorbed, totally engaged. She was also drawn to his calm analytical mind. In fact, everything about him seemed to attract her. She couldn't get him out of her thoughts.

Several weeks passed and spring slipped into summer. Colin visited on weekends, but they hadn't gone back to Cleveland since the day of the soccer game.

"I was thinking we should have a Fourth of July picnic," Pam said. "Why don't you ask Kwasi? He must be lonely."

"He probably has other plans," Mila said. "He'd come if you ask; he likes you."

Pam flipped open the address book on the shelf below the telephone. "If you'd like him to come, here's Uncle Clifford's number."

Mila dialed the number and Kwasi answered. "Hi. This is Mila...you know, Colin's friend..."

"Sure. It's nice to hear from you," he said.

"I hope I'm not interrupting your studies."

"No, not for now. Finals are over."

"Next week is our Fourth of July celebration and we're planning a barbeque at Pam's house. Colin is coming and we wondered if you'd like to come too."

"Sure." He laughed, and added, "I'd like to see Painesville – the name is intriguing."

"It's not much, but Pam's house is warm and welcoming. It'll be nice to see you."

"Can I bring something?" he asked.

"We'll have plenty of food." She took a deep breath. "Colin is coming out the day before; Pam's kids are with their dad. There's plenty of extra room for you to stay here too."

"Okay. That sounds good. I'll give Colin a call. What's his number?"

When she hung up she rushed to find Pam. "He's coming!" she said. "I told him he could sleep in one of the kid's room – is that all right? I'll clean it."

Pam smiled, and teased. "Joy-joy-joy."

CHAPTER TWENTY-SEVEN

▼

Painesville and Cleveland
1962-1963

At the end of the evening Pam and Colin went upstairs. Kwasi and Mila remained on the couch talking and listening to music.

"I brought some African high life, since you said you didn't know what it is. My younger brother just sent me a tape from a radio station from home.

The music soared around them. "It's wonderful," she said. How do you do it? Do you have a partner, or what?"

"The women form a line inside a circle and move in a circular motion to the beat. The men are on the outside and move in the opposite direction. Two moving circles," he said, "filled with life."

She felt comfortable talking with him and decided to ask something that had been on her mind, "How do you feel about living in the States? Do you feel accepted?"

Without hesitating he said, "If you're talking about blacks and whites I'm most comfortable with the international students. Your blacks think I'm putting on airs because of my British accent." He paused and glanced over at her. "And, the whites - well - their preconceived ideas confuse them when they hear me speak. They don't know *what* to think of me."

"I hope you don't include me in your generalization."

He laughed softly. "I'm not here to win a popularity contest. Once they learn I'm from Africa and not Harlem they're more willing to accept me, but then they expect me to act like what they imagine a "*boy from the jungle*" would act like.

"That's a little harsh," Mila said. "Maybe they weren't being derogatory. Maybe they think you're exotic; curiosity is natural. I'd never seen a black person before I came to this country, nor yellow, or brown, only plain milky white people."

Mila had dated a few students she'd met at her night classes, but no one had captured her interest until now. Their bodies seemed to fit just right when they danced. She was surprised by his strength, his arms felt strong and powerful. He was husky but without an ounce of fat – pure muscle. At the soccer game she noticed his legs were muscled like a dancer. Why was she so attracted to him? Was it curiosity? A way of showing her independence? Or somehow meant as an act of defiance against society, or Frances, or Donald? She'd responded from the beginning on some deeper level. She felt intrinsically she could trust him.

The record came to an end and they both reached for it at the same time. Their hands touched and they glanced down, aware of the stark difference. "So different the skin," he said, "so alike the form." He traced his finger along her hand and she drew in her breath.

"Do you think our differences are only skin deep?" Mila asked.

His eyes never wavered, but met hers. "I'm afraid I have trouble trusting white people in America. Have you ever dated a black man and been subjected to the stares of disapproval? It's safe and comfortable here, in your friend's house, but what about the rest of Painesville?"

"Cleveland is different from Painesville," Mila said.

"At the International Students Union maybe, but that hardly represents the rest of the city. How would your parents feel if they saw me holding your hand?"

"The woman who adopted me is an attorney; she has Negro clients," Mila said; then she thought of Donald.

"That's business. I asked a couple white girls out for coffee at the university. They liked showing me off, like a trophy animal, especially if I dressed in my tribal robes. I was colorful."

"That's not fair," she said. "Do engineers make decisions based on so few samples?"

He drew his hand away and she regretted their lost connection. She longed to take it again and press it to her lips. Instead she said, "You must miss your family. Do you see your sister and brother - the ones here?"

"I speak to Matthew occasionally, but since we have different mothers, we're not close. I've only been able to visit my sister in Canada once. I can't afford the money or the time. What about you?" he asked.

"Pam is my family," she said. "I was adopted from Finland and I'm estranged from my family here, except for my brother, Zeke who's away at military school."

"I like Pam," he said. "She's cheerful and upbeat, and she doesn't pry."

The house settled into quiet. Dawn was beginning to end the night and they stood by the front window, knowing they should get some sleep.

"Mila - it's like music - me-la; a lovely name. It suits you."

His soft accent lulled her, he pulled her next to him and gave her a friendly hug. She was once more aware of how perfectly their bodies fit. It felt natural to nestle her head into his shoulder. She lifted her face toward his and he kissed her gently, softly, and she was reluctant for it to end. She'd never felt so accepting. Everything so right.

"It's nice to be around someone who doesn't like to drink, and can still be fun and interesting," Mila said, the next morning. Alcohol makes me sick and I don't like the feeling of not being in control of what I'm doing. I tried it mostly so I wouldn't seem so young."

Pam agreed. "It gives me migraines. I take the occasional cocktail, or a glass of wine, but I've never felt I had to drink to be popular or as an excuse to relax. Even Colin and his pot," she laughed. "I've tried it and can't be bothered. If that makes me *uncool* so be it."

"Kwasi's intelligent; a thinker. I'd like to know him better. He reminds me of Sammy. We've sent each other a couple of postcards, but it's not the same, I miss talking to Sammy and it would be nice to have a friend like him."

Pam didn't disagree about Kwasi, but Mila could feel a reservation.

"Is there a reason for your hesitation?" Mila asked.

"I don't really know him," Pam said.

"Then what's wrong?"

"Nothing, exactly." She paused. "It's just that you've mentioned he doesn't intend staying in this country after he gets his degree. I don't want to see you get hurt."

"We're only friends. I was seventeen before anyone kissed me and if you're worried, I'll probably be a virgin forever."

Pam shook her head, "I doubt that," she laughed. "You just have to meet the right man."

Except for Kwasi formally calling to thank them for inviting him to the picnic, he neither returned to Painesville nor phoned again.

Weeks passed and they were sitting at the kitchen table studying as usual when Mila blurted, "I guess Kwasi's just not interested in me. I was so positive he liked me as much as I did him."

"You could always call him?" Pam suggested.

"No. I can't keep doing that."

Still she couldn't get the memory of his kiss out of her mind. It took kissing to a new realm for her; it seemed to go to every part of her body. It was the last thing she thought about before going to sleep. During the next three months she thought of a hundred reasons for calling, but dismissed each one.

"The teaching shortage might work to your advantage," Pam said. "I saw this on the bulletin board." She handed Mila an article. "They're starting the Ohio Cadet Provisional Teaching program. It allows you to start teaching before you graduate once you've finished your student teaching. You're so close to your degree, you could finish with only a few night school classes."

When Pam told her it seemed a perfect reason to call Kwasi. In her nervousness, she dialed the wrong number and when she dialed again her hands began to shake.

"Hello. This is Mila." She rushed on, "I thought you might be interested in hearing my good news." She told him about the cadet program. "I have to come to Cleveland to fill out some papers. I thought we could get together for coffee, or something," she ventured.

"I spend all of my time studying," he said, "but a break sounds good."

The call hadn't gone as she'd hoped. "I can't figure him out," she told Pam.

"He did agree to meet you."

"Not with much enthusiasm."

It was a long trip and required two buses. They met at Jack's Flap Cafe near the bus station. The strain and artificial formality were unbearable.

"I guess I shouldn't have bothered you, but I wanted to find out something and I guess you've given me the answer."

Kwasi stirred his coffee with total concentration before finally asking. "What did you want to find out?"

Her irritation made the words come in a rush and she felt like her voice sounded too loud. "Do you like me or not?"

Again his answer seemed slow in coming. "I've been seeing someone – Gloria. It's not that…that's pretty much over."

"Then what is it? I thought after what happened at the picnic that… well…that you liked me."

"I do like you - very much, but you know that I was sent here to gain engineering skills, and bring them back home. The easiest way to avoid all of the problems is not to get involved since it can't lead anywhere. My people would never accept you. Besides," he said with the beginning of a grin, "I'm sure you don't have the requisite number of cattle or brothers to give to my father for a dowry. An old tribal custom."

Mila smiled at the thought of Zeke in the wilds of Africa herding cattle.

"Don't I have anything to say about that? Why don't we try being friends before we plan international travel or taking cows to Africa? Anyway, you promised to take me dancing."

His laughter restored them to equilibrium.

"Okay," he agreed. "If you don't mind the bus ride from Painesville. How about next Saturday night?"

CHAPTER TWENTY-EIGHT

▼

Because of the bus schedules Mila often met Kwasi at the boarding house. Uncle Clifford was like a maiden aunt in a relentless vigil at the bay window. Owning the boarding house was a perfect outlet for him and he considered those who lived there as family. As Mila's visits continued they became better friends and she now accepted his bizarre dress like everyone else did, without giving it a second thought.

She sympathized when he complained that his legs always felt cold, in spite of the fact that the doctors said he had no feeling in them. They'd been injured in the Korean War. She learned he was an avid reader and they began to exchange books and discuss the classics and the latest plot of the science fiction novels he devoured.

His head was bald and shiny when he wasn't wearing his curly blond wig or straight auburn number with bangs, but no one thought of him as an object of ridicule. He knew everyone and everything that went on around him and exercised a benign authority in the neighborhood and was respected by all.

"Does Kwasi ever mention me?" Mila asked.

"He doesn't talk to anyone much. He's always studying," Uncle Clifford said. "That boy is *so straight*, and so proud. In Ghana white men do business with his father and treat him as an equal. Here it's different."

The more she learned about Kwasi the more she understood what it must be like for him to be in such a different culture, to have his place in society changed so radically. Perhaps it was that feeling of displacement, even though the reasons were so different, that gave them a certain connection.

"But things are changing," Mila insisted. "People are making a difference. The marches are helping make a better world."

"We'll see," Uncle Clifford said.

"In my student teaching class I have my students get in a circle and close their eyes, then I reposition them in the circle and ask them to guess what color the person next to them is. I try to teach them that our only differences are skin deep - just the top layer - and in the darkness you can't tell what color someone is."

"Naive, my dear" Uncle Clifford said. "Mankind *is not* blind. You think the difference is only skin deep? Black people learn that the difference goes down to our bones."

"Aren't you inspired by Dr. King? I believe him when he says: We *shall* overcome!"

"We'll see," Uncle Clifford said again, but he did allow her to address him as "UC," and took her under his kimonoed wing.

Mila and Kwasi grew comfortable with each other, though he remained intent on not letting the relationship advance to a deeper level. She was never invited to his rooms; instead they visited in the front room or in the kitchen until a Thursday in December. He had a test coming up and didn't want to contend with the downstairs traffic.

He lived in two small rooms, one he used as a living room, at the other end an alcove held his bed. The abundance of electrical wires in the apartment led to a big Grundig short-wave radio playing soft rhythmical music. They could hear Uncle Clifford downstairs talking to one of the Black Muslims who routinely came to the door selling Mohammed Speaks Bulletins and natural baked goods. Kwasi sat at the table lost in working on a long mathematical equation and jotting numbers down on a piece of paper. Mila curled up on the couch to work on lesson plans until it was time to leave.

"You two been studying all this time? Uncle Clifford asked on their way out. He shook his head and looked at Mila, "I think you're as serious as he is. You need to do something just for fun."

"We go to soccer games and we go dancing." Mila smiled and patted his shoulder in reassurance.

"Two of a kind." Again he shook his head, smiling. "You see to it this girl gets on the bus safely. This is no neighborhood for her."

When they were apart, Mila thought of him continuously and spent her time anticipating the next time she'd see him. She and Pam were sitting in the kitchen working on lesson plans and correcting papers when Mila let out a sigh. "How do you know when you're in love?"

"I suppose it's a little different for everyone," Pam answered, without looking up.

Mila persisted. "How was it for you?"

Pam rolled her shoulders and rubbed her neck. "I wanted to be with him all the time – everyone else seemed inane – he seemed to be with me no matter what I was doing."

"Are you talking about Colin?"

"No, my husband – ex-husband. I'll never feel the same about anyone as I did about him; when he touched me I melted."

Mila sighed. "That's the way I feel about Kwasi. I daydream about him. When we dance or he holds my hand or puts his arm around me it feels like an electric charge."

"Don't confuse passion with love," Pam admonished her. "You said you only wanted to be friends."

"I'm sure that's all he wants. We can study for hours, walk, listen to music, but he's so proper; he never seems interested in anything more."

"I can't tell you how to seduce someone, if that's what you're asking." Pam rested her pencil on her chin. "I wouldn't be in a hurry. What if you fall in love and he stays aloof?"

"Isn't that just life?" Mila asked.

"No, it's not. It's suicide."

Pam's answer surprised her. She seldom expressed such strong sentiments. Mila tried to concentrate on her lesson plans, but couldn't help wondering. Was she hiding her head in the sand? No, it would all sort out, she argued, although Kwasi never failed to remind her he'd be leaving when he finished school.

If their schedules allowed, Mila sometimes met Kwasi for a sandwich or coffee. He remained skittish and doubtful about being seen in public places. She was so intent on him she failed to note the stares or pay attention to the heads turned who whispered their disapproval. And over and over she told him it didn't matter.

"It does to me," he responded. It taints things – makes them seem contemptible and shoddy."

Neither of them had money to squander, their evenings out consisted of Friday night dances at the International Students Union. When they got on the city bus a group of hostile teenagers monopolized the rear of the bus, loud and aggressive. Kwasi directed Mila to a vacant seat near the rear exit and they sat quietly gazing out the window.

"Hey, man, you getting some white pussy?"

At first the words were a soft buzzing, accented syllables requiring attention to unscramble, but they became louder and more demanding, tauntingly repeated.

"Hey, *bitch*, you like sucking black dick?"

Mila felt Kwasi tense and her heart raced. There were too many of them for him to fight without getting hurt. Silently he reached across her and pulled the cord for the next stop and helped Mila. The cluster of bodies pushed against them, blocking their way, shoving, nearly knocking them out into the street, the sound of their laughter followed like hornets whose nest had been dislodged.

Kwasi was like a caldron of molten metal ready to spill. They walked in silence. The International Students Union was packed. The music was a counterpoint to the internal rhythm of anger and insult. It was a relief when the first notes of African highlife started, the distancing of the circles making it safer. She became entranced by the rhythms of the music that took over her body. Many of the dances could be done without a partner, but she had no lack of invitations.

Mila came out of the ladies room to the last notes of the Motown hit, *Gloria*, and saw Kwasi talking to an attractive black woman. He had his arm on the wall, leaning toward her, laughing, and her look of proprietorship sent waves of jealousy through Mila. They had the easiness of two people who had been intimate. As Mila walked toward them Gloria allowed her look to linger and languidly put her hand on Kwasi's arm. "Thanks for requesting my song," she said loud enough to overhear. "See you later," and turned without acknowledging Mila.

"Who was that?" Mila asked.

"Gloria, the woman I was dating."

"Why are you dancing so often with her? Are you still interested; she acts like she's still interested in you. You told me you'd stopped seeing her."

"It doesn't mean anything," he said. "We just like dancing together."

"You've been ignoring me all evening," Mila said. "What's going on?"

"Nothing's going on," he answered. "What's going on with you? You're certainly shaking your booty for everyone. I've told you to watch out for the East Indians. They have only one thing in mind."

Mila felt so hurt neither tears nor words seemed adequate. She walked away and sat in a chair against the wall, hidden by the bodies on the dance floor. Old feelings gripped her; she wanted to hide, to escape, and to be anywhere but here.

She felt a hand on her shoulder. Kwasi stood with her jacket. "It's time to leave," he said.

They didn't speak on the way to the boarding house. She wanted to get her things, get on the bus, and go home. Uncle Clifford smiled when they came in. He was dressed in his favorite getup, a bright red satin robe he kept rescuing from the spokes of his wheelchair. They climbed the stairs and opened the door in silence. Kwasi sat down and began reading a journal. "Am I so unimportant to you that you can just sit there and act as if nothing of importance had happened and ignore me?" Everything exploded and she grabbed the first thing that came to hand, a heavy textbook and threw it.

Kwasi covered his head with his arms and looked at the dent in the wall. He moved toward her before she threw something else and drew her into his arms. "I knew there was another part of your personality waiting to get out." She collapsed in his arms.

He petted her hair and held her close. When she finally looked at him an expression crossed his face she couldn't read. He reached for her hands and pulled her to the alcove and she was sure he could hear her heart thumping.

"I never planned for you," he said. "I never planned to feel like I do."

Slowly he undressed her, kissing her, stroking her, until she felt a strange mixture of calm acceptance and arousal. Only then did he undress, and Mila watched shyly. She stared at his full erection with wonder. He seemed oblivious until he became aware of her gazing. "It's just a part of me, like a foot or a leg, well, not exactly," he smiled. He was in no rush to enter her.

She tensed with the initial penetration and he waited, as if there was nothing but time. The rest was easy. She hadn't expected anything like this, the closeness, the feeling that she wasn't alone.

"I love you," she said.

She woke later, still wrapped in his arms, and felt a deep contentment watching him sleep beside her. "I'm not a virgin anymore," she whispered in his ear.

CHAPTER TWENTY-NINE

▼

Acceptance came from the Cadet Teaching Program. Paul had been as excited as she was when the letter arrived. "You'll be splendid," he assured her, and Greg said, "Just be yourself, darlin'. They won't be able to resist you." She wished she felt as sure as they did.

The morning of the interview she was awake at dawn trying to remember all the advice Pam and Paul had given her. Since sleep was impossible, she showered and dressed in a straight navy skirt and a white blouse with a navy tweed jacket.

She boarded the bus armed with her transcript, her evaluation, the recommendation from the classroom teacher where she'd done her student teaching and two references. Only her grades made her apprehensive and she hoped the extra units in special education would counter-balance them.

She closed her eyes and listened to the hypnotic drone of the bus anticipating the next time Kwasi would hold her and they would make love; her lips curled in a contented smile and a warm rush of anticipation swept over her. Now she knew what it was like to have a man to love. Instead of Frances's criticism, Kwasi and her friends encouraged her and told her she could succeed and even excel. She looked out the window thinking how much her life had changed. Still, as the bus approached the outskirts of Cleveland her nervousness mounted. She was on her way to the first interview of her professional life. She took deep steady breaths to calm herself.

As she walked up the sidewalk to the front door of the Board of Education she rehearsed what she'd say to Mr. Porter, the assistant superintendent who would interview her, when her feet went out from under her on a patch of ice and she landed on her knees and hands. Her nylons were shredded and her white gloves were filthy from the muddy slush. She could hear Frances's voice: *How could you be so clumsy?*

"*Baska*," she cursed. She brushed herself off; relieved no one saw her fall. Inside the building she rushed to find the rest room, took off her pantyhose and felt grateful she'd shaved her legs. She stuffed her mud-soiled gloves into her purse, applied lipstick, combed her hair and walked to the receptionist's desk.

"Mr. Porter finished his last interview early, so he can see you right away. He'll be glad you're early because he has a meeting." She led her down the hall. "Miss Robertson," she announced.

"I called the janitor to salt the sidewalk again. Are you okay? You had a nasty fall out there," he said.

"I'm not hurt, just embarrassed. I hope I'm as lucky falling into this job."

"Good," Mr. Porter said, laughing out loud. "You'll need that type of recovery with the children. Let's see what you've brought me." He read over the papers. "Tell me why you want to teach."

His warmth helped her relax. "I like young children. They're not jaded like adults and they respond to me. I can get ideas and lessons across to them. I was responsible for my brother as a child and now I help with my room-mate's children." She caught herself, afraid she was babbling. "Maybe it's not important, but teaching will personally allow me to be independent because teaching is a job I can do anywhere." After the words were out of her mouth she realized she was talking as much to herself as to him. She smiled at him tentatively and then grinned outright.

Mr. Porter waited for her to go on. When she didn't he jotted some notes and without asking any more questions he rose and held out his hand. "A refreshing interview," he said. "I'll pass on my recommendations and you'll get a letter in a few weeks." As Mila turned to go he added, "I think you'll make an excellent teacher, Miss Robertson."

She was euphoric. When she got to the sidewalk the janitor was pouring salt where she'd fallen and she glanced back at Mr. Porter's window.

"*Baska*," she repeated, with a smile, surprised at the ease with which the Finnish word escaped. Horse manure. It was like the other word that came back to her, *Sisu*. She decided to find a Finnish tutor. She also decided to buy a present for Zeke, to tell him she missed him.

Her acceptance to the cadet program arrived two weeks later. "My life is too good to be true," Mila said, turning to Pam. "I'll be teaching Special Education at the Douglas Elementary School in Cleveland, the Hough area. Grades one through three and only sixteen students per class."

"You'll have your work cut out for you," Pam ventured. "Who's the principal?"

"Miss Mercy."

They laughed. "I hope that's not prophetic," Pam said.

Mila poured a cup of coffee and joined Pam who swirled her spoon around in her coffee and looked thoughtful. "It's too far to commute to Cleveland everyday. You'll have to find a room. Maybe Colin will have some ideas."

"I hadn't thought of that," Mila said. "I don't want to leave you and the kids. You've become my family."

"Don't look so stricken," Pam said, "it's not as if you're dropping into a void." On the way to the cookie jar she gave her a hug. "You'll always be welcome wherever I am."

She wished she could share the news with Zeke and when she received his letter she took a chance of reaching him while Frances and Donald were at work. They arranged to meet the following Saturday.

"School is awful," he complained.

Mila didn't argue with him, but let him talk. She was also careful not to talk too much about her own happiness in the face of his misery.

"Mom insisted on college and now she's upset because I dropped out." His look challenged her. "I'm not like you. I hate school."

"You don't think you'd feel different if you gave it more than a few months?" Mila asked. "What would you like to do?"

He let out an exasperated sigh. "I told you. I want to go to sea, but mom's forbidden it."

Hearing his laments brought back the misery she'd felt at Frances' determination to force her will. She wanted to urge him to follow his dreams and regretted being unable to offer him nothing but an understanding ear. A twinge of guilt made her duck her head. She'd been so involved in her own life she'd neglected Zeke. He sat folding and unfolding his napkin while she tried drawing him out, but he was clearly miserable and reluctant to discuss any of the subjects she attempted. Her heart felt heavy when they hugged good-bye.

She wrote him a long letter to try and reinforce her concern and encouragement, but could never be sure he received her letters. His letters arrived more and more infrequently.

Because she was happy, she couldn't understand why her dreams were confused and troubled. Night after night she woke with a feeling of apprehension and fear that it would all end abruptly, be snatched away from her.

The dreams left her flooded with feelings of rejection, inadequacy and disappointment in herself and those upon whom she depended. It took moments before she could fix herself in time and place.

What bothered her was elusive, like trying to remember the right answer on a test, those hidden words that hovered in the corner of her brain until the last second of recall. It was something in Kwasi, a reluctance to surrender to her love - and love was what she felt, there was no doubt.

It was a low-key Sunday evening. Kwasi wore his native dress; he wrapped the cloth about his body and gathered it at one shoulder so it fell in drapes of richly colored graceful folds.

"It looks like a cross between a sarong and a Roman toga," Mila told him the first time she saw him in it. Now it seemed natural.

She had started leaving some of her things there so she wouldn't have to carry them back and forth each time she stayed. She slipped into a robe, picked up a book and curled her feet under her on the couch.

"I guess I'll look for a room before much longer," she said. "What would Uncle Clifford say if I moved in here?"

"Here?"

"It's not too far from where I'll be teaching."

"I don't know."

"We'd have more money if we pooled our expenses and I'm here most of the time anyway."

"I'm not sure it's safe," he said.

"I've never been hassled," Mila said. "Between you and Uncle Clifford, I feel safe."

Kwasi let the subject hang.

"The guy on the top floor has moved out," she said. "Uncle Clifford told me."

"He didn't exactly move out," Kwasi said with a wry smile. "He got the DTs and jumped."

"But the apartment is empty and it's bigger and not much more expensive, Uncle Clifford said." She sat on Kwasi's lap and put her arms around his neck. "What is it?" she asked.

He looked into her eyes. "You mustn't forget what to expect when I graduate; nothing has changed. I have commitments at home."

"I haven't forgotten," she said.

"Only a year," he said.

"That's a long way off," she answered.

Kwasi was listening to The Voice of Africa when the phone rang. He presumed it was his friend, Adopo, calling back with another math question and answered in their native dialect. Mila watched his face change from greeting a friend to one of puzzlement. He held the phone out to her, and she mouthed, "who?" Kwasi shrugged.

"Hello, this is Mila Robertson." The phone was silent and she was ready to hang up.

The voice was strained, but familiar.

"Mila," another silence followed as if the caller was having trouble saying more.

"Dad?" Kwasi turned down the radio and stood looking at her.

"You have some letters here, and something from college."

"Oh! It must be my diploma."

"You mean you haven't picked it up?"

"They wanted $50.00 and it's not on my list of priorities." She paused. "How did you get this number?"

"I called the woman you live with. One of her children gave me this number. Who answered the phone?"

"Kwasi, my boyfriend."

"Can't he speak English? It sounded like gibberish. What language was that?"

"He's a foreign student," she said.

"Where does *he* live?"

"Here." She rushed on. "He's going to engineering school. You'd like him."

"What kind of a name is Kwasi? What country is he from?"

"Ghana."

This time the silence was prolonged. "From one of those black countries in Africa?"

Mila wanted to hang up.

"That's the last straw. I always stuck up for you, protected you, and for what? This is how you repay me?"

Her temper flared. "Protected me? You never protected me."

"He's a *nigger*! No daughter of a mine could do such a thing. Ulle was right about you. I don't ever want to hear from you again."

The receiver buzzed in her hand.

Do not weep now, tree so green,
Leaf-bedecked and girdled white!
You will have a merry future,
New and joyous life awaits you.
Soon now you will weep for gladness
And sing out in ecstasy.

Ibid, Runo 44, Lines 160-165

CHAPTER THIRTY

▼

Lintavaara, Finland
Suburb of Helsinki - 1965

Tarja stood on the crest of the small hill leading to their duplex. Her hair was pulled back from her face and hung in soft waves, the ends of the scarf she wore fluttered in the breeze and her summer dress outlined her long silhouette. Her beauty still stunned him. Patrick chased his ball, laughing. When Tarja saw Anders she waved and Patrick rushed to his father to be lifted in his outstretched arms.

Lintavaara was convenient, scarcely half an hour from Helsinki but a world away. A creek wandered by the houses, the clear water skittering over shiny rocks. Tiny white wood flowers blanketed the ground under the birch and spruce trees, and bushes ripe with blueberries were plentiful in fall.

Finland burst forth in summer, Anders thought. Instead of bundled solitude, the streets came alive with smiles and shopkeepers whistled as they opened for business; summer lightened life. Problems that loomed like shadows seemed less threatening.

The twenty duplexes were mirror images of each other with a communal sauna running the full length of the units and separating them. Martti and Rauha, his wife, lived in the other half of their duplex with their two-year-old daughter, Riina. In exchange for reduced rent, the brothers shared maintenance responsibilities. Martti installed shutters, Anders painted, and the women planted brightly colored flowers. It was the nicest place they'd ever lived. Rauha worked as evening supervisor of a meatpacking plant five miles away. Her hours began when Tarja returned from her teaching day so they could share responsibility for the children.

Anders worked with the owner of a small electronics store and one other employee, Marko Nummi, a far better technician than salesman. Marko held a university degree. At lunch Marko confided to Anders that he was applying for another job.

"I hear Valkonen has an opening for a District Manager in their Sony Products Sales Division. I'd be a fool to pass up a chance for this opportunity. Openings there are rare."

"Maybe I should try too," Anders said.

Marko dismissed the suggestion. "You're always joking, Ahlgren."

"Good luck," Anders said, straightening vouchers to cover the sting of Marko's words.

Anders thought about the conversation the rest of the day and told Tarja, as they got ready for bed.

She stood at the mirror brushing her hair. "Why don't you apply?" she asked.

"They'd just laugh. With only three years of school in Finland and another three in Sweden I don't have the education. Without a degree employers won't even look at my application. You know how it is here."

The importance of education was acknowledged every May first. Whether in Parliament Square in Helsinki or the village market place, the custom was for all university graduates, no matter the year of graduation, to gather and congratulate each other, tossing their white caps in the air, the proud mark of their status. Tarja had her white cap and Anders knew she didn't join her friends in the celebration out of consideration for his feelings. The whole concept rankled him.

Enrollment in university was impossible without passing the qualifying exams at the end of high school. He was self-conscious and angry about his lack of education and saw no way out. He had neither the money nor the time.

"You have language skills," she argued. Anders learned foreign tongues with an astonishing ease. "What harm can there be in trying?" Tarja insisted. "It's not like you."

"I'll think about trying," he promised.

Marko's remark and Tarja's challenge was the impetus he needed to his spirit of competitiveness.

"I've decided to apply," he told Marko the next morning. "What have I got to lose?"

Marko stirred his morning coffee, raised an eyebrow and looked doubtful. "I've got more experience, they only want applicants with degrees."

"I know. Don't remind me about your white cap."

Anders stopped by Valkonen before going home. On the tram he read through the employment form, scanned the pages asking for his job history, education, foreign languages fluency, technical experience, training, hobbies, likes, dislikes. Once home he took out his pen and filled in his name and address and social identification number, wrote: *no phone number, chess* under hobbies, and left the rest of the four pages blank. In Finnish and Swedish he wrote:

If you are looking for someone to push your products, then I'm your man. I have experience selling Sony products and understand them thoroughly. Anything technical I can learn from your engineers.

Below that, he wrote:

I also speak Swedish, Norwegian, Danish, and English.

The following week Tarja held up the envelope, slowly waving it back and forth, smiling as she tried to keep it away from him until he caught her in his arms, kissed her, and snatched it from her hands.

"What does it say," she asked.

"It's from someone named Nortamo. At the Valkonen Company. I'm going in for testing the day after tomorrow."

Tarja glanced at the letterhead. "He's the owner of Valkonen!" she cried, clapping her hands. "I told you!"

Anders was astonished to learn that the tests referred to measured intelligence and psychological health and had nothing to do with the company's products, nor were any technical questions asked. When he finished, he was told he'd be contacted in a week. He left thinking the entire experience had been a waste of time.

The arrival of the second letter informed him he'd been scheduled for an interview with Nortamo. Anders got another surprise when the receptionist ushered him into a large plush office. Every businessman wore his rank like a costume, dressed in the latest fashion. Informality was considered an eccentricity in the stratified business and social climate of Scandinavia. Nortamo, a tall shambling man, dressed casually in jeans and a denim shirt, rose from behind his desk, introduced himself and shook Anders's hand. He motioned him to one of the chairs grouped around a table at the end of the room.

"I'm intrigued," he began. "I've never had an employment questionnaire like yours. Why did you do it like that?"

"I decided you didn't want to hear what I don't know."

Nortamo opened the folder on his desk. "Are you pulling my leg? About your education?"

"No."

Nortamo studied the papers in front of him. "Your test results are quite impressive. And with no university background."

"If schooling is your only interest, I'm wasting your time. If your interest is selling your product, I know how to get customers to buy."

They went over Anders' history, bantered about peripheral subjects, spoke of family and travel. He wished Nortamo would cut to the chase. Tarja had been wrong, he suspected. There would be no job offer.

Nortamo straightened some papers on the table, looked up and addressed him in rapid Swedish. "This job involves extensive travel in Finland and the rest of Scandinavia to familiarize the owners of radio and television dealerships with the products and to get orders. More than a hundred men have applied for this position, all with degrees. It's obvious you're plenty smart and speak the requisite languages, but why should I chose you over the others?"

Anders thought for a while, smiled and replied in flawless Swedish, "I'm stubborn and I don't give up. That's the key to sales, no matter what the person is called, District Manager or Clerk. I love meeting and talking with people. I enjoy travel. And, even if I can't afford to buy them, I'm familiar with your products from my current job."

"What if a technical question came up?" Nortamo asked.

"I'd ask your engineering staff. They know the answers, but they don't sell your products."

"What if you're sent to Lapland or Sweden and a store owner has a technical question?"

"I would say, 'That's a good question. Let's look it up together in the manual,' or 'let's call the firm's technical experts back in Helsinki.'"

Nortamo laughed. "I suspect I'd probably buy anything from you! If you can push the product like you can switch languages, you have the job."

Anders wasn't sure he'd heard right.

"How much are you making now?" Nortamo asked scratching numbers on a piece of paper.

"Three thousand markka a month." Anders answered.

"Plus commission?" Nortamo asked.

"No. Not yet."

"I'll give you fifty percent more."

The words were out of Anders's mouth before he could think. "Make it double."

Nortamo considered. "You're probably worth it, but it wouldn't be fair to those who've been here a long time. I'll give you ninety percent."

Anders took a breath and sat straighter. "Okay. Give me three months probation. If you're not satisfied, I'll leave, if you are, you can pay me the other ten percent, plus commission."

Nortamo smiled and nodded. "You drive a hard bargain. He buzzed his secretary, Barbo, explaining to Anders, "You will be given felt boots and a felt coat, blankets, matches, and a gun."

"This is what your District Manager gets?" Anders asked in surprise.

"It's the law. If you hit a moose or a reindeer, and it happens all the time in the forest, you're required to kill it and then report it to the police. The government reimburses the owners for their dead animals. The problem is most prevalent in Lapland; the Sami people have herds of reindeer which are given the right of way."

Anders laughed. "Matches and a gun. I think I can do it."

Anders burst through the door that night, picked Tarja up in a bear hug and swung her around. "I got the job and a big raise. Now you can quit teaching and stay home if you want to."

With a satisfied smile, Tarja gave him a kiss. "Yes, and we can have another child."

Anders sobered. "You know I'm against that idea. My health - ", the sentence hung unfinished. Always in the back of his mind was the thought of his mortality.

Undaunted, Tarja dismissed his doubt. "You worry too much. You can't predict the future."

"Perhaps you're not realistic enough," Anders said.

At the end of three months at Valkonen he received the additional ten percent and was sent to Sweden for an intensive course of study at the American styled business school. He was taught the subtle nuances of the business world as well as how to fill out forms, how to read quarterly reports and interpret balance sheets.

The sequence he found most helpful was the course on presentation. The men were filmed on Sony videotape. Anders was appalled when he watched himself. He talked too much, used too many superlatives, too much slang, said 'you know,' too often as well as 'un huh.' He vowed to improve.

The course did not prepare him for Nortamo's announcement when he got back. "I've invited fifteen store owners for their annual weekend in Helsinki. I'll have Barbro arrange hotel accommodations, but I want you to take care of the dinner. Have it at the Hotel Scandia. They have an impressive restaurant.

Anders was overwhelmed. He returned from Sweden thinking he had learned all there was to learn about business. His restaurant experience was limited to his work as a busboy at Sundstrum's in Stockholm and stopping for coffee and pastry in the small cafes attached to the gas stations through- out Finland.

But overnight he came up with a plan. He went to the Scandia Hotel and asked to speak with the Chef.

"My company has a reservation for dinner on the fifteenth and I'm in charge. I've never arranged such a thing before." He had decided on a large sum of money. "This is for you," he said, handing it to the chef. "You have a free hand. Send the bill to the Valkonen Company."

The chef agreed. As an afterthought, Anders said, "For me, I want a rare filet and boiled potatoes. I like my food simple." What he didn't say was that he had never tasted a filet and it seemed like the perfect opportunity.

Next he spoke with the *sommelier* about choosing the best wines.

He was running on all cylinders, his mind and body never relaxing from the challenges.

Tarja had flawless taste, and he asked her to help him purchase a good suit. "My costume," he said.

"You are turning into a real hot shot," she said with pride.

"I don't like being a hot shot. I don't like that about myself." He was repulsed by the competitiveness and phoniness he saw in the other District Managers. They were womanizers, heavy drinkers, arrogant. He was happy with the trappings that went along with the position, but he didn't want to become like them: jealous and backstabbing. He knew there was already talk by the other men on the sales staff that he lacked a degree. Anders exacerbated their hostility by remaining private, while they stressed their professional standing and eschewed the stigma of being salesmen. To them, salesmen worked behind counters in stores. Anders was more realistic. We are salesmen, he thought. Glorified, well-paid salesmen.

Nortamo called him in. "Your dinner party was a huge success." He lifted a stack of papers from his desk. "Your bills," he said. "I've never been presented with such huge bills."

"And you've never been presented with such a huge stack of orders," Anders answered.

Nortamo grinned at him, unable to disagree, then inquired, "Do you drive the Trabat?"

"Yes," Anders answered.

"An East German tin can on wheels. Go to the Fiat dealership and get a decent car. I'll authorize you to buy whatever model you like."

Though he had been satisfied with his Trabat, Anders didn't protest.

CHAPTER THIRTY-ONE

▼

Cleveland, Ohio

Please don't let me be pregnant, she prayed to no particular god. Anything, but make me un-pregnant. Mila returned to the bathroom several times an hour to see if her period had started. She'd already tried baths so hot she could hardly lower herself into them, she tried laxatives, she tried jumping from the table, and she tried drinking gin, which only made her nauseous. She tried anything and everything she'd heard women talk about, short of using a coat hanger.

April 23, 1965 – I'm worried – This is the second month I've gone without a period. Just when everything is going so well, that's the last thing I want. Dr. Pollock told me the chances of pregnancy were practically nil after my operation. What if I died and my baby went to strangers. It's a nightmare thought. Anyway, I decided long ago not to have children. What do I know about mothering?

The years with Frances had left her filled with doubt about herself and her genes. She wouldn't risk having a child suffer as she had done by being unwanted. Kwasi was too busy worrying about studies and his father to think of anything as mundane as birth control; besides she'd reassured him she couldn't get pregnant. And, he'd always made it clear that marriage was out. She dreaded telling him and felt angry with Dr. Pollock. He could have given her some warning.

She needed to talk to Pam. Like old times they sat at the kitchen table over untouched coffee. "I don't know what else to do," she told Pam. "I'm driving myself crazy. Kwasi has obligations, he's always made that clear, and eventually he'd hate me for complicating things. All the choices seem impossible." She picked up her cup and thumped it back onto the table. "I can't have a baby."

"It's not easy but lots of women end up doing it."

"No. What if I died and someone like Frances got their hands on my child? I won't take that risk."

"You could put it up for adoption."

"No. It would be the same with adoption." She shook her head. "I couldn't live with the uncertainty of knowing if my child was safe and loved."

"What does Kwasi say?"

"He offered to stay here, but I know he's upset."

Pam got up and hugged her. "I'm so sorry you have to go through this, but you're strong – stronger than you know."

Mila sighed. "The only thing left is an abortion."

Pam took a deep breath. "I've heard awful stories about abortionists here."

"Someone told me about a doctor in Japan who performs abortions in a hospital," Mila said, "but we could never get enough money for that."

"What about Puerto Rico?" Pam suggested. "There's a teacher at work who went to a clinic there. I think it was a little expensive, but sanitary and safe. I'll talk to her and then the two of you can get together."

"Maybe I can go over the Memorial Day weekend. I don't know how we can afford it, but if we can get the money together by then," Mila's voice trailed off.

After Uncle Clifford failed to convince them to have the baby, he pitched in two hundred dollars. Mila took the money she'd saved for summer school and Kwasi had a small amount he'd put aside for rent during the summer. Mila was sure Pam and Colin gave more than they could afford. Their friends amazed and touched them with their generosity. They counted the money out on the bed in their apartment.

"There's not enough for both of us to go," Mila said.

"I don't want you going alone," Kwasi said.

"We've been over this," Mila said. "It's not a matter of what we want." She took his hand to comfort him. "I'll be all right." She tempered her words so they sounded less strident. "It's best this way."

It rained overnight and low clouds hung in the sky as Mila looked through the window. They got out of bed without talking, each lost in separate dread of the trip. Buttoning the waist of her suit skirt was troublesome. She willed herself not to get sick.

Khalid, Kwasi's friend, drove them to the airport. Speeding along the roadway it seemed like they were setting out for a holiday but as they got closer to the airport they sat squeezing each other's hands, their resolve ebbing and flowing.

"If you change your mind, we'll work it out," Kwasi told her.

"We're doing the right thing," she said hoisting her book bag over her shoulder and picking up an overnight bag. "Don't go in with me," she said, kissing him and putting on a cheerful face. "I'll see you Sunday."

It was her first airplane flight and she wished it were under different circumstances. She stood in the middle of the airport confused, passengers rushed and bumped into her; the loud speaker was a blur. The walk to the gate seemed endless and she paused often to put her luggage down and rest. She transferred in New York for Miami and from there took another plane to San Juan.

"Finishing school work before your vacation?" the man next to her asked, seeing her textbook. She nodded, not wanting to talk, fighting back her solitary fright.

"You kids have it easy," he said. "Going away to school, going away on vacation. You'll have to face reality someday," he predicted. He put earphones on and Mila heard him click through the channels until the sound of Frank Sinatra's voice leaked through the air next to her.

As the plane descended Mila felt her stomach lurch and held tightly to the chair rests as the wheels hit the tarmac. As passengers stood up, she felt panic, the reality of her mission overwhelming. She wanted to scream at the crush of people pushing against her.

Her books and luggage felt heavier than in Cleveland and her suit too warm in the humid air. People jumped into waiting taxis. One pulled up to the curb in front of her and she shook her head, but the driver jumped out and opened the door for her. He had gray hair and a grizzled moustache. His dark eyes held hers; lines of life creased his face. He cocked his head. "American?" Mila nodded. His smile was paternal, encouraging. "Get in," he urged.

She pawed through her papers pulling out a page with the doctor's address and handed it to the driver. "I don't have much money...no mucho dinero," she added. "Is it far?"

"No not far," he said, pushing down the meter and after a few blocks he pulled up to the address. Mila paid him and gave him a small tip.

"Please wait a minute." Within minutes she returned and found him waiting at the curb. She slumped back into the cab and put her hands over her face. "His office is closed," she said. Exhaustion and desperation over-whelmed her and within minutes she blurted out the story of why she was there, why she couldn't get married, why she had no money.

He twisted toward her from the front seat so he could look at her. "It is not a new story. I see many young girls like you - with their mothers, with or without husbands. I can spot them. What hotel do you want?" he asked. "Where are your reservations?"

"I don't have any reservations," she said.

"I'll take you to a hotel. It's plain but clean and reasonable." He held out his hand. "My name is Miguel," he said. Relief flooded her. In her despera-tion it never crossed her mind he could be a charlatan, or worse. She felt an innate trust. "The café on the corner is inexpensive." He pointed to a faded rose-colored building, the window frames and doors trimmed in blue. "Get chicken with rice. I'll write down how to ask in Spanish," he said. "I will ask my wife for the name of a doctor. She knows about such things. At the hotel he carried her bag to the lobby. "In the morning eat only dry toast. I'll come for you at eight."

As Miguel promised, the room was simple and although she couldn't see the beach, a fresh gentle breeze cooled her as she relaxed into exhausted sleep.

The next morning she climbed into Miguel's waiting cab. They drove for several blocks and turned into an alley. Mila's face was ashen with apprehen-sion as she looked at the faded wooden door.

"It is the back entrance. Knock and tell them Esperanza made your appointment."

The woman who answered motioned for Mila to follow her upstairs to a small reception area where an older woman sat beside a teen-aged girl. The nurse motioned for the girl to follow her and disappeared. The nurse returned and started unwrapping paper bundles. Mila stared in horror at the metal instruments. They looked like medieval torture devices and she shud-dered, feeling faint. She wanted to run from this room, from this building, run to Miguel and tell him to take her to the airport, tell him she'd made a dreadful mistake. She dug her fingernails into the palms of her hands and steeled herself to wait for the doctor.

Finally it was her turn and she was led to a small room. "Take off your clothes from the waist down, then get up on the table," the nurse told her in English. There were no gowns, only a thin paper sheet. She wished Pam could be there with her calm assurances. The teenager before her had her mother. What would Frances say if she could see her now?

A man came into the room. He looked at her without smiling, his faced wrinkled.

"Where did you get my name?"

"I don't know your name. A taxi driver brought me."

"Where did you meet him?"

"In a line of taxis at the airport."

He shook his head.

"Where is the father?"

"He's a student back in Cleveland - in the States."

He sighed. "When was your last period?"

"Three months ago."

"Put your feet in the stirrups." After he finished his examination, he said, "You are at least twelve weeks pregnant, probably more. It is too risky."

"I have to have an abortion. I can't go all the way back home," Mila protested.

"Between twelve and sixteen weeks is a dangerous time. You run the risk of hemorrhaging and infection. Go back, stay pregnant, get married, have your baby."

"That's impossible," she said. "Please. Help me. I have money."

"I can't take the chance," he said. "You can work it out. You're a good-looking woman. Find another man." He pushed a buzzer and the nurse came back. "Next patient," he said.

Miguel saw her come out and drove slowly down the alley to pick her up. "Everything is okay? You look pale."

"He wouldn't do it. Please. I have to find someone. Do you know anywhere else?"

After a moment Miguel snapped his fingers. "There is a woman's clinic," he said. "We'll go there."

"How long will I have to wait? My plane leaves at five and I can't miss it."

"I'll wait for you," Miguel assured her.

The woman at the desk was on the telephone. A number of women were waiting, some clearly American, but most Puerto Rican. The woman gave her a sheet of paper, "Fill this out."

She watched the clock jump in two-minute increments. After an agonizing wait her name was called and a nurse led her into an examining room.

"How much money do you have?"

"Five hundred dollars."

The woman scoffed. "My dear, that's not half enough."

"It has to be!" Mila pleaded. "Please, help me. I have to be back at work on Tuesday."

The woman studied her face. Finally reaching a decision she said. "All right. It would be easier for you if you had anesthesia, but you'd have to wait here at least four or five hours; you'd be too woozy to travel."

"I can't wait that long," Mila said.

"It's your choice."

Two young assistants came into the room and stood on each side of the table. They held her arms. Mila lost focus of everything but the pain. It was beyond anything she could have imagined. It traveled through every nerve ending, until she feared she couldn't endure it any longer. As one cramp ended, another began. Finally, she felt something pulled from her body and heard a plop of something in a metal vessel.

"It's over."

The instruments were removed. Snapping off her rubber gloves, the woman said, "Here are some pads, in case you experience cramping and bleeding. The nurse will show you where to rest until you have to leave."

Miguel came in to check on her and found her on a cot in a small waiting room.

"You are pale," he said. "You should delay your flight."

"I can't," she insisted, hanging onto the table for leverage. Miguel guided her. "I have a ticket for today. Why are you being so kind?" she asked. "You don't even know me."

"We had a child, a daughter. I was strict with her." His eyes clouded and he raised his hand as if to brush a fly from his face. "She was afraid to tell us she was pregnant. They were young, with no money and tried to take care of it without help. She didn't want to shame us, afraid we would no longer love her." His voice cracked with emotion. "As if you ever stop loving your child. And now? She is gone and we are alone."

Miguel helped her into the cab and drove her to the airport in silence.

"I'll never forget you," Mila told him. "I don't know what I'd have done without you."

"It is all we can do in life," he said, "try to understand and help each other. It makes us human."

She forced her last twenty dollars into his hand. "I wish I had more."

She refused the meal the stewardess offered her. She wished things were different, that she could have a baby that was a part of her, to have her own family like everyone else. Tears seeped through her eyelids. Was it a boy or a girl, she wondered? What would it have looked like? What color would its skin have been?

When the plane landed in Cleveland, she was the last to get off and before she reached him she saw Kwasi watching each passenger, bending to see behind them until he saw her and rushed to her. He held her for long moments and gently released her enough to search her face. "You were supposed to phone me," he said.

CHAPTER THIRTY-TWO

▼

Still weak, Mila resumed teaching after a few days, anxious for the semester to end. She attended her evening classes and made a half-hearted attempt at finishing her term papers, unable to rouse from her stupor, feeling emotionally and physically drained, ill, and weak.

Each night it took greater effort to climb the two flights of stairs to their rooms. She opened the door to the hodgepodge of their improvised life and gazed around the room with tender eyes. The desk Kwasi made from an old door sat atop two saw horses, orange crate book cases were shoved into every inch of empty wall space, the sofa Pam donated was the only comfortable place to sit. In the center of the room, the table salvaged from Uncle Clifford's attic was painted red. The bed on a raised platform in an alcove at the far end was shoved next to the small bathroom. She thought of their lighthearted joy when they moved in together, adding each piece like the grandest treasure.

Kwasi was in the throes of finals, but insisted on doing the shopping and cooking. "You have to get back your strength," he said, and made her stay in bed when she was home, holding her each night like a child until she fell asleep. After a few hours of restless sleep she woke to see him across the island of the room bent over his books or sometimes staring into space. A silence had settled between them, an avoidance.

He tried putting on a good face when he saw how drained she was, but in the early morning hours two weeks after the abortion when neither of them could sleep, Mila broke the black stillness to ask him how he felt.

"Just fine."

"You don't act fine. What are you not saying?"

"Nothing is the matter. All the time studying. You know I hate exam time."

His curtness surprised her. Her feelings were so delicate it felt like a slap, like she was intruding on his privacy.

"I think we need to talk about it - talk about the abortion."

Kwasi's face tightened. "Let's wait until school is over," he said.

"We can't go on not talking about it," she insisted. She searched for his expression. Only the light for studying illuminated the room and he was cast in shadows. With a shock she saw his hands covered his face and when he looked up tears glistened against his dark skin.

"I shouldn't have allowed it." His strong voice cracked with emotion. "I was a coward for not insisting we keep our baby."

The Thursday before school ended Mila opened the door to find music playing for the first time since Puerto Rico. When she walked in, Kwasi smiled. She changed into her robe and sat on the sofa watching him stir a pot of soup and slice the bread. He turned the fire down and sat beside her.

"By now you know, it's not my custom to do things the way you do. I don't understand why Americans feel it's necessary to say 'I love you' at the drop of a hat." He paused at the bewildered look on Mila's face, withdrew a small package from his pocket and handed it to her. She folded back the paper revealing an oblong bead of deep green with flecks of pale yellow and white. Separated by a knot on either side of the graceful central bead was a carved ivory bead. Kwasi took the soft leather strap on which they were threaded and held it for a moment. "My giving you this," he said as he placed it around her neck, "*means* I love you. In my tribe, when a man gives these particular trade beads to a woman it means 'my heart belongs only to you.'"

It would normally be time for her period; perhaps, since it was the first one since the abortion, it was more severe.

When Kwasi came in he put his arms around her as she stood at the stove. "Smell's great," he said. "Mind if I turn on the soccer match?"

The pain intensified and she tried to hide it. She didn't want to spoil their evening. She was drenched in cold perspiration and staggered across the room unable to silence her moan of pain. Kwasi saw her swaying and jumped up to help her to the bed.

"What's wrong?"

"I think it's my period."

"I'll bring you some aspirin," he said.

By the time he got back a huge gush of blood had pooled between her legs and she cried out. His face was a mask of terror. He whispered something in Ashanti. "You're bleeding to death," he said. He brought back folded towels and put them under her hips and between her legs. "I'll call Khalid. You've got to go to the hospital." Mila passed out.

The next morning she awoke alone in a sunny room. In a blur of memory she recalled being placed on a gurney, rushed through the doors of Emergency, and pushed down a long corridor with Kwasi running along beside her. Then her memory froze.

The knock on the door startled her and reflexively she pulled the blanket around herself.

"I'm Doctor Fennel," the man in green scrubs told her. "You're looking better this morning." He turned the pages of her chart. "I performed a D and C on you last night." Seeing her puzzled expression he explained. "That's dilation and curettage, a procedure to clean out your uterus." Mila felt her neck and face turn hot. "It's obvious you had an abortion recently." He paused. "You're lucky. When you arrived you were on the verge of shock from acute blood loss."

She didn't know how to respond and rolled and unrolled the sheet before asking, "When can I go home?"

"If you don't have more bleeding, and I don't think you will, and if you don't develop a fever, you can be released tomorrow afternoon," he said. "I think we should talk about birth control."

"My other doctor told me I'd probably never be able to have children," she said.

"Well if he told you that, he was wrong, as you discovered for yourself; one ovary is plenty. No sex for four weeks. Your body needs to heal." He tempered his lecture by taking her hand. "You should do fine, but if you have any bleeding or run a fever after you go home, call me immediately - don't wait."

The D and C scraped away the final remnants of their child. It wasn't just the tissue that had disappeared. The curtain through which she screened reality was also torn away. Before, their love had been like electricity, taking the path of least resistance. Now they hesitated, foremost in both their minds the knowledge that they must avoid another pregnancy, now caution and love perversely nudged them apart.

Letters began arriving from Ghana, which Kwasi read without sharing the contents. She could feel him distancing himself, his thoughts focused on another continent, another life. She remembered a science class in which she studied the ocean plates. Their lives were like those plates, colliding and moving apart - unable to fuse.

She lived each day knowing their time was finite and knew she didn't want to be there to watch him leave. She couldn't imagine life after he was gone. She knew Pam would listen, but her feelings were lodged deeper than talk. She knew she would be welcome again with Pam, but that place belonged to

Colin now; she wouldn't remain at Uncle Clifford's where each day would be a reminder of the life they no longer shared.

She was an avid bulletin board reader, in stores, at bus stations. She scanned the notices placed on them about used washers, kittens and puppies needing homes, calls for baby sitters. Habitually she read the one in the teacher's lunchroom. There was a plea for teachers in the Peace Corp. She smiled to herself. It reminded her of the poster: Uncle Sam Needs You.

She flew eastward, she flew westward,
Flew to northwest and to southward
But she cannot find a spot
Even in the worst of places
Where to build her needful nest,
Where to take up her abode.

Ibid, Runo 1, Lines 183-188

CHAPTER THIRTY-THREE

▼

Cumanacoa, Venezuela

Leave taking in Cleveland was swift. They shaped and kneaded their words, but the words seemed unstable, like rising dough easy to collapse with a punch. Mila gazed at the small diamond on the tiny face of the watch Kwasi gave her as a farewell present, "To remind you to think of me," inside were her initials and the date, September 1967. But the past with Kwasi must cease to exist; it was the only way to survive.

In Tucson, study of Spanish was demanding: two hours in the morning, one after lunch, and another two after dinner. The current crop of Peace Corps volunteers were drilled in Venezuelan history, politics, culture and customs. They were inoculated for every conceivable disease.

Nights, lying in the humid room at the YWCA, listening to her three roommates' snores and tossing and turning, she considered quitting, and returning to Cleveland, but for what? She recognized another feeling, like an ancient echo of a past she'd forced from memory. She yearned with all her being for a place to belong.

As part of the Peace Corps Training Program, Mila was assigned to Tapalpa, a small village in the mountains north of Guadalajara, where she lived with a native family and taught English at a local school. It was four weeks of intensive cultural and language immersion. Two more volunteers dropped out. The original forty-two had dwindled to thirty. After training she would be sent to the small community of Cumanacoa deep in the jungles of rural Venezuela where she would set-up a community development/teaching English as a second language program.

They traveled east through low-lying slashed and burned jungle, then started climbing through the mountains. The bus hugged the mountainside and the driver maneuvered with skill, but still Mila felt nervous and opened the window to keep from getting sick.

They circled a dusty plaza surrounded by a broken concrete walkway with a few benches and scraggly trees. A mass produced statue of Simon Bolivar stood in the middle of a slab of cracked concrete around which an attempt had been made to plant flowers, drooping from lack of water.

The Dominguez family lived near the school in a two-story concrete blockhouse. Senor Dominguez taught mathematics and history and Senora Dominguez was an administrator. They had two children, Mauricio, eleven, and a teenage girl, Rosa. A grandmother and widowed sister also lived with them as well as a maid who stayed in a one room shack behind the house, near the outdoor toilet.

The kitchen opened into its own courtyard where an avocado and two shade trees grew and where the grandmother tended a flower garden. Next to the toilet was a makeshift shower with a hot water container on the roof above. The roof housed chickens, clotheslines for the laundry, and an herb garden. On Monday Mila woke to the unfamiliar sound of roosters and Rosa's gaze, a cross between a question and a welcome. Rosa took her into the kitchen that looked like a color wheel. The table was rustic planks of wood with gaily-colored chairs of blue, yellow, green, pink, orange and red. They smiled at her as if she were some kind of exotic animal, not quite sure how to treat it. Breakfast was a family affair of fresh rolls, crumbly white cheese, and coffee. Mila answered Senor Dominguez's queries couched in a semi-formal series of questions about her trip. Senora Dominquez framed her words in basic Spanish as if incredulous that Mila would understand. Mila, in turn, was impressed by their knowledge when she asked her own questions.

"How large *is* Cumanacoa?" she asked.

"About twenty-five hundred people, plus the ones who come to market twice a week," Senor Dominguez answered.

"Is there any industry?"

"A small sugar cane factory about three kilometers from town," Senor Dominguez answered.

"Is the land fertile?" she asked, thinking the area too rocky and dry.

Senora Dominguez answered. "We grow vegetables: corn and squash."

Mauricio joined in the conversation, beginning to feel more comfortable. "Wait until the rainy season," he laughed. The only thing worse than the dry season is the rainy season. Our road turns into a lake of mud and it's the only way in and out of the village."

The coffee was hot and strong and Mila wrapped her hands around the cup and breathed it in, smiling at her new family.

She walked to school on the west side of the plaza, a concrete building with a tin roof. School started early, seven-thirty, but let out at noon. When classes ended she met Rosa and they walked home for the main meal, black beans, rice, and plantains that looked like bananas but were hard. They were usually fried, but sometimes boiled and rolled in sugar. And always *arepas*, round balls of cornmeal dough, flattened a bit so they were an inch thick and literally stuck to the stomach. It explained why most of the women had protruding abdomens. Senora Dominguez patted her stomach, "*arepa* belly", she said, then laughed, but Mila looked forward to market day and the sight of fresh fruit and vegetables.

Between the heat and the heavy meal everyone but Mila collapsed for a *siesta*. Mila accepted the primitive arrangements such as the shower that had one weak light bulb and undependable electricity. It was impossible to see to shave her legs; a custom Latin woman didn't follow. *Siesta* seemed like an opportune time and she put on a bathing suit under her skirt and blouse and went up to the roof with her razor, soap and a towel where earlier she'd placed a pan filled with water now warm enough to use. She was twisting around to reach the back of the first leg and hadn't noticed the maid who was taking down the wash until she heard a terrified scream. The entire family rushed up to stare at Mila in open-mouthed wonder.

"She was going to kill herself," the maid screamed. *Pobrecita*, poor thing, she's gone over the edge," she pronounced.

"No, no," Mila assured them and explained why she was there.

"Crazy *gringita*" the maid said in disgust, "sitting in the midday sun.

The weeks passed and her mail arrived randomly. In the latest batch there was a letter from Zeke telling her he was attending Wilberforce College in Ohio, but was thinking of dropping out and becoming a policeman in Painesville. He enclosed a photo of himself on his used sailboat. "I bought it during the summer," he said. Mila thought he looked as happy as she'd ever seen him. There had also been a businesslike letter from Frances telling her that Grandma Marta had died and Betty was in ill health. The news left her sad; Grandma Marta and Aunt Betty were among the few pleasant memories of childhood. Frances wasted few words with sentimentality. A letter from Pam enclosed one of Sammy's erratic postcards, this one from London with a picture of the Tower: *Haven't lost my head, yet.* And a letter from Kwasi.

Hello my dear Mila. I am having a complete lapse of memory, even forgetting my own name, honey, exhausted from travel and the family. Everything has changed. Only my mother and younger brother, Michael, are happy to see me. Had my hair cut yesterday. The barber was drunk and messed it up. Another barber re-did it, but not the same as when you cut it. My bed is a sad and lonesome place. Somebody is missing from my side. Nobody is here to wake me up. Nobody is here to give me orders. I miss you very much. Good night to my precious love, Kwasi.

Rosa helped assuage the loneliness. In the early evening she often accompanied Mila to the *tienda* where she could purchase needles, thread, and yardage and together they stitched simple blouses and skirts by hand. Rosa, along with the few other students who planned on going to a larger town for high school, attended the more advanced of Mila's English classes.

The weeks turned into months as Mila settled into the routine and language of her life. An idea for community development projects gnawed constantly in her mind. She was unclear about what constituted community development and her various queries failed to help. She wrote the Caracas Peace Corps office hoping for guidance and suggestions. They wrote back suggesting hikes in the mountains where it was cooler, but she had no desire to stray too far from Cumanacoa. She took a book from the box provided by the Peace Corps after dinner and tried to concentrate but instead listened to the faint conversation of the villagers strolling in the cool of the evening as twilight softened the village.

On alternate Saturday evenings wooden benches were set up in the courtyard of the school and electrical cords snaked along the ground to the projector. The kids crowded around Mila as a battered screen was hoisted in place and the film rolled. It was a 1960 Russian film with Spanish subtitles and the electricity faded in and out. Looking around at the children scattered in the audience her mind again grappled with ideas for a community development project. The children helped their parents on their farms part of the time, and the rest of the time hung around her. Summertime would be here before she knew it and they would have long hours with nothing to do.

On the walk home from school she noticed how the women struggled with all of the packages they carried and an idea formed in her mind. Everyone could use a way of carrying things. Why not make a bag large enough to put the many things the women struggled to carry? She knew that the Catholic organization in Cumana, a larger town fifteen miles to the west, distributed relief supplies of beans and rice and the next Saturday she took the bus to Cumana, and begged them for their used burlap sacks. On the first sunny day, she and the kids washed the sacks and spread them in the sun to bleach. "They're for our summer project," she told them. There were still details to be worked out, but Mila intended to create a cottage industry in the shade of the school courtyard.

She placed a call from the cinderblock building that housed the post office, the regional mayor's office when he came to Cumanacoa, and the only phone line in the village. She'd applied for a five-day visit to Peace Corps headquarters in Caracas, but the approval papers failed to arrive. When a free line became available the children ran to the house to tell her. A voice barely audible above the static confirmed her authorization to travel.

She looked forward to visiting and getting news from the other volunteers. She also wanted newspapers and books and hoped there was mail waiting to be forwarded to the interior.

The bus was loaded with people, and poultry in wooden cages. It took an unpaved dirt path to join the paved road. After a few miles, she wondered how she would survive the sixteen hour three hundred mile ride. The decrepit bus negotiated hair-raising turns on roads barely more than bridle paths skirting the faces of thousand foot precipices. The other passengers chattered among themselves, casting quick glances her way and then looked down if she tried to make eye contact. As they rounded another curve she felt her stomach heave and nervously said, "*Yo tengo mucho mierda.*" In a split second, she realized she'd used the wrong word. She intended to say *miedo*, fear, but instead used *mierda*, shit - I have much shit. Her cheeks burned, for a moment there was absolute silence, then the tension was broken with laughter. For the remainder of the trip she was offered food and answered question after question until they arrived in Caracas.

The bus dropped her off at the Peace Corps headquarters where she learned how many volunteers had gone back home. Several of the single women found service in the rural areas too lonely and returned to the States shortly after arriving. Mila was congratulated for sticking it out and advised to apply for a transfer, if isolation got to be too much for her. The thought uppermost in her mind was getting to the pension to take a shower only to discover it was *ocupado*. She decided to leave her bag in the room and explore Caracas. The noise and activity were heady after Cumanacoa. She dodged the big city traffic and gazed into the window of a Caracas equivalent of Saks Fifth Avenue. The lessons of the Peace Corps about taking responsibility to represent her country well at all times faded from memory as a heavenly aroma wafted her way. Forgetting she was dressed in a faded wraparound skirt and still grubby from the trip she followed her nose through the glass doors and was absorbed in the muffled Musak. It was a far different sound from the cacophony of the swampy jungles as was the unaccustomed luxury of the deep pile carpet, the textures and smells of the fabrics around her.

In the center of the room she found a buffet table groaning with an array of gorgeous food and helped herself to the dainty canapés, hot hors d'oeuvres, and glass after glass of punch. She was sure the beautifully groomed guests were exercising Latin courtesy by moving away to give her more room at the buffet table, until she got a whiff of herself. She smelled like *eau de* chicken and Venezuelan dust.

As inconspicuously as possible she edged away from the table. She needed to find the ladies room and stepped onto the escalator that went from the first floor to the mezzanine, cutting off her retreat to the front door. Mila stopped an elegantly dressed man rushing by, *Senor, adonde esta?*" Before she completed the question he put his fingers to his lips and hissed, then ignored her. The problem grew severe. Her only thought now was escape and the only means was the escalator.

Between ascending and descending a fashion show had commenced. The models were introduced from below and embarked one-by-one to be swept into view with royal aplomb and the rustle of polite applause. As the next model stepped onto the escalator, Mila stepped on, trying to hide behind her. For a moment she considered walking backwards, but more models stood every few steps with frozen smiles. As they descended the announcer described each dress and the courtier house being honored.

Her only hope was to reach the door to the street before the store manager reached her. As she got off at the bottom she felt someone grab her arm and an incredulous voice. "Mila?" A tall man with unruly hair and tortoise shell glasses stood looking at her. The jacket of his suit was slung over his shoulder and a familiar crooked grin spread over his face.

She searched his face and as recognition dawned she heard herself say, "Sammy? I have to pee!"

CHAPTER THIRTY-FOUR

▼

Peace Corps, Venezuela

"Are you a big shot?" she asked Sammy.

He looked up from the bread he was slathering with butter. His expression was devilry. "I'm a Stanford graduate; do I need more big shot credentials than that?" He took a huge bite out of the bread, licked the butter from his lips, and grinned crookedly.

"You forget, I knew you when you tripped over your feet," she said. "You have to be more specific: what kind of big shot?"

"Ah!" he said, "The big shot explains to the humble peasant."

Mila laughed. "Who ever thought we'd see each other again so far away from Painesville."

"Of all the gin mills, in all the..." Sammy mimicked Humphrey Bogart.

"Your mom told me you were an attorney," Mila said, "that you worked for some engineering firm."

"Latham and Beck Engineering."

"Do you like it?"

"Interesting question. My biggest accomplishment so far is being called Sam instead of Sammy." Mila laughed.

"Most of the attorneys are my age and competition is fierce. Typical Corporation - only so many slots at the top of the pyramid - lots of politics and backbiting. You go where they send you or get lost in the dust."

"And I thought you came down here to find me," Mila said.

"Of course, since you never came to San Francisco," Sammy said, "what other choice did I have?"

Mila shook her head. "Remember Pam? The friend I lived with? She forwarded the postcard you sent from London. You're the last person in the world I expected to see in Caracas."

"Mom wrote you were in the Peace Corps but I didn't know where. You two seem to have become good friends," Sam said.

"Yes, Leah starred as Nurse Cratchet in *One Flew Over the Cuckoo's Nest* at LEC. I loved her. I missed seeing her after I moved to Cleveland."

"She had a choice between a part on Broadway or having me. It's a family joke. I've often wondered if she regretted her decision," Sammy said.

"I don't think there's any doubt she feels she made the right decision. She's terribly proud of you."

"Which brings us back to you. How is the Aadams Family?" Sam asked.

"You know the word *estranged?* That would sum it up. I hear from them on an 'as needed' basis, except for Zeke."

"Give yourself a pat on the back. You made it despite her," Sammy said.

"I'm not sure I've made much of anything. Let's change the subject. Are you married?" Mila asked.

"Not yet. I'm serious about somebody. Mae. She's Chinese. We met at Stanford."

"What would the folks in Painesville think?"

Sam smiled. "Painesville isn't the problem. I haven't met her parents. She's afraid they won't approve. She's applied for med school in the east. What about you?"

"Talk about families not approving - I lived with someone from Ghana for three years," Mila said. "I got pregnant and had an abortion. He had to return after graduation."

"That doesn't sound like you," Sammy said. "Why would you get into a situation like that?

"I was in love," she said. She looked down at her napkin and straightened it on her lap, feeling defensive. She thought about accusing him of the same thing.

"That must have been tough." He said it kindly.

"It was, but he told me from the beginning. Not that it made it any easier."

"The abortion must have been hard to get over."

"It was all hard to get over. I haven't yet."

They were silent for a few moments. Sammy took a sip of water. "Any plans after the Peace Corps?"

"Not yet. Soon though," she said.

They walked back to the hotel in the same companionable silence they shared in high school and gave each other a friendly hug good-bye.

"I'll look forward to your next fashion show," Sam said. "Maybe Paris or London."

"Don't run out of postcards," Mila said. "Good luck with Mae."

She still smarted from Sammy's questions. She knew she had a tendency to compartmentalize her life, to protect herself and avoid thinking about difficult things. She'd started as a child, inventing her boxes, her tunnel. It was time to face the reality of her situation with Kwasi.

Before she returned to Cumanacoa she checked in with the Peace Corps office just as the mail arrived. There was a letter postmarked months earlier.

Dearest Mila. I finally received your Christmas card. I too am sharing your Peace Corps experience. My whole digestive system is overturned, upturned and interrupted violently. I am still confused but if things continue as they are I'm thinking of returning to the U.S. (but not to that crummy Cleveland). Can you suggest someplace where I can use my degree and we could be together?

He went on to say Ghana held only disappointment.

My eldest brother has squandered Father's money and without capital and government connections a person can do nothing under the present government. I cannot see myself hiding in some civil service job. I would like to bring my younger brother with me so he can attend a junior college until I earn enough for university for him.

Just when she'd resigned herself to a life without Kwasi her hopes were buoyed up once again. She felt a twinge of anger over the emotional gambit he put her through and then empathy for what he must be going through. Still, she wasn't an elastic band that could be stretched taut over and over without the eventual loss of elasticity.

Each time she dealt with the bureaucracy, her disillusionment with the Peace Corps grew. She asked for guidance about community development, but the country director was in Washington and his bubbly assistant suggested sport's programs. She nearly laughed at the idiocy of the suggestion since the temperature rose to ninety degrees by eight in the morning.

Toward the end of the term on her way home from classes she noticed a group of children gathered near the village's only cafe. For a moment she thought perhaps it was the Regional Peace Corps Director checking on the site after her visit to Caracas so Mila slowed her pace to get a better view without appearing obvious. A man in his late thirties with dark curly hair, a strong nose, and a chiseled face was reading a newspaper and eating lunch.

His short sleeved shirt showed strong muscled arms and his shoes were polished to a high gloss, unusual in the dusty countryside. A town beggar wandered up to him and Mila expected the stranger to wave him off, but instead he reached for a pile of change on the table and handed him several coins.

At lunch Mila asked casually if anyone knew the stranger sitting at the cafe. Rosa immediately rolled her eyes and enthusiastically answered, "*el jefe* engineer from Caracas."

"What's he doing here?" she inquired.

"He's here to build a bridge. He came while you were gone."

"This bridge will help our town," Senor Munoz said. "We can ship out more sugar cane and get supplies faster."

"His name is Francisco Paolo Colombo," said Senora Munoz. "The children follow him everywhere. They keep his shoes shined, his car polished, and he gives them coins but I think they would do it for nothing they like him so much. He's Italian, but he's lived in this country many years."

"Silvia Catalan wants him for her *novio*," Rosa giggled. Silvia Catalan taught school too and initially had joined the other teachers in suspecting the blond haired, blue-eyed Mila wanted to steal their husbands and boyfriends. It didn't take long to dispel that fear and they had befriended her.

Senora Dominguez scolded her daughter. "Be quiet and don't gossip. That's no way to speak of a teacher."

"And is he engaged?" Mila asked.

Rosa looked over at her mother and with shiny black eyes shook her head, no.

At bedtime Mila took out Kwasi's letter so his words were the last thing she read before she went to sleep.

The following Saturday she washed her hair, dressed with more care than usual, and accompanied by a gaggle of children walked the few kilometers to the bridge site. Massive piles of steel rods and girders lay piled along the riverside and bulldozers with umbrellas over the drivers' heads were preparing for a crossing some ten yards from the old wooden bridge.

The chief engineer was in conversation with another man, but the children's noise distracted them. They smiled as Mila approached and held out her hand. "I'm a teacher with the Peace Corps. The children were curious to see the bridge site, so I thought I'd come with them."

"Paolo Colombo," he replied, "and this is my partner, Xavier Ramirez."

They all shook hands. "Xavier is making one of his rare visits to the interior," Paolo said. "Unlike me, he prefers the city. It works out well."

"I prefer seeing my wife and children," Xavier said.

"It's a perfect match. He's good with business, I'm good with building."

Paolo gave the information with a restrained formality, and she felt uncomfortable and pushy to have interrupted. She got a whiff of after-shave lotion. His dark eyes seemed to be evaluating her without smiling until he made a sudden move to reach over and tickle one of the children who screamed with laughter. With that invitation to play they were all over him begging for money. He reached into his pocket like a rich uncle putting coins in each outstretched hand.

"I heard the Peace Corps had arrived," he said. "Please call me Paolo. If you're interested in bridges, I can show you around."

More than a month passed with little more than a nod between them, and always with children surrounding them. Every school day Mila passed the little cafe that existed mostly on his largesse. Paolo took his noon day meal there and Mila learned that he'd bought the espresso machine so he could enjoy his passion for the thick brew. He worked long hours at the bridge site and each month he left for Caracas and was gone for several days.

Her community development plan was on top of her and she felt the pressure to make the last of the arrangements. A few weeks before school ended, she approached Paolo and the few businessmen in Cumanacoa for seed money to buy supplies, bright yarns and paints. Before school ended, Mila already had the kids busy. They fashioned the burlap sacks they'd pre-pared earlier into *bulsas*, shopping bags that they decorated by appliquéing bright flowers onto them with the yarn. Next they painted wooden dowels in cheerful colors, or braided hemp for handles. The meager proceeds went to the kids who in turn gave it to their families.

The children were always hungry while they worked and she came up with another plan to supplement snacks. She again approached the business-men to contribute powdered milk and kool-aid mix producing pink, orange and green milk and next convinced the bakery to donate day old rolls that could be softened by dunking into the colored milk.

Before long nearly everyone in town had at least one *bulsa* and Mila decided to branch out. Twice a week a handful of children accompanied her to early morning market in Cumana where they placed the *bulsas* under an awning made from a sheet and tree branches. News of their program traveled to Caracas. The Director arrived with a cameraman and the story was printed in the Peace Corps newspaper distributed throughout the system.

Waiting for the bus after a long market day, she heard someone call her name. "I was hoping I'd catch you," Paolo said. "I have to inspect the Manzanares River Site this weekend and I wondered if you'd like to go along."

"Yes, I'd like that," she said. "It would be great to see something besides Cumanacoa and Cumana.

"Can you be ready early, by six?"

"Sure," she assured him. "I'll be ready."

She hardly slept, afraid the alarm wouldn't go off and Paolo would leave without her, or worse, think she forgot or changed her mind. Then she caught herself feeling guilty. All summer Kwasi monopolized her nighttime reveries before sleep came; tonight he hadn't been foremost in her thoughts.

The Dominguez family was askance, particularly grandma who clucked and shook her head. Senora Munoz took Mila aside. "It is improper for an unmarried woman to travel with an unmarried man," she warned.

Although Mila assured her "It's for the Peace Corps. They encourage trips," it was Paolo who eased the tension, after Mila told him.

"There's a great sense of what is appropriate in this culture. We have to be careful of your reputation. I'll speak to Senor Dominguez. Let me handle it."

Senora Dominguez may still have harbored doubts, but when Paolo picked her up in his beige Volkswagen, the family greeted him cheerfully.

"Do you know any American songs by the Beatles?" he asked. "Sing them for me. Radio reception is non-existent out here."

"You don't want to hear me sing," she protested. "I can't carry a tune."

"But I do want to hear you. Please."

Mila began with *Yesterday,*" emphasizing the words by moving her hands, as if to dismiss yesterday. She followed with *Michelle,* keeping time on her knee, and ended with *Norwegian Wood,* smiling and taking a bow.

"Unique interpretation," he said.

"If I didn't know better I'd accuse you of being tone deaf," she smiled.

"It was lovely," he said. "You sing with passion."

"Okay. Now it's your turn," Mila said.

It was a popular song Rosa sang constantly. *Yo soy quel que cada noche no te olividan,* I am the one every night who cannot forget you.

"Now *that* was beautiful. Have you studied voice?"

"I studied the violin as a child," he said.

"A child prodigy, I suppose?"

"Something like that." He rolled down the window and rested his arm. "I still play in chamber groups in Caracas, but no longer professionally."

"In Italy?"

"How did you know that?" he asked.

"You're a main topic of conversation," she told him. "Where do you come from in Italy? Not that I'll recognize the name."

Paolo's smile looked like a toothpaste commercial, perfect white teeth set against his sun-tanned face. "Your candor is charming. In Brecia," he said, adding "in Northern Italy."

"Why did you leave? They must need engineers there too."

He seemed to consider before he answered. "There were more opportunities in Venezuela. I needed a change, adventure."

"Are your parents still living? Do you have brothers and sisters?"

"You're full of questions. My father is a doctor, retired now. I have two older sisters, one is a nun and the other is married, but unfortunately no children. My parents are anxious for grandchildren, especially mine, to pass on the family name. Before you ask, I've never been married but I was engaged for a year and it didn't work out."

"Such a large family. They must miss you. Do you visit?"

"We write, mostly." His accent added to the richness of his voice, full and mellow. "What about you?"

"I have a brother in Ohio. I'm adopted. I was born in Finland."

"Finland? That sounds like an interesting story."

"That's one way of looking at it," she said. "Was it easier to converse in Spanish because Italian was your first language?"

"I'm far from fluent, but I knew Spanish before I came, as well as some English."

They had been going downhill for sometime and as they came to a wide curve, Paolo said, "There's the river. We have to get to the other side."

"Can we drive across the river in this?" Mila asked.

"The river is shallow further down. I've done it before; these small cars are best; they almost float."

He turned into the riverbed, and they drove mid-stream before the wheels got stuck in the littered rocks. The more Paolo tried to get out, the deeper they sank. They both sat in silent shock as the water washed over their feet. He revved the motor but the wheels simply spun without going anywhere. Mila waited for him to explode or apologize or show some reaction, instead he opened his mouth and in Spanish began singing, "yesterday...all my troubles seemed so far away..." They doubled over laughing.

"I'll help you unload," she offered. Their clothes hung in wet folds. To lighten the car, they carried load after load of equipment to the bank and then rocked the car back and forth. Mila got a good purchase as Paolo stepped on the gas but as the car lurched forward suddenly, Mila sat down in the mud. When Paolo got to the other side he waded in and helped her to shore.

"Everywhere I go in this country I seem to end up in the mud," she laughed.

After Paolo finished re-loading, he snapped his fingers. "I know. Let's go to *Puerto la Cruz*."

Mila had heard the name. It was an exclusive resort on the coast, about twenty miles north. The white stucco hotel was tucked behind landscaped grounds, and tranquil fountains. The guard at the entrance gate stopped them. He looked disdainfully at the muddy car and equally muddy passengers.

"What is your business," he asked.

Mila didn't catch what Paolo told him, but abruptly the guard's attitude changed. "*Si, senor. A sus ordenas*, at your service." Paolo drove up the circular driveway and the doorman opened Mila's door and helped her out of the car. She carried her burlap bulsa with the bright orange flowers and followed with all the aplomb she could muster. The bellboy showed them to a small two-bedroom suite with a common sitting area and an ocean view.

"I want to replace the clothes you ruined," Paolo told her. "There's a shop downstairs, please buy what you like. Get a bathing suit and something special to wear for dinner. Just give the sales person the room number."

Mila stood mute. She wondered what he expected in return. As if reading her doubts, Paolo smiled. "Don't worry - it's your enthusiasm, Mila. The way you handle whatever comes along. It's a wonderful quality you have and refreshing after the women in Caracas."

CHAPTER THIRTY-FIVE

▼

Both Painesville and Cumanacoa seemed worlds away. For the first time she experienced pure luxury and reveled in it. Paolo remained as unpretentious as ever, as much at ease in their plush surroundings as he'd been in the muddy waters of the river. In contrast to the other men in suits and ties, he wore his usual outfit of dark slacks and a short-sleeved shirt open at the neck. "The blue linen sheath is perfect for you." His compliment made her feel sophisticated though his praise brought color to her cheeks.

"I resisted the latest tropical evening wear. It reminded me of the children's' *bulsas*," she quipped.

He smiled and studied the elaborate menu. "The grilled fish and vegetables are fresh here, unless there's something else that appeals to you."

Relieved not to be eating arepas, Mila nodded agreement.

"And a bottle of the local white wine," he told the waiter. They ended with espresso and Amaretto cookies wrapped in red and white tissue paper.

"I feel like Cinderella," she said. "Is it midnight yet?"

"Almost. Just the right time to go dancing."

They went from a chic disco club to an outdoor pavilion where they danced in the warm dark breeze off the ocean. Whether the music was disco or tango or something in between, Paolo moved with equal grace. Highlife seemed a long time ago. When she thought of Kwasi she felt a twinge of guilt; what would he think if he knew she'd gone to a hotel with another man?

Paolo seemed responsive to her when they danced, but made no overtures when they returned to the suite. He opened the mini-bar and looked at the array of bottles.

"Would you like a night-cap?" he asked.

"I've had plenty," she said.

"Me too," he agreed. "I guess I'll turn in. It was quite a day."

In a way she felt relieved that he maintained a distance but her sense of pride made her question why.

When school resumed in the fall, she noticed Carlos; a wiry nine-year-old student who remained after the other kids had raced out.

"What is it, Carlos? Looking for homework?" she teased.

"When will we make *bulsas*?" he asked, his expression full of concern.

"We've run out of material. It was only a summer activity." Carlos remained standing, clearly troubled. Mila put down the papers and studied the child's expression. "Is something wrong?" she asked.

"I need to make them," he said. "My father has lost his job. He injured his foot with a machete cutting cane. We need money for food."

Mila had heard nothing about the accident, but Carlos's distress touched her. "I'll see what I can do," she promised.

Paolo had been busy at the bridge site since they got back so it was a relief to see him at the cafe. Mila was incensed by what Carlos told her and didn't know where to turn for help. Paolo put down his newspaper and listened attentively as she poured out the story.

"Yes, the treatment of the workers is very bad in these rural areas. The owners do as they wish without regulations or laws to protect their employees. Juan Gonzales was lucky. He got a week's severance pay."

"Lucky? That's terrible," Mila said. "Is that the way your firm operates too?" She was ready to unleash her wrath on him. The memory of Frances's work for Workmen's Compensation flashed through her mind.

"No. We have provisions for injured workers, but it is our choice."

"There must be something I can do about it. I'm going to talk to the owner. Do you know where he lives? If Carlos worked day and night making *bulsas* he wouldn't earn enough to feed his big family."

"The owner lives in Caracas. He never comes out here. He leaves everything to his foreman. I can get you his address, but he wouldn't be any help."

Undaunted, Mila started a campaign of letter writing. After a month Carlos ran into the class early one morning and thrust a basket of homemade tortillas at Mila. They were wrapped in banana leaves to keep them warm.

"My father and mother...thanks you," he said in halting English and then rushed to add in Spanish, "Papa has his job again."

The irony of the situation didn't escape her. She'd acted with the same unrelenting conviction and stamina as Frances. Frances obtained compensation for her father and the other men injured on their jobs and Mila for

Carlos's father. To her surprise she found herself longing to tell Frances what she'd accomplished.

She waved to Paolo on the way home from school. "Hi," she said, taking the other chair at his table. "Senor Gonzales has a new job driving a tractor. He can do that with only one leg."

He smiled warmly. "All I did was get an address."

"I was wondering," she said. "May I ride with you the next time you go to Caracas? I need to talk to the Peace Corps office; I can't get any answers by mail. Not that I'll get many in person, but..."

"My pleasure," he replied, but you'll have to be on your own." He took a sip of his espresso, "I'm there only briefly on business. Xavier and I are meeting with the president and the governor of this district."

"The president of what?" Mila asked.

"Venezuela." Seeing her surprise he said, "It's a small country, not like the United States. You get to know people."

"Will I be in your way?"

"Not in my way, but I couldn't be with you."

They resumed their camaraderie on the trip, but when they got to Caracas Paolo dropped her off at *Los Pinos,* a cheap hostel where volunteers stayed. She grabbed her small bag and her backpack. "Call me at the office. I have to get back day after tomorrow," Paolo said. "I'll leave a message with the secretary about when I'll pick you up."

Mila felt frustrated by everything: her inability to get answers from the Peace Corps, by Paolo's matter-of-factness, and the fact that she hadn't heard from Kwasi. The Peace Corps office was the same as the last time, the person with the information was away on business. She walked by the department store where she'd bumped into Sam, and since it reminded her of him she sent a postcard: *No fashion show, no dinner, no fun. Caracas isn't the same without you.*

The next day Paolo picked her up. "How did things go with the Prez?" she asked.

"Okay. There's always a lot of haggling and, what is the term? Greasing of the palm on these projects."

They stopped for the red light and Paolo drummed his fingers on the steering wheel until the signal changed. "What did you find out at the Peace Corps?" he asked.

"What happens when I get out, how many stool samples they need, and how soon I get the money they've saved for me."

"Will you teach?" Paolo asked.

"I'll try. I haven't had a letter from my boyfriend. My plans depend on whether he comes back to the States."

"I'll miss you."

"Will you?" Spontaneously she put her hand over his on the gearshift and reached over and kissed him on the cheek. "I'll miss you too. You've been a good friend." He only smiled.

Mila had written Kwasi several times a week outlining her plans and hopes. She assumed he was too busy to write and so she was unprepared for the letter waiting upon her return to Cumanacoa.

Hello Mila. I have received your letters. Drop these daydreams; my plans do not include personal contact with whites. I must fulfill my duties and responsibilities to my family. I am married now and we are expecting our first child. I am unable to correspond as a friend, and suggest you forget writing. Do not try to bring any part of the past to me. Stop weaving dreams.

He signed his name in full: Kwasi Bwacho Achampong.

She read it twice and stared at it in disbelief. The thought of his having children with another woman ripped through her. She remembered Kwasi telling her about this girl he would marry, that women's worth was measured in cows. They'd both laughed. Lying in bed in Ohio he assured her, "I've been gone so many years. She was a child when our parents made the arrangements. She'll be married to someone else by now."

The rational part of her knew he must have tremendous pressure from his family, but rational thought couldn't contend with her pain. She gathered all of his letters, took off his watch and his trade bead and put them into the childhood suitcase she carried with her everywhere. She had forgotten anything could hurt so much.

She knew she was reacting to more than just Kwasi's rejection. Her thoughts were forced back in time: to her loneliness and fear on the boat to America, to the isolation and fear she'd experienced under Frances's control. She wrote a long letter to Pam pouring out her misery. Somehow she taught class, performed her daily routine, but her appetite deserted her and what little weight she had fell away.

The rain was relentless, like a drumbeat on the tin roof, and her room a prison. Outside she sloshed through the streets in the downpour, coming back chilled and damp. After a week she went into a decline that left her weak and unable to get out of bed. Rosa was beside herself and finally sought Paolo, working down river, to enlist his help.

"My God," he said. "How did this happen?" He turned to Senora Munoz. "Get her things together," he said. "I'll drive her to Caracas."

"The Peace Corps," Mila said in a whisper. "They have a clinic."

CHAPTER THIRTY-SIX

▼

Mila woke to see Paolo standing at the opened window with sheer curtains puffed out in the breeze. The room smelled fresh and she stretched, feeling she hadn't moved for days.

"I hoped you'd wake up before I left," he said.

"Where am I?"

"This is my home." Paolo waved toward the sky outside, "*Los Cumulos.*"

"The clouds? Looks like heaven. I don't remember very much."

"You were a very sick young woman. You had pneumonia and were anemic and it will take some time to recover. I thought you could stay here until you get your strength back."

"Have they thrown me out of the Peace Corps?"

"I've cleared it with your supervisor. Right now your only job is to get well."

A small elderly woman came into the room, smoothed her black dress, smiled benevolently at Paolo and dismissed Mila with a nod. Paolo said something in Italian and she said, "*buon giorno,*" to Mila.

"This is Sophia. She'll take care of you."

"She doesn't look too happy about it."

"She'll be okay. She's too old to do much work, but as you can see from her plump figure, she cooks. She came with me from Italy. She thinks of me as a son and protects me from unchaperoned women in my home," he laughed.

The house was a sprawling one story complex, everything simple and cool. The floors throughout were of Italian tile. Most striking was Paolo's art collection, a mixture of antique Italian and modern, predominated by a starkly simple abstract bronze of a mother and child.

In addition to Sophia, there was a full time caretaker who cultivated the tropical plants and trees on the spacious grounds. His wife did the cleaning and they lived with their young son in a small building on the property.

The house stood on a hill above the city; below sprawled numerous shantytowns held together by tin, cardboard and luck and were often swept away during the rainy season. Gazing at the blue sky dotted with airy white clouds high above Caracas, she understood why the estate was named *Los Cumulos*.

Sophia dedicated herself to fattening up Mila while keeping up a constant patter in Italian. The only word Mila understood was *mange:* eat!

The days of recovery left long afternoons to dwell again on Kwasi's letters and she couldn't gather the energy for any new challenges. Instead she was filled with lethargy, her body heavy with loneliness. At the end of the week Paolo came back. "Do you think you're well enough to travel?" he asked.

"Yes, I need to get back and finish the school year before I'm too big to waddle out of here."

"I'd like to show you more of Venezuela before returning you to Cumanacoa. The Peace Corps sends volunteers and then doesn't give them a chance to see the country," Paolo said.

On their last evening Paolo took her to a seaside resort. True to South American fashion of dining late, dinner didn't start until nine o'clock. The hotel was surrounded by jungle and the air was humid. Paolo never displayed a tendency to drink, but Mila watched him order one drink after another all evening; she wondered what made him ill at ease.

She excused herself early saying, "I'm feeling a bit weak. I think I'll take a shower and get some sleep." While she was brushing her teeth, she heard a soft knock and opened the door a crack. Paolo stood unsteadily, smiling.

"Can I come in?"

Mila assumed he wanted to talk over the following day and went into the bathroom to finish rinsing her mouth. When she came back, he was on the bed, propped up on the pillows and he patted a place beside him. The moment she sat down he began kissing her, at first softly then more earnestly. Two years had passed since Kwasi held her, she was lonely, and Paolo was attractive. He removed his clothes and held her next to him. Though he was passionate, he didn't have an erection.

Flopping back on the pillows, he said, "It's the liquor." He closed his eyes for a minute and then started fumbling around with the sheets and the pillows. Taking one of the pillows, he slipped it beneath her nightgown and gently lowered her against the other pillows.

"Beautiful," he said. "You would make a beautiful pregnant woman." He patted the pseudo-stomach and said in Italian, "*Cara mia...cara mia*, my dear, my dear." Some part of Mila's mind was aware that the episode was strange, but not wrong, and she responded with tenderness by pulling him close, over the pillows. He continued to caress her, until she realized he was penetrating her, all the time murmuring endearments in Italian until the act was consummated.

"*Bene*," he said and fell asleep. He left sometime during the night.

He waited for her at the Peace Corps office when they returned to Caracas. She needed to complete her paperwork and when she got back to the car, he put his hand over hers. "I meant what I said last night. You would be a beautiful mother, a good mother. All the little ones in Cumanacoa love you."

Mila felt confused by his uncharacteristic behavior. He suggested that they stop for a late lunch. "You'll leave Venezuela soon," he sighed. "The time has gone quickly."

"Maybe for you," she said.

"Why not stay here? I like traveling with you; I like being with you. Besides, from what you've said you have no reason to return, you have nothing there."

It bothered her that he had dismissed her previous life so cavalierly, although she doubted he'd meant it that way. Her thoughts flashed back to her Naturalization and Frances's words. She felt offended by his accusation that she had nothing and corrected him, and Frances in her mind: she had nothing of her own - yet.

Paolo stopped at an intimate Bistro on a narrow out-of-the-way street.

"I meant every word I said to you and I have something to say that I ask you to consider carefully." He ordered a bottle of wine. "To a new life," he toasted, looking at her seriously. "I want you to marry me."

"Marry you! But we're friends."

Paolo burst out in rich deep laughter. "That's one of the reasons I love you," he said. "Of course we're friends."

She was afraid she'd stammer if she opened her mouth. It was tempting; it would solve so many problems. In fact it sounded too good to be true. There was a missing link - something she didn't understand.

"I'll think about it," she said.

His eyes sparkled. "We will make beautiful children," he said.

When they started the climb to Los Cumulos she wondered why she hesitated, why she didn't jump at such a chance. He was wealthy, well connected, and intelligent, she enjoyed his company, but love? No. She'd loved Kwasi with all her heart and she didn't have those feelings for Paolo. She loathed the thought of being dependent, obligated to someone as she'd been with Frances. If she said yes it seemed she'd have everything, but at the same time, still nothing of her own.

Before they got to the front door it was flung open and a man in his mid-fifties burst out. Seeing Mila he quickly lost his welcoming smile. He was dressed in tight trousers with a wide black belt. His loose fitting artist's smock had floppy sleeves and the tie was undone leaving a wide expanse of gray chest hair. If Sophia had been unfriendly, this man was outright indignant.

He spoke in Italian, and Mila assumed he was asking about her. After a rapid exchange, Paolo turned to her.

"This is Victor," he said. "A friend from Italy."

With a heavy accent, Victor said, "I live here…on and off."

Paolo corrected him. "Victor has an apartment downtown, not far from his shop. He decorated the house."

Victor had made drinks from passion fruit and vodka and Sophia had made a tray of antipasto and pinched Mila's arm still encouraging her to "*mange.*" Victor cast black looks in Mila's direction.

"Shall we have a game of cards after dinner?" Paolo suggested.

Mila sipped her drink and looked from Paolo to Sophia to Victor. The drinks made her giddy and she started to giggle, and then said, "Fellini." All heads turned to her. "This is a movie by Fellini."

Paolo and Victor exchanged looks and finally seeing the scene as Mila had, burst out laughing. Sophia looked at all of them and shook her head.

Her future seemed formless, but she made one decision and wrote to Pam, *I can't come back to Ohio. Everything would remind me of Kwasi. I think I'll stay on the west coast. Paolo suggested San Francisco.*

In August Mila stood at the ticket counter, Paolo beside her moving her bags as the long line moved up.

"You don't have to stay with me," she said.

"I know."

After she got her gate pass and seat assignment they went into the bar where it was quiet. There was still over an hour before take-off and they ordered a Cinzano. She folded the napkin around her glass and watched the condensation from the ice moisten it. She hated the dead time before leaving, the uncomfortable contemplation of separation.

Breaking the silence Mila said, "Maybe you'll visit me in San Francisco."

"Yes, perhaps."

"It seems like I've been saying good-bye all my life and it never gets easier," she said.

"I want to say something to you," his face was serious with concern. "Your family in Finland. Have you ever tried to get in touch with them?"

"I don't remember their names. I have some letters from a lawyer who might know how to get in touch with them if he's still alive."

"You should try."

"Perhaps someday. We'll see."

He held both of her hands in his. "There's something else I want to say - about your future. The help you gave Juan Gonzales impressed me. Your arguments were cogent and you enjoy helping people. Have you ever considered law as a profession? I think you would find it a different challenge from teaching; something more suited to your intelligence."

"Law? I don't think so. It reminds me of someone I dislike."

He laughed. "We all know lawyers we dislike. Caracas has an excellent law school," he said and smiled, "if you change your mind."

The loud speaker announced the flight in Spanish, then in English and German. "*Arrivederci, cara,*" he said. "I'll miss you."

Her eyes clouded. "Thank you - for everything," she said "Even for the advice."

His laughter followed her, like a warm breeze.

CHAPTER THIRTY-SEVEN

▼

Ferry from Helsinki to Aland
June 1971

As Anders's career flourished, his marriage floundered. Tarja resented the very job she'd urged him to get and he questioned the wisdom of her latest pregnancy. This vacation was their first in three years, an attempt to re-establish the closeness of their earlier years.

Tarja had miscarried the previous winter and refused to believe that the roads were closed by ice and he couldn't travel the three hundred miles from Vassa. Even when he arrived with a huge bouquet of flowers, rare and costly in winter, she remained cool and distant and continued to reject him. She accused him of caring more for business than for his family.

He didn't want to face the problems in his marriage; he was exhausted from working non-stop. As his migraines grew more frequent and his temper flared more easily, he worried about ending up back in the sanitarium. The ferry was filled with people, yet he felt alone, remote.

Two guards marched in front of the iron gates at the President's palace, while next to it the Swedish embassy glowed golden in the summer sunshine. He never tired of the view and the rhythm of life around Helsinki's harbor. Before they boarded, Tarja and Rauha bought enough provisions in the harbor market to feed another twenty people. The flurry of housewives still buying the morning's catches of fish and fresh produce continued; florists picked over flats of flowers; tourists bought locally made baskets and carved wooden art.

Anders pushed away from the railing with both arms and stretched, try-ing to unkink the knotted muscles in his neck and left shoulder and hoped the holiday would give them a chance to patch things up.

He and Martti had rented a large cabin for their families in a sheltered cove on the southwestern coastline of Aland where the best fishing spots were. Aland, the largest of the islands in the archipelago between Finland and Sweden and a favorite summer vacation spot, always made him think of his grandmother Ahlgren. When he was a few years younger than Patrik she had shown up unexpectedly, bringing money for Lars and toys for him and Martti. She said she'd come to make amends for not keeping Lars after his birth and tell him she'd learned too late he never saw a penny of the money she sent for his care, but she'd followed his life and had worried about him when he ran away at fourteen.

"You were ashamed of me and your sin in conceiving me, your bastard child." Lars spat out the words and threw her money on the floor.

But Anna Ahlgren held her ground. "I've inherited the family ship build-ing business and my life has changed. I can do for your son what I couldn't do for you. Let me take Anders home to Aland and educate him."

His voice was icy. "Why should I salve your conscience?"

Kaija begged him to listen, but it was useless. "Think of Anders, forget your pigheaded pride. Allow your mother to make our lives easier." But Lars wouldn't relent and his grandmother never came back, even when Lars died.

Anders visited her in an old peoples home before she died, and although confused she remembered him. "It looks like you turned out all right," she said.

Anders couldn't help wondering, what if...what if... What if Lars hadn't refused surgery? What if Kaija hadn't sent Mila away? What if he hadn't been crippled with tuberculosis? What if Tarja hadn't gotten pregnant, would they have married? He shook his head, it did no good to think about *what ifs*. Right now was the reality of his life.

Usually the sea calmed him but now, gazing at the horizon, at the sky and the receding shoreline, he felt disquieted, his mind a storm of thoughts. As a child he'd imagined himself Captain Ahlgren, manning the wheel in heavy waters, fighting the waves, righting the ship. He wished for a ship of his own. He knew he romanticized, but the sea was like a siren song. How wonderful it would be dealing only with nature's primal elements. Even now, if he went to a seaport, he wandered the docks watching the sailors work, noting how they removed their caps to wipe their suntanned foreheads - dreamy looking, as if they knew secrets, their eyes full of wisdom from long hours of reflec-tion.

As the ferry pulled away from its mooring, nine year old Patrick stood at the railing comparing the model sailboat he and his father had made with the boats gliding around the granite rock islands. He adjusted the lines on the sails of his ship accordingly.

"Dad, there's the fort. Let's go there again. I want to explore Suomenlinna Island and check out the old cannons."

"We'll go when we get home," Anders said.

"That's what you always say, but we've never gone back," he said, his mouth turning down like his mother's.

"Okay," Anders said. "The day after we get back we'll all go, maybe have a picnic."

"No," Patrik said. "Just the two of us. Mom is always angry."

Anders felt a stab of pain fearing he caused Tarja to deflect her dissatisfaction of him onto their son. "Just the two of us. Okay. We'll let mom do something she'll enjoy too," Anders said.

"Promise," Patrik insisted and stuck out his hand following their long-standing custom of shaking hands when they agreed. Anders looked down and ruffled his son's unruly red hair, even though he knew Patrik considered himself too old for head rubs. The physical connection helped stave off a feeling of melancholy. He would do better for Patrik, he thought, better than he had for Martti or Mila; he'd help him become whatever he wanted to be.

"Can I have some money for a coke?" Patrik asked. Anders reached into his pocket and held out a handful of change that Patrik took before running off.

He was debating when to tell Tarja he was planning to make a short trip to Halstahammar, a small town outside Stockholm, to visit Harold Hedlund with whom he'd lived during the war. Shortly before leaving on holiday he'd had another note telling him Harold's last wish was to see him, he was ill, near death. From nine to twelve he'd led a normal boy's life thanks to Papa Harold and Anders wanted to see him one last time.

Tarja would question why he'd go to visit someone who had hurt him so much as a child. She'd view it as another abandonment and even though he didn't want a fight, he was determined to go.

By twelve Anders was thin, but tall for his age, and with the trust of a child, regarded the Hedlunds as his family. That brief spate of an ideal boyhood ended when he contacted tuberculosis visiting one of the Hedlunds' elderly relatives.

He spent the next year in a sanatorium north of Stockholm with the disease that still plagued him. He was pronounced "non-infectious" and assumed

Papa Hedlund had come to take him home. Instead, a stranger stood before him, shifting from foot-to-foot, not looking him in the eye.

"Mrs. Hedlund thinks it's too dangerous to have you in the house," he said. "She's afraid for Trudi."

"I can live in the room next to the sauna," Anders said. "I won't go near Trudi."

Harold Hedlund looked at him sadly. Anders tried to convince him. "Please let me stay," he begged. "I don't want to go back to Finland. I'll get stronger. I'm not sick anymore. I don't have any infection. I'll work hard," he promised.

Hedlund shook his head in firm decision, and Anders, stricken, tightened his jaw refusing to give way to tears. Anders' innocence ended that day. When Hedlund offered him his outstretched hand, Anders refused to shake it.

There was no plane to take him back to Finland. Instead, Harold Hedlund bought him a train ticket, handed him a package of warm clothes, food for the trip, and money for Kaija.

During the trip up the coast of Sweden to the tip of the Gulf of Bothnia, to Tornio on the Swedish border and down the length of Finland he relived the rejection. He vowed never to become dependent again on another. He would never trust anyone. He would rely only on himself.

He was roused from his thoughts by an insistent tug at his pants by five-year-old Riina. "Where is Patrik? I want him to play with me. Auntie Tarja and Mamma are making sandwiches in the cabin and I'm supposed to stay below deck, but there's nothing to do." Riina, standing with the sun in her golden hair, with her never ending curiosity, and quickness of speech was so like Mila, Anders felt his eyes sting with sudden tears.

"And do you understand why?" he asked.

She sighed. "Yes. They're afraid I might go through the rails, but I'm too big. I tried."

"What if you'd fallen in the water? That's dangerous," Anders scolded. "We don't want to lose you."

She put her hand in his. "Don't be angry. Will you tell Papa?"

He tried to look stern. "Promise me you won't do it again."

"I promise," she said solemnly. "Can we shake hands like you and Patrik do when you promise?" They shook hands and then Anders scooped her up into his arms and gave her a ride to the cabin as she tried to catch the wind with her hands.

After lunch Riina napped and Patrik worked on his sailboat, while Tarja and Rauha relaxed in the afternoon sun. Anders and Martti stood at the rail watching the small wooden houses drift by, each on its own rocky granite island. A woman stood fishing from a short pier.

"Kaija should be here instead of riding the bus to Moscow," Anders said. "It's a long hot ride just to pay her respects to Stalin's grave; it's nonsense."

Martti scowled. "Nonsense to you maybe, not to her. You refuse to see the benefits of communism."

"You know she'd enjoy the fishing here, but I guess she only wants to fish with Aleksis so the two of them can drink together. Besides, the years haven't made her like children any more."

"It was a good opportunity for her. A number of other people from the Socialist Workers' Housing Complex are going, so she won't be alone. Aleksis's busy with the job at the airport. I've got to get back to it too," Martti said. "Some of us have to work for a living, not just drive around the countryside."

Anders tried not to rise to the bait. "At least Aleksis wouldn't be caught dead in the Soviet Union - or maybe I should say that's the only way he'd be caught there." Anders smiled at his joke. "I can't understand how you allow yourself to buy into all the lies the Soviet bosses dish out. They're busy rewriting their history however it looks best for them and the masses muddle along as they always have." Anders chided him. "You're too smart to fall for that brainwashing."

"It's easy for you to pass judgment since you're a District Manager with a big capitalistic company. No wonder you don't understand the plight of the real working man any more."

"What about you? You've been promoted to chief foreman," Anders said.

Martti gripped the railing, his back rigid. "That's different, the building sector helps the people. They need homes."

Anders raised his voice. "And people need things to put in those homes." He caught himself, and put his hand on Martti's shoulder, then threw up his hands in an 'I give up' gesture. "I want this to be a good trip. We're on vacation and neither of us is going to change our views. Let's forget about politics."

"Forget about politics? Life *is* politics. You'll never understand that." Martti spat into the water and walked away.

Life was perverse Anders thought, the better their respective lives grew, the further apart he and Martti grew.

Tarja looked up from her book when she heard their loud voices and after a moment joined Anders. "You've got to go easier on Martti," she said.

"Communism is his religion. Lars and I both failed him as father figures; we failed to provide him with answers, so he turned to Communism."

"His heart is in the right place," Tarja said. "Remember when Patrik was born and you were still in the hospital how he took time off work to help me?"

"Yes. I let you both down, I guess. I know he needs approval," he said, "we all do."

Tarja patted his arm. "Fish. Play chess. Be brothers," she advised. "Mend the fight. You've been through too much together to let something drive you apart."

"And does that go for us?"

There was a wistful tone in her voice when she responded. "That's more complicated," she said.

The afternoon wind made Tarja shiver and Anders put his arm around her, drawing her next to him. "You are a fascinating woman," he said, "and still the sexiest I've ever known."

For once she looked pleased, and the color rose in her cheeks.

"Sexier than your secretary?" she teased, but there was an edge to her question.

"I've never loved another woman as much as I love you. You grow more beautiful each year."

Her voice grew deeper. "Then why don't you stay home more?"

"I'm here now," he said.

"That's what makes it difficult," Tarja said. "In the past, when we were together we were truly together no matter what we were doing, dancing, talking, making love. You were there a hundred percent; the rest of the world was blotted out. Now, I never feel you're really there even when you are. I don't know you anymore."

"Each time I pack and unpack I feel part of our marriage break away," he said. "I intend to make up for all those lonely nights when I couldn't hold you. Let's see if one of the cabins is empty. We can talk and rest."

"Rest?" Tarja laughed.

Tarja welcomed him on his return from Halstahammar and Anders was grateful. Visiting Harold had been the right thing to do. He was telling Martti about the building boom in Sweden as they drank beer and grilled the day's catch while Tarja and Rauha chatted about the children when Tarja mentioned that Riina could walk to school with Patrik when she began kindergarten in the fall. Rauha had tried changing the subject but Martti interjected.

I'm sending Riina to school where she can learn to speak Russian," he said flipping the fish onto the plates.

Anders couldn't help himself. "What? You're going to let them brainwash Riina too? Next you'll be enrolling her in the Communist Youth Program. Can't you at least let the child make up her own mind when she's older?" He could hear the demanding tone of his voice and knew Martti's reaction would be hostile.

"I didn't interfere when you sent Patrik to that Finnish-Swedish speaking school where he's learning the language of our former oppressors. Talk, talk, talk. You do that real well. Well, I'll tell you something for a change. I'm moving my family when I return to Helsinki. I've found my own place. I'm fixing it up. Now you can expand into our space."

Later that evening when they discussed the blow-up Tarja suggested, "Rauha might be able to change Martti's mind."

"Rauha won't fight him on this. She doesn't agree with his politics, but she knows there's no changing Martti's mind when it's set on a course of action." Anders shook his head. "I'm angry with Martti and angry with myself. It's like the civil war in America, brother against brother - history repeats itself. I've allowed politics to divide us. I'm sad, sad we've grown apart, sad I'm losing my best chess opponent."

The honeymoon bliss with Tarja lasted only until they got home from their holiday. Like an alcoholic who fell off the wagon, the time away from the bottle hadn't stopped the escalation of the disease. He felt guilty in the face of her accusations because in spite of its pressures, he loved his work, the freedom of travel, learning the technology, the panoply of business.

When he returned from his first trip, Tarja raised her voice in condemnation. "Why bother coming home at all? I'm tired of running a hotel."

Anders dropped into a chair, tired, longing for peace. "Can't you stop feeling sorry for yourself long enough to think about me?"

"I'm sure Barbo is proud of you," Tarja shouted.

From the beginning Tarja hated his secretary and Anders's loyalty to her, but Barbo taught him the paper ropes, the ins and outs of surviving in a big firm and she continued to do so. Barbo was always there with words of encouragement and sympathy. He appreciated the fact that secretaries frequently did more than the men they worked for. When he started he hadn't known a contract from a racing form. His mistake was praising her in front of Tarja. Tarja constructed a scenario of his deceit and deception and believed his travel wasn't business but pleasure.

He grew weary of her accusations. Her endless haranguing left a canyon between them that deepened with each quarrel. He longed to share his success, to ask her advice, to pour out his doubts, but a barrier stood between them. He no longer knew how to please her.

"Nothing I do makes you happy," he said. "What do you want? When it's time for the baby, I'll be home; I promise. I won't be gone again."

"It's too late. Don't bother." Tarja said. "It's not your baby."

CHAPTER THIRTY-EIGHT

▼

San Francisco, California - 1971

The basement apartment near Stern Grove was perfect: a small kitchenette, bathroom, and bedroom/sitting room. The sparse furnishing included a bookcase and a desk; several windows faced the backyard to keep her from feeling claustrophobic.

Miss Wylie, the owner, was all business. "I keep it clean and expect you to too. I don't want anyone moving in with you, no over-night boyfriends and no smoking or loud noises. I expect you to respect my need for quiet. The rent is due on the tenth of the month."

Mila nodded in agreement and handed her the check.

After the steamy summers in Venezuela, the first few weeks she'd felt chilled to the bone, but now after too many days of warmth, she longed for the fog like a native. The steep hills, the odd buildings that at first failed to enchant her she now found charming.

Those first weeks she learned there was no reciprocity of teaching credentials between Ohio and California. Pam was enthusiastic about Montessori teaching methods, but they required two years of training. Mila decided if she had to go to school that long, why not an additional year for law school? She did well on the Law School Admission Test, and sent for her transcripts. She could just eek by with her mustering out money from the Peace Corps and a student loan. The private universities were too expensive and she decided on Hastings Law School.

During Orientation, the new students were asked why they chose law school. Her younger, idealistic classmates answered that they sought justice, truth, righting wrongs. Only a few honestly admitting they wanted to make money. The word "autonomy" popped into her head. She recognized that her primary motivation was to be her own boss and acknowledged to herself that her role model, at least in the law, was Frances.

When students were asked whether there were any cases they would not defend, without hesitation she'd answered, "I wouldn't represent a child abuser or a child molester. Never."

The professor raised a fuzzy gray eyebrow. "Interesting," he replied, "but what if you worked as a public defender and that was your job?"

"I'd pass on the case. There are a lot of people in the PD's office."

"But don't you think everyone is entitled to representation? Aren't you judging the person's guilt yourself, Miss...Robertson?"

"If I felt my own prejudices prevented me from doing my utmost then I'd be required to pass on the case. We've all heard there are too many lawyers in California. It shouldn't be a problem. I'd do a conscientious referral," she answered.

Again he raised his eyebrow as a slow smile turned up one side of his mouth. "Fair enough. Anyone else willing to put himself or herself on the line?" he asked. There was not.

The Greek of Contracts, Torts, Constitutional law, Real Property, made her fear her learning skills were too rusty. She felt like the proverbial accountant who glued: *debits on the left, credits on the right*, in his top desk drawer. She wrote over and over: plaintiff equals good guys; defendant equals bad guys, except that didn't always prove true.

She spent all of her spare time in the library in a never-ending grind of study. She felt alienated by the age difference between herself and her classmates and remote from the natural merging of the younger students. Some Friday nights she joined the group that went to Hamburger Mary's, south of Market Street, and then headed for the Stud Bar in the same area. Friday night was Motown dance night; no partners were needed. The place hung with warm bodies. Dancing was her main outlet and San Francisco was a great town for walking.

Since returning from Venezuela, she wrote often to Zeke and corresponded infrequently with Frances although her hope that law school would be a common ground for them proved to be true to a degree. Frances wrote that her law practice was getting to be too much for her to handle by herself and hinted that if Mila agreed to return to Ohio they could practice together.

During the first hectic months of law school, she failed to phone the number on the business card Sam gave her in Caracas. When she finally did phone she learned that he was assigned to London.

"When did he and his wife leave?" she asked.

"His wife? As far as I know he's a bachelor," the secretary told her.

Mila hoped he hadn't been hurt with Mae, but the news that he was single cheered her and she bought a postcard with the Golden Gate Bridge and wrote: *Dear Sam, Great… I move to San Francisco and you flee to London. Don't lose your head in the Tower.* She put her address at the bottom.

Professor Graham was in love with the United States Constitution, and they got off to a bad start.

"He lectures caressing a green pamphlet of the Constitution." Karen Allgood, her study partner, told her. "He worships at her feet."

"*Her* feet?" Mila scoffed.

"Yeah. His greatest regret was not being one of the original framers. He calls it a visionary document of freedom."

"For whom?" asked Mila.

The first week of class Graham pontificated about the beauty of the language in the Declaration of Independence, "All men are created equal; they are endowed by their creator with certain unalienable rights," he quoted, "among these are life, liberty and the pursuit of happiness."

His unbending manner, the way his finger stabbed the air, reminded her of Frances and with precipitous abandon Mila held up her hand, interrupting the flow of his words.

"The fallacies in just the first two lines of the Declaration of Independence are enough to cast doubt on the Constitution. Although the sentiments expressed therein," she said employing the legal lingo, "are noble as far as they go, being applied to white, land owning men, and since the Supreme Court has been comprised almost expressly of such men, what can you conclude about justice and equality? Only one thing: all people are *not* created equally, nor do they receive justice equally."

"Ms. Robertson, is it?" Graham drawled out her name. "Are you familiar with the Amendment in the Bill of Rights, which grants you the freedom to speak," he paused dramatically as his voice rose on the last phrase, "without the full facts?" The room was silent. "Well, perhaps then, you're familiar with the Amendment which prohibits slavery? The amendments giving one and all the vote? NO?" He thundered. "If and when you've mastered the Constitution, perhaps then you'll be in a position to debate merits."

His challenge made it necessary for her to learn the finer points of Constitutional law. She developed her own outline as she went along so that she understood it in depth. She employed aggressive learning rather than passive rote reading and word of her outline got to Professor Graham who called her into his office.

"This is impressive," he said. Even more surprising was his invitation to become his teaching assistant during her second year. She was prepared to refuse until she learned that she would be paid.

Her latest challenge was Torts and the issues centering on Negligence and Causation. Her notes and outlines were spread out on the kitchen table. She was plowing through the material for the thousandth time attempting to understand Proximate Causation and whether a person's actions were the proximate cause of the suffering parties' injuries. It seemed deceptively simple, but there was intervening causation. She felt agitated and got up from the table to pace her tiny kitchen. Prosser and his torts made her furious. And, where in the hell was the happiness guaranteed by the Constitution now? She resented how hard she had to study, especially over Thanksgiving weekend. She wished Karen was there, at least they could study together. She wished she had the money to fly back to Cleveland to be with Pam and Colin. A small turkey that would be food for the rest of the weekend was roasting in the oven and she indulged herself by buying a pumpkin pie, her favorite. The sun was shining for a change, and she was filled with the injustice of being indoors, studying, and alone during the holiday.

It felt like she couldn't stuff one more word into her brain, that her eyes couldn't absorb one more fact, that it was impossible to remember one more case reference. She felt like a blotter black with soaking up ink.

She grabbed the heavy Torts book and flung it with all her might right out the kitchen window breaking the glass, then collapsed on the bed, going somewhere deep inside herself, her sobs rumbling only to be muffled by her pillow. The words were stuck somewhere inside but wanted to come out: *Aiti*, mother. *Don't leave me alone.* She longed to be held as mothers held children in books and movies, mothers who smelled like soap and loved her, like they were supposed to do. They weren't supposed to ever send their young daughters away.

She sat up and blew her nose. Why now, after all these years? She thought she'd buried those feelings. She dialed Pam's number but there was no answer. She wanted to hear a familiar voice, Zeke, but what if he doesn't answer? Slowly she dialed the number, and then hung up. She could hear her heart thump. Hell, she thought, what can I lose? It's Thanksgiving, I don't want to be alone; I want to be with family. She took a deep breath and dialed the number again and heard it ring, one, two, three, four times. Then she heard Frances's voice.

"I'm studying Torts," she began. "I'm having trouble understanding causation."

"What specifically?" Frances asked. "Does it have to do with the injury? Is there something that intervened? Ask yourself questions about the order of all intervening events."

Frances cited recent cases for Mila to read. "Keep trying. You'll get it. Law school's hard, but a lot more interesting and rewarding than college." Mila felt heartened, but Frances couldn't resist adding an admonition. "You should have taken my advice and attended Ohio State. You're stubborn and have to do things your way." For once she tempered it. "It will get easier with time," she said.

Mila hung up and sat on the edge of her bed feeling better hearing Frances's clipped answers to specific questions. It was ironic, Mila mused, that the factual, impersonal nature of law allowed them a semblance of communication.

She posed a question for herself. Was her *real* mother the proximate causation of her injury, her misery, her loneliness? If Frances were a kind and nurturing intervening cause, would she have felt abandoned? No, if Frances had wanted me, I don't think so. *Curious*, yes, but *abandoned*, no. But, the situation is what it is. The law likes remedies, but the law wouldn't get involved in a case like this. Was there a remedy? If so, most likely the statute of limitations had long expired.

Was she understanding torts? Was the remedy finding her mother? But now the turkey was burning and wind was blowing in the broken window.

CHAPTER THIRTY-NINE

▼

Christmas loomed. Karen invited her to spend the day with her family, but Mila declined deciding a family setting would exacerbate feelings of being an outsider. Tucked amongst the few Christmas cards was a letter from Pam. She and Colin were buying a house and Pam was involved in establishing a Montessori school in Cleveland Heights. She urged Mila to come for a visit.

Classes let out early on Friday for vacation and she decided to walk downtown and look in shop windows. Gump's and Podesta Baldacci captured a spirit of the fantasy she carried in her mind of what Christmas should be like and inspired her to buy a small tree and some decorations to take home to her apartment.

The phone rang just as she plugged in the lights and she nearly knocked the tree over thinking for a moment she'd done something to the electricity.

"I've been trying to get you all afternoon. Where have you been?"

She didn't recognize the voice, and snapped back, "What possible business is that of yours?"

"I understood you were a *friendly* American and might be willing to show me a good time."

Realizing with delight it was Sammy, she asked, "How much are you prepared to pay?"

"How do you bill your time?" he asked.

"I cost more than you can afford."

"We'll see about that. Meet me in the Lobby of the St. Francis Hotel and wear something sexy and red so I'll recognize you."

"Do I have to bathe?"

"You can do that here."

"Are you serious?"

"Quite. I'll send a cab in an hour."

He was waiting in the lobby when she came through the door. It seemed natural to watch him walk toward her, as if they'd seen each other a few hours earlier instead of three years ago in Caracas.

It felt like some invisible gears clicked into place and settled. Everything around them seemed to freeze as they stood staring at each other. "We have reservations at *Le Bebe Agneau* at eight."

The restaurant had touches of a French Bistro. Edith Piaf's songs of love and pain and loss served as a backdrop while they caught up on their lives since Caracas. Mae had chosen medical school over marriage.

"You don't seem heartbroken," Mila said, stirring her coffee and savoring the creme Brule.

"It fizzled out when I got back from Venezuela and my assignment to London added the finishing touches."

"How long will you be there?" Mila asked. "Do you like it?"

"I'll be coming back to the States next summer," Sam said. "London is a fascinating city, trite but true. I've seen a little of the continent, Paris and the Italian Riviera. I'd like to travel more, although I do plenty for Latham & Beck. London can get pretty gray and dismal during the winter."

It seemed like they existed on two planes. They were holding one conversation with words, another with their eyes. Sam's dark curly hair was no longer unruly and she found herself wondering if it was as soft as it looked. Where had the broad shoulders come from? His body had filled out. She wondered what it would feel like to kiss him, to have him hold her. She hadn't been involved with anyone for months, maybe longer. She'd lost track. Slow down, she warned herself, don't get carried away, but her stomach was already queasy with nervous excitement.

"What about you?" he asked. "Law school? How do you like it? Anyone in your life?"

"Law school is harder than I expected and I feel older, uncomfortably older, like part of my brain has atrophied. I thought seriously about going back to Venezuela. There was a man there who wanted to marry me, but I'm here - not there."

The waiter brought the check and after paying Sam took Mila's hand. "Come on. I have a surprise for you. I'm making restitution for missing our Senior Prom," he said helping her on with her coat.

"You're not going to fall down and break your leg again?"

"No, I'm taking you dancing. I've found a place that plays music from the fifties."

"Your dance classes paid off," Mila teased after they'd danced their way through one long set without stopping. "You must have practiced."

"I had to learn all the social graces so I wouldn't embarrass myself," Sam said. "The corporate world, or at least Latham & Beck, expects a well rounded executive. It's a little like the star system at MGM under Samuel Goldwin."

"Follow the yellow brick road?"

"Yeah. Something like that."

It was close to midnight and the music turned romantic. They were swaying to Blue Moon, Mila's arms around Sammy's neck and his arms around her waist while the vocalist sang ...*and then you suddenly appeared before me, the only one my heart would ever hold...* Sam pushed her away far enough to look into her eyes, ...*and when I looked the moon had turned to gold...* he kissed her.

He picked up his key at the desk and the elevator carried them to the twenty-second floor. His suite had a view of Union Square and a cable car clanged by on its way up Nob Hill. Rain was beating on the window; she looked down at the city lights refracted through the drops, then kicked off her shoes and tucked her feet underneath and sat on the small sofa. She wanted to go to bed with Sam, she knew, but she wanted it to be more than a casual encounter. Sam handed her a glass of wine and sat beside her. They touched the rims of the glasses. She put her hand on his arm and his pulse seemed to beat through the sleeve of his shirt, racing, and every beat ran through her fingers and up her arm and through her body. They put their wine glasses down and Sam gently pulled her up so she was standing in front of him, his large hands resting on her shoulders.

The room began to sway and she felt her stomach rising in protest, her head spinning. "Where's the bathroom?" she asked, already feeling the beginning nausea. She put her hand over her mouth and Sam rushed her to the toilet.

He stood beside her, rinsing the towel. Finally she stood up. "I'm sorry," she said. "I just can't drink and I've been studying so hard and then the excitement of seeing you, not that you make me sick to my stomach," she said, grinning slightly.

"It's all right," he assured her. "You'll feel better if you shower," he said. He undressed her slowly.

"I do feel better," she said, as he helped her into the tub and adjusted the shower temperature. He undressed and climbed in beside her, soaping her. His long limbs moved with ease, all traces of teenage awkwardness left behind. When he touched her breasts and traced their roundness, her breathing stopped, her nipples hardened. His fingers were gentle as he explored her body, caressed her and drew her tightly against him. He dried her, rubbed her hair with the towel until it no longer dripped, and carried her to bed.

"You need a good night's sleep," he tucked the covers around her. "Sweet dreams," he said and kissed her closed eyes.

The next morning, slowly waking to the sound of rain, Mila felt exquisitely complete, as though returning to life after a long sleep. The sight of Sam beside her seemed perfect and natural. Without opening his eyes he smiled and pulled her close.

"Where have you been all these years?" he murmured into her hair. "What have we been doing away from each other?"

CHAPTER FORTY

▼

They'd made no commitments to the future except for a tacit under-standing that when he returned from London they would be at a juncture of decisions. They put off saying good-bye until the last second; they couldn't tear themselves away from each other. Sam had promised his parents he would spend his last week with them, but kept phoning them with excuses until his visit to Painesville was reduced to just three days.

Dear Sam,
You make me feel wanted. Even though you are stronger than I am, you don't shove me around. You laugh at my jokes. You touch me. You walk with me. And there are other reasons too numerous to mention, even if I could think of them.

Their letters crossed in the mail sounding like a continuing dialogue, one voice imitating the other. Mila put his on the refrigerator door with magnets, knowing it by heart.

My Darling,
I will try to tell you why you are so important: You don't mind my jabbering about my work, my concerns. You don't mind when I boast. You smell nice. You have erotic breasts and you kiss like an angel.

Their letters linked them and served as a chronicle embracing every sub-ject and corner of their daily doubts and successes. Her ears seemed able to hear the mail drop through the walls of her apartment.

My dearest,
You might think that through the press of events certain things are unnoticed;
that when life and obligations, real or imagined, make everything bigger than it
is, that I would forget. But let me say this: I remember the red blouse that clung
to your body that you wore at my request. And I remember talking of love and
passion and raspberry tarts.

And Mila wrote back:

And of feeling comfortable while kissing the animal warmth of your neck.
And I remember joy.

Sam was like her alter ego where her studies were concerned. She could
hear his voice as she sat in class or poured over case law. He assured her she
would breeze through her final year and pass the Bar Exam on the first try,
and though she failed to take such a cavalier attitude herself, from a continent away the power of his words made her feel safe, loved, and less apprehensive.

Each letter was a visit that turned like the facets of a jewel, catching a
new light of insight and depth. She unfolded the familiar tissue thin tablet
paper on which he wrote to her with the same thrill she felt when the dozen
long stemmed roses arrived on New Years Eve with the reminder at midnight
to drink the champagne he left, that he would be doing the same and promis-
ing the following New Years they would be together.

What you do to me is: You let me be myself. I feel free to tell you anything. I
know I can expose all of my emotions and fears and inadequacies, and you will
understand. You hear what I'm saying. You let me say stupid things – and don't
then jump on my ego. You let me feel intimate with you.

She put a pot of water on and made herself a cup of tea. His quiet confidence in her gave her hope, and great happiness, and desire, and love. He
made her happy to be alive.

Mila was enmeshed in preparing for moot court when Paolo's letter
arrived saying he would stop in San Francisco the following week on his way
to New York on business.

They'd kept up a regular correspondence and any other time she would
have been excited by the news, but between pressure over trial preparation
and thoughts of Sam, she let out a sigh. She wouldn't dream of hurting Paolo,
and arranged her time to accommodate his visit.

She wrote a quick note to Paolo saying she would meet him, and a longer
one to Sam in which she mentioned Paolo's visit. She studied for another

hour and walked the three blocks to the mailbox to revive herself with some fresh air.

She'd forgotten how handsome Paolo was until he walked through the doors of Customs. He wore a black cashmere sports jacket and a camel's hair topcoat over his shoulders. On someone else it might have seemed pretentious, but on him it assumed a sophistication and naturalness that made heads turn as if a celebrity had walked by.

"Finally," he said after they made their dinner choice and sipped their Campari and soda. "Study agrees with you. Your eyes seem even more alert and bright, but you seem pale from too much time inside, and thin from spending more time studying than cooking," he said.

Mila laughed. "I need Sophia around to tell me, *mange! mange!*"

"Those were happy times," Paolo said.

Mila watched him smile, thinking his eyes seemed sad.

"How is she?" Mila asked.

"Sophia? Much the same."

"And Victor?"

"Ah! Victor. A different story altogether."

"Why? Did one of his clients object to chintz bedspreads or Florentine wall sconces?"

Paolo gave a mirthless laugh, more polite than amused.

"Victor is the reason you left Italy and broke with your family, isn't he?" Mila asked.

"Yes. It seems easier to talk about it here," he indicated their surroundings, "away from Caracas."

Mila put her hand over Paolo's. "He's more than a friend, isn't he?" she asked softly.

"Yes," he nodded.

"I always knew, somehow, although it wasn't until I left Venezuela that it became clear to me."

"We were children when we became friends. Sophia is Victor's mother. She worked for my parents and we lived in a villa outside Sienna. Victor's interests besotted me. He was older by ten years and I was flattered by the time he spent with me. When my parents found us together they were appalled and could think of nothing but the scandal. They sent me as far away as possible hoping it was only a stage I was going through. I used their liberal allowance and sent for Victor and Sophia."

"Sophia knew?"

"We've never addressed the subject. She'd been a surrogate mother to me, and she dotes on Victor, so it all seemed perfectly natural."

"But your parents? They must be pleased you've succeeded."

"It is typical of our strata of society to speak only superficially. They want an heir to carry on our name and fortune." He reached for her hand, "but that is not the reason I proposed. I proposed because I love you and nothing would give me greater joy than to have a family with you. You are the kind of woman who would be a partner in her husband's life. There is an excitement about your enthusiasm for living. Not many women would join the Peace Corps and live in Cumanacoa. Your interest in my work and your willingness to go into the field with me was wonderful."

"There must be many acceptable women who would marry you."

"Many of the educated women in Venezuela are lesbians because the men are such pigs and treat them so poorly."

"You'll never know how close I've come to taking you up on your offer," Mila said.

"Why didn't you?"

"I care about you very much, but it would never have worked out. And, now I'm involved with someone I knew from high school, of all things."

"I hope he appreciates you."

"I think we appreciate each other. You'd like him."

"Perhaps you're right," he said shrugging lightly. He rearranged the salt and peppershaker. "What is the news of your family?" he asked.

"My brother, Zeke, gave up on college. He's a policeman and seems happy. As far as my parents, I have hopes of establishing a better relationship with them now that I'm almost a lawyer. Perhaps I'll get some respect, if not love. She's a lawyer too, you know."

"No, *cara*. I mean your family in Finland."

Mila shrugged and flipped her hand in a motion of dismissal. "I'm sure they've forgotten me. They've never tried to reach me and since my mother sent me away, I can only assume it was because she didn't want me. I used to hope I'd hear from them, but… it's been so many years."

"Perhaps we both need to try harder," Paolo said. He looked reflective. "Time slips and shifts like sand."

Their farewell was bitter sweet. "I'll call you the next time I'm here on business," Paolo promised. He gently touched her cheek. "Keep writing," he said.

"Maybe I'll come down for a vacation after I pass the Bar."

"You're always welcome." He turned and waved after he went through the checkpoint.

Mila won her case in moot court as well as finishing her finals and rewarded herself by going out for a beer with her classmates to celebrate. Two pieces of mail were waiting for her. One showed a return address of British Air that she assumed was an advertisement. She ripped the envelope open and found an airline envelope and inside a ticket from San Francisco to London. The second piece of mail was a small brown package with the admonishment: OPEN THIS FIRST. Inside was a tape. Her hands were shaking when she pushed the play button but when she did the room broke into a smile. Sam was giving a rendition of Blue Moon and when he got to the line… *the only one my arms will ever hold…* his speaking voice interrupted the lyrics. "Do you realize a blue moon is a rare occurrence – two full moons appearing in one calendar month – as rare as us falling in love. I should be doing this in person, but failing that, let me tell you that I, who usually can't plan more than one day in advance, walk around making plans for trips five years from now – with you. Fly to me. Marry me."

Her return telegraph read: *My darling, Yes, yes, yes.*

CHAPTER FORTY-ONE

▼

Helsinki, Finland; Cleveland, Ohio
1980

Patrik came home after midnight to the house on Saimaantie Street where he lived with Anders since his parents' divorce seven years earlier. Like his father at eighteen, Patrik was tall and broad shouldered, but unlike Anders he was powerful and muscular from years of playing sports. He found his father propped against the sofa, gasping for breath, unable to talk, pointing to the telephone across the room.

Patrik wrapped him in a blanket, grabbed the car keys off the table, and carried him to the car. "Don't die on me," Patrik said. "*I'm* taking you to the hospital. It'll take too long for the ambulance to get here."

The car skidded along the icy road, but traffic was sparse and they made good time. Oblivious to the snow and wind swirling around him, Patrik kicked the car door closed and shifted the bundle in his arms for a better hold. The night was a dark void except for the lights along the walkway which lit the bony planes of Anders's face in ghostly shadows, his limp body dangled in his son's strong arms as the doors of the emergency entrance swung open. The startled receptionist stared at the young man with wild red hair streaming behind him like a Viking of old offering up a human sacrifice.

Patrik's voice boomed with authority. "This is my father. He is very sick. Get a doctor and make him better."

It was three days until Anders opened his eyes to see his old friend and lung specialist, Dr. Rikkala, sitting beside his bed.

"Ahlgren, you're one lucky guy. You have less than one lung but I didn't save your life at Meltola to have you die of something preventable. Even a cat has only nine lives. If you don't stop smoking, you'll be dead before you're fifty." To emphasize his point, he added, "If you don't care about yourself, think of your boy. He wouldn't leave your side. When he wasn't at school he was here, checking up on you. He needs you."

"You smoke more than I do," Anders answered.

"I don't have pneumonia and chronic asthma," Rikkala said. "It's nothing to joke about. I'm ordering a three-month leave of absence from work effective immediately. Go to the Canary Islands. There's a good Finnish Health Station there and you more than qualify. It may be the only thing that can save you. Two other doctors have agreed with my diagnosis. Take the time off and get away from this arctic weather. It only adds to your problems."

"I'll think about it," Anders said.

Anders was released two weeks later and for the first time in memory was without something to do. Patrik brought him books from the library and they played chess, but Anders remembered what it was like to be young and was reluctant to ask him to stay home. He insisted Patrik continue working with his dog sled team for the upcoming competition.

Tarja called and the sound of her voice made him nostalgic. Being off work gave him time to reflect on the failure of their life together. He would never love another woman with the same intensity. The one time in his life he'd been drunk was because of his jealousy over Tarja's affair with a colleague from work.

During convalescence his thoughts returned with regularity to his little sister. It was hard to believe she would be thirty-six. She must be married by now; maybe she had a family. His inquiries and letters to Mrs. Robertson in Ohio had gone unanswered, but as the days tumbled one after the other in static regularity, his resolve took form.

Martti came to visit from Turku, on the west coast of Finland where he now lived. Although Turku was less than two hundred miles away, it might have been a thousand for the distance that had grown between them. Martti was less interested in their chess game than in bragging about the success of his own construction firm and their time together remained strained by the chasm of divergent views.

"I've made up my mind to go to America and find Mila," Anders told him.

"Why would you bother with her after all these years?" Martti said. "Why waste your money on a wild goose chase? She's never written to us. Not even to our mother."

"It doesn't matter," Anders answered.

When he told Kaija of his intentions she crossed to her bureau, opened her dresser drawer and withdrew some papers. "Mrs. Robertson is as good a place to start as any. This is the last address I have for her," she said. "I don't know if attorney Arnerio still has an office. You could try. He might have more information." Then she picked up the picture of Mila taken shortly before she left and hugged it to her chest surprising Anders by her display of emotions. As a child he'd longed for her hugs, but other than a rare pat on the head she'd always been preoccupied with her own concerns. He rarely hugged his mother, unable to show her the affection she craved without feeling counterfeit, but he crossed the room and held her. She felt fragile and he felt her heart beat erratically against his chest.

By May Anders felt strong enough to travel, but the long plane ride left him weak. He arrived in Cleveland, rented a car, got an Ohio State map and checked into the Hilton Hotel near the airport where he attempted to sleep for a few hours but he was too restless and tired to relax. He showered and changed clothes to get rid of the stale smell of the airplane.

He liked the casual attitude of the hotel staff, efficient but without the formality of the better hotels in Finland. The receptionist, like most Americans, spoke rapidly and at first Anders's mind blanked on the words, but when she discovered he was a foreigner, she spoke not only slower but louder.

His phone was ringing when he returned to his room. "This is the receptionist, Mr. Ahlgren. We were just talking downstairs. I've located a lawyer by the name of Frances Robertson in Painesville at the same address you gave me. Do you want me to dial the number for you?"

Anders's palms were damp as he held the phone. "Not tonight, it's too late. I'll place the call in the morning."

During the night he decided surprise would be better, not to phone but to confront her face to face. The next morning was like Finland at its summer best. The air was soft and balmy, the Chevrolet responded to his every touch.

On the plane he'd read that Cleveland once claimed a thriving steel industry, but at present was economically depressed. The area had a rundown look. He remembered European news coverage of riots in Cleveland years before in which they'd emphasized the downtrodden status of Negroes in America. He wondered if the Negroes were regulated to this area of town since he'd never seen so many in one place. The receptionist at the hotel was charming and helpful and didn't seem downtrodden. He enjoyed the soft cadence of her voice. He wondered what the truth of their life was in America. He'd ask Mila.

Finland remained a conservative society where racial bigotry existed. There were few blacks in Scandinavia, although Anders had encountered a few African students in Helsinki. Outside of seeming exotic in an almost total white population, he found they were no better or worse than anyone else.

He'd always wanted to explore the United States and he decided to take Route 20 rather than the freeway and traveled northeast from Cleveland through the heart of a number of small towns: Euclid, Willowick, Eastlake, Mentor; the foreign names sounded exotic. The number of small businesses and gas stations he encountered between towns surprised him, so unlike Finland where you drove for mile after mile on straight, level roads through endless pine and spruce forests before arriving at a crossroad with the inevitable two gas stations.

Painesville seemed idyllic, better than the descriptions he'd read about small towns in America. As he drove around the park in the middle of town he noticed the old fashioned bandstand. It wasn't any different from the ones in Europe. He wondered if they too had Oompah bands.

He arrived at lunchtime and stopped at Isley's. He'd read about ice cream parlors. He wondered if Mila had sat laughing with her teenage friends in the red leather booths. He pictured her, still speaking quickly and persuasively like she had as a small child. Perhaps she too was a lawyer. It didn't matter. All he wanted was to see her.

He asked directions when he paid his bill and now stared at the name in heavy black letters: Frances L. Robertson, Attorney at Law. Maybe Mila was here. He took a resolute breath and knocked firmly on the door.

Anders smiled and held out his hand to the elderly heavyset woman who answered and took his hand automatically. He assumed she was a housewife earning money working as a receptionist until she spoke.

"I am Frances Robertson," she said and transformed into another person. "How may I help you?"

"Anders Ahlgren. I am here to see Mila." A fleeting expression of unease flicked across the woman's face.

"Come in, Mr. Ahlgren. Have a seat over there." She indicated a chair on the other side of her desk and seated herself behind the broad expanse of wood. He noticed the determined set of her head in her fleshy neck. Her eyes had grown darker, her thin line of mouth set firmly below her imperious nose. Only her bountiful hair wrapped around her head in a braided coronet gave any softness to her features. He felt wary. His skill at assessing people told him to let her lead the conversation.

"I'm afraid you've made the long trip for nothing," she said. "We could have handled this by phone."

Anders let the statement hang in the air. "You failed to reply to my letters about my sister."

"I have no proof of who you are, sir. You can't expect me to give information to a stranger."

"Mila has two brothers; I am one, Martti is the other. Mila was born 1943, twenty-eight day of June, in Sweden. Her father is Lars Ahlgren; her mother is Kaija. Mila came to America in 1950 on the ship GRIPSHOLM."

"This information is available to many people. It's public record."

Anders didn't respond, instead he opened his briefcase and placed Mila's birth registration from Sweden, his own passport, and a packet of Frances's letters to Arnerio in front of her.

"It is obvious I'm not making myself clear in English," Anders said and switched to Finnish.

Frances's eyes flashed and her mouth twisted downward, but she stared at the wall for a moment and spread her hands over her desk. "Marja Leena has chosen not to keep in touch with her father and me," she replied in flawless Finnish. "We made sure Mila had a college education. Afterwards she taught school in Cleveland and then in Venezuela. She's had her difficulties, but there's only so much one can do to help. The rest is up to the person." Her face took on a look of sad resolution. "We've heard nothing from Marja Leena for some time," she said.

"When was that?" he asked.

There was a slight hesitation. "She was in South America in the Peace Corps."

"What is this Peace Corps you mentioned?"

"It's a volunteer organization. Frances opened a file drawer and rummaged through it. "Here is an article about her." Frances handed him the Peace Corps newspaper clipping.

Anders studied the photograph of Mila in three quarter profile. "I would still recognize her. She's beautiful," he said. "She still has the mischievous way she looked as a child." He studied the article. "Shopping Bags and Food for Cumanacoa Children Program," he read aloud, and then said, "It has been a number of years since she sent this to you. Surely you've had other information from her."

"The occasional postcard only - that's how we learned she'd gone to Venezuela in the first place. She sent a card to our son. Later she sent another card saying she would probably stay in Venezuela after her term with the Peace Corps was over. She was vague, something about a job. She hasn't been forthcoming since she left home. We've felt sad that after high school she basically left us for good."

"It seems strange she'd send you an article if she severed contact with you. May I see her postcards?"

Frances rummaged through the top drawer of her desk and handed him a postcard addressed to Zeke Robertson. It had a picture of sailboats racing outside the Caracas Yacht Club. The writing was similar to Kaija's, free, and flowing. "*Dear Zeke, My Peace Corps days are drawing to a close. I'm thinking of staying here as I've been offered a job as translator for an engineering firm. Once I know what's going on I'll write to you. Maybe you could come down and visit - the sailing is great! Love, Mila.*"

When he finished reading, Frances said, "We didn't keep the others, since there wasn't really any information."

"Can I speak with Zeke? Perhaps she wrote to him again."

"We have no home delivery, so I'd know if there had been others. The mail comes here to my office."

Anders felt something wasn't right. He noted the tense set of the woman's shoulders. He persisted. "Perhaps the Peace Corps knows where she is."

"The Peace Corps is a government agency located in Washington, D.C. I've attempted to reach Marja Leena through a woman friend whom she lived with when she left home, but to no avail."

"How can I reach this woman?" Anders asked.

"She's moved. Remarried. No one seems to know where she is. As I told you, Marja Leena had problems."

"What problems?"

"She chose to live with someone her father disapproved of. It made problems for our family. We hoped she might straighten out."

"You mean a man? She's a grown woman. Was he a drinking man?"

"He was an African, a black man. Apparently it didn't work out."

"Are you sure? Perhaps she married the fellow," he said. "Then she might be teaching school under a different name."

"It's doubtful. We would have heard." France's voice was edged with impatience. "I'm sorry I can't help you, but I have clients coming and a great deal of work." She stood up.

Anders remained seated. Perhaps he was simply disappointed, but he felt there was something slippery about her answers and her sympathy wasn't sincere. "I'm staying in town a few days. I'll visit the police department and see if they have any information. I'll contact you tomorrow."

"The police would have contacted us," Frances said. "You must try and understand. This is Mila's way. She is very stubborn and spoiled; used to having her own way."

Had something happened to Mila in Venezuela, or before that? Without more facts his mistrust was speculation, but he felt uneasy.

"If anything changes - what was your address in Finland again?" she asked.

Anders felt deflated, as if all the air had been sucked out of his lungs. On the drive back to Cleveland he had to pull to the side of the road in a deep spasm of coughing. A few droplets of blood stained his handkerchief. If he couldn't find Mila, it was time to stop fighting.

CHAPTER FORTY-TWO

▼

Mila sat daydreaming about her honeymoon. It had been eight years since her flight to London to marry Sam. She gave a silent thank you to whatever cosmic force had brought him back into her life. In her wildest daydreams she couldn't have imagined the fulfillment and love she knew as his wife.

Mila looked out her office window at the Bay Bridge, reflecting on her life. If there was any flaw in their lives it was the amount of time Sam traveled. She dreaded the nights he came home and announced he was being sent to Saudi Arabia, or Japan, or some other far off place. She was expecting him back from Africa today.

It was a given that as far as his career, it would be suicide if Sam refused to travel. Latham and Beck wanted only indentured servants of the highest caliber who were judged not on years of selfless service that often ruined their health, but on their last successful project. The ones who didn't go along with the program watched their careers shrivel. She'd seen them at social events, poor cripples hanging on by a thread. Their earnings kept them hobbled and groveling to maintain their mortgage payments in expensive neighborhoods, and keep their children in private schools.

Sam and Mila lived near Golden Gate Park in the same flat they moved to after their marriage. It was a large Queen Anne with lots of big and comfortable rooms. They went house hunting periodically.

"It's a hell of a lot of money for something without land around it," Sam remarked after such expeditions. "Back in Ohio we'd have a couple of acres."

"Don't you think Thomas Wolfe was right when he said you can't go home again?" Mila asked.

"It depends on what you're going back to."

Mila enjoyed the intellectual challenge of the law, was overly prepared when she went to court, hard pushed to relinquish control of even the smallest details of her cases. She was a perfectionist, and a successful one, but the trade-off was the hours required in preparation and worry over details that woke her during restless nights and littered her sleep with concern.

They'd been so busy with their careers that it came as a surprise when Mila discovered she was pregnant a year after they were married. Her reaction was the same as it had been with Kwasi; the thought of bringing a child into the world flooded her with anxiety and panic, and without consulting Sam she went to her gynecologist to discuss abortion.

"My dear," the doctor said, "You say you are happily married, so why would you even consider such a step? Does your husband agree?"

"It's me," she blurted out. "I'm so afraid I won't know how to be a good mother. What if my husband and I both died? I couldn't bear the thought of someone else raising our child," a shudder went through her, "our baby in the hands of strangers who didn't love or protect it," and to herself added, "or even worse, in Frances's hands."

"I have a feeling this little baby is insistent about being born," he said, placing a hand on her shoulder. "I don't usually say this to my patients, but I've known you for a few years now and I think this baby is important for you. You have time, please consider your decision carefully."

When she told Sam she was pregnant his reaction was so joyous, the thought of hurting him by admitting her visit to discuss abortion faded. Now, almost six years later, she wondered herself how she could have considered such a thing, she still shuddered at the thought of Emily without a mother.

She remembered looking at Emily when she was born, searching her looks, this miracle child that carried the secrets of her own beginning, her genes, her ancestry. From the love she shared with Sam they created this perfect human being. If her birth family ever saw Emily would they comment about resemblance to distant uncles and aunts, to grandparents? Her mind stretched to capture the past that slipped away like sea spray washing back into the retreating surf. A wisp of pine, a snatch of a lullaby, the strong hand of an older brother.

For the first time in memory Mila knew a sense of family and belonging. There was no need to be afraid to love and she loved Sam and Emily more than she thought it was possible to love. And she was awed by their love for her.

Mila picked up the enlarged snapshot framed on her desk taken during Christmas vacation in Lake Tahoe. Sam and Emily had made angels and in the snow wrote: we love you, Mommy.

They lived a quiet life. When Sam was home they spent most of their weekends in the park. Sunday afternoon they took long walks, packed sandwiches and listened to concerts, or took Emily to the aquarium. Now that she was old enough, they rode their bicycles. Mila smiled thinking of Emily's reluctance to remove her training wheels. When Sam suggested taking them off she shook her blond curls and told him, "Mommy said I'd do it when I was ready."

Mila knew she indulged Emily. She'd insisted on hiring a Hispanic baby sitter because she felt they were loving with children. While one part of Mila was grateful another part felt frustrated, worrying about Emily's childhood slipping by while she sat in her law office. Emily loved Ampara who picked her up from Montessori each day and drove her home to a waiting snack and an afternoon of games. Mila felt a stab of jealousy when Emily ran to Ampara after a fall, or brought school art projects to Ampara as gifts.

Her law career was flourishing; although she knew it took too much of her time and a vague sense of apprehension seemed to perch on her shoulder. It was worse when Sam traveled. During those times she woke from dreams in which she was scared and angry. The fear of death began to haunt her. She rose from bed shaken, paralyzed by her fears. Why now? She wondered, when my life is so complete. Why am I terrified that it will end, that it's too perfect to last?

She shouldn't leave work early, but justified her defection on the grounds that Sam was flying home after being gone for three weeks in Khartoum.

She'd been feeling the stress of the office before Sam left and her appetite had fallen off. It seemed he was forever expressing his concern that she was losing too much weight and working too hard. She remembered the look on his and Emily's face when she lashed out, so unlike herself. "Stop nagging. I'm not hungry." She compounded the episode by a reluctance to make love.

"I'll be gone for a month, honey," he whispered, and then asked in a Groucho Marx voice, "Wanna have a little fun?"

"Do you have to kid about everything," she asked, presenting her back to him like a wall of ice.

She made it worse the following morning when he asked her to drop him off at the airport. "I'm preparing for an important trial, but of course your job comes first."

As Mila started the approach to the Bay Bridge and home, she asked herself for the hundredth time: *what's happening to me*? She felt the tightening of her neck muscles and rolled her head from side to side trying to relieve the tension.

As the cars slowly moved toward the tollgate, Mila edged to the lanes that would feed out to the middle of bridge traffic. She crossed the bridge morning and night and realized that more and more she was drawn to thoughts of disappearing in the water below. She drove in the inside lanes to avoid swerving to the edge, wondering if the car could break through the guardrails and plunge into the waters of the bay. It was irrational, but she fantasized what it would be like, the first bracing coldness, the slow sinking of the car, an inability to open the door as she plunged to the bottom and gasped for the last bit of oxygen. Her dark thoughts frightened her.

She forced the images out of her mind and began planning the things she had to do before she and Emily picked Sam up from the airport. Thank God he would be home for Emily's birthday. She looked out over the Bay where a passenger ship headed in to dock and rolled down the window and breathed deeply to control her nausea.

O good woman, tell me, tell me,
Which way do I go to get there?
What direction should I travel?

Kalevala, Runo 34, Lines 113-115

CHAPTER FORTY-THREE

▼

Mila thought about bolting. The door was black lacquer with neat gold letters: F. Rubenstein, M.D. No reference to psychiatry. F. Rubenstein, the similarity in names caused Mila to consider another therapist. She picked a straight-backed chair in the waiting room, furnished in soft dark colors and hushed with an Asian feeling of tranquility. The lighting was soft too, inviting quietness. Mila tried to relax and compose herself.

"I'm Fran Rubenstein. Please come in Mrs. Lammi."

Mila was relieved to see that she looked nothing like Frances and that she called herself Fran. Dr. Rubenstein was small, smartly dressed in a beige woolen dress with a silk scarf caught with a garnet and pearl pin. Her hair was black with wisps of gray at the temples, short and neat. Mila noticed her hands. They looked gentle. Her dark eyes were deep set and her lips were generous and soft. Her smile reminded Mila of Pam. There was a hint of mischief, and Mila felt an intrinsic trust.

"You told me on the phone you're obsessed with driving off the bridge. That you are unable to make decisions at work. That your appetite has disappeared and you feel you're driving your husband away. What do you think is happening?

"I don't know." She gave a short uncomfortable laugh. "I don't know what it takes to make me happy. I have an interesting career and I'm successful. So is my husband. Our daughter, Emily, is a happy, delightful little girl."

Mila felt dwarfed in the upholstered softness of the chair, like a small bird trapped in a bog of brown velvet. Her eyes reflected the fear of being cornered. The groan that came from her mouth seemed to belong to someone else, then, a voice sounding hollow like a distant echo, protested.

"I can't talk. I can't do it. I'll talk later. Not now." She was coming unglued, powerless to help herself. Her body alternated between feeling loose as Jello or rigid as stone in an attempt to hold herself together.

Dr. Rubenstein sat patiently as Mila averted her gaze. After a moment the doctor handed Mila a box of tissues to dry the tears falling like small waterfalls.

Mila gave a short nervous laugh and wiped her glasses before putting them back on.

"You said your daughter's seventh birthday is coming up. What were you like when you were that age?"

Mila's throat convulsed and her mouth wouldn't open. She looked at the doctor in terror. Fran Rubenstein returned her gaze with eyes that invited confidence and an air that she'd heard everything and nothing would shock her.

"Please help me. I can't breathe."

Dr. Rubenstein waited and then in a kind voice said, "Why don't you tell me what happened?"

"It was the first week of school," Mila began. "I was dressed in a red corduroy jumper and white blouse with puffy sleeves. I even had new shoes and white socks. I loved my new clothes. But I was frightened because I couldn't speak English, only Finnish. Everything was different."

Mila sat on the edge of the cushion frightened, ready to run. She considered just that before deciding to continue. "The woman heaped a bowl full of Cheerios and started screaming at me to finish eating so she could get to work. I tried to please her. My stomach rebelled. I vomited on my clean blouse and she grabbed me and dragged me by the arm to the bathroom. I stood over the toilet bowl, Cheerios streamed out of my nose and mouth. She rammed my head straight into the toilet bowl as far as it would go. I remember my eyes and mouth were wide open. Up and down, up and down, endlessly. I tried to breathe. I choked."

"Finally, she stopped. I had bumps on my head from hitting the sides of the toilet. I cowered on the tiles, trying to hide, to get away from her. She stood over me with a bucket and threw cold water. I remember crying for my mother. I remember her saying my mother was never coming, that she'd sent me away because I was no good. The limp ribbons in my hair hung down my back. I smelled of urine and vomit all day."

"Where was your father?" Dr. Rubenstein asked.

"He wasn't even my father yet - they hadn't adopted me. I'd only been there a few weeks. He'd gone to work, my brother Zeke was only three and just sat there. Terrified I suppose." She could feel her voice growing quieter, without inflection, as she told the story her voice faltered and then stopped.

There was a long silence.

"That was a terrible experience for you. You must have been utterly terrified," Dr. Rubenstein said.

"My head felt so big, like a balloon blown past the bursting point. I hurt everywhere and there was blood from the side of my face and my knees were skinned from being slammed on the floor, but she sent me to school anyway. I felt so alone," Mila said, "so alone in America."

"How does talking about this make you feel?"

Mila hesitated and in a soft voice said, "I've never been able to tell anyone. It was too embarrassing and humiliating. First, that it happened; second, that someone would do that to me; and, third, it's a shameful thought that I could allow such a terrible thing to happen. I felt I must have done something to deserve it, but then I couldn't figure out what it was."

"A child has no control over what adults do. How old were you when this happened?" Her voice was factual.

The ordinary question of her age was a comfort to her shredded emotions. "I turned seven in June and arrived in America in August. My mother had told me how wonderful America was, but I just wanted to go home. I missed my family and I was scared all the time."

"How did you get along with the rest of the family?"

"All of the externals were in place so we looked like a happy family. I grew to love my brother, Zeke, and was comforted by our dog, Mr. Peepers. I think Dad was as intimidated as the rest of us. He never did anything to hurt me. He never hit me."

"But he was a parent - your father, who was supposed to protect you. How did that make you feel - that he didn't?"

Mila thought for a long time and started slowly, searching for how she felt. "Disappointed. And angry. It made me angry when he didn't help. He was a weak man. I liked him at first, when I was small, but I learned not to count on him to protect me. I can't imagine Sam not doing everything in his power to protect Emily."

"No one knew what was happening to you?" Dr. Rubenstein asked.

"Oh, yes, other people had some idea, but not the extent. I tried to tell my Aunt Helen, and the minister. A teacher at school tried to help. The woman exercised financial control over her siblings and held a position of power in the community. Everyone was afraid to go against her."

"I'm afraid our time is up," the doctor said. "I wish we could go on, but... I would like to work with you. It seems we've already gotten started."

There were six people in front of Mila as she stood in line with her grocery basket. She went over her list to make sure she'd remembered everything this time and feeling relieved she stared at the bulk candy thinking perhaps she would duck out of line long enough to get Sam and Emily some jelly bellies. She opened her purse to make sure she had enough money, then decided she would put it on her Visa card, but remembering this was a heavy month of purchasing, thought it might be better to keep the cash and write a check. Her mind grappled with the problem of what to do. She was sure those around her knew how hard she was struggling with the problem and she became more agitated because she couldn't make a decision. She pushed the cart out of line and rushed from the store and sat in the car grasping the steering wheel with white knuckles.

She managed to get home and dial Sam to pick Emily up from school but she remembered little until she heard them open the front door and call for her and she realized it was dark out. Emily exploded through the bedroom door and bounced onto the bed.

"Mommy, I did all of my problems perfect today, and we got ice cream on the way home to celebrate," she said.

Sam's forehead was wrinkled with worry. He sat on the edge of the bed and took Mila's hand without speaking, then bent to kiss her while Emily continued to tell Mila about every minute of her day, and ended by asking, "Why didn't you pick me up from school?"

"Mom's not feeling well, Pumpkin. How would you like it if we order a pizza tonight?"

Emily looked at her mother before her excitement erupted. "Mom says..."

"I think that's a wonderful idea," Mila said and watched the look of joy break across Emily's face.

"And a coke?" Emily asked.

It wasn't until Emily was in bed and they were sitting in the living room that Sam asked, "What happened today?"

Mila tried to explain. "I can't make decisions anymore, and you know that's all you do in the law. I'm scared and so tired. Everything is spinning out of control. I've talked to a Dr. Rubenstein today, the therapist I told you about. I liked her." Mila hesitated, "I'm considering going on medical disability. She said I'm going through a severe depression."

"What can I do?" Sam asked.

"Hold me. I'm scared."

Sam cradled her in his arms. "We can work this out together," he said.

"My life is finally together, but I'm falling apart," she said into his shoulder.

"Maybe that's why you feel safe to let go of some of the past. I knew things were bad for you in high school but I was too young to know how to do anything about it."

"You were a lifeline even then," Mila said. "You were a friend when I didn't have any."

"I'll tell the office I'll be unable to travel for a while. Would you like me to ask my mom to come out and stay? She could help with Em," Sam suggested.

"Let's try to handle it ourselves for now," Mila said. "All I know is, I don't want to live like this, feeling so down. So hopeless."

PART THREE

▼

1980 - 1982

I am waiting, I am thinking
To arise and go forth singing,
Sing my songs and say my sayings
Hymns ancestral harmonizing....

Kalevala, Runo 1, Lines 1-4

It occurred to me...
In my brain it rooted firmly
To return there to my birthplace...

Kalevala, Runo 34, Lines 113-115

CHAPTER FORTY-FOUR

▼

Mila saw Fran Rubenstein for four months, twice a week, and had been back at work for three weeks.

"They gave me another paralegal so now I have four, plus a secretary, but my caseload is the same. They also agreed to a thirty hour work week, but my first week was forty and it's escalating, although I'm still not up to my usual sixty."

Mila twisted on the couch trying to get into a comfortable position. "Not that much has changed."

Dr. Rubenstein was quiet.

"And before you ask, I've told the senior partner." They smiled at each other and Dr. Rubenstein nodded. "And your husband sounds supportive."

"He's my rock. We've been talking about our future. We'd like to simplify. Sam doesn't want to travel so much. He's interested in environmental law and has a friend, Bob Miller, from law school that practices in Cleveland. He's offered Sam a partnership."

"Cleveland? How would you feel about moving back where Frances is?"

"Maybe I'm deluding myself, but I could live anywhere if Sam and Emily were there. Besides, Sam's parents are getting older and his Dad's in poor health."

"You're talking about everyone but yourself. What about your career?"

"I'd like to get away from litigation. I've always thought I'd like to teach law, since I was a Teaching Assistant in Constitutional law. Litigation requires a total commitment in time. I want to spend Emily's childhood with her. She'll be seven soon."

"And Frances?"

Mila shrugged. "Frances offered me a job while I was in law school. I had fantasies in which she finally accepted me. I don't believe that will ever happen and I could never risk anything that might harm Emily."

"Hold it," Dr. Rubenstein said. "You told me that in law school you said you wouldn't take child abuse cases, and you obviously think Frances is a child abuser. Why would you even consider letting Emily around her?"

Mila fidgeted on the couch, and moved a pillow behind her back.

"Are you remembering something?" Dr. Rubenstein asked.

"A Saturday, a fine Indian summer afternoon. I was ten. Before Frances left for her law office, she told me to weed the garden. Zeke and Donald were upstairs painting a bedroom."

Mila grew quiet remembering how warm the sun felt as she lay on the ground by the flower garden in the back of the house with Mr. Peppers nestled next to her. "My cousin Annie had loaned me a new Nancy Drew. Usually I kept a vigilant ear for Frances's return, but I was absorbed in finishing my book and I was startled when I heard the car door slam."

She paused.

"I threw the book into the bushel basket and tossed weeds and flowers alike in after it. I knew she was angry when I heard the screen door vibrate. She came in the backyard. A heavy wooden hoe lay next to the basket of weeds. She loomed above me, hands on hips. 'You haven't done a damn thing in the house. There's dirt on the living room rug and spider webs hanging all over. What have you been doing all day, madam? I'm off working and the rest of you are taking a holiday."

Mila interrupted her narrative to explain that Frances always talked that way, and her own voice had grown flat as she continued to describe the scene in a factual voice without emotion, drawing inward rather than making the event dramatic. On some level she was appalled by her memory of that day, and flooded once more with the feeling that somehow she brought out the worst in Frances.

"Am I the only one who knows how to work? No one helps me. I have to do everything: shop, cook, clean. I'm the one who takes care of all the details, lends the money, keeps idiots out of jail, and protects the workers. *I'm* the one who *earns the money*. Who helps me? Not Donald Robertson. That's all beneath him.'

"It felt like an electric current ran through me," Mila said. "Her voice became more strident, spit hit my cheek. From the corner of my eye, I saw her grab the hoe and then everything happened at once. Mr. Peppers whimpered and started to bark. I curled into myself as I felt the first whack of the wood handle, a terrible pain ran down my lower back. I was sprawled face down in the dirt. She kept hitting me, and hitting me." Mila hugged herself, remembering. "The pain was terrible."

"Did your father do anything?"

"Yes, he yelled from upstairs for her to stop and then he ran outside. I remember Zeke was with him looking scared. Dad was pulling her away, telling her she was killing me. I could hear his voice and see his feet when he bent down to touch me and his hushed voice when he said 'I think you've knocked her out. My god what if you've killed her?' I remember wondering if she'd be sorry if I died. If she'd go to jail.

"Dad put his hand on my shoulder and asked me if I could hear him. I thought if he was there I'd be safe for the moment because his voice was full of concern. I wanted to make him feel better so I struggled to answer and tell him how much it hurt. Zeke stood crying next to him and Dad told him to go back inside and play with his trains.

"Didn't they call a doctor?" Dr. Rubenstein asked.

"No. I heard Dad say they should, because I looked so bad. I could hear Frances in the distance still breathing hard. 'Quit pretending,' she told me, 'and get into the house.' I was so used to obeying, I tried, but I was unable to move."

"Dad made another half-hearted attempt, 'Ulle, what if it's serious?' But she was in charge again. 'We don't need that kind of trouble. No ambulance. She'll be okay in a few minutes.' He covered me with his shirt and stroked my arms. She bent over me and told me to move my legs. I moved one leg a little, but I thought I'd pass out. All she said was 'See. I told you she was all right. Pick her up and get her to bed.'

"Dad did tell her he didn't think they should move me, that they might make it worse, but she was intractable, and insisted I was all right."

"You mean you never saw a doctor?"

"No, and I think I knew by then that I couldn't depend on Dad to stand up for me. He was weak and I was learning there was no one I could trust. He tried not to touch my back when he carried me upstairs. There was no position that wasn't painful. I wanted to lie on my back or curl up, but any movement felt like a knife had been thrust into my spine. Dad put me on my side and brought a warm washcloth and washed the dirt off my face. I asked him if I'd be all right and he looked away without answering. The woman brought me milk and cookies. Dad gave me aspirin and sat with me soothing my covers and told me to get some sleep. I asked him not to leave. Instead he put his hand on Frances's shoulder and urged her toward the door telling me he'd check on me in a little while.

"I was trying to sleep when the door creaked open and Zeke tiptoed toward me holding one of his stuffed animals. I stayed home from school for a week."

Dr. Rubenstein asked. "Were you left alone?"

"They hired an elderly neighbor from Scotland, Mrs. Eves. She came a few hours each day and fixed lunch. Before she left for work each morning, Frances brought a clean nightgown and a pan of water for a sponge bath and told me not to show Mrs. Eves my back. I couldn't stand being touched by her. While I was alone during the day I worried about being permanently paralyzed and forced to stay at B-B all my life. Whenever she was around I could feel myself floating above the scene in the bedroom. I heard her words beat against my temples but the other girl, the girl who hurt, retreated into her tunnel."

Mila's feet were flat on the floor, as if to ground her. Her body had grown still. "Just when I think I'm getting better, more of this stuff comes out."

"How long did you use the tunnel?" Dr. Rubenstein asked.

Mila thought, her voice barely audible. "At least a few years. I thought maybe I was crazy."

"Your tunnel was a safety device, a form of protection, something we see when people are abused or tortured literally beyond endurance. They depersonalize themselves from what is being done to them. What made you stop using the tunnel?"

"I became worried I was spending too much time in it. I was retreating into it even when nothing bad happened. I thought someday I wouldn't come out of it and my family in Finland wouldn't be able to find me. After that I escaped more into reading and started planning how to murder her."

Dr. Rubenstein laughed out loud. After a moment Mila joined her.

"I can hardly wait to hear how you planned to murder her," Dr. Rubenstein laughed. "She was a very sick woman."

Mila felt a weight had been lifted. "Yes. She was."

Therapy was a slow process. Mila often felt that for every step forward she took two steps backward. It took time to grow comfortable with each hard won insight. She'd never grown comfortable with those silent moments at the beginning of the session. Usually she felt awkward, hesitant about starting, but not today.

"Lately in my thoughts the image of my seven year old self alone on the boat to America is sharp as glass. Then my images fade into the shadow of a woman and try as I might, I can't get the face into focus. I'm sure that face is my mother. I remember during my second year of law school, I think it was Thanksgiving, I was trying to understand the concept of Negligence and suddenly I thought of my own mother, wondering if her sending me away, abandoning me, was the proximate cause of my misery and loneliness."

Dr. Rubenstein looked up from her notes.

"Then I did what I always did until I learned differently here, I shoved the memory and my misery and my anger away until that black box exploded." Mila sat straighter, as if coming to a conclusion. "I want to find my family in Finland."

Dr. Rubenstein nodded. "Yes."

"I'm ready," Mila sighed. "All those years of hearing *your mother sold you, your mother's a whore, and no one wanted you.* How could anything I find be worse than that?"

Dr. Rubenstein echoed herself - "Yes."

When Mila returned to her law office she asked her secretary to hold all calls, took out a piece of letterhead and began to write.

Dear Mr. Arnerio:

I hope you will be able to help me in my search for my Finnish family. Your name appears on a number of letters, which apparently were written at the request of a Kaija Ahlgren. I believe she is my mother...

CHAPTER FORTY-FIVE

▼

Mila felt adrift when she discontinued her weekly therapy sessions after fourteen months. Dr. Rubenstein assured her "I'm as near as the telephone." Six months passed since Mila felt the need.

Her work schedule was staying in manageable limits, but it seemed some evil force was conspiring to snarl things up today. Monday was never her favorite day of the week, but this one didn't bode well starting with trying to find a pair of panty hose without a run. She spent more hours than she'd planned or wanted going over interrogatories with her paralegals. Her plan to finish work early so she could have a leisurely bath and relax without rushing went awry. Bridge traffic slowed because of a wreck and by the time she got home all she wanted to do was fix a simple dinner, spend a quiet evening at home, read Emily a bedtime story and curl up next to Sam.

Instead they had to attend one of those excruciating dinners with the big shots from Latham & Beck. She recalled with a shudder that her inability to make decisions when she'd been depressed extended over what to wear. Daily, for months, she dressed in the safety of navy slacks and suits and white blouses. As she recovered she'd donated all of her *blue* clothes to Goodwill, never wanting to see them again. She went through the closet, deciding on her aubergine wool challis suit and taupe pumps. That should satisfy the censorious tastes of the Latham & Beck wives. Mila opened her jewelry drawer. She didn't have much jewelry, only things she treasured and loved. She took out the Georg Jensen broach Sam gave her for their ninth anniversary, the simple elegant design for which the Danes were noted. Sam's taste was flawless, especially in the jewelry he selected for her. It was not cloyingly dainty, but scaled for someone of her stature.

The dinner was held in the Carnelian Room at the top of the Bank of America building where people wandered about, a drink in hand, looking at the view of the city. Mila thought of drinks in the singular at these functions since not being in control of one's drinking was frowned upon, and not being able to have a cocktail and maneuver through the wine courses at dinner was equally frowned upon.

They found their names, written in calligraphy on place cards. It was a ritual of placement, first how close your table was to the head table, and next the importance of the vice presidents who served as hosts at your particular table, and then whom you were seated next to.

Mila and Sam were in a neutral location with Gordon Bailey, a vice president who was in tenuous decline, but renowned for his ability to rally. Mila was surprised to see him ask the waiter for another highball and Marion Bailey look at him with a chilled displeasure before she turned to Mila.

"We haven't seen you at the Women's Club," she said.

"No. You may have forgotten that I work," Mila said. "It's almost impossible to know what my caseload will be or when I'll be in court."

"I see. So few of the wives have outside employment." Marion Bailey grasped a memory from her storehouse of useful facts. "You've been having medical problems, haven't you? And that's why your husband can't travel?"

Mila recoiled. She felt appalled that her private life was under the scrutiny of these strangers, as if she were sitting at the table nude. "I enjoy the intellectual challenge of the law, and the chance to help people."

"Bridge is enough of an intellectual challenge for me," Marion said. "Do you play?"

Louise Hubbard was new to the department. Her husband, Rudy, had recently come to work for the firm and Louise displayed the eagerness of a wife who wanted her husband to move ahead and knew her importance in that process. "I love to play bridge," she interrupted. "I played duplicate in college at Mills."

Mila smiled at the subtle exchange of information.

"Really? I'm a Mills grad myself," Marion said, turning away from Mila.

She could hear Sam talking to Mel Brower who looked upon all of the other attorneys in the department as a gallery of moving ducks that must be shot down before he walked away with the panda bear.

"I see old Jacob Hiller is here. That's a surprise. I thought he got the can tied to him," Mel said.

"He's coming back as a consultant. After he retired they realized how valuable he was," Sam said.

"Yeah. One of those over-achieving Jews. If he's such a brain he should be smart enough to know he'd never make it with this company."

"Why's that?" Sam asked.

"Where have you been? They may hire a couple minorities here and there, but they never make it to the top. The blacks stay a couple years and split. The Jews move ahead at first, but only rise so far. The lucky ones like Jake come back as consultants for a few years."

As if to validate the truth of Mel's announcement, their conversation was interrupted by Gordon Bailey. "What do you call five hundred Jewish lawyers at the bottom of the ocean?" His voice carried over the din of voices and Mila noticed the conversation stop even at the head table. Barely able to control his mirth, Gordon chuckled "a good start," and repeated, "a good start," as if to make sure everyone heard him.

Mel turned to Sam, "So how's your golf game coming?"

"I've never cared much for golf. It's all walk and talk and getting lost in the rough," Sam replied.

"You'll get further ahead with golf," Mel advised him.

"My game's tennis. The balls are bigger."

Mel laughed, and then added, "It's the game of choice, my boy. You should work at it. Did you hear we got the contract for El-Marrakech?"

"No. I knew we were bidding on it," Sam answered. "I don't keep up with the scuttle the way you do."

"It's a great opportunity to score points by going overseas. Of course it means living in Saudi for a few years."

"And I couldn't do that because I'm Jewish," Sam said, airing the innuendos Mel had made all evening.

Unflappable, Mel dismissed the statement by shrugging his shoulders. "You know Latham & Beck. One's entire family must enter the project with enthusiasm."

Mila rolled the window down and let some air into the car. "I can't wait to get home and take a shower," she said. "I want to wash off the entire evening. How can you stand it?"

"It seemed worse tonight. I feel like a fraud most of the time. They'd probably fire me on the spot if they knew I'd voted Democratic in the last election."

"I thought that kind of bigotry died during the sixties. It was like listening to Donald Robertson."

"I'm sorry you have to go through it," he said. "I get a little inured until one of these evenings. Are you doing all right?"

Mila reached over and put her hand on his leg. "Thank God for you and Emily."

He covered her hand with his. "I just don't want you to be unhappy."

"It wasn't your fault. It had been coming for a long time. I think it was probably a blessing in disguise. I made some real breakthroughs about my childhood and you can congratulate me, I haven't had to call Fran."

"I feel like I'm being offered the gift of getting to know my new wife," he said. "I kick myself for failing to realize how hard you were peddling just to stay in place. I always sensed there was a part of you I couldn't reach, a part you kept hidden."

"Not just from you. I didn't understand it myself. I thought it was my fault and I was ashamed."

They stopped at the signal and he leaned over and kissed her. "We're a unit and stronger together than separate. Promise me you'll tell me - if things are - "

"Getting out of hand?" Mila said. "I promise. I've been so wrapped up with myself; I've failed to pay attention to what you're going through. Is it catching up with you?"

"I've gotten good experience with Latham & Beck, but I've gone as far as I can. Tonight was a good indication. Anyway, environmental law is what I want." As the light changed, he said, "I'm not going to put up with Latham & Beck's crap much longer, this is the time for us to make the change we've been talking about. You've said you'd like to teach and I'd like to accept Bob's offer to join his firm."

"Let's do it," Mila said.

The message light on the telephone was flashing when they let themselves into the house. "Shall we wait until the morning to find out who called?" Mila asked.

"It's up to you. Personally, I don't want to hear anyone's voice but yours."

"It might be about Emily," Mila said. "She hasn't slept over much. Maybe she wants to come home."

She pushed the button and listened to the tape rewind and then Zeke's voice. "Hi, sis. Will you give me a call when you get back - no matter how late it is."

Mila looked at Sam. "I hope it's not bad news. It's been a rotten day."

"Do you want me to call him?" Sam asked.

She shook her head, no, and dialed the number; surprised Zeke picked up on the first ring. "I'm glad you called back tonight," he said. His voice sounded hoarse, like he had a cold. "Dad died this afternoon. They think it was a heart attack. Mom has already arranged for the funeral. It's in two days. Please come. I'd like us to be together."

CHAPTER FORTY-SIX

▼

San Francisco/Painesville

Mila's anxiety mounted as the plane landed. She realized now there was a certain amount of whistling in the dark when she assured Dr. Rubenstein that she felt strong enough to handle things

As she walked up the steps to the Funeral Home her stomach churned at the thought of seeing Frances. She tried to relax the taut muscles in her neck and shoulders. She took some deep breaths and gained control.

"Are you all right?" Sam asked.

Mila nodded, and held his hand tighter. "I'll be okay," she said.

Frances had aged not only in years but also in physical stature. She still wore the royal coronet braid wrapped round her head, but the auburn crown was gray. The imperious set of her head was the same, but her lack of taste in clothes now appeared as personal neglect. Her mouth was puckered in an etched scowl and she was puffy with overweight. Had her inner ugliness of spirit broken through at last, Mila wondered, and found herself thinking *short squat toad.*

On the way out of the funeral home Frances stumbled and Mila instinctively reached out to catch her. Touching her, Mila felt the same revulsion she'd known as a child. She smelled stale and metallic.

"I got him the finest casket money could buy," Frances told her and anyone else within earshot. "He always had to have his way and I know that's what he'd expect. Myself, I just want a plain pine box," she said

Carmie, Donald's secretary, was unable to control her tears. Mila wondered if Donald had ever turned to her on those nights he disappeared from the house for hours.

Zeke rode with his mother in the first limousine and Sam and Mila rode in the second.

As they drove to the cemetery, Mila said, "This funeral is a travesty. She hasn't changed a bit in that respect. It's all appearance in front of people."

"She seems to be in her element," Sam said.

"The open casket? Yuck. Zeke says she's even having Taps played. She can't resist reminding everyone that he was a veteran."

"Ritual serves a purpose. It helps people mourn," Sam said.

"I looked at him in the casket and realized I had no feeling for him. As for Frances, she's lost her power. I may never fully understand her, but I feel free," she said and smiled at Sam.

There was a reception in the church basement after the ceremony at the cemetery and in the evening the family gathered at B-B. Sam's parents were included. Mila couldn't help but feel the irony and wondered if Donald's spirit hovered in a malevolent cloud of disapproval.

"It's been a long day," Mila said. "We should get going." She rose to gather their coats.

"Before you go," Zeke said, "I want you to have this." He removed the ring from his finger and held it out to Mila. "It's pop's ring. I know he'd like for you to have something of his to remember him by." It was a heavy gold band with diamonds and a large ruby. "You can have it cut down," he said.

Frances's lips tightened and her body grew rigid.

"That's a lovely gesture, and I'm touched by your thoughtfulness, but you should keep it. The ring will always remind you of dad and your close relationship." She returned it to Zeke and Frances sat back in her easy chair, looking relieved.

Zeke walked out to the car with them and waylaid Mila. "Pop told me he set up a new Will about six months ago and hadn't forgotten you. I guess mom got to it right away. He always kept the key to his safety deposit box on his key ring and told me to get it after he died, but it's gone."

"I don't want anything from him," Mila said.

"Will you go with me tomorrow morning?" Zeke asked. "Mom's going over the will and I want you to be there with me just to make sure she doesn't pull any tricks."

"A bunch of weak sisters with their sympathy and sniveling. What a charade - all these flowers - what a waste of money." Frances's first words to Mila the next morning crackled with anger. She was no longer the brave widow thanking family and friends for their homemade bread and casseroles. "And look at this stack of letters," she said waving her hand over them. "I'll never get all of them answered. You can bet they're all after something from me."

"People simply meant well," Mila said.

"I'm surrounded by stupid clients and uncaring children. I made you what you are today by beating some backbone into you, and you've never shown an ounce of gratitude. None of you know what it is to suffer."

Mila found she could listen as if to a stranger, an unpleasant stranger. Before she could respond, Zeke arrived.

"This won't take long," Frances said. "I've already prepared a waiver for each of you to sign. In essence all it means is that you waive your rights to receive a copy of the Will."

Mila felt the hair stand up on her arms, but before she could contest Frances's statement, Zeke spoke up. "Why should we waive those rights? Pop said he'd drawn up a new Will. I'd like to read it."

"I have no idea where you got such an idea," Frances answered. "I went to the safety deposit box and all I found were the stock certificates. There was only one Will, the one from ten years ago."

"That's not true," Zeke said.

Mila felt the old injustice rising in her. "It was wrong of you; not only wrong, it wasn't legal for you to open the safety deposit box while matters are in Probate."

Frances scowled. "Of course you'd show up at the funeral because you expected to get something. You were written out of the Will. You have nothing to say about this. It's none of your business."

Zeke stood up. "Mila's here because I asked her. I wanted her to be here."

"Thanks, Zeke, but you needn't justify my presence here. I've known since I was nineteen that I'd been disowned," she gave Zeke a hug and turned to Frances. "But Dad loved Zeke and there's no reason for him to sign a waiver."

Frances stood up behind her desk; her eyes glazed over, her right arm and finger grew rigid as she stabbed at the air, thrusting it at them. "I'm the one that put up with Donald Robertson all these years. I'm tired of both of you and I was tired of that senile old man. He wouldn't have been anything without me. None of you would. I did everything."

"What about the jewelry Dad gave you over the years? The gold bracelets and the diamonds? Mila should have some of it, and I might want to give it to my wife when I get married."

"I never wore things like that," Frances said. "It was a waste of money. I intend to sell them."

Mila saw the horror of her words wash over Zeke's face and her heart ached for him.

Zeke sat in mute disbelief. "You're going against pop's wishes."

"You're pitiful," Mila said to Frances. "You've betrayed not only yourself but all of us by losing your humanity. I wouldn't be you for anything in the world. I'm surprised, but I do feel sorry for you. You're all alone in the world."

"Don't waste your sympathy on me, Madam. No one needs to feel sorry for me."

Mila's voice was quiet. "You've never let anyone get close to you - you pushed us all away, except perhaps Ollie. You're a bitter, sick, evil old woman."

For a brief moment Frances's eyes cleared and she stood still. Then a look of cunning crept over her face. "Ah, but I'm wealthy." Her eyes gleamed. "Donald's stock is worth millions and added to my millions, that makes many, many millions. And it's all mine. Everything. I control it."

Mila stood up. "I'm leaving to go to my husband and my child. Zeke, I'll have a lawyer for you in the morning."

When she joined Sam at his parents she relaxed. Leah brought her a glass of sherry and she called Pam.

"It sounds like you're still alive," Pam said.

"I'll give you a blow-by-blow later, but right now I feel washed out."

"I'm not surprised. We'll have all summer to talk about it. I can't wait to have you back," Pam told her before they hung up.

The next morning, Mila called Zeke from the airport. "We're leaving, but I wanted to make sure everything went okay with the lawyer."

"Yeah, thanks for your help. I'll keep you up-to-date when I have some news."

"Let me know if there's anything else I can do - or Sam.

"Thanks, sis. Have a good trip."

It was a relief to board the plane and sit in familial security. At another time Mila might have felt crushed in the confinement of the middle seat, but now she felt protected by the bookends of her husband and daughter. The stewardess gave Emily two extra packs of pretzels and an entire can of soda for herself.

"Well?" Sam said. "Do you still want to move back to Ohio?"

She smiled, "If therapy served no other purpose, it allowed me finally to look at her with detachment. Yes, I'm looking forward to the change."

Sam took her hand, and pressed it to his lips and kissed it. "Good."

She shook her head remembering the scene at Frances's office. "I wanted so much for her to like me and I wanted to like her. In law school I thought we might at least find something in common and become friends. I wonder when she's dying if all her hatred will flash in her mind, if all her stocks will help her then. It was cathartic for me, but I'm glad it's over. Zeke needed us," Mila said. "I didn't expect anything, but Zeke certainly deserves something from his father." Emily patted her mother's hand. "Are you sad that your daddy died?"

Mila considered the question, careful as always of her answers to Emily's questions. "Grandpa Donald was old and sick for a long time. It's sad when people die. Nothing is quite the same afterwards."

If Emily was worried about losing Sam, Mila knew the question would come up again, but she didn't want to burden Emily with adult problems or project her memories onto her child.

Mila turned to Sam. "When did you tell Bob you'd start?"

"He's bogged down with work, but he's reasonable. He understands it'll take time to wrap things up in San Francisco."

"I'm excited about the house in Chagrin Falls," Mila said. "It has a lovely old fashioned feeling. It will be fun having seasons again and some space."

"Chagrin Falls. Who in the hell thought up the names, I wonder," Sam asked.

"At least Chagrin Falls is better than Painesville. That was too apt for comfort."

The plane taxied down the runway and took off. It circled over Cleveland and started west. Sam looked out the window.

"It always strikes me funny," Sam said, "that I expected the west to be open spaces, but this part of the country has a lot more areas of rolling hills and woods."

"And creeks. I've always wanted to own land that had a creek running through it."

"It was nice to meet Pam after all these years. I didn't realize she and mom are such good friends." He laughed, "She's a solid sort of person, and I like Colin. I can understand why she was so important to you."

"Like you," Mila said. She kissed him on the cheek.

Emily's ears perked up. "We'll get to see Uncle Zeke, and Auntie Pam and everybody when we move, won't we?" Emily asked.

"Yes, of course."

"Grandma Leah and Grandpa Harry?"

"Yes, all the time."

Emily hesitated. "What about Grandma Frances? Will we have to see her?"

"Do you want to see Grandma Frances?"

From her earliest years Emily had sensitivity to the feelings of others and Mila noted her hesitation before saying, "She's not very nice."

"We'll probably never see her," Mila said, "but if we do you'll never be alone - daddy and I will be with you."

Follow on along the river
Passing by three foaming rapids
Till you reach a point of land
At the tip-end of a cape.
On that point there stands a cabin

                                        Kalevala, Runo 34, 147- 152

So why should a poem not weary,
Fragile verses tire of tinkling
Through the long delights of evening,
From the songs at set of day?

                                        Ibid, Runo 50, 525-528

So, I'll cease and stop and end it,
In a ball I'll wind my verses,
Twist them in a storehouse loft,
Bolted there in bony locks
That they cannot be released
Never, never be untangled
Till the bones themselves are loosened,
Teeth pulled out and jaws pried open
And the tongue be freed once more.

                                        Ibid, Runo 50, 537-546

CHAPTER FORTY-SEVEN

▼

Helsinki, Finland
San Francisco, California

Anders opened the door to bring in wood for the stove and felt the wind wrap around him, finding every buttonhole and opening of his clothes. He felt like a troll returning to his den. The short days of winter had forgotten the sun, and snow flurries brushed against the windows. He was proud of this home he'd built from trees he and Patrik had hewn. He loved working with wood. It was alive. He could feel its warmth as he formed and shaped it. The wind whistled through the chimney as he added wood to the fire. His mind strayed, as it did so often, to Mila.

The isolation of winter made him reflect on his life, spotted with more sadness than joy. He glanced at the stack of books, a fortress for his isolation. He thought of his father and how his early death had altered the path of all their lives. Now that Kaija was dead he could find some sympathy for her. Her life hadn't been easy. When she was young she escaped her black emptiness with alcohol and men. Later it was communism, the only hope for the working class, she thought. She died of pneumonia with the poster of the long dead Stalin above her bed.

The fire blazed and he stared into it. Every so often the hiss of the flames lapped at a damp log and sent fire motes dancing. His thoughts were like that, random, hissing and flying in all directions. In his mind Mila remained a lively child of six for whom he carved toys.

He'd spent most of the fall with Patrik who lived in northern Finland, but before returning home he contacted Arnerio.

"I've been trying to reach you," Arnerio told him. "I received a letter months ago from someone who claims Kaija Ahlgren may be her mother. It must be your sister."

He now held Mila's letter in his hand, trying not to let his hopes once more get dashed in disappointment. He had a telephone number. If this too proved fruitless, he'd abandon his faith in finding her. He dialed the long overseas number and listened to the phone ring thousands of miles away.

The phone cut the night in two like an ambulance siren. Sam fumbled with the light. "Hello. No. No. Why don't you look when you dial?" The phone thunked into the cradle. "Damn," he said, flopping under the covers, but before he got settled the phone rang again. "No. There's no one here named Ahlgren."

Mila knew with a flash of clarity it was the call she'd been waiting for. So much of her life felt unsettled, as though she were trying to recapture the contents of a dream. She was across the bed, ripping the phone from Sam's hand. "Yes," she said. "Who's calling?"

Through the static she heard the deep male voice, and a whisper of memory as she heard him say her name. "Mila?" The phone shook in her hand. "Is it finally you? This is your brother, Anders. I knew someday I'd find you."

Mila's whole body started to shake. "Is my mother there?" she asked.

"Our mother died," he said.

"Dead?" She felt a stab of regret. Her dreams of reconciliation, her hope of understanding and resolution were dashed in one word: dead. "When?" she asked.

"About a year ago. Did Mrs. Robertson tell you I was at her law office in Ohio looking for you a couple of years ago? She didn't know where you were."

"No," Mila answered, "she didn't tell me."

"Our mother regretted sending you away and tried to contact Mrs. Robertson to send you back to us."

"I've waited a lifetime for this moment. I can't believe this is happening," she said.

"The only thing that's important is that we can be together again. We have to take back thirty-two years, Mila - a lifetime."

Sam was fully awake, his face full of expectation. Mila replaced the phone and burst into tears and Sam held her as she sobbed against his shoulder.

"It was my brother. His name is Anders," she said in wonder. The full impact of his call settled on her. She reached for the box of tissues. "It's like a dream. All the years I've waited, hoping someone cared enough to find me. He said he'd never stopped loving me. He loved me always." Still reeling from the call she clutched a pillow. "My mother is dead and I think there's something wrong with my brother's health, something with his lungs. I couldn't understand everything he said. Just think. I have two brothers and all sorts of nieces and nephews. An entire family who all want to meet me."

"You must go to Finland," Sam said.

"Yes," Mila said. "How soon can we leave?"

Sam held her to him, kissed her eyes, her hair. "I think this is a journey you must take by yourself."

Mila sat in the heaped bedclothes. "Yes," she said. "I think you're right. What about Emily?"

"Em and I will manage. Mom will help."

Lying in bed after Sam fell asleep, she hugged her feelings around herself. Each word of their conversation was etched in her mind. With absolute certainty she knew that nothing in her life would ever be the same and that in a split second her entire world changed.

The cat's claws made a gentle racket on the wood floor before she jumped up on Mila's side of the bed to curl herself around Mila's feet. In the stillness, the faint iodine smell of the ocean came through the open windows.

The arrangements went smoothly. Not many travelers were interested in visiting Finland in the winter. Pam had been jubilant, but Mila hadn't reached Zeke. She tried the number again feeling it was important to share the news with him.

"That's wonderful," Zeke said when she finally reached him and told him the news.

Mila heard a reserve, a pain she remembered from years ago when she told him she had another family.

"I've finally found my family in Finland, but you'll always be my little brother," she said.

The land below was white on white, a pale sun fading and a foggy dusk settling in. The plane hit the tarmac with a thud and slipped in the slushy snow. She was tired, but had been unable to sleep on the plane. She felt on fire, her blood flowing too fast.

She resented customs, the waiting for luggage. What if no one was there? What if no one recognized her? What if she had mixed up dates? Finally she snapped her luggage closed and headed toward passport control. Through an enormous glass window she saw a crowd of people pressed against the glass, waving and smiling.

The doors swung open and a tall man coming toward her blotted out everything and everyone. He was smiling and his arms opened and Mila rushed into them.

"Mila." The warm, gentle pronunciation of her name felt familiar, foreign, but just right. He smelled like pine boughs, like the outdoors.

Gently he released her and they stepped apart. She became aware of those around her, their faces wet with tears and smiles. They introduced themselves in a jumble of foreign sounding names. They brought exotic Hawaiian flowers in the middle of the Finnish winter. Anders continued to hold Mila's hand and pulled it tightly toward him. Her hand felt safe, tucked into his much bigger one. In this public place, she felt intensely private.

The airport was hot and smelled of damp wool and perfume. Relief and intensity overcame her, and she gasped for breath as Anders led her through the glass doors and they walked into the coolness of steadily falling snow.

The End

ACKNOWLEDGEMENTS

Our deep gratitude goes to Suzanne Hartman Byerley for her encouragement, subtle suggestions, quiet direction, editorial skill and friendship. Thank you to Charlotte Gullick for her careful reading and wise editorial suggestions. I would like to acknowledge Rita as a collaborator par excellence. When we innocently started this novel we thought it might take a year, at longest. During the following years I learned many lessons in humility, patience, and the profound importance of friendship. At times we grew to think like one person, but at all times Rita was ready with intelligence, support, ideas, understanding and a sense of humor. My respect is infinite. FP. Fauna and I were walking along the Mendocino Headlands when she proposed we collaborate on a writing project. This is the result. Without her dedication, writing expertise, and critical eye, this novel would never have seen the light of day. Words on a page can not express my thanks for her untiring work, nor for our enduring friendship. RKR. With love and affection to my husband, Robert M. Read. His steadfast encouragement, and extreme patience in all matters technical, have literally kept me from "booting" my computer down the cellar stairs. RKR. With gratitude to my husband, Harry Perkins, for his encouragement, patience and belief. FP. Cathi and David Read: I owe you multiple salads and pizza for your patience and humor when advising me on "writing programs". Thank you. RKR.

ABOUT THE AUTHORS

Since childhood I have been in love with words. In Mendocino, California, I am surrounded by writers and artists and became a serious wordsmith. The first time I had a story accepted I felt I'd won the Pulitzer. I am presently working on my second novel, You Were Fashioned for Me. Fauna Perkins

Rita K. Read has traveled and lived in many areas of the world. She and her husband reside in a small community in the Northwest where she is a regular contributor for the Panorama Voice. She has just completed a memoir, My Daughter, My Life. Her next book introduces Finnish detective Solve Haldersson.

Printed in the United States
143587LV00004B/1/P

9 780595 475100